THE TAVERNER NOVELS

RECOVERED CLASSICS

The Taverner NOVELS

Armed with Madness
Death of Felicity Taverner

Mary Butts

Preface by Paul West
Afterword by Barbara Wagstaff

McPHERSON & COMPANY

THE TAVERNER NOVELS

 Published by McPherson & Company, Post Office Box 1126, Kingston, New York 12401. This book has been issued with assistance from the literature programs of the New York State Council on the Arts and the National Endowment for the Arts, a federal agency.

Published by arrangement with and authorization of The Estate of Mary Butts.

Library of Congress Cataloging-in-Publication Data

Butts, Mary
[Armed with madness]
The Taverner novels / Mary Butts : preface by Paul West : afterword by Barbara Wagstaff.
p. cm. — (Recovered classics)
Contents: Armed with madness—Death of Felicity Taverner.
ISBN 0-929701-17-8 (cloth)—ISBN 0-929701-18-6 (paper)
I. Butts, Mary Death of Felicity Taverner. 1992.
II. Title.
PR6003.U7A6 1992
823'.912—dc20 91-32693

Printed on pH neutral paper.

Manufactured in the United States of America.
3 5 7 9 10 8 6 4 2

CONTENTS

PREFACE

The Hummingbird of English Prose

Stylists get overlooked whereas experimenters don't. Stylists modulate voice, tone, rhythm and pace whereas experimenters just keep on asking for attention. Stylists work on you like radioactivity or radon where experimenters do it with a bang. Asked if he experimented, the composer Edgard Varèse said yes he did: first, he said, he experimented, then he composed.

Mary Butts rarely bids for attention, but she hones and shines her prose with self-absorbed joy. One can see why she vanished into jet-vortices left by Woolf and Pound; a great deal of what she most wanted to say had no public visage, no exoteric face to be called up by. After all, a woman obsessed with "visible Pan" is probably not going to tout it too well on the Rialto. For Butts, the finding and rendering of this Pan was enough. She knew that a good thing would out and did not require commercials; indeed, she thought it better to leave a thing to find its own way, gently propelled in roughly the right direction by style, then left to float into others' lives like a baptized butterfly. You can see what she is by reading *Scenes from the Life of Cleopatra,* her lushest last novel. She was a Sitwell of the Grail, but in many ways she was a European author, on one occasion talking pure Valéry when she said what interested her above all: "Nothing but spiritual development, the soul living at its fullest capacity." In other words, *implexe.*

Her prose is startling without being ostentatious. Perhaps some of the most elliptical prose in English, it reveals the space between things, inciting the reader to fill the space or begin to commune with what is there already, in between. That is why her prose seems so sliced, sometimes devoid of cumulative rhythm. She writes staccato anthems, training the reader to apprehend autonomies she then puts side by side, saying these, ladies and gentlemen, are the collocations of a universe. Where nothing is, is most. Perhaps she is a metaphysical writer, one who believes in jumps and bridges, stiles and leaps. While the rest of the world that is going to be famous busies itself with transitions and causative euphony, Butts points to the gap, which is really the portion of the figure's ground that happens to be between two salient figures. She's looking at saliences, yes, but much more at the big buzzing blooming fusion that lies behind things, around them. She is the celebrant of context. An unfortunate role, this; it makes you an usher rather than a soloist, attuning the reader to your Pan-mindedness of course, but hardly making you a lordly delineator. Woolf derided her first novel, *Ashe of Rings,* perhaps because she felt she'd been scooped, much as Nathalie Sarraute in *The Age of Suspicion* derided Woolf, and for similar reasons. Butts, on the outside socially, and always diffident, went her own way esthetically, knowing she was right, and that her punchy, trenchant, almost jactitatory English proved her so.

Her most conspicuous originality consisted in her resolve to depict worst things, or things at their worst, with a view to transforming them, which means assimilating into one's being a sense of Creation's massive, impersonal onslaught. Try to steal its thunder by feeling a little godlike, by getting proprietorial with the tornado that swipes you, as if it were your own. I call this *deinosis* and link it to certain primitive rituals that enhance the human being with the chills of grandiosity. Her paragraphs contain a great deal of isolation, almost as if she is trying to stunt the mind's ability to connect one thing with another. Take this, picked at random from *Armed with Madness:*

> *They went in. Pine-needles are not easy to walk on, like a floor of red glass. It is not cool under them, a black scented life, full of ants, who work furiously and make no sound. Something ached in Carston, a regret for the cool brilliance of the wood they had left, the other side of the hills, on the edge of the sea. This one was full of harp-noises from a wind when there was none outside.*

See how she uses the annotative disjointedness of the clinician or the lab assistant, striving not for euphony, but for carefully built dislocation. She does it all the time, not to be staccato or telegraphic, but because things that look isolated are not. Butts conveys holism through short breaths and a host of long, similar pauses.

I see two things: her inclination not to be gracious or polite, and her love of outlandish things—themes that others might find fey, daffy, far-fetched. She may have modeled herself on Charles Williams and M.R. James, but she often seems to have more in common with such novelists as Nélida Piñon and Clarice Lispector, Brazilians both. Whether she is addressing her prose to the Holy Grail, Bradbury Rings, or whatever drove Alexander the Great, Butts finds the style that suits her matter, not her reader. There is a reportorial pertness to her prose, not quite genteel or considerate, and you have to get used to it. Some would think her rather dotty, even on the strength of this peremptoriness joined to her weirdo subject-matter; but she was only trying to get across to us her private sense of the universe, an enterprise that hardly conducted Blake, Messiaen, and Ensor to extremes of amenity or what tends now to be called reader-friendliness. *Il faut avoir un aigle,* said Gide, or your work will be just a gentle pit-a-pat. Well, Butts has her eagle or her demon plucking at her and drawing her away from the hallowed bows and scrapes we associate with more circumspect authors. She's a bit of a redneck in fact; she's something of a Djuna Barnes, minus the addictive wordplay.

There is an instructional tone in what she writes, a touch of what in the military we called Station Standing Orders. She shows the ecstatic, suppositious mind reeling itself out into the arcana of life along a rubber band that eventually snaps it back into the company of all those crisply registered finitudes. Trenchant she is, with a penchant for gossip overheard from people who take part in an atavism they are not aware of. I do not see her laboring among movers and shakers to make her career a success; rather, her vision sustains her, revealing what she needn't do. She has this uncanny sense of something's always being slightly wrong with the universe, almost like an early intimation of the absurd—or at least of the finding that the universe is not absurd, whereas we are. Everywhere, she says, "there was a sense of broken continuity, a dis-ease. The end of an age, the beginning of another. Revaluation of values. Phrases that meant something if you could mean them. . . . She wished the earth would not suddenly look fragile, as if it was going to start shifting about. Every single piece of appearance. She knew it was only the sun, polishing what it had dried." This is bracing stuff for 1928. Her prose becomes more fluent, more protracted, but she never loses her addiction to the thing *per se,* to the phenomenon considered in its own right. She is the hummingbird of English prose.

The best account of her, with critical aperçus shining through his gentle kaleidoscope of her image, is by Virgil Thomson. One expects a composer to tune into her daimon, for a while at least. Thomson extolls Butts the gentle-born roisterer who wore a single dollar-sized white jade earring under a man's felt hat tipped-up, who "toddled" because one of her knees came easily out of joint, and who revelled in the pub-crawl. Socially, her act was to lead people on until they shot the works. Literarily, as Virgil Thomson says, she preferred revealing people caught up in something overpowering, "so irresistible that their higher powers and all their lowest conditionings are exposed . . . an ultimate clarification arrived at through ecstasy." Glowing at the center of a cyclone she created, she eventually proved too much for Thomson. I would like to think her time has come again, though she is essentially a Parisian author, similar in some ways to Auden, as in this:

O Lord, call off the curse on great names,
On the "tall, tight boys,"
Write off their debt,
The sea-paced, wave curled,
Achilles' set.

She envisioned some perpetual good husbandry of the planet that could be learned through opium or emotional upheaval. Was it the storm goddess, as Thomson dubbed her, or the seemly earth-ecstatic who wrote these lines?

Curl horns and fleeces, straighten trees,
Multiply lobsters, assemble bees.

—Paul West

Armed with Madness

Armed with madness, I go on a long voyage.

Chapter I

IN THE HOUSE, in which they could not afford to live, it was unpleasantly quiet. Marvellously noisy, but the noises let through silence. The noises were jays, bustling and screeching in the wood, a hay-cutter, clattering and sending up waves of scent, substantial as sea-waves, filling the long rooms as the tide fills a blow-hole, but without roar or release. The third noise was the light wind, rising off the diamond-blue sea. The sea lay three parts round the house, invisible because of the wood. The wood rose from its cliff-point in a single tree, and spread out inland, in a fan to enclose the house. Outside the verandah, a small lawn had been hollowed, from which the wood could be seen as it swept up, hurrying with squirrels, into a group of immense ilex, beech and oak. The lawn was stuck with yuccas and tree-fuchsias, dripping season in, season out, with bells the colour of blood.

Once the house was passed, the wood gave it up, enclosed it decently, fenced a paddock, and the slip of dark life melted into the endless turf-miles which ran up a great down into the sky.

The silence let through by the jays, the hay-cutter, and the breeze, was a complicated production of stone rooms, the natural silence of empty grass, and the equivocal, personal silence of the wood. Not many nerves could stand it. People who had come for a week had been known to leave next day. The people who had the house were interested in the wood and its silence. When it got worse, after dark or at mid-day, they said it was tuning-up. When a gale came up-Channel shrieking like a mad harp, they said they were watching a visible fight with the silence in the wood.

A large gramophone stood with its mouth open on the

verandah flags. They had been playing to the wood after lunch, to appease it and to keep their dancing in hand. The house was empty. Their servants had gone over to a distant farm. The wood had it all its own way. They were out.

There were two paths through the wood to the sea. A bee-line through the high trees, of fine grass, pebble scattered, springing and wet. Then, across the wet ditch that was sometimes a stream, a path through the copse in figures of eight, whose turns startled people. As the wood narrowed, this way ended in a gate on to the grass, the nearest way to an attractive rabbit-warren. These were the only two paths in that country, except a green road which led from the house over the down to the white road and from thence on to the beginnings of the world, ten miles away.

There was only one house except a shepherd's cottage, and a little fancy lodge, the wood had swallowed, which they let to a fisherman in exchange for fish. The fisherman was a gentleman, and a fine carver in wood. The shepherd was a troglodyte. He came home drunk in the moonlight spinning round and yelling obscene words to the tune of old hymns. They were equally friends with both. They belonged to the house and the wood and the turf and the sea; had no money and the instincts of hospitality; wanted everything and nothing, and were at that moment lying out naked on a rock-spit which terminated their piece of land.

The cliffs there were low and soft, rounded with a black snout, but based on a wedge of orange stone, smooth and running out square under the sea.

Up and down the channel, high cliffs rose, airy, glittering, but some way off. Their headland was low, their valley shallow and open, spiked only with undersea reefs, no less lovely and disastrous than the famous precipices which made their coast their pride.

"Mare Nostrum," they said, in Paris or in London, at

the sea's winter takings there. An outlet for a natural ferocity they were too proud to exercise, too indifferent to examine. Also a kind of ritual, a sacrifice, willing but impersonal to their gods.

Meanwhile the weather was good. One of them sat up, and rolled off the reef's edge into the sea.

A brother and sister to whom the house belonged, and a young man they had known a long time. They called her Scylla from her name Drusilla, altering it because they said she was sometimes a witch and sometimes a bitch. They were handsome and young, always together, and often visited by their friends. It was Felix, the brother, who had swum out. His sister sat up and watched him with the touch of anxiety common to females, however disciplined. "Be careful," she called, "the tide's turning." He wallowed under the sea.

"Leave him alone," said the other man, "it's the last day's peace," and rolled over on his face and ate pink sea-weed.

She approved because it was good for his complexion, wood-brown as they were fair, but she stood up and watched the boy's head popping in and out of the crisp water. Naked, the enormous space, the rough earth dressed her. The sparking sea did not. But the sea at the moment was something for the men to swim in, an enormous toy. She thought again: 'He won't drown. Besides, why worry?' Lay down again, and fed an anemone with a prawn.

"Ross, why do you say 'the last day's peace'? You like people when they come."

He answered:

"One always enjoys something. But this one's an American."

"No, we've never had one before."

"I don't mind 'em. I always like their women. But take it from me, all we shall get out of this one is some fun. He won't like the wood. The wood will giggle at him."

"It laughs at us. . . ."

"We don't mind—it's our joke." He laughed, sitting upright staring down-Channel, his head pitched back on an immensely long neck, his mouth like a wild animal's, only objectively pre-occupied with the world. She thought: 'Grin like a dog, and run about the rocks,' accepting him as she accepted everything there. She said: "Give him a good time and see what happens." That was her part of their hospitality, whose rewards were varied and irregular. None of them, with perhaps the exception of Felix, could understand a good time that was not based on flashes of illumination, exercises of the senses, dancing, and stretches of very insular behaviour.

Something long and white came up behind them out of the sea. An extra wave washed Felix a ledge higher. "Thank you," he said and skipped across. "Oh, my dear, I'm sure an octopus caught my leg."

"D'you remember," said Ross, "the chap last winter who killed them with his teeth and fainted at the sight of white of egg?"

The pleasant memory united them; they became a triple figure, like Hecate the witch, amused, imaginative. They put on their things: Felix's pretty clothes, Ross's rough ones, the girl, her delicate strong dress. With their arms round her shoulders, they crossed the rocks and went up the cliff-path, and through the wood to the house.

Chapter II

THEY WOKE to a clean superb day. The high trees broke the sun, and Scylla admired the form of them, standing straight to the east in the natural shape of trees, their tops curled to the west, tightened and distorted against the ocean wind.

Below them the copse was a knit bundle, almost as firm as stone. Still there were long shadows as she dressed, still dance and flash of birds. The wood was innocent, the house fresh and serene. At breakfast, in a quicksilver mirror, she saw the men come in. The eagle over it had a sock-suspender in its beak, but between the straps and the distortion she did not like the look of them.

They meant not to help her with the American, whom they had ordered like a new record from town. Who would have to be met.

They were like that. She was like that herself, but did not manage to give in to it. Which made her despise herself, think herself too female.

All three had work to do. She got hers done, and at the same time believed herself the sole stay of her men. Separated and bound to them because of her service they seemed unable to do without.

Ross was saying, cautiously: "That man's coming today." She wondered what he was thinking about in the train. Staring about and trying to remember the name of the station. A name as familiar as their own. Nothing to him. Fun to make it part of his consciousness? Fun for them. The men were saying: "We really ought to go over to Tollerdown and see if the others have turned up."

Ross's hair curled like black gorse, Felix's spread like burnt turf. "And not to Starn with me?" she said. A long day off they would have on the turf together; Ross poking about for rare plants, Felix making up a tolerable poem. Ten miles she would walk, also alone in the hills. At the end there would be a point of human life, a station shed a stone's throw from a crazy square, old houses tilted together; the gaping tourists, the market-day beasts; the train poking its head suddenly round an angle in the hills. There she would be eventually accompanied by a stranger, neat, interested, polite.

Then back in a car, flight after the steady walk—which would end where she was now, in a place like a sea-pool, on the lawn grass, in the cool rooms, under the trees, in the wood.

"All right," she said, "I'll go—if you order six lettuces and four lobsters, a basket of currants; and Felix does the flowers." There would be six lobsters and four lettuces. She needed to be alone as much as they.

She took her hat, and ashplant, and left them.

For a while she climbed the green road, worn down in places to its flints, black glass set in white porcelain rings. Below her the field-chequered sea-valley collected a haze. The sea was a hardly visible brilliance. On the top of the down, she looked inland, across another valley to another range, and far inland to Starn on its hill, the hub of the down-wheel, set in its cup of smoke and stone. A very long way over the grass, a very long way down a chalk-road. A longer way through a valley track, called Seven Fields into Starn. Seven Fields, because Felix said there were seven different kinds of enclosures, all unpleasant. A yellow field, a dirty field, a too-wet field, a field where you stubbed your feet. A field with a savage cow, a field with a wicked horse. Always something wrong, whichever way you walked it, except the fourth, which was not a field but an open copse, treed and banked and prettified. 'Midsummer Night's Dream,' true greenwood. And hope, one way, of Starn in a mile and a half. She needed it by the time she reached the copse, in spite of her light stride and airy dress. The boys were off by now, somewhere on Gault cliffs, which was not a nice place, but a wonder and a horror, overhanging a gulf over a wood full of foxes the surf lapped, where even she had never been. The boys would be sitting there, dangling their legs, the gulls fanning them, an unsailable bay under them, transparent, peacock-coloured, where under the water the reefs wound like snakes.

It was all very well. She had told Felix to collect mushrooms and not allow Ross to experiment. He could get them in Ogham meads—What was she worried about? Money, of course, and love affairs; the important, unimportant things. Hitherto God had fed his sparrows, and as good fish had come out of the sea. But everywhere there was a sense of broken continuity, a dis-ease. The end of an age, the beginning of another. Revaluation of values. Phrases that meant something if you could mean them. The meaning of meaning? Discovery of a new value, a different way of apprehending everything. She wished the earth would not suddenly look fragile, as if it was going to start shifting about. Every single piece of appearance. She knew it was only the sun, polishing what it had dried. Including her face, her make-up had made pasty with sweat. There was something wrong with all of them, or with their world. A moment missed, a moment to come. Or not coming. Or either or both. Shove it off on the war; but that did not help.

Only Ross was all right— He never wanted anything that he did not get. Life had given it up and paid over Ross's stakes, because once his strong appetites were satisfied, he did not want anything in human life at all. It was something to eat and drink, to embrace and paint. Apart from that, he knew something that she was only growing conscious of. And wouldn't tell. Not he—laughed at her for not knowing, and for wanting to know.

Felix was quite different. Felix was scared. Fear made him brittle and angry and unjust. Without faith.

Faith was necessary for the knowledge of God. Only, there were fifty good reasons for supporting the non-existence of God. Besides, no one wanted to believe that any more. That was the point. And it was a shame for those two men to make her go all that way through a valley, while they were grubbing about in the wind. The next stile was a beast. She crossed it heavily. A long corner to turn, and there would be Starn to look at. There was that horse again, knotted and stiff and staring at her. It was too far to come. Miles behind her, a white road stood on its head over the hill that led to the green road that led to their house. She had come down that road, a long time ago, turning her back on the sea, to get to Starn, to meet an American, who would like her, not for long, and no one else— Someone had barbed-wired the gap, damn him! She flung herself on her back and wriggled under, jumping up with too great an effort. What was she really doing, out in this burning valley at mid-day? 'They force me with more virtue than is convenient to me. Not innocently— How can we be innocent? I am going to let things go. A witch and a bitch they call me. They shall see.' She flung into the inn at Starn, ashamed of her appearance, red and dusty, and ordered a long drink.

Chapter III

COOL, RESTED, made up, she went to the station. It is always pleasant to collect someone expected out of a train. She wished it had been someone she wanted, someone known or necessary to be known. Michael, who went with the house—Tony, she wished to know better—Vincent, she might get off with—the peacocks of her world. Then she reminded herself of the pleasure it would be to shew a stranger their land, as they knew it, equivocal, exquisite. From what she had observed of Americans, almost certain to be new.

Then she was flying through lanes, an attentive, intelligent old-young man beside her.

"God! What a beautiful place," he said. When 'beautiful' is said, exactly and honestly, there is contact, or there should be. Then, "This is the England we think of. Hardy's country, isn't it?"

"Yes, don't rely too much on the weather and the food."

"Don't worry about me. I've done some camping."

Nice man. But when he stood in the verandah and looked about him, he said: "I couldn't have imagined it."

At tea, he said: "It seems to me that you have everything. No luxury, but all the beauty there is."

Slightly overdoing the beauty business— Beauty is a too concentrated food. And what did he mean about luxury? There was a sort of lean splendour about their things, anyhow. Still, his repose and his careful manners flattered her. She wondered when the men would be back, smelling of turf and thyme, and settle him in. Not a sign of them, and she'd told him they'd gone out to get mushrooms, usually picked at dawn. She took him up to his room and left him. Alone, he sat down on the bed, pensive. "Lord!" he said, "how did I get here?" The properties of the room included a bidet, a chart of the coast, and a still-life of poisonous-looking wood flowers, Felix's work. He thought that the berries were deadly night-shade, which they were. He looked out of the window, the verandah roof sloping beneath him, of slate flags, patched and bound with lichens and ferns, and wondered when and how it had all been put together. His eyes travelled to a yucca, bent like an old man, and opening in a single three-foot spike. Then the wood. He had come out of simple curiosity, and to see something in England off the regulation road. So that was what this Paris bunch did when they got home? What did they do? What was there to do? Where were the men who had asked him? Some kind of trick to leave him alone with the girl?

Getting mushrooms? He decided, for the first time, that mushrooms grew. And that he must carry on, attentively. With immense deliberation the sun was moving west. He stretched his neck out of the window, and saw the crest of the down turn black, and draw up like a tower. He drew in his head. He did not want to see that hill with the stars trembling over it. How did they light the place? *I know moonlight, I know starlight.* Very sensitive to the arts, he admitted that he might soon be justified in singing that. *Lay this body down.* What an idea, but he might soon have to do it. To him, straight from London, Paris, and New York, the silence was intolerable.

The wood sighed at him. Just like that. Two kinds of life he did not want. The ash-fair tree-tall young woman downstairs, and the elaborate piece of leaf and wood, that was one thing and many. The wood and the woman might be interchangeable, and it wasn't the sort of thing you wanted on a visit. He had nerves, too, a great sensibility to take impressions. Always in relation to people. Life to him was an elaborate theatre, without scenery. Here the scenery seemed to be the play.

He got as far as that when he remembered that downstairs there would be certainly something to drink, and began to change, beautifying himself, scrupulously and elaborately as a cat.

He had a cocktail; he had two. A woman came in. Scylla told him she was her old nurse. Was it truth, or a comedy, when she said:

"I found the lobster and the fish Mr. Felix got in the ditch."

And Scylla answered:

"Where are Mr. Felix and Mr. Ross?"

And the nurse had said:

"You never know. I'll bring in dinner."

So they ate together; an eatable meal, fresh-tasting wine, and the inevitable whisky after. A rabbit crossed the lawn. A rat came under the verandah and stole a piece of bread. Two bats flew in. Scylla said:

"They're full of lice, worse luck."

Nothing went on happening: the delicate quiet waited on them.

"I expect," said Scylla, "that they went over to Tollerdown, and found our friends had come to the cottage."

He thought: 'The mushrooms are wearing thin.' "Where is Tollerdown?"

"One of the hills in this part of the world. You know this country was given its first human character in the late stone age. That's all the earthworks and barrows you see. Two of our friends have a cottage there. They dress up like the Prince of Wales, and quarrel like dogs. It will be fun if they are there."

Well, it might be. Anything which would give Dudley Carston a human scene. And if there was one thing in history one could hope was over, it was the stone age. But the young woman's mind was distracted by the thought of it. She was laughing to herself. Laughing at the stone age. Real, abstract laughter. She had forgotten he was there. That her brother and her friend had disappeared. She might be mad, but she was good-looking. Women lovely and mad, or only lovely and only mad, should not be left alone in woods. Literature did not help him. He could only think of La Belle Dame sans merci, and she wasn't that kind. She should think of him as a real man, not one of her flighty shadows too careless to be there to receive the stranger they had invited to follow them some hundred miles.

"Shall I go and look for them?" he said.

"Where?" she said— That brought it back— "The openness here is deceptive, and they might come a hundred ways. I'm ashamed of their manners."

She was telling herself: 'Something has happened, I think. I told myself this morning I'd watch the scene and not try to make it right. My boy friends can go hang.'

The silence went away, and left nothing.

There was an iron clang. Carston sat tight.

"It's the gate on to the grass," she said, "here they are."

Two heavy men syncopating their walk. Must be a march of trolls in the night through the wood. Nothing natural was coming. Four tall young men crowded into the room.

"So you've collected Carston?"

The men from Tollerdown, of course.

He saw three men about thirty years old. One tall and black, with close-set eyes and a walk affected to hide his strength, called Clarence. One rougher, shorter, fairer, better bred, called Ross. Then a boy, Scylla's brother Felix Taverner, the english peach in flower, lapis-eyes, the gold hair already thinning where the temples should have been thatched. Then, last, the tallest they called Picus, grave as a marsh-bird dancing and as liable to agitation, his colour drawn from the moon's palette, steel gilt and pale, the skin warmed to gold by the weather, cooled to winter in the dark crystal eyes.

Clarence and Picus crowding off to eat in the kitchen. Scylla followed them, but came back.

"Something has happened, I think. If it's what I think it is, it will be a diversion for you."

Not so sure, he waited. They came back. Their fatigue was different from his, an affair of the muscles. They seemed drunk on fresh air. He found himself faced with his usual problem, how to make a fresh event serve his turn, relate it strictly to personalities, especially his own.

That was the situation for him, as he listened, translating, to the story Felix had to tell. Felix said that Ross and he had been to a place called Gault, and he'd sung to it. Presumably a dangerous place. They had then decided to call on distant friends, who might or might not be inhabiting a cottage on a place called Tollerdown. Anyhow, supposing they were not there, a rare species of hawk known as a honey-buzzard might be observed in the vicinity. On arriving they had found their friends (Scylla seemed to be the only woman in the group, a point for reflection) in difficulties owing to their well, shrunk by the drought, yielding nothing but dead hedgehogs. A digression on the use of soda-water to make tea. An excursion down the well to clean out the hedgehogs had led to a discovery. An odd cup of some greenish stone had been found, rather like pea-soup carnelian. The state of the well had necessitated the transfer of Picus and Clarence for an indefinite stay. "You're done in this country if your well gives out. Wait till ours does." Carston was not interested. This might interfere with his making love to Scylla, which he had decided was to be his expression of a successful visit. Unless he found out how to use it.

Then Ross produced the cup suddenly, out of his pocket, and handed it round. Carston said:

"That means nothing to me."

"Been cut by hand," said Felix. "Is there a kind of opaque flint glass? Keltic twiddles, I think, very worn round the rim."

A good deal was told Carston, casually, about Kelts and

Saxons and Romans and early Christianity; things completely over so far as he knew— Not that they talked about what he hadn't heard. Only they talked as if there was no time, no progress, no morality. He knew, of course, that there was no progress, and no morality.

Then Ross said, roughly and softly, as though he was loving something:

"The thing was that we fished it out with a spear."

Scylla said, "Ross, that's odd."

Clarence fidgeted attentively. Felix stared, and Carston saw the boy's tricky brilliant eyes light up. Picus was grave, a man so tall and thin he seemed to go on for ever. Unnaturally supple, he had seen him pick up something behind him as if it had been in front. He tried to think what a spear had to do with it.

Felix said, sharply:

"Good old Freud."

"Idiot!" said Ross, and turned away furious and contemptuous.

"It seems to me," said Scylla, "that people had to start some way of thinking of things. What they saw once they'd learned to think might be quite different from the things they'd learned on."

Then, to Carston, she said that odd things were always happening, and old patterns repeated themselves. That it was sometimes alarming when they did, and Freud very useful in the case of irrational fear. Very true, too, when there had been a row, and no one could feel what was just and what was not. Always look out for the suppressed wish that's taken a wrong turning. But that what had happened to-day was objective and odd.

Carston said:

"I think I'll have to ask you to explain a little more than that."

But Ross had turned round again. "I'm awfully sorry," he said. The insolent insincerity was not meant to be lost on Carston, but it was. "Put it down to the solstice or the heat."

"Tell us the news," said Felix. "We couldn't get back without our tea. Ross believes in perspiration. I don't."

Carston had come with elaborations of the best gossip. They listened to him—rather too attentively, he thought. At the same time there was something that spoiled his effects. It was the place, the faintly lit room mixing with the starlight outside. A shallow little green dish was lying among the glasses. Might have been made out of star-material. The woman had called it a diversion, but they weren't going to let him play. He began suddenly to dislike them, wish to humiliate them. Far too troubled to think how to do it.

Even Ross saw there was something wrong when he left them and went up to bed.

But this Carston had seen. Four ways of saying the woman good-night. Ross nodded to her. Felix embraced her. Clarence kissed her gallantly, with a flourish indicating affectionate indifference to their difference of sex. Picus, busy with a syphon, crooked his fore-finger at her across the room.

Chapter IV

THE MORNING RESTORED Carston to kinder thoughts. Last night might have been spent under the sea. If they had drawn him down, it was possible that they had not done it intentionally. His room was comfortable, if mad, full of little bits out of the sea. A ship in a bottle pleased him. On a hook was an old cap with an anchor. A ship was painted inside his morning cup of tea.

After breakfast he had the sea full; bathing with Felix who treated the sea like a living animal. Carston was content to show how well he swam. Very content, that he swam so well, better than the boy. Looking from the rocks inland, he thought it might really be quite all right if there was not too much scenery that called for a too high quality of attention. At least he could not go back next day. Pride forbade it. He must stay until he had some power over them. That would be his compensation for a week's boredom and acquit him.

Scylla he was reconsidering. To make love to her would be too hard work, too easy. The sort of woman who forgot all about you next day.

To have power at a moment's notice, it is as well to begin by knowing a secret. He remembered the cup still on the table at breakfast, and used by Ross as an ash-tray. Then, that Felix had not used it.

"You know," he said to the boy, "that I was very interested in what you were saying last night. But I didn't quite catch on."

Felix was thinking that here was something nice and new, who did the things they did, a little differently. With the fundamental error that being an American, simplicity and kindness would be his chief characteristic. He surprised Carston with his quickness to explain.—"We got over there, and found Picus saying he was ill and Clarence doing all the work. As usual. So, after tea with soda water, I went down in the bucket. The others hung on to the windlass and Picus strolled out. Got a fishing spear with him, because he said high hedgehogs aren't things to handle (they smell water and fall in, poor brutes). I raised that cup along with the corpses. We were looking at it, and Picus began to whistle. You must hear him whistle; it's like Mozart. Said he was perfectly well again. He and Ross are mighty queer birds."

"Tell me more about your friends."

"Picus is Clarence's 'old man of the sea' only he's young. Clarence doesn't know it. Scylla says I'm hers. He only does one or two small things like whistling, but he does them perfectly. Riding and blowing birds' eggs. You saw how powerful his body is, but he's like a bird. Off in a flash. Hence the name. Picus was the Woodpecker.

"Clarence fights for him and with him. What he fights for, I don't know. Clarence is quite all right. A bit insincere, because he's afraid. And what he's afraid of, I don't know."

Carston could only say: "Tell me more."

"Scylla's a different egg. If there is anything wrong about my sister, it's everything. I've said the word 'fear' at least ten times lately. This time it's my own." He horrified Carston—he was like a desperate butterfly, angry, petulant and white.—"It's she at one end, and Picus at the other, who get me going. It's because she wants everything to happen to its last possibility. That's how she gets kick out of life. Once a thing's got going, she'll understand it and manage it. And enjoy it. She'll never tone it down. Sort of woman who'd have mothered the house of Atreus, and though I owe her everything, it's wasted on me. She'll enjoy—"

"What will she enjoy?"

"What will happen out of what happened yesterday. Don't you see. That infernal Picus is a psychic if there ever was one. Or if there is such a thing."

"Does she believe in that?"

"Believing doesn't trouble her. Only what is going to happen. She doesn't create situations. She broods them and they hatch. And the birds come home to roost. Some mighty queer birds. Truth isn't everyone's breakfast egg. She isn't happy till it's hatched. Calls it knowing where you are. I wish I knew where I was—"

Carston revised his ideas again about Scylla as a lover. He could only say: "But what can she and your friend Picus make out of what happened yesterday, anyhow?"

"Don't you see? It was fishing it out of the well with that old spear—they always went together."

"What went with what?"

"The cup of the Sanc-Grail, of course. It and the spear, they always hunted in couples. You've heard of it. All sexual symbolism. I wish I hadn't."

"Does sexual symbolism get you?" It would be news if it did.

"I should worry. But the Sanc-Grail was a very funny thing. People used to think it was a shallow greenish dish. And the cup's a shallow, greenish dish. Those well-shafts on the downs might be any age. So might it. Tollerdown had a bad reputation, and I never heard of the Sanc-Grail doing anyone any good. With that moron Picus behind it, and that demon, my sister, in front of it."

Carston took stock of several things: what he remembered of the Grail story, the possibility of anyone behaving as if it had happened, and what that implied in human character. Felix's youth.

He said at last:

"Don't tell me your sister is superstitious."

"Not she. Better if she was. She'd read it up and do processions and things. It might be like that. But with her it won't get its home comforts. It will get vision."

On the last four words he changed, and Carston saw the sister in the brother, in the elegant, frightened boy now explaining that what he wanted was not vision, but fashionable routine.

"Of course, there is nothing in it. I only meant that the find's a reminder."

"Reminder of what?"

"Of what it would remind you, of course. Oh! I see you don't know. Never mind, it's a long story."

Carston gave out. He was not pleased. He had been atrociously taken into confidence, and he had not understood. His earlier dislike of them returned, with an uncomfortable respect. The Sanc-Grail did not call on everybody. The boy was a young thing, telling him how much he hated poverty and dreams. What a snob he was. All about the things you could not do. Felix remembered that Ross had prepared them to be misunderstood. It did not occur to him that he had no right to expect that Carston should understand.

Chapter V

Picus was alone in his room, modelling the body of Scylla in wax. One of the little things he did. Clarence was a serious and accomplished painter, discovered and produced by Ross. Picus played about with wax, which grew more transparent as he touched it. Exceedingly powerful in body, he looked like wax, in a gauze-thin blue sweater rolled up his neck. He looked out of the window at the wood swimming in the mid-day heat, let out a little breath and waited an answer from the wood. He smiled and began to dance, like a marsh-bird, swinging up a leg, effortlessly, in any direction.

Then his face expressed pain. He put up his hands to his head and pressed them in. In a kind of despair, he turned and dug his nails in the wax of Scylla's flesh.

Carston came upstairs to wash, bewildered by the dark stair, the corridor crossed with sun motes. He walked into Picus's room by mistake. There he saw him, very gracious, in a room shabbier than his own, making the portrait of Scylla in wax. He saw brightness, nakedness, a toy. A liveliness of colour to remind him that she was a young woman alone among young men.

"I don't like it," said Picus, and broke it.—"I'll make another after tea." Carston could have cried. The waste of richness, the shocking petulance, a toy that excited him shewn and taken away. For a moment he had embraced Scylla. Another of the little things they did in their spare time.

Pushed out of his politeness, he said:

"You're the one who discovered the cup, aren't you?"

"No," said Picus, "I only thought of the spear to poke about with. It was Felix's find."

"Miss Taverner's brother seems a bit upset about it."

"Does he?"

"You shouldn't have broken that statue."

Picus covered up both statements like a perfect young gentleman, rather a stupid one. It occurred to Carston that he was stupid; also that perhaps it had scandalised him to have shewn Scylla naked to a stranger, and hoped it was that.

They went down to lunch. It was his first lunch, but he felt as though never in his life had he done anything but eat there. Once he had lived in America, once he had come to Europe, but that did not count any more. That theatre was as another earth, and the plays were not the prologue to his play. For this play there had been no rehearsal and he did not know his part. Or, if he had a part, he had to improvise it, and it must be a good part. Lost in a green transparent world, he was blind. Beginning to see in a new way he disliked, a seeing like jealousy, without arrangement; principally a sensibility about Scylla, likely to become a fury of desire. He remembered its modest beginnings the night before, his rejection of it on further acquaintance with her brother. That it had started again in Picus. Somebody said: "What do we do this afternoon?" The heat answered that. Laid down on the verandah in a wicker chair like a shell, he lay still, face to face with the wood. One by one the others disappeared.

* * * * *

Ross went up the hill, carrying his painting things. The place he wanted could not be seen from any shade there was on the down-top. He planted his easel in the full light.

The cliffs down the coast were too good-looking. He chose the somberest patch of barn and field in the next valley and drew it hard, his shirt-sleeves rolled up his amber arms, his back square to the house in the wood, several hundred feet together.

Presently he noticed that it was becoming difficult always to distinguish between a sheep and a shrub, and that that meant thunder. With his back to the house and the wood he was being stopped working from the other side. He drew in a tree-shape rather hard. The white haze gathered. The more he looked, the less he saw. Instead, he began to see shapes in his head, not outside it, an exercise he avoided, because it interfered with precision of hand. Unwillingly he felt that he would have to return before he meant to, to a place where there was a martyred ass called Clarence, lying alone for a moment in a verandah, a little distance from a young American, who was keeping remarkably silent. Whom his instincts were against. Not because he disliked him, but because the town-bred contact between them had died. They were all stuck down there in a bewilderment, which had happened because they had forgotten the duties of hospitality and had left it to Scylla to fetch the stranger from Starn. If they had not done that, two of the party would have died of the hedgehogs, or else come straight over to them without raking up a well. Not that he was sorry that it had happened. Then he whistled as he drew, out of tune, but as though he was loving something. No nonsense about being the thing he loved, but like a lover, aware of the presence of what he loved everywhere.

There was a hard, explosive sound. Several mixed noises. A bird tore out of a thicket and crossed an open space, indirectly, frantically, and disappeared. He imitated its call and burst out laughing. "Woodpecker up to his tricks again." Then he went back to his work, straining his eyes.

* * * * *

In the verandah, Clarence slept. He dreamed that he was walking, at night, on a thin spit of rock across the sea, Picus's slender height and great weight against his shoulders, in his arms. Picus was dead, and he was glad he was dead and it was over. The difficulty was to get rid of the body, which was coming alive somewhere else and following him. It could only be got rid of at the end of the rock, and he could not go on much longer like that. There were dark hills round the sea, and in them was the living Picus, not his at all, but another, the real one. It was such a bother, his feet were covered with blood. It wasn't till the dead Picus was in the sea, that the real one would come out of the hills and play with him. No use waiting for day, because it was always dark in that country.

He often went there when he was asleep, often with a dead bird, Picus the Woodpecker, in his hand and in his arms. Sometimes it was an image for Picus. Sometimes him. There came a point when he would say: "This is a play, made out of my wishes and my disappointment. Truth is quite different. I am unhappy because the boy has things wrong with his character, because he has things wrong with his inside. Or, because we all think, somehow, that Picus is a bad lot." After this correction there would come the final idea that saw behind these images and their rationalisation another truth. He stirred, shifted and fell asleep again, not knowing at all that Carston, awake, was wondering why he seemed so wretched, and why he had dictated them and taken offence at lunch. That Carston liked him, and admired his good looks, who could only see how worn they were beside the American's ageless set trimness.

He dreamt again: another Picus came walking up the rock-spit, carrying a glass dish which was the cup of the Sanc-Grail, saying: "It's the *lapis exilii,* the stone of exile. What I'm walking on is the *lapis exilis,* the slender stone. All the same, my dear." Then the neat reminder that no grail texts were clear what the thing was really called. Then his private fancy to call it the *lapis exultationis,* the stone of joy. That the thing had never existed. The joy-stone. Freud again. Had he ordered more wax for Picus to play with? A letter with a stamp like a black star, shifting along a river which carried the London post. Too slowly. It must get there quick, or Picus would be angry and say he hadn't sent it. He woke to remember that that had been an old quarrel, and the stuff had come. Also that he ought to talk to Carston, wide awake in a basket chair, five stone pillars away. That he was feeling horribly shy, raw, ill-adjusted, sick to assure himself that the others thought he was good for something. Had the American seen through him? After all, he'd seen war. Half an hour's more sleep. Perhaps the dreams would be more comfortable, or wouldn't come.

Carston was wondering if he was expected to come over and talk. He liked to hear Clarence talk about war. He had seen some rough stuff himself in Russia. A good soldier the man must have been. Wondered why he hadn't stuck to it, and was now rather overdoing the art business. The others did not overdo it. Quite a good painter, too. Then he saw Scylla in the tree-tops. A limb of ilex, detached from the main height and formed perfectly. Lifted up, glittering in the insolent sky. She was upstairs, broken in pieces, in preposterously pretty, sexual wax. Picus might be there, making another. He'd go up and see. Creep in, if he wasn't allowed to enjoy it.

Almost as good as having the girl, to have that thing of her in wax. This was as far as he got. It was quite true that the statue would have done as well. Desire in Carston was almost mental, a redecoration of his memories. Only at the moment he was between the two, the statuette and the girl, the shoulders he saw in leaf and wax and flesh, and was troubled by the repeats.

While Clarence, asleep again, dreamed he was meeting Picus as he had met him in the war, wearing his shrapnel helmet, a queer glass dish someone had found in a well. Rather a worry.

"Big magic," said Picus. He was a boy then, his smile already gracious and timid, contrasting with a loose, haughty walk. He had said, laughing: "If you take it off,

off comes my hair." That was important. The queer fairy cup his bird wore. Some day Picus would take off his cap to him. He woke up. Something had broken in him, the sense of wrong adjustment was easier. It would come back, but now it was perfectly easy to talk to Carston, by this time also anxious to bridge the gulf between lunch and tea.

Chapter VI

TEA WAS a reasonable meal, with a real human being at it, the doctor having come over from Starn to attend to Picus's health. Carston held his attention, improvising brilliantly on aspects of his native land, wondering if he could interpret Scylla's cordiality into the beginnings of desire. Quick work, he knew, but life in the infernal stillness was going at a pace that had New York beat. It became the doctor's turn to talk. Carston noticed how they played in turns, the second guest after the first. "Pass the buns," said Felix. That was the cue. Carston listened to stories of medical practice in a remote district; after a time to an accompaniment he did not at first locate. Later that it was Picus ringing with a spoon on his medicine glass.

The doctor said:

"I don't wonder you two left Tollerdown. It's a cheerless place at best. I only knew it in winter, going out there to deliver the shepherd's wife. So I think of it as the darkest place that exists."

Scylla answered: "I know. Even now when it is burnt white. I think of it the only time I was there in winter, in a storm. Wind roaring over the flint-crop and snow whirling. Lying an instant and vanishing."

Ross said: "BE PREPARED FOR LAMBING—You hear them mewing in the dark, and see a light in a wooden box on wheels, and out comes a shepherd, with his hands covered with blood."

The doctor said:

"Shew me the cup you got out of the well." And when he had looked at it: "The luck of the country's with you. I'm glad to find a few roman pots. It isn't glass at all, too heavy. I think it's jade. It may have been set once. I tell you, it might have been the cup of a chalice." Intelligent interest. Carston felt quite friendly now towards the thing. The others were giving polite attention. Five people at once thinking about a spear. No, six. He was.

"One has time to remember things, shooting about this country in a Ford. Do you know it makes me think of what I remember of the cup of the Sanc-Grail?"

Picus said, meekly: "What was that?"

Carston thought: 'How was that camp, or wasn't it? Would one of them pick up the challenge? Of course, it was a challenge.' Ross said: "That's a long story," but Scylla leaned forward, excited, and said: "The best way to get that story out is for everyone to say what he thinks or feels or remembers. The Freud game really. Start, Felix!"

"Tennyson," said Felix.

"Oh, my dear," said Clarence, "those awful pre-Raphaelite pictures put me off it long ago."

Ross said: "A mass said at Corbenic."

"Wagner," said the doctor.

"A girl carrying it," said Carston, staring at Scylla and trying to play.

Scylla said: "*Quod inferius, sicut superius est.*"

Picus said: "You haven't told me much."

"Second round," said Scylla,—"people enlarge on what they said before."

"I said Tennyson," said Felix, "because I hate the Keltic Twilight. And nearly all its works. I hate it because it's a false way of telling about something that exists. No, a messy way. Responsible for the world's worst art. Now and then it nearly comes off. Milton left it alone, and I don't blame him. Tennyson made it idiotic with his temperance knights. Fixed it, too, enough for parody. Killed the unstated thing which I don't mind telling you scares me."

Clarence said: "I agree with Felix. I can't stand bad drawing."

Ross said: "At Corbenic, wherever that was, there was a different mass. It may have been the real thing."

The doctor said: "Parsival is like a great religious service to me."

Carston, embarrassed at his turn coming, saw their pained faces. He said: "I supposed the girl who carried it was the female spirit of life."

Scylla said: "I quote again: *'Here lies the Woodpecker who was Zeus.'*"

"Thank you," said Picus.

Later, Carston asked her to take him for a walk. The doctor went with them to the gate, and she asked him what he thought about Picus's health.

"Everything is wrong, and nothing," he said. —"I don't mean by that that he invents it. His aches and pains are a mask that conceals something. What that is, I've never been able to find out—"

"Does Clarence know?"

"I shouldn't care myself to know too much about Picus. Despair's a bad bedfellow."

Scylla said: "We know what despair is." As if she were saying that she knew how to take a temperature. Carston went with her down the wood to the sea. Twenty-four hours before he had been alone with her for the first time. Alone with her the second time, he was almost in pain because he wished to use the moment, and did not know how. The more he planned the less he'd be able to do, who had rarely failed with women. Now the sun struck aslant, the light-chequers broadened into patches. It was damp and delicious. The evening birds were tuning up. A little sympathy is generally judicious.

"I took a walk this morning with your brother. He seemed troubled by what you found yesterday. Even now, after the talk at tea, I'm not clear what it is all about."

Not a hint of his sex had crossed her mind. An american boy, very polished and friendly. No reason not to tell him anything there was to tell.

For the third time Carston heard the sentence: "That's a long story. You must help me to explain."

He answered: "You said two things at tea. The Latin bit, which means, I think, that the things underneath are the same as the things on top. And something I don't get at all: *'Here lies the Woodpecker who was Zeus.'*"

"Yes."

"Then you said another thing—you said that you all knew what despair is. How can that be true?"

Scylla said: "Well, I take it that we have to know everything about being lost."

Lost. He did not get that. If ever there existed a group sure of themselves. He mentioned it.

"Swank," she said, "and instinct. To cover quite intolerable pain. You see we know between us pretty well all there is to know. That's why we rag all the time. To keep things clean, and because it's the only gentlemanly thing to do. We have our jokes, our senses, and our moments of illumination which always take a turn for the worse. See? We live fast and are always having adventures, adventures which are like patterns of another adventure going on somewhere else all the time. A very different sort of affair, a state suggested if you like in a good work of art. The things down here seem hints of it, but there is nothing to make us sure that it is a reality. Let alone that it is worth what it costs us. Quite the contrary. We get into trouble over it, it runs after us, runs away from us, runs away with us, makes fun of us and fools of us. Because of it we have no money, and the wrong lovers, and our instinct for power is starved. For we come of families which have never been without power before. And the name for all this is our subconscious minds. And between Freud and Aquinas, I've managed to tell you about it completely wrong. For another of its names is intellectual beauty, and another, the peace of God."

"D'you believe in God?"

"I don't know. All we do know is what happens to faith based on catch-as-catch-can visions."

"Weren't all religions based on that?"

"They were, and look at them! But now you see why we felt we were being laughed at, dangerously, when we lifted that cup out of a well on the point of a spear?"

Carston pulled himself together. "What did you mean by the other thing: *'Here lies the Woodpecker who was Zeus'*?"

"A little poetry, a little witchery, a little joke. It's the same thing as I said before. Now I'll tell you something worse than what I said before.

"Along with faith fit for people like us, and good taste which are where morals end, there is no goodwill left anywhere in the world. Which started to go first, or if they all went together, or which pushed the other out, I don't know. I've an idea that something else, a principal we haven't named yet, got rid of the lot."

Beginnings for an erotic conversation.

A turn of exasperation seized him. She was leaning on the red arm of a pine tree which stood by itself outside the wood, a crooked blue mushroom moulded by the wind. The scent from its cap mixed with the smell of wind off the tide-stripped rocks.

"Now you see why that cup upset Felix? If it is anything, it is only a Keltic mass-cup. And that, perhaps, is not certain. I don't think you do see. As Felix would say: 'I don't blame you.' But an american poet said: *'Memory, you have the key.'*"

"I have no memories," said Carston.

"We are all wishing we hadn't; because memory produces imagination, and imagination is a state by itself. Memory was the Muses' mother, and the muses are nine names of the imagination. I told you you'd see some fun. Now I must go over to the coast-guards and order a car. We want to take you somewhere to-morrow. See the thunder clouds banking up? I must get back before the rain."

Carston thought: 'Getting rid of me. In an instant she would be off like a hare.' He said:

"Stay a minute. Maybe it's because I have no memories, but I don't see where the fun comes in."

"Don't you call it fun to watch how violently, strangely and in character people will behave? Watch Ross, watch Clarence. Watch me." He was watching her. Green, pointed feet in plaited shoes, bare arms, pointed breasts under a dress full of air. *Blow away the morning dew.* That was remembering something. Like open fir-cones dipped in fire and cream, the thunder-clouds were piling up the sky. Mounting the hills, a wing of them rising out of the sea. Inshore, a breath of wind clashed the pine needles.

Another memory.

Love only me.

Donna Lombarda.

Love only me.

Love only me. Because the tune was what the needles brushed out, and the words the wish that made his body ache.

"Can I come with you?"

She looked at him candidly. She wanted to be alone. "I must go to the farm as well; I do the housekeeping at this time. It's a hot flat walk. The others have gone down to the rocks to fetch a drift-wood log. If you liked to help them to get it up. It's bleached white, and when it burns it will go up in blue and green sparks." He saw that there was something pathetic in the way they made a game of their poverty.

"I'll go to them," he said, "but you haven't explained what the american poet meant when he said that memory had the key?" She had moved away from him.

"He said:

> *Mount. . . . .*
> *Put your shoes at the door,*
> *Sleep, prepare for life.*

And called it: *The last twist of the knife.* Adieu."

The log, as he expected, was large and most unwilling to be moved; the cliff-path more a gesture in broken clay than an ascent.

He saw her in his mind, dew blowing away over burnt, empty grass towards a formidable other world, its edges drawn in fire, the thunder-clouds now half-way across the sky.

Before dinner, he remembered the library, the middle room of the house. Alone there, he looked for something, not Tennyson, to enlighten him. He found a book, and sat in a window with it. Presently he noticed the entrance, one after the other, of Clarence, Felix, and Ross, and that they all went, reticently but eventually, to the same gap in the shelves.

Chapter VII

THEY DINED WITHOUT Picus or Scylla. He saw Clarence, uneasy, and heard that Picus had gone out alone because the doctor had told him to take walks. The earth was now closed in a hot, purple air-ball, the lightning flicking on and off. Without any regard for the weather, Ross arranged their chairs in the verandah while the storm banged about. Carston was silent. He was not accustomed to invite the lightning to visit him under trees. And Clarence seemed fatuous to him when he turned on the gramophone to play against the sky. They were not disturbed about Scylla, who might be out walking alone in the livid night. Apparently the farmer had an old father who gave her beer and told her ghost stories. It was Clarence who swung up and down, turning disks, and saying teasings that were brittle and raw, in his rich, sad voice, tortured and made petulant by the uproar through which his friend's feet could not be heard coming through the wood.

Carston thought that it was like the place to leap up from its equivocal quiet into an orgy of cracking and banging. He wanted to go and meet Scylla. To see her safely home. Why were they so careless of their women? She had told him that love had left them. Had courtesy? She might come a hundred ways. It was the same as on the night when the men had been lost. They had come back safe from adventure. He wanted her to enter with him. He was an american gentleman in an uneasy place. Yes, he would go at once and fetch his young hostess. A proper thing to do. He felt at ease for the first time.

Ross advised not: "She knows her way. You'd never find it. It will rain in a minute. You'll see to-morrow morning the freshest earth there is."

"Prepare for life,
The last twist of the knife."

For the freshest earth there is. 'Phat' went a raindrop on a flag, and a double uproar began. For an hour it rained, through sheet lightning, and thunder like a departing train, the hills calling to one another. The gutters of the roof rushed and sang and leaked, single notes from which the ear eventually picked out a tune. Syncopation, magic, nature imitating Mozart? Carston came to hear it as an overture, for some private earth-life, mercifully and tiresomely apart from his.

Things going on singing, not to him. Escaping also, not finishing, or finishing somewhere else. Beginning again, to enchant him with fragments. He admitted that he was enchanted— When would Scylla wind up the charm by coming through the wood?

The storm tuned up again, the rain striking in rods, filling the air with fine spray. The others were enjoying it, the first row of the stalls for a nature-play. Discussing other spectacles. Then he saw Scylla and Picus run out of the wood and across the lawn, laughing, wet as dogs. He heard Clarence order Picus upstairs to change, to be ignored, while Scylla squeezed out her hair.

"We ran back together. It was too good to miss. Tell me, Carston, does the lightning get you when you're under a tree, or when you're not? We tried both."

That was all there was to it. But how had they met? All prearranged he supposed. No, Picus had done it. Loped off another way to meet her at the farm. She was saying: "You're lucky that you didn't come with me. Admit you'd have hated it?" Was that flirting with him? He asked her what she meant. "Storms aren't in your schedule." So wet they both seemed naked. They all went in. He made hot grog for her over the wood fire, the acid smoke bringing water to his eyes. They looked like real tears to Ross, who wondered. Scylla came down in blue, her hair tied up in a gold cloth, unable to stop laughing. Clarence followed her. Ross said: "Got Picus to bed?"

"No: insists on shaving, and to spite me stands about in his skin." There was more behind what he said than self-pity, yet Carston felt that Clarence had better have hit them in his exasperation than have pitied himself. Why, he wondered? Scylla had said that goodwill had left the earth, but he had noticed that they were compassionate. Perhaps it was that they knew pity's value and feared a sudden demand. At the same time he had no sympathy for Clarence, and they had, who were looking askance at him as though he had said a tactless obscenity. Scylla was saying:

"Warm inside and out. Carston, you're sound on grog."

Picus came down, flushed and transparent, and asked him for some. He found that he could not say 'Help yourself,' forced to wait on him.

"Let's dance," said Scylla; and they danced together, the six of them, but Picus infinitely the best. One of the little things he could do, but not one with Scylla, who moved about with her brother, limbs of the same tree.

There were only five glasses when they all wanted drinks—Picus came over with the cup for Clarence to fill with whiskey and soda. "I don't mind using the ash-tray," he said; and Carston heard through the jazz and the slackening rain a voice which might have been a woman's or a man's: "He doesn't mind using the cup of the Sanc-Grail for whiskey and soda," and another voice, which might have been a man's or a woman's: "He doesn't mind using for a whisky and soda, the cup we use for an ash-tray, the cup of the Sanc-Grail."

The last of the lightning winked at them, the rain turned to a sweet shower, an after-thought.

What'll I do? the gramophone was saying: *What'll I do, what'll I do?* Make love to Scylla, thought Carston. Hadn't they ever thought of that? Shew then that they had among them a living cup. He remembered the new records he had brought them from London, and went upstairs to fetch them. Outside Picus's door he remembered. They were making a noise downstairs. He could look in. More Scylla. A whip-up for senses which were, perhaps, older than theirs. Not refreshed—he thought of it with a sneer—by memories and the past. They should create his memories for him.

He fetched the records, and, a little elated by drink, opened the door of Picus's room. The draught from the window made his candle stream. He saved it and looked. There was no statuette. Even the broken pieces had been cleared away. His light under control, he looked round. Clothes in exquisite order, chaste, ivory dressing things in rows. Scent bottles with a silver strainer, a hollowed bunch of grapes. Nothing to read. Like Ross there. The other went about weighted with books. Something to read. Somebody's book on early church vessels. So Picus had a rationalist mind? Not much read. Time to go.

Below, he was greeted with cheers.

Airs went to his head.

Waiting for the moon to rise and shew me the way
To get you to say
I love you.

"Will there be a moon, soon?" he asked Ross—"after the storm, I mean?"

"Sorry; she's over. To do her tricks, I mean. Aldebaran's very bright just now."

Damn the stars. *I know starlight.* And the penalty. Leave the stars to them. Carston turned a disk: "I think you'll like this. Not come to London yet."

They did. Incarnated him responsible for *O Lady be good,* as for everything else in America. Scylla, dancing with him, smiled as he sang *I've been so awfully misunderstood,* with candour, with friendship, with something spilt over from a reserve of joy. He derided the men because not one of them knew what she was, because an American would discover a treasure worth a hundred Sanc-Grails. There was Picus dancing about like a marsh-bird courting, with an old cup on his head. Up and down and sideways, and never a drop spilt. Tilted his head sideways and caught it as it fell, and it was empty all the time. "Now I call that cheating." In a moment it was back again and full, and never a drop was spilt.

Then Carston showed them the Charleston, and tumbled with them up to bed, shaking hands at doors, easy at last, and full of goodwill.

The air that filled his room was moist and strong, preparation for the freshest earth there is. The elation went out of him and left content. The visit had given him wonder. That was good, because one got brittle and lonely travelling round, and quick to mistrust. How simple it had been to win on these lordly young men. Love their women. Their place was his now. And the wood. It stood like something punished under the rain. He blew out his candle, and lay down in bed.

A minute later the tail of the lightning winked. The rain quickened. The door next his opened. The gutter outside began to run fast again. Through the finale of the storm, he heard a gull crying. Then, outside his door he heard a whistle like a glass flute. How loud, how long he could not judge, startled by it, teased by it. It was outside the door where Scylla slept. All he could do was repeat the words of the call, as it poured out, with grace notes and repeats:

Oh, sweet and lovely lady be good,
Oh, lady, be good to me.
I've been so awfully misunderstood,
So, lady, be good to me.
Oh, lady, please have pity,
I'm all alone in this great city,
I'm just a lonely babe in the wood,
So, lady, be good to me.

Scylla's door opened, neither noisily nor stealthily. Carston was out of bed, his ear to a split panel. He heard her laugh, her stage notion of an american accent. "I should worry." Her door shut. He felt like a weight on his body, the three feet of stone between them. On the other side of that they were lying together, in the quiet of the wood. After a time, he went to the window to listen. But only the casement farthest from him was open, and there was no light. Shocked, almost whimpering, he went back to bed, falling, thanks to the strong air, very quickly asleep. Outside, the night cleared. Over the wood Orion hung up his belt and sword. In the pommel, Aldebaran shook; the star some time before Ross had offered to his attention.

Chapter VIII

THE MORNING was a merciful bustle, with Ross's promise come true of the freshest earth there is. The car arrived, and there seemed to be a controversy where they were to go. To pay a call or see some antiquity. Felix put his foot down on the antiquities.

Carston saw Scylla, preoccupied, perfectly and hideously gay.

They took him to Starn and shewed it him: as if it was a live thing; and did not notice that he resented its life, and was making attempts to kill it. Principally he remembered it because it was half full of people from the world outside. Not peasants, people in vulgar clothes, on motorcycles, in Ford cars, come to stare because it was summer, whom his party treated as if they were a disease.

After lunch the object of the expedition leaked out. He was told that there was a farm, some way off, where mead was made and could be bought. The price of whisky and drinkable wine had turned their thoughts to it. There was no road to the farm. About the distance they were delicately indefinite. They spoke about a track across a place they called the Heath.

Carston had seen the Heath, had crawled along it for miles in the train. It had seemed purple and endless, and he suspected full of traps. The other side of these people's world of hills and the sea. Their idea was that it was time for Carston to visit it, covered with a gauze of every variety of heather, the sweet blood-bright burning crop out of which the honey wine was made.

They rested a little and set out.

Ross caught up Scylla, walking ahead, picking out the track. "A word with you," he said, "don't let anyone know."

"Why not?"

"Because of the American, because of Felix, because of Clarence."

"Why shouldn't they know that Picus and I have an amourette and have magic between us?"

"There's something wrong to-day with Carston."

"At worst he'll leave and blast my reputation for a bit. What of that? And, anyhow, how did you find out, a floor up with Felix and Clarence?"

"Felix and Clarence snoring. Carston quiet, Picus whistling."

"Ross, why have that tall bird and I become lovers? I want to know that. I think it is the kind of thing we shall find out about when it's over, and wonder at." Ross said:

"There is trouble about. The kind that comes with brightness. Can you see that?"

"I can," she said. "Do you mean that Picus is up to no good? I rather agree."

"The first rule," said Ross, "is that Picus is never up to any good."

"Allow me a little fantasy about him."

"Remember that I told you."

"You are being one of the enemies of the rose. Why should you? You always do what you like. Leave that to Clarence."

"I'm telling you to be careful."

"Are we never to have any peace, only adventure and pain? And you, Ross, have a sacred peace."

"So have you. It's the others. That's why they had better not know."

"Perhaps not Felix. Brothers will be brothers."

"Carston's bored. To-day he's upset. Satan's looking for a job for him. I think you were to have been the job."

"First I've heard of it."

"We didn't tell him how long he was to stay."

"You mean that our 'come down and see us' is going to add an episode to what Felix calls the family horror?"

"I mean that anything that's going to happen that shouldn't will find him useful to happen through. Also, a thing you will be too vain to see. This is a move against Clarence by your fancy-boy."

She looked across the purple land to where it ended in the waters of an estuary, more transparent than the sky. "Remember what has to be remembered, too—that Picus and I are young and handsome, rather in love. That he is full of fun and dancing, and bird-calls. Like I am. These things count as well."

"You'll see."

"You are not counting on me?"

"If you can keep things steady, you'd better."

"Perhaps I'm tired to keeping things steady for you. This is my pleasure and my game. And Clarence is unreasonable. Think of it another way, Ross: that Picus is giving us an excuse for the sacred game."

He answered sullenly: "Americans are bad players. At bridge or gardening, or life; especially when it is life as the sacred game. And it isn't his game here, anyhow."

Scylla said: "I'll tell you something. Picus doesn't want Clarence to know. He's afraid of that."

"So he should be. Where would he be without him?"

"Dead, perhaps. That's why I'll do my best to be decent. And now, I want you to tell me what you think about the cup?" He turned away and beat the heather with his stick.

"It's too late, Ross, to be petulant, because you know too much or too little. When you said there was trouble about like brightness, you spoke of things which are nefas, and you've got to go on. Remember Freud."

"We aren't worthy," he cried.

"Worthy? What's worthy? Was anyone? And you've forgotten Gawaine, the knight of the world and of courtesy."

"I didn't know he came into it."

"That comes of never opening a book."

"I detest women."

"Never mind detesting me, which is what you mean. If that cup is anything at all, if it was once an old cup of the sacrament people called 'big magic,' if it's anything or nothing, we can't hurt it, and it can't hurt us. We have our courage and our imagination. We have to be as subtle as our memories. That's all. And but one thing: Picus has given the cup to me."

"Considering your relations, I suppose he had to."

"Then forward, damsel of the Sanc-Grail."

"How dare you!" said Ross, "how dare you!"

She looked at him stoically, "I thought better of you, Ross. Thought there was something hard and great in you. I'm tired of being disappointed. Hear the words of the lover of a bird. He is light and winged and holy. And I mean by holy all there can be in the word; I mean, tabu. You are heavy, wingless, and sacred. And you are a very sensual man. You should understand."

"I understand that you're up in risky air, because you've got off with the worst of the lot of us."

"I can fly." She waited a moment and then spoke cheerfully: "The first thing I understand is that you and I are being unpleasant to each other. The difficulty in this business will be to see the obvious. If Picus is up to his tricks, he's won the first round. And I've tried to pretend that Picus means less than he does to me. To please you, and because it sounds chic. I take that back. And we shall all see."

Ross stood still, his face wrinkled like a pony, sniffing.

"Where are they?" he said. They looked back over magenta risings, yellow sand-holes, black bunches of trees. Quite different from the ravishing gauze seen from Starn on its hill. They waited, but neither one body nor four could be seen moving out of a pocket or over a ridge of the huge, broken honeycomb. Scylla said:

"Has Carston got lost?"

Ross did not suppress a laugh. "He's got three of us with him."

"We're not heath-people."

"Picus knows it. Spends days prowling about here." That subject, delicately picked up, was dropped. "Let's get on."

"No, let's wait."

"Why should we?"

"Because of the mead. Think of us, sweating back with a dozen between us."

Bing. A large black bee slapped Ross's cheek and swung out along the ribbon of sand-path across which the heather stalks whipped their ankles.

"Follow the bee," he said, "it won't be the last walk we shall take together."

"Good!" she said—"at worst they will only be lost. Who minds being lost when there is so much to see? They can steer by Starn. We'll collect what we can, and get home with some martyrdom in hand."

For the last time she looked back over the blazing plain from which an army might pop out. Ross did not look back. He stood with his head flung up, his mouth stretching into its wild-animal smile. With violent, silent amusement, he said:

"It's beginning."

Chapter IX

AT A CHOICE of tracks apparently parallel and similar, Picus had led them to the left. He had trooped them through a wood and sweated them over a crest, to drop them again in a sunk road, made for running contraband a century before. He was asking: "Where are the others?"

"I want my mead," said Felix. "The farm's ahead on the water's edge, where the heath runs out in a point."

Sunk roads are filled with loose sand. They go from nowhere to nowhere now. They trap the sun and keep out air. Their banks curl over in a fringe of heather wire. Adders bask on their striped sides. From this one Starn was invisible, and the eventual blue water bright as dew.

Carston plodded beside Clarence, his feet chafing with sand. They left the wood and crossed another ridge, and saw on their right a creek of yellow grass running inland behind them. They walked another mile till they came to the base of the point, and saw cottages under a crest of dark land. Felix cried out: "We were wrong. Look over there!" They looked across the creek, now filled with water, and only bordered with its grass. Two miles on the farther side, on a patch of green land reclaimed from the heath, was a noble group of trees round a white farm.

"We should have gone there," said Felix—"this comes of Picus's swank about knowing the heath. This leads only to a place we called Misery, because they starved their dogs."

"I saw no tracks in the sand," said Carston.

"I supposed you knew the way." He heard them screaming like gulls over dead fish and would have preferred the birds' company. Abusing each other for what they would forgive in two minutes. Consider rather a joke.

Forget. They none of them saw that Picus had done it on purpose. Then Carston admitted that he might not have thought of it himself if the night before Picus had not slept with the woman he wanted. Why had he done it? He had separated himself from the woman, to mislead them.

They were lurching back through the sand the way they had come. But they had forgotten where they had entered the sunk road that led nowhere in particular; followed it as it wound into exactly the middle of everywhere, and looking over its bank found the airy roofs of Starn lost behind a line of high black trees.

Forgiveness woke in them and fatigue. Picus had been mocked for vanity, had mocked back, and set them off laughing. They were nervous, sweating, flushed. Felix shrieked when a snake flicked across his shoe. But it was all part of a game. Hardly able to see more than the sky, they trudged the road the sun had made into Danae's chimney, down which God came in a shower of gold. Clarence led them. Picus followed. He had deprecated Carston's suggestion that they should try and cut across the creek and make for the farm. "Bad bog," he said. "Marsh-king's sons," said Felix, "that would be the end of us," and Clarence that he had seen a pony lost there. At this choice of pleasures, Carston had followed them; and the sunk road, having come to the middle, stopped in a circular sand-bank round a foul pond bordered with marsh-grass where there was no way out. They flung themselves down.

It occurred to Carston that it was all nonsense. They had only a few miles to go. Keeping towards the long hills, they must strike a road and eventually, Starn. At Starn there was water, tea, lime-juice, gin, champagne. The liverish grass and thick water displeased him. "We can't stay for ever in this cup," he said.

Picus was asleep, Clarence bending over him. An odd sort of pietà. Felix was sinking in the mud, collecting a plant he said was for Ross. All careful of each other's needs and pleasures. He heard Clarence call softly: "Wet a handkerchief, Felix, I want it for his head." Saw it brought over, and Picus jump up in a flash. "None of that sort of water for me, thanks." To spite the men who took care of him? Probably. Carston felt that he was being given an opportunity to hate and that was good. "Hadn't you better try and get us out of this?" The tall creature looked at him, sadly. "I'll try; but you'll have to leave it to me again, you know." He sprang up the hollowed bank, kicking mouthfuls of sand into Carston's face, and vanished. Carston crawled up to watch, hiding behind the heather rim. He saw Picus run a few yards and fling himself down on his face. He waited and saw him get up, heard him call "It's this way," saw him glance round and make off. Carston called back to the other three, heaved himself over, and they set off on a slight track towards the belt of wood.

They went in. Pine-needles are not easy to walk on, like a floor of red glass. It is not cool under them, a black scented life, full of ants, who work furiously and make no sound. Something ached in Carston, a regret for the cool brilliance of the wood they had left, the other side of the hills, on the edge of the sea. This one was full of harp-noises from a wind when there was none outside. He saw Picus ahead, a shadow shifting between trunk and trunk. Some kind of woodcraft he supposed, and said so to Felix who said sleepily: "Somebody's blunt-faced bees, dipping under the thyme-spray"; a sentence which made things start living again. Would they never have enough of what they called life? There was no kind of a track over the split vegetable glass. A place that made you wonder what sort of nothing went on there, year in year out.

The end of the wood was a little cliff, pitted with rabbit holes; and where the hills opened, Starn towering, not too far.

"We get down here," said Carston, trying the loose lip of the cliff.

"Into what?" said Felix. Then they saw that the wood was surrounded again by marsh, the end of the creek which had separated them from Ross and Scylla, curled round on itself. Cutting them off from Starn this time. Clarence said: "Where's Picus?" and Carston hoped that young man was about to get what was coming to him. Only he had gone. They began to think of their sins. Except Carston, who did not think of sins at all. There was raw heath on the other side, but the marsh was wide, and Carston was assured deadly. They left the little cliff's edge, and re-entered the wood. He heard Felix saying: "Where has Picus gone?" Gone to find Scylla? Carston wondered. By a quick turn which would bring him suddenly face to face. And at the folly of three strong young men, tramping about, lost and sapped.

"Call for him," he said. "He'd not answer," said Clarence—"he may have had one of his bad pains again." Carston wished one on him, making an image of him in his anger, until he thought he saw him, walking towards them, transparent and powerful, malicious and shy; his hat perched, to remind them of hooded birds. Remembered his magic, and forgave him. Grew angry again and dazed. Envious also, because he had no part in Picus's dance. "Leave him alone," he said, "he's gone to find a way." Clarence put a hand on his shoulder; thanks, he supposed, for taking it like that.

At last, from the extreme end of the wood, in the least propitious place, they saw across the marsh a clear causeway of stone.

They scrambled down, crossed it, found a path which led them under the hills by a white road into Starn.

About the end of the walk, the less said the better, until at the inn the landlord answered their faint cries for drink. He wanted to know why they had left six and come back three.

"Lost 'em," said Felix.

"You should have stuck to Mr. Tracy. He's the one for the heath. Knows all the paths, and the people who bide out there."

The talk petered out. The evening marched gravely down. The two undoubtable shops put up shutters. The tourists had gone. A man came through with a bunch of sheep. The bar of the labourer's inn turned on a gramophone. From time to time, a huge man came in from the fields, making for his beer. The cries of children stopped. Mothers came out. A fast touring-car shot across the square. A mist rose, an intangible gauze, refreshing them. They dined in the inn garden. When Carston saw in the west a large star watching, he though of the lights on Broadway. Felix saluted the star. Clarence worried, but without, for once, worrying them.

They set out to watch the square again.

Then Scylla appeared, and Picus and Ross.

"We found him, sitting on a stone, saying he had lost you: that you ran away from him on Hangar's ridge."

"He lost you first," said Ross. "I don't blame you."

"He did," said Felix, "and cleared off when he'd made a final mess of it. I know his ways. Have you got the mead?"

"Bottles," said Scylla.

They were surprised when Picus, who had thrown himself into a chair, got up and said: "That's how you take it. It was not my fault."

Clarence sprang beside him.

As he went out, Scylla touched his sleeve with her fingers. He took no notice, but Clarence did.

Carston's fatigue had passed into charity. They were all over-tired, of course. The developments of over-fatigue were caprice and anger. What had Picus been up to? Helping himself with accidents, of course. But exasperating himself.

"There were no bones broken," he said, "you've got the mead, and we've all got back." He was furious when Clarence ignored him, and went out into the half-light after the man who seemed to combine all the elements of a family curse. Felix began:

"God! I'm sick of this. Why can't we be at Biarritz leading a reasonable life?"

A negro song came into Carston's head: *Bear your burden in the heat of the day:* but it did not occur to him to tell it to the boy, whom it would have helped.

Clarence came in again. "I've ordered the car. We ought to get back. I'll tell the others." Carston saw him go into the dining-room and heard Scylla call:

"Well, we want to eat. Tell it to wait."

"We must go home."

"Take it home then, and send it back for us."

Silence again. Question of expense.

Carston saw Picus come into the dining-room from the garden and sit down at a table by himself. He heard Scylla call:

"Clarence, leave your fancy-boy alone."

That had done it.

Picus was eating alone. Anything might happen, only it was time for sleep. Half an hour later they had packed into the car and shot away, up into the hills the night wind had now made exquisite, to a different wood from the one in whose red-glass darkness Picus had lost them, moist and shimmering, a repetition of the tremblings of the stars.

Chapter X

THE NEXT MORNING the sky was white round a blue zenith. Carston came down, not pleased, because through every discomfort of soul he was feeling well, his body content with itself, a steady animal health. He should have been all of a tremble, and he was hoping that there would be fish for breakfast, lots of fish. There was fish, and after it the toast came up, hot and hot. He remembered again to make opportunity serve him. Health would give him power. Also he would desire Scylla more. Desiring her more, and not wholly as panache he might get her. Picus was bound to let her down. He was saying: "I'm sorry I lost my temper. It was trying to lose you three like that. You know how one is." Scylla said:

"Served you right, when you'd lost them."

"How did you do it?" said Ross.

There was no answer. Picus was giving the impression that he was about to flirt his tail and vanish. Carston was irritated again. There came droning into his mind an ugly sentence, a haunting from barren New England: *Thou shalt not suffer a witch to live.* He was hearing Picus say: "How's the cup this morning?" and saw Scylla get up for it.

It was not on the card-table, folded over in a half-moon. It was not on the chimney-piece, or on the sideboard among the candlesticks, whose silver had worn down to the copper and polished rose.

They passed the morning entering and leaving rooms where the cup was not. Not in the kitchen, the lavatory, or the library. In twos and threes and singly, getting more silent as they passed each other. Up and down the curved stairs whose banister was a rope run through rings. Carston saw a good deal in that journey. Scylla's room which had its objects of luxury, where the first time he stared at the bed, he suffered and desired to throw himself on to it. In and out of the room several times, he became indifferent, content with repeating to himself: "I shall sleep there." Picus's room, non-committal, in exquisite order like a manly woman's and Clarence's, full of frivolities. Then he remembered something he had read about an Emperor's collection of hats and wigs 'which sometimes solace the leisure of a military man.' There were no wigs and no hats. But no memory in that place ever had a straight point. Only his room was a sad, gay, desperate display of something like toys. He pitied, without humour, having no humour; slightly wanting for himself a glass orange, each of whose fingers came out and held a different kind of scent.

All their things for art or sport were cared for like tools or choice animals. In Felix's room there were leopard skins; in Ross's a Buddha in a red lacquer shrine held a crystal, a reflection for their mutual contempt.

And the beds were humble and the linen darned, the bare floors solid like glass rocks. He could feel the weight of the blue slate roof, cooling and darkening the rooms, holding the house to the earth, while they searched it like serious children for a thing which could not walk. In and out and up and down a house much larger than it seemed, cooler than the wood's heart.

Dazed Carston played too, arrived at the long attic, roaring dark, directly under the roof. The roar was from bees who hived under the slates, and the smell their fresh honey and the black clots, old combs. There was Felix opening a victorian work-box made out of an elephant's foot. A place where it was utterly impossible for the cup to be. No more impossible than that it should have been overlooked anywhere else. Short of idiocy, a miracle, or a trick, the thing was off the map. A conclusion they had reached by lunch-time, after a morning's exercise indoors.

It was a quiet meal. Two things had been lost. Picus

and a cup. Picus had found himself. As for the cup, they had reached the time before the time for real consideration, when the instinct is to find something else to do. Carston, no more than the others, was quite ready to say that, since six pairs of eyes had failed to see something, then that thing must have been hidden, and hidden well. Instead he was made unhappy, because he heard Picus say to Scylla: "We don't want to bathe to-day, do we? Come over to Gault Cliff and I'll shew you something—"

"Birds?" He nodded once. "I'm coming."

They were in the library, the sacred neutral zone for arrangements that had no reference to their life as a group. An arrangement Carston could not be expected to have understood. It was a very dark room. From a window seat he saw their bodies straining to be away. And hated it. Like a man put in a bag and shaken up, instincts were stirring in him, like muscles unused in years, and sore and strengthening.

The american appears to the english everything that is implied by saying over-sensitive, touchy, or abnormally quick to take offence. Our reaction is usually bewilderment, grief that our intentions have been misunderstood. Followed by a desire to give them something to cry about.

Carston thought they had seen him, could not have understood that no one was seen in that room. And they had not seen him. If they had, they would have supposed that he was there not to be seen. Scylla was sitting on the top of the library steps, made like everything in the house before the days of cheap furniture, shabby and characteristic as an old dog. She said to Picus:

"You idle baggage, what have you found on the hills?"

"Come and see!"

"Let me down!" He put his hands under her arm-pits and let her down, so gently that Carston did not hear her feet touch the floor. He saw their colours; her white; Picus's blue and grey. He saw their beauty, their own, and the beauty of their passion. And another thing; that the man's right hand ought not to belong to his body; that it was red and thick and swollen at the joints. He remembered the delicate adaptability of Ross's, Felix's, Clarence's hands. This gave him a key. To a very old feeling about sin and fleshy lust. A refinement on sensuality, he knew, but an excuse for rage. And a warm feeling that what would relieve him would be right. Right for him to possess Scylla, if he had first rescued her. That would give him the claim on her body. Rescue her from what? From passion for a tall delicate man with coarse hands. Also because he had glory, a kind of lost god. From what was the glory? From the devil. How did one shame the devil? By taking the honour out of his sufferings. *Thou shalt not suffer a witch to live.* And the reward would be Scylla.

What would he give her? Respect, for he did not respect her, or at least admire. Sincerity, loyalty, virility—after what? He was sure Picus did not respect her, was not sincere with her, had no loyalty, and he didn't know about the last. The fantasy in this sequence escaped him, because of the naïveté of his cult for women. He had made a martyr of a person who was not a martyr, or to nothing which would have moved him. In the world there is a fifty-fifty deal of pleasure and grief. The excuse of that band was that they knew it, and that they had something else to occupy their attention, something that the wood knew.

When they had gone, Carston went to the wall where a map hung, to look for a place called Gault Cliff. As well to know where they were going. He followed the coast with his thumb, and found it. About three miles away. There was a track they would probably take; and a way where no track was marked over God knew what to God knew where, which might get him there before them.

The others seemed to expect him to want to be left very much alone. Praise their country and give them the slip? Or take Felix down to the sea and make him talk?

He decided to do that.

Chapter XI

PICUS AND SCYLLA went out of the house along the green road, walking separately. They sprang up the hill, the air from the sea fortifying them, against the mid-day, against the desire to anticipate in thought a distance their muscles must cover.

They came to the coast where Ross had sat and painted, his back to the house. "This way," said Picus, and turned through a gate into a tunnel of hawthorns where a bird had flown out before Ross. There Scylla paused, but he took no notice, and she fell behind him, following his stride.

The way became hard, no way at all, but climb and drop over unmortared stone walls, bound with bramble and thorn. They crossed them, without reference to each other, steady as hunting dogs. In time they came to the edge of Gault.

"Let's go down!"

"How?"

"On the soft side, where the landslide was last winter. Can you do it?"

"I suppose so." She looked where a coast-path ran to the edge, straight out into mid-air.

Some time later they were in the unvisited wood under Gault, where the low trees grow to the edge of the sea. Where there is no bay, no beach, no landing-place, no way round. Taking advantage of a great fall of earth, Picus had created a way down.

From the immense crag water dripped, and ran out under the roots of a thorn over the tidemark of the open sea. They followed it up to where it ran over pebbles across a circle of grass enclosed by low trees. Greenwood within whispering distance of the unharvested sea. She said:

"What have you found here?"

"What d'you mean?"

"The way down—and this—"

"Foxes, badgers, fifteen ways of looking at a finch. They don't mind you here."

High over them the gulls squalled like sorrow driven up. At long intervals the water tapped the rocks like memory driven away. She knelt over the stream and washed dust and clay and a smear of blood from her bare arms and neck. Pulled a trail of thorns from her skirt. Threw away her hat.

"This is Bari," she said, "the warm wood."

"Which one was that?" said Picus, off his guard.

"Baldur's wood," she said, very carefully, not to make a mistake with him.

Gault Cliff hung over them, a terror to look up at, its seamed head raw in the light, but dark underneath and broken into bog and scree, interlude between the earth of pure stone, and the earth of wood and spring. No interval between the wood and the sea, it was that made the place incomparable. They lay on the grass on each side of the foot-wide brook, paddling their hands.

"Not bad for a naked sword," she said. He kissed her over it. "Hush!" A bird appeared. She cried out: "That's a Great Black Woodpecker."

"I've been looking for it all my life," he said. "Chuck!" said the bird at them and went off. They saw the scarlet ribbon on its head.

"What else is there here?"

"There's a badger that bit me, and a vixen I can almost nurse—there's the skeleton of a man—"

"We won't look there now—"

"Not to-day, love." She crossed her hands on her breast. He had given her all he had. This place. A fountain where saga and love were mixed. She looked up into the sky at Gault Cliff, where the mica glittered like sweat.

Again Picus said: "Hush!" She listened, loving him. The bird was back, the largest and rarest of the woodpeckers.

"I saw him when I was looking at the skeleton. In a tree."

She said: "He was a famous bird once, Picus Martius. He was Zeus." He nodded, as if he was saying: "I thought as much." But she had turned the corner where love sees. When she saw that she was lying by the same thing. That what she had said to confuse them prettily, to hide love by revealing, had been about this. Between the tree and the skeleton there had been the bird who had been god. He had seen it, who was called Picus the Woodpecker, who was a man, who was the same thing. Now she knew, who was her lover. And what was she now, the lover of a bird?

Even Leda found a blue egg. She laughed. How long was this going to last? What was this? It was all right; worth whatever it hatched.

Only he must make love to her there.

He had rolled up the sleeves of his blue sweater. He put out his arms, one marked with a badger-bite, across the stream and slung her over.

It was late afternoon. They were lying again on either side of the stream. Gault over them, a little blacker with the sun turning behind it.

"How did you come to find this place?"

"Last spring, looking for young gulls. I looked down and thought if I found a lover—"

"Any lover?"

"I have only found one."

She kissed him over the ribbon of water. He said:

"There's a nest in every crack of the rock. It's still pretty full." That took away her fear of Gault. For the terrible crag was soft with birds, and where the birds ended the spring rose. None of the sequence without grace.

They were coming out of the trance of love into a time which would have to be put up with until luck turned them birds again. He had given her his treasure. If he rose and strangled her, she had that to remember to him. There was trouble in his face, the old trouble, Picus's grief. That was not named or rational or tamed or shared. Untractable, inexplicable, near to wickedness.

The water divided them. She crossed it. He moved his hands as though he would be rid of them.

"Shew me the skeleton!" He shook his head.

"Make the bird come back! I want to see him again."

"Woodpecker-Zeus," she said, "leave your skeleton under the tree. Stop flirting with us. We know who you are. Eagle. Kingfisher. Swan. We have met you before. I am Leda. You know best who he is."

She waited, hoping for the best.

"There it is," said Picus. She could not see it. The shadow of the cliff was moving towards them.

"In the thicket." She clapped her hands, and the bird flew out.

"There," she said, and saw him suddenly pleased and changed.

Then he said:

"Wonder what that chap Carston'll make of it?"

"Make of what?"

They were looking at the other out of the corner of their eyes. Picus paddled one hand in the stream.

Scylla said:

"There is one thing which may have surprised him already. His room's between ours."

"Well, that ought to interest him."

"Only," she said, "if he wanted me."

"He may be wanting you. Perhaps you'd better sleep with him. It would be better than his coming down here. Where nothing has been spoiled, love."

"I see. Mais comme tu taquines éternité."

She thought again: 'I have no business to be glad that

Clarence does not know, nor ask if he will be taken here. I came first.' This was an excuse, not only in honour, but in letting life alone.

He got up and drew her on to her feet. He walked her along the grass between the thickets and boulders, so that her feet never touched a stone. Up the landslide she hardly felt the slant of the earth, held as if he were walking with a tree. At the top of the cliffs he gave her no time to look back. In their triumph they walked alone a little separate from each other.

At a gate he caught her up.

"What y' thinking about?" She saw his head on one side.

"Carston and the cup. That ought to get him going more than us."

"Perhaps it will."

"Picus, demon, where did you hide it?"

"Hush! love."

Chapter XII

After an accident in the sea with a small octopus he would sooner have avoided, Carston returned to the house. Felix had not talked to him, said that it would be wiser not to talk, because there might be big magic about. Could not Carston feel it cooking up? Convinced that the boy was enjoying himself, he went up to his room. And what was there to do but think of those two, up somewhere high in air, kissing, or finding some strangeness in Nature and forgetting to kiss. He lay staring and fretting, until with slow alarm growing like a dream, he saw the lost cup, by itself, on the end of his mantelpiece. And earlier in the day, they had passed in and out of his room looking for it there.

His first impulse was to run downstairs with it, crying. Crossing the room to take it, he slipped on the glassy boards, and the fall and anger from pain turned him. He did not want to touch it. There might be something about it after all. Working a splinter out of his hand, it occurred to him that they had put it there; that the morning had been a farce played for his benefit, a vile joke to make a fool of him. Those people who made love under his eyes, who had lost him on a moor. They had not let him into their lives. They would not believe his innocence. Under the shock of his fall, his imagination galloped reeling. He felt very lonely. He was very lonely. It did not cross his head that they would believe what he told them. Still less that it did not matter whether they believed him or not. Behind this, a dead fever reviving in the blood, was the literal fear of the cup, that it was uncanny, tabu. He passed a dreadful minute, staring at its impressive antiquity. His sensitive intelligence raced through a variety of panics, till the shock of his fall subsided and he began to arrange alternatives. To go down to tea with the cup and say: "I found it in my room. I don't know how it got there."

To hide it in his baggage. In the house. To put it somewhere—say, in Picus's room. To destroy it.

The first would make a fool of him, the second a thief, the third impossible, the fourth a trickster; the fifth might bring bring him to a bad end. This was what had come of his nosing round for power. Scylla would be coming in, burnt with kisses. Perhaps she had played off this trick on him. How many years had he been living in this chinese box of tricks? If he could have believed in their belief of the possibility of a possible sanctity, gone down to them and said: "Here is something that may be precious," he would have walked into their hearts. But that would not have served him, because he did not want their hearts. Did not want hearts. Wanted scalps.

On a final sweep of rage he went downstairs with a cup in his hands to Felix and Clarence and Ross. He said: "Here's your cup. I should like to know which of you played this off on me. I should like to know who put it in my room."

"Oopsey daisy," said Felix.

"If that's your notion of hospitality, it doesn't coincide with mine."

Clarence said: "If you don't like us, what d'you come down here for?"

"What we mean, is," said Ross, "that we don't understand why you should think such a thing."

"Are you trying it out on me that the thing got there by itself, and that none of you knew?" Felix said:

"If we had known, why should we have spent a morning perspiring over it?"

Carston cried at him:

"I'd not put it past you. The day I turn my back on you

all will be the best I've spent. I can tell people then what I think of you."

Felix answered: "And we might as well tell the world that your thirst for antiquities led you to steal a family chalice. Nice kind of mind you've got. You know none of us put it in your room." That was what he did not know. What he could not have done, others could do. There was a stupid, broken pause. Then he said, who had had time to think:

"I suppose the alliance between Miss Taverner and Mr. Tracy explains it."

"What alliance explains what?"

Carston looked at the brother; felt like a man pulling up blinds.

"Love made them mischievous, I suppose."

"What love?"

Warm, sunburnt, they came in. They were in the room, leaning on their ashplants, serene, apart. After a silence, "What's wrong?" said Scylla.

"The cup's turned up," said Ross, "in Carston's bedroom. Did either of you put it there?"

Knowing Picus behind her, she laughed. Lovers' jokes are sacred, pleasantries of a man who discovers the sea-wood, the rock soft with birds, the meeting of pure water and salt. Come down out of that to enchant and rule her equals.

"Count us out," she said. "What's biting you, Carston?"

If she had shewn a little decent concern it might have recalled him. But he went on:

"Then I suppose your friend did it. Not content with keeping me awake all night."

They stared at him. Clarence was practically invisible with frightful emotion.

"Put what where?" said Picus, laughing.

"Four mysteries," said Carston, "since I got here. First, you found that thing. Then Tracy vanished, after leading us a dance in an infernal prairie. Then the thing vanished. Then it's found in my room. I'm waiting your explanations. I've gotten my own."

"Let's hear 'em," said Ross.

Scylla spoke: "It is my cup. My lover who gave it me. We who have enjoyed it. Carston can think what he likes. I did not put it in his room. It is he who will not play. If he wants to find out what has happened, he will find out. We will tell him when we know. Which we don't at present. Don't be a fool, man. No one has tried to trick you here."

All fairly true, but Picus had done something. Just a little devilry. Her heart caught at a beat, she tasted something in her mouth, salt like pain. Pain so soon after. Other side of the halfpenny. She sneered and sat down, tapping the bright boards with her stick.

Carston felt disintegrating, sticky, a loser, afraid. Still standing, he stared out at the wood, at the ilex-limb, each leaf a white-fire flame. He became aware of all the noises of the wood, that it was cackling all the time, a frightful old long gossip about dirt and the dead ends of lies. His subtle brain raced on, took a glorious chance. He said:

"I can tell you something then. Tracy has a book up in his room. On somebody's collection of early church ornaments. He brought the cup down from London to work this off on you all. You remember how he stunted his ignorance? Just a little game to make you think something of yourselves and let you down. You may like being kidded. I don't. I reckon I've done you a service—"

"Bright idea," said Felix. "True, Picus?" He flew at them, with the menaces of a bird.

"What d'you mean? Scylla's been talking. You are all a pack of old women intriguing against me. Making my life hell. Like Carston, I'm sick of your hospitality. Especially when it includes him."

"*Our hospitality,*" said Felix. Quotation wasted on Picus, caught Carston.

"Yes, a decent vendetta would be better than your poisoned fun."

"We don't seem to have cleaned up anything," said Clarence.

"Cleaned up," said Picus, chattering at them. "Accusing me. Boring me. Interfering with ME." In this there was something that was not comic, in the dis-ease he imparted.

"An aborted thunderstorm," said Scylla. "I'm going up to change."

Five left, hating each other. Then Felix modestly, like the youngest: "I'll go down the wood, and see about the dinner fish." Four left. "Work to do," said Ross. Three left. "Have you a time table?" said Carston. Clarence said: "Hadn't you better stay till we know the truth?" Carston turned his back on him, and went out neatly through the library door. Two left.

"What is this about you and Scylla?"

"I suppose I am free to sleep with whom I like?"

"Why her?"

"Why not? You don't want her."

"God, no. But you might have told me."

"I thought I heard her tell you."

"So you and Scylla are one voice then?"

Picus laughed again. "She shouldn't have told." Clarence smiled back at him faintly, as if he had to smile under pain, his own, anyone's. And Picus chattered on, all of him dancing together, subtle, venomous, absurd.

Clarence listened, till the time came when he could listen no longer, and hid his face, the awful pain rising in him, drowning Picus's presence. And he was thankful for it. Escape into infinite suffering, a deadly grey land, and he was thankful for it. Away from Picus for ever. Not even to meet the true Picus, but to the country where there was no Picus. When that had gone away for ever. That nerve dead. *Free among the dead.* He raced away on that black heath. Of course, the place where Picus had lost them the day before. But that country had been sapphire and purple, wild with bees. He was out there now in December.

The North cannot undo them.
With a sleepy whistle through them.

True for trees, but what about the 'gentle girl and boy'? He had hidden himself a long time in the pain.

When he took his hands away from his face, Picus had gone.

Chapter XIII

SCYLLA WENT UPSTAIRS, and lying on her bed in her shift felt her elation and clean fatigue replaced by shabby weariness and fear.

Picus had played that trick on Carston. Picus had spoiled her pride in him. Why had he played a spiteful joke? She had not begun to think it possible that he had arranged the story of the cup. Only the trick on Carston was ill-mannered, a little cruel. Also irrelevant. It had made the business seem empty, like the effect got at séances where the interesting, the decisive, the clear is always on the point of arrival, and invariably fades out before the point is reached.

Like the mass of keltic art. Like, now she considered it, the whole Grail story, the saga story *par excellence* that has never come off, or found its form or its poet. Not like the Golden Fleece or Odysseus at Circe's house. There was something in their lives spoiled and inconclusive like the Grail story. It would be her turn next for Picus to insult, as he had played a pointless joke on a foreign guest. A number of unpleasant emotions followed that thought, chiefly disturbed sexual vanity which sets the earth by the ears. Life was ice-bright, and disagreeable as flint. It was a maudlin dream. Chance couplings, little minds setting to partners. Victory of ants over the sphinx in flesh: over birds.

She watched the flies flashing across the window, a bee searching a flower head in a jar of mixed wild stalks Felix had put there. Then to detach herself she played an old game, that she was lying out on the wood's roof: translating the stick and leaf that upheld her into herself: into sea: into sky. Sky back again into wood, flesh and sea.

It did not work, as it was meant to, to deliver her from herself, but it made her see Picus's proceedings diabolic. Why so? Parody of a mystery. A mystery none of them believed. That reduced it to a bad taste. They did not quite disbelieve. Dangerous fooling then? Parodied also in her bed. Very cruel and so wrong.

But under Gault Cliff there had been no parody. That she had to love Picus by, as much of a creation as any growth in nature. Or ritual, or rite produced by the imagination. As little symbolic as the result of any mystery propitiously performed.

As she attended to what she was thinking, she laughed, her immense vitality racing back. Her entry had made his trick glorious. Dinner would be difficult. What had been wrong with Carston? She would go and talk to him. What about? She would propitiate Felix. How? They will all hate me. Without whom Picus would not have turned creator. Woman's place indeed. Clarence wanted that job. He did the work, and I wear the crown. Not my fault. Chances of the sacred game.

Swept off into stadium of the game; which is the pleasure in actions for their own sake. Done for the love of playing. Done for the fun of it. Done for no pompous end.

That Felix was just a little nervous about.

Played by Alexander, and young Cleopatra in a bundle at Caesar's feet.

Played by that demon Picus, when he had whistled up mystery with what was now undoubtedly a victorian finger-bowl.

Played by Malatesta having Isotta sculped for the Madonna; and the man who broke the bank at Monte Carlo.

Played by Chaucer who loved everything for what it was. A sword for being a sword, or a horse. And they for what they were, the 'gentle girls and boys.'

Good thinking, good eating. All things taking care of themselves. Each thing *accordynge to its kynde.*

Would there be a train for Carston to go away by? Good idea of Picus to say it would be better for him to be slept with than visit that wood.

Was there anything to eat for dinner, anyhow? She jumped up and went out discreetly through the kitchen. In the scullery there was Felix, cleaning a basket of fish. Too much fish. Enough for half to go bad, and the rest infuriate Picus, who would say he had been given it to encourage his brain. Felix said:

"I thought I might as well help. Nanna and Janet are at it all day. Nothing like getting in a stock. Had a good walk with Picus?"

The basket, full of fish-shapes, was wet, black-ribboned inside, a shell sticking here and there, a live whelk walking up. Sea-smelling, almost living food, still running with the live sea. She took a knife and a fish, and cut down on the slab of dark blue slate used for cooling butter. Felix had covered it with scales and blood.

"We'll do it together," she said.

"You're not very good at it," he said.

She hesitated, testing the contact with him.

"We'll do other things together, then."

"Don't we pretty well always?" —His knife scraped down on a bone— "I mean, it's only half the time I don't understand."

She thought: 'So he went and gutted fish for me.' She said: "What, my dearest dear, did you understand to-day?" He answered: "When you came in with Picus I saw your beauty. After Carston had been talking, and surprised me, rather. After the things which have happened lately. It was a kind of answer. A sudden opposite to what I was thinking. To what the world is usually, I suppose. You see, I would sooner have you or even Picus in the right. Only, I haven't faith."

She thought: 'Try and have faith. No. Don't try and have anything. Be with me.'

And in answer, she told him about the wood. The bird, Picus. *O lady, be good.* Everything. That she could not have told the others. She heard a thought in his head: 'I shan't be able to keep this up, but to-day I am my sister's.'

More love for her now, handed back through Carston's spite; peace in the scullery with her flesh and blood. Fish blood and flesh on a stone between them. In one day, two kinds of perfect love. Life with Picus. Life with him. (He had understood love for Picus. Picus would not understand love for him.) Life without Picus? Life without him? She remade Antigone's discovery that you can have more lovers and more children. Not another brother, once your people's bearing days are gone.

Life with the two gone. Life with Clarence, Carston, Ross? She thought she heard a voice saying: "You will soon be left alone with them. You will be without Felix. Because there is coming to you the opposite of what you've had. Must come to you. More than separation; avoidance, treachery. Equal to what you've had. At one point, life without them will mean that."

"Not if I can help it!"

Behind this somewhere was an immense discovery, a huge principle which made it immaterial if she could help it or not. She rested in the knowledge that it was there. Their nurse came in, and they thought at once of washing and going away to change. Mounting the stairs, their arms round each other's shoulders, Carston saw them from his room, and was inexpressibly shocked, unable to understand how Scylla had persuaded her brother that her relations with Picus had been misunderstood.

Chapter XIV

As Felix said, "pep" had been the *mot juste* for the way Carston behaved. When he had found that there was no train that night, he had walked across the valley. There he had discovered a coast-guard, and, practically unaided, the system by which the station wireless picked up the lighthouse, and from there communicated by telegraph with Starn. From this, he produced a taxi and a lodging for the night. He walked back and packed vigorously, kneeling on the floor, his back to the window and the wood. When he had seen Scylla passing upstairs with her brother, he had shut his door, ceased to hear the silence of the house, heard instead the wood, a little restless, its branches changing places in a wind risen suddenly off the sea.

Odd that he would not see the place again; have no part with its men, or possess its woman. Never found out what had really happened.

He was still on the crest of the energy he had spent in denouncing them in a general sensation of burned boats. There had not risen yet doubt of himself, scrutiny, not of his motives, he knew better than to do that, but of the figure he had cut. Yet, his angry elation was like a fir-cone fire, needing baskets of brittle wood-shells. He had a fine story for his friends, something to think about. Scylla written off as a bad job, as a romance. It seemed equally impossible to say good-bye, to leave without saying it. Then the old nurse knocked, told him that his taxi was there, and that Mr. Felix, Miss Scylla, and Mr. Ross wished him a pleasant journey. He tipped her enormously, slipped across the verandah, fearing heads that were not watching. With jars and jerks, the taxi crept up the long hill.

Divine escape. On the down-crest, the earth was a map of naked beauty he saw in the piece and understood. "I've been living inside a work of art"—living what was meant to be looked at, not lived in; not to be chewed, swallowed, handled, kissed. He lay back, rocking over the grass track, almost satisfied with this. A piece of life, definitely over for him, with the stone age, and the Middle Ages, and— A patch of purple gauze ahead, smoke of no earthly fire, now a patch of those tall, bee-shaken spikes they called foxgloves. As they passed it, he saw thin legs stuck out of it along the earth, a body backed against the flower wall. It was Picus out there, up there. Looking out at nothing; out to sea. Sitting on the top of the world.

Chapter XV

AT STARN he was refreshed again with contacts from outside. There was an unusual number of tourists, two and two on the hillpaths, swarming the square. They did him so much good that he crossed to the station to meet a down-train that held more. Not many get out at evening, where there was nothing to do but stare. All he noticed in particular was an old gentleman.

He was beginning to enjoy the country. Enjoy Starn. Would have liked to know more, its history and contemporary life. He thought the old man with a red face, in grey flannels, a local landowner; thought him back to some dignified house, and was surprised later to see him dining at the inn.

He was not known there, it seemed. There was a difficulty about a room for him. Carston felt that he should leave graciously, suggested that the old man should have his room, and he a bed anywhere. There was consultation, hesitation, acceptance, thanks. After an interval, they had settled down to coffee together.

It was easy to be charming to him. An obvious number of right things to say. In a flash that, too, had passed.

"So you've been staying over at Gault House with the Taverners. Did you meet my son there—Picus, I think they call him? My name's Tracy."

Carston thought: 'Be cautious, be very cautious indeed. Don't tell lies. The old man will be going there. His eyes are the colour of his flannels. What we call stone, and never is. Stone takes light.'

"Yes," he said, "he is staying there with his friends."

It became suddenly necessary to observe with every faculty he had. He had no idea why; not for distraction, not with reference to himself. The impression was that he was opposite someone very old—not particularly in years, but in something built by centuries of experience, and now no longer in flower. The same could be said of his son and his son's friends, only that they were in flower, and might not cease flowering once their bodies' bloom was done. Centuries had gone to his construction. Carston was surprised at his attention to this, until he noticed that their setting outside the inn was the setting of a play.

Before he had wished for drama, and had not found his rôle. Now he was too much of a man to take himself off.

The stage surpassed all romantic expectations, a town with towers, in hills high enough and low enough to set and display it equally. A fleece of stars over it, thick as the flocks on the down-sides, turning, turning with the earth.

"Do you like this country?" the old man said.

"I like it immensely. I am sorry to leave. I only came down for the week-end."

"Still, you prolonged it. This is Friday."

Carston thought: 'A nice slip to start off with. I'd better be a bit more frank right away.' "To tell you the truth, I'm a stranger, and I found things a bit difficult over there."

"Would it surprise you to hear that I've heard that said before?"

"Not at all."

They laughed together. Carston began to think backwards. The eighteenth century had produced this type, had set him in culture and conviction that Nature had appointed certain old men to approve and modestly direct her arrangements of air and fire. The Renaissance had kicked off that ball, now frozen into the marble and stucco that he was sure adorned his park somewhere. Behind that there was the matrix; the Middle Ages, feudalism, Christendom. Faith in a childishly planned universe as one thing. *The earth one great city of gods and men.* His history lessons were taking life at last.

"I detest impertinence," the old man said—"I don't

think it will be necessary to go into that; but other people have found my son difficult. Was it anything to do with him?"

Carston thought: 'Picus again. In for some more. No good pretending.' He said:

"I reckon. Perhaps I didn't catch on—that he was fooling me."

'Like talking to an old stone idol; live stone idol; stone idol that walks: after something. I ate their bread, and I was rude to them. Be careful, be very careful, indeed. . . . '

"People, I hear, have left the house before, after what I could only wish was my son's sense of humour had come into play."

Carston saw that it was a question which was going to lure the other on. And he longed to tell someone something.

"Who are down there now?"

He gave the names. No harm in that.

The old man meditated: "Ah! the heart of the band?"

Why a band? More news.

"My son has a bad habit. He is fond of other people's property which may never be his. In this instance I am speaking for myself. He has a book of mine that I want. Also, it interests me to know why he should want it. And I may say that your quarrel interests me, whatever it was."

"Don't call it a quarrel. I just didn't like his way of going about things."

"And the rest of my family? We are all more or less related."

"I was to blame in part. Lost my temper and said more than I should, and they let me go."

"Very characteristic; of England, I mean. I am sorry. I suppose, by the way, you didn't see about the house a book on early Church vessels? If you had, it would be easier for me to call my son to order."

'Say no; say no; say no. A fool I shall look. He's seen I hesitated. What in hell does it matter?'

"I sort of remember a book like that in the library."

"Not in my son's room?"

"No, I was never there."

The old man did not seem pleasant; silent after he had been told a lie. Then he began to speak fast.

"As you have acknowledged a difficulty, I feel that I might as well tell you why I have come down—at least to find out whether that book is there or not. Why should he want it? He's quite illiterate. Only if he has it, I shall be on the track of what may be cropping up again. You know what I mean—romantic ideas, now that we know they are lies, which are liable to fall into very silly and very evil practices. Excuses for perversions."

Carston thought: 'It's coming out. The old man has a drink in him. *In vino veritas:* good old Montparnasse.' Again his curiosity, he said:

"There was nothing like that down there."

The old man said: "My book's gone—and if he has taken that he may have taken something else. There's his cousin, Scylla, there—"

"She is beautiful—"

"I am glad to hear she is up to your new-world standards. But an affair with her mixed up with superstition and theft."

"What is superstition over here?"

"A disgusting relic of non-understood natural law."

"I'm at sea."

"Of course, you are, and I'm glad to hear it, and that you saw nothing objectionable. In spite of your little difficulty, whatever it was."

"Tell me," said Carston, "what do you expect me to have seen?"

The old man considered: "A strained, shall we say, morbid situation between my son and Scylla Taverner. Repetition in another key with Clarence Lake. Remember, the idea of the first comes from you. The latter, I have frequently observed with disgust. So long as there has been no mention of a cup—"

'Cup. My God! And I'm half in mine.' Carston heard a noise like bells he distinguished for the blood in his ears. Then there rang over Starn a variation on three notes, flood-tide pouring into the hill circle, passing out down the valleys, striking and hushed at once on the grass cloth of the hills.

"Don't tell," said Starn bells. "Don't tell. Don't tell!"

He thought: 'I must tell something, I need to. There must be something I can tell. Not tell on them.'

The old man was talking with something in his voice of a stallion's scream:

"My son's after Scylla Taverner with a piece out of my collection. As if I didn't know where I got it, and all about it. And what put him up to it? And what'll that neurotic hussy make of it? But if he did it, I've got a surprise for them. Its story'll be the surprise, if he doesn't mind being turned out with his fancy girl—"

Not tell on them.

Carston said: "It isn't what you think, at all, Mr. Tracy. I've nothing against your son in general. I reckon now that I was jealous. You see, I'm in love with Miss Taverner, and his easy ways angered me. That's why I left."

At once he ceased to be an object of interest. But he was believed. Fooled the old man who was down there, up to less good than anyone else. The bells stopped. There was a feeling that the air had been emptied for ever. A cow mooed. Life started again. He went on easily:

"Funny how a love you feel is hopeless spoils your judgment. Goodness knows I never noticed anything of what you suggest. I just couldn't get inside their life, and I wanted to get into hers—"

"There was that book in the library," said the old man.

Inspiration came lightly.

"You half talked me into that. Now I remember it had

a book-plate in it, Felix Taverner's." 'If I fool him too much, he'll go to bed. And I ought to warn them. Warn them of what? That the old man knows the cup's gone. Certainly. Picus is the sort to take it out on Scylla. The Sanc-Grail theory's bust anyhow. Tell 'em that.' He listened to a theory of the rights of owners to their property which sounded exaggerated even in the mouth of an elderly english collector.

The old red lips moved unpleasantly in their thatch of dead-white hair:

Prupperty: prupperty: prupperty.

The earth one great city of gods and men.

He began to live again in moments of insight. They were exceedingly unlike the flashes by which they are generally described, more like obstructions removed, revealing a landscape that had always been there.

The old man seemed to have come out of the Roman world. That was difficult to understand, except on a theory that times are grouped otherwise than in sequences. What had his kind been doing at the time of the Roman world? When they had been pouring out of Britain, who had been pouring in? The ancestors of the peasants Carston had seen; but it was not a question of ancestors. There had been a story then of a king, a *comitatus* called Arthur, whose business had been divided between chasing barbarians and looking for a cup. A kind of intermezzo in history, in a time called the Dark Ages, which had produced a story about starlight. Suns of centuries had succeeded it, while the story had lived obscurely in some second-rate literature, and more obscurely, and as an unknown quality, in the imaginations of men like Picus and Scylla, Felix, Clarence, Ross. A very bad old man was putting an unpleasant finger into that pie. Carston was sure of one thing, that he disliked him more than his son. The old man was studying him, with coldness fired by brandy.

"I can't exactly promise to avenge your wrongs, Mr. Carston. But I assure you my son will regret it if he has tampered with my collection. If he has with him a small jade cup, quite ageless in appearance, and slightly ornamented, and if he has persuaded himself that it has some superstitious history, my visit may afford you some satisfaction."

Carston thought: 'He is mad about property, and he hates his son. And his son's lover, and youth and imagination, and all there is to love over there. He believes in something too. In the thing which he accuses in his son. Whatever that is. Something I can no more imagine in Picus than that Picus doesn't wash. The devils believe backwards. I can't grudge the man a trick or two with that behind him. Now I know the father, I can't hate the son any more.'

He noticed the bad moral that if he had stayed over there and behaved himself, he would not have had this interesting insight into his late hosts' private lives. Another brandy went down. He wanted to go for the old man on their behalf, and excited with drink he needed to talk. So long as he did not say the word *cup*.

"I assure you, sir, you won't find anything a father would object to in that house." 'He knows why I am saying this, because I've seen him.'

"They strike me as people who have loved and suffered a great deal. That purifies."

"From what?"

"From being like what you say— From only thinking of yourself." It is not agreeable to be dismissed like a baby. He had to remember that the old man hadn't seen through him.

"If you were to ask me, I should say that they were looking for something. Miss Taverner told me one day that what they wanted had been lost out of the world."

"When and what?" said the old man.

"I don't quite get their dates. Might have been any time, the Middle Ages, or the day before yesterday—a thing that's been lost—"

"There was only one thing lost of a symbolic value in the Middle Ages," said the old man.

Then Carston's cups influenced him to obvious caution—then to dreams. He saw Picus making pretty things, Felix laughing, Ross painting, Clarence sleeping, Scylla running away into thunder over burnt grass: running in, in love, through a rain wall.

The energy that had got him away must get him back, and damned early. He arranged to be called, arranged for a car, without question that the morning would find him in the same mind.

Chapter XVI

NEXT MORNING Carston was by no means in the same mind, and hardly in the same body. It occurred to him, as he looked out on to a village square full of bellying sea fog, that sleeping above him was an impeccable old gentleman of considerable resource and command, tracing a son who had robbed him. At the same time that the old man would be making an early start, or might be watching him from his sleep. That in going back he would be taking sides in a peculiarly unpleasant family row. If there had been a train before mid-day, he would have taken it. Instead, he took exaggerated precautions, sure of only one thing that he did not want to meet the old man again: told the boots he was driving to a farther village to see the church: hoped he bribed the driver of the car to silence.

Not until he was on the down-track again, by the foxglove patch, did any of last night's elation return. He yielded to the idea that he was on a pilgrimage, dismissed the car, left his suit-case under a wall and walked the last mile. Over dew, through gauze and long sun-shafts down to the house.

Seven-thirty o'clock. The old nurse in an older dressing-gown was waking up the kitchen life. He asked for Scylla, the easiest and the hardest person to see, and waited for her below. She came down, heavenly sleepy. He told her that he was sorry, and what had happened at Starn.

"That's all right," she said, "everyone gets worked at times. I only wish you had not sprung it on Clarence—I'd like you to be sorry for that—no, *not* because it was bad manners but because it was cruel and damned silly—"

That punished him, though he did not understand her aversion to cruelty, that kind. She went on—"But a worse thing has happened, it may be for the best. It usually is—" Suddenly, the complications of the story came over her, and he heard a sort of cry: "What is it all about— I don't like this," and he saw that he meant to stay if he had to sleep out on the earth and gnaw grass to help her. Then she told him to go down and bathe before breakfast, while she told the rest, and gave his case to the old nurse.

"Take it up to Mr. Carston's room. He did good work for us last night at Starn."

A little breakfast with the Borgia's. Poison anyhow, hurrying up over the hills. No woodpecker, no appetites. Clarence handing back with interest his insolence of the day before.

Scylla said:

"Clarence, we must be practical. Go and find out what Picus has tried to do." And Carston could have kicked the man when he assured her that it was now her business.

"It's not become that," she answered, steadily—"go you and manage him, as you have always done."

No, Clarence would not. Waited to be entreated to have more fun in refusing.

"Are we going to lie, or aren't we?" said Felix.

"That depends on Picus." It did.

"Whatever we do, he'll do the opposite." Felix got up and put the cup in a drawer.

"The book goes on the fire."

It is not easy to burn a book. He was banging it down on the kitchen fire when Mr. Tracy walked into the house. Carston retreated backwards through the kitchen, where Felix pushed him into a cupboard, and kindly got him out again, and up the backstairs to the attic and left him alone with the bees. There he meditated on what was going on below, whether the bees would attack him, and what it would be like if they brought the old man up there.

Below, Scylla thought: 'Keep things amiable: keep things casual: pay out what rope we have.' She constrained Picus's father to breakfast, because his son was unwell, and noticed how Clarence slipped away to warn him, now that the worst had come to the worst.

"It was nice of you to come," she said—"just as the place is at its loveliest." Ross despised her for that, and Felix admired, while her spirit was falling away into pockets of pain like dropped heart-beats, because in everything Picus was a lie. Excepting under Gault Cliff, and they would never go there again. Never again. That brought up bubble upon bubble of agony each time they rose, with attention to the unpleasant details of his father's visit. That sinister antique was saying:

"Call that old nurse of yours. I want to ask her a question." And she did not dare to be anything but unspeakably civil, while he said:

"Did you unpack for Mr. Tracy, and if so did you find a green bowl in his case, or a book that wasn't a novel?"

Trust Nanna. She almost put Mr. Picus's father in his place. Felix's business to have done that. Felix had gone out. Oh, God! to collect more fish?

Ross helped: "Picus is pretty unwell. Shall I take you up?"

And she managed to say, coolly: "I don't see why a book not a novel or even a cup should be out of order in anyone's luggage. I could have asked Nanna that myself."

That bothered the old man's exit. Ross went too, and she sat alone, wondering where Carston had got to. "He's up with the bees, honey," said her nurse. Tell the bees. Nanna did that when one of them died. Which of them was going to die first?

Picus had taken his father's cup.

Picus had stunted its origin.

Picus had had an idea, or why the book?

Picus had run into small mystifications.

Picus had made love to her.

Picus would not make love again, because they had been found out.

Picus led Clarence a hard life.

No one could go to Picus and say: "So much for your silly devilries. *Turn ye to me.*" And I even thought of marrying him because of his beauty. I did not catch the joy as it flew. Damn female instincts. Picus should not have pretended it was the cup of the Sanc-Grail. That will do in weaker minds and more violent imaginations than mine and Ross's.

Meanwhile, Carston had discovered a dormer in the attic roof, and saw her walking the lawns. He stuck his head out, powdered with the shells of dead bees, and called. She ran in and up to the attic door.

"Couldn't you," he whispered, "get him over to Tollerdown to look for himself? Get Clarence to take him. That will give us time."

"Good," she said, "I'll go down and try it." They both saw that the real need was to get rid of the old man. But as she opened Picus's door, she heard:

"Go over to Tollerdown to satisfy myself. Why? You've got it and you can keep it. Would you like to know its history? In India it was the poison-cup of a small rajah I knew. He was poisoned, all the same, drinking out of it. I saw him with a yard of froth bubble coming out of his mouth. Burnt up inside, I believe. I brought it away and gave it to a lady, who was frequently at Tambourne when you were at school. When she contracted tuberculosis she had a fancy for it as a spitting-cup. That is, so far as I know, any interest that attaches to the thing."

"Your mother drowned herself, didn't she, Picus?" said Ross, with that impersonal interest in the event which was sometimes too strong an antiseptic, never a poison.

"Yes," said Clarence.

"You see," said the old man to his son—"since that is your selection from my collection you may as well know your choice. You know now, and that your efforts to identify it as a mass-cup will hardly succeed."

"Picus," said Felix, "it is up to you to tell us if you have this thing."

"You fool," said the old man, "I saw him take it, when he thought I was asleep before the fire."

"What does it matter if he did, when we have none of us seen the thing?"

Picus raised his shoulders out of the sheets:

"Oh, cut that, Felix, when it's where you put it, downstairs in the bureau drawer." They noticed the father in the son. Then Scylla's turn came—"From the bridegroom to the bride. Hardly as propitious as one would like."

"That is superstitious," said Ross,—"Scylla's no bride for any son of yours, and the cup's bitter history concerns no one but the dead."

"Why did he pretend it was the cup of the Sanc-Grail?" said the old man.

"How did you pretend he did?" said Ross.

"A snip of an American called Carston told me last night at Starn. Another candidate for your rather second-hand beauties, Scylla—"

"Felix, will you fetch him?" said Ross.

Upstairs, through the bee-roar, Carston heard the boy say:

"So you did give us away last night at Starn!"

"I'm damned if I did. That's his bluff." He thought: 'I knew I'd have to go down. I'm in this. How life arranges itself without our tugging and kicking.' "Give me a run-over what's been said."

"He wants us to have it," said Felix. "It was a rajah's poison cup. Jade is supposed to shew poison. Of course, it doesn't, and the man died. I shouldn't be surprised if old Tracy hadn't a hand in it. He brought it back and gave it to a female tart. That was a bad story, because Picus's mother pined about it, till they found her in the stream beneath old Tracy's house. Picus was a kid at the time, and he adored her, and the old man had the woman to live with him at Tambourne till she died of t.b., and the cup was one of her belongings. Sort of thing which wouldn't work out so badly to-day with divorces and fresh air. The old man's loving it; spotted that Picus has given Scylla the cup."

"Then why on earth the stunt about the spear and the well?"

"I don't know— He's the old man's son. Come down."

Carston felt his position false again. Somehow he had given a clue to this hag-driven ancient: he was a little in alliance with him: he protested. Picus's father said:

"Quite enough, my dear boy, quite enough. You were obviously startled, and I had my theory of what startled you. I'm sure Scylla will forgive you in time, and I must be off now. I'll leave you your treasure, but I should like my book on the mass-cups back. You see now that it will be quite useless to try and identify it from that."

"Ask Felix," said Picus. No one knew whether to help him out or not. Carston thought of its boards smouldering on the kitchen fire, making it, as Nanna had pointed out, unfit for proper use.

Scyllla said, coolly: "I can't part with the other half of my wedding-present."

And this infuriated the old man. It was evident, even to their over-hurried perceptions, that he was more than insulting and exultant, he was in earnest. He began to frighten them. They could not decide whether to economise the truth or not. The old man seemed in need of exorcism. A bib. Altogether too gothic now.

Then Felix cried out: "I burnt the damned thing when Carston told me that you and Picus were playing us up."

The old man began to laugh. "That'll do," he repeated. And quite soon after he was gone, and they dragged out chairs and lay on the lawn at different angles, no one wishing to speak.

Chapter XVII

CLARENCE FIGURED it out. Picus had done this to get away from him, falsifying the devotion of years, flaunt a pretty cousin, marry a pretty cousin: because she had some money: because she was a bird and bee woman: because Carston was after her, must be after her, or he would not have come back from Starn. Or why should any man run back after such an exit, to help a woman, a mime, a baggage, a bag of excrement? There is a great difference between a sportsman, a painter, a man that feels the earth, between Ross and Scylla and his terrible green Sdi creature, and Clarence's feeling for decoration best served by cities, a blasted heath no more than a site for his palace. He was on Carston and Felix's side, never satisfied with the earth sacrifice the others munched, wanting *décor* as Carston a stage. Picus was his set-piece, his jewel. His jewel had lied, his palace was unsound, the beautiful basket in which he had put all his eggs was broken. He had no more eggs to lay. A very serious man unable to exercise his sobriety, because he had made *fausse route* with his friend, because his education was insufficient for his abilities. Not for the first time he did not try to correct himself, thought about his wounds and his wishes until they took phantom shape and he slipped off uneasily with his gun down the wood. Scylla made a face after him. Ross shook his head. Carston had an impulse to follow.

"Gone off to invent excuses for Picus," said Felix, "for you to listen to— It's the occupation down here."

"Come and pose," said Ross. "I want a model."

Carston was alone with Scylla. He said:

"I think I've an excuse now to say 'explain a bit'." It was parching hot, gritty as if a storm of microscopic dust had filled up the holes in the leaves, in the grass-blades, in the skin.

"Reassure me, at least," he said, "that this would have happened without me."

"Of course. Much worse if it hadn't been for you." They stopped talking.

"I tried to help you," he said, "it is your turn." Saw the effort she made, thought how easy these people were to spur.

"Let's go up and tackle Picus," she said—"there is one thing about staying in bed, it runs to earth."

"No," said Carston, "you must excuse me. I've had about enough of that chap."

"So," said Scylla, "for the moment, have I."

"Seems to me he played a mean trick on you all—What I don't see is why. Or why it should have got you."

The other side of the house Ross was seeing Felix flung in a chair, hearing the nervous sobbing his own cool voice could not control. Nor could he control in himself his aversion to speak or to help.

"What in hell do we come here for? I told Scylla to sell those shares and we'd have been at Biarritz."

"It would have been the same at Biarritz."

"You might be. I should be different there. You're looking for something. I'm not. And I hope when you get it you'll like it. Looking for the Sanc-Grail. It's always the same story. The Golden Fleece or the philosopher's stone, or perpetual motion, or Atlantis or the lost tribes or God. All ways of walking into the same trap. And Scylla gets into bed with old Tracy's son."

"That is not the point. What is it about a trap?"

The boy got up and looked a little madly and very insolently at Ross, the blue eyes cold between lids red with weeping. Ross was surprised to find himself edging away, like a man who is to be shot at.

"We're through with the baby-brother business."

Upstairs, Picus had finished shaving, his body worked

on as delicately and scrupulously as a cat. Whistling to himself while Felix was sobbing, whistling back his power as their idol, like a god summoning an element or in confidence like prayer. He set his tie for the last time, shook himself, laid himself down on the window seat, and drew a ring with a pearl on to his atrociously powerful hand.

And Clarence out on the high turf was not looking at the sea or the terrible crest of Gault suspended in the haze. Or at the small enamel floor he trod on, flower and leaf stars and bars and rings and crosses: or at a dozen rabbits hurrying: or at one hawk not hurrying, until he dropped faster than the eye and there would be one rabbit the less. He walked slowly, inside himself, petting his phantoms, especially a phantom of Picus, the body up at the house was behaving more and more unlike. He wondered also why Scylla had called him "mediaevalist," because she said he assumed a form from inside and made things fit it, instead of compelling what is to do his construction for him. Hadn't Picus invented a lying fancy to please her, to get off with her? Lying and lecherous his bird was, for a woman who had snapped him up for her body's sake and her vanity. This went on until he saw the names he called her take body and walk to meet him out of the wood. Vanity, lechery, falsehood, and malice lolled along together across the grass, out of the trees. And because she called him mediaevalist, he saw them in archaic dress.

Scylla said to Carston on the lawn:

"So, you see, what sounded romantic excitement about the Sanc-Grail cup was real. And unfortunate?"

Carston wondered, deplored and detested the european faculty for taking the skeleton out of the cupboard. Rattling it, airing it, lecturing on it. She was winding up a discourse without enquiry into his feelings. On what he supposed was the skeleton, the world skeleton. He heard:

"If the materialist's universe is true, not a working truth to make bridges with and things, we are a set of blind factors in a machine. And no passion has any validity and no imagination. They are just little tricks of the machine. It either is so, or it isn't. If you hold that it isn't, you corrupt your intellect by denying certain facts. If you stick to the facts as we have them, life is a horror and an insult. Nothing has any worth, but to tickle our sensations and oil the machine. There is no value in our passions and perceptions, or final differences between a life full of design and adventure and a life crawled out in a palace or a slum. The life of Plato or Buddha, apart from the kick of the illusion, was as futile as the lives of the daughters of Louis XV. Old talk, you say, and remember *In Memoriam.* But notice what is happening now people have become used to the idea. Any little boy in a Paris bar, who never heard of physics knows. Everyone gets the age's temper. With results on their conduct— 'Why be good any more' they say, and the youngest ones not that. And it's not intellectual beauty the culture-camp admire. It's themselves for having such fine subconciousnesses. Such an elegant sublimation of their infant interests. Watch the world with the skeleton acclimatised! Even when I was new we tried the bad to see if it might not be good. But the new lot aren't interested. Don't give a button for the good any more.

"And there is no evading it by any 'service of humanity' game. Unless you're one of the people who get sensual kick out looking after things, why help humanity? Think of Wells's Utopias. Birth-control, and peace and drains. And nothing left to do but report on the fauna of a further star. Our visiting-list extended to super-birds, or intellectually developed spiders. *Nothing* but physical adventure. Especially as we've picked up one priceless truth off the road, that every action brings with it its toxin and its antitoxin. If, instead of becoming cynical or scared, we started enquiry again from that—"

Felix shouted melodiously:

"I'm post-War. I'm just through getting clear of you. I admit you can scare me, but in reality you bore me. I don't care any more. I may be a mass of inhibitions, but I'm out for myself—"

Through the grilling haze, Luxury, Malice, and Untruth strolled over the grass to Clarence. In Ross's heart there twisted ache and dislike. Carston gave in to spiritual upset, while his body lay in a garden chair. Scylla ended:

"So even the memory of a great magic turned out to be a bird's joke."

Picus thought how he would appear downstairs and bewilder them again. Had enough of Scylla. Wished now he hadn't given her that cup. Caught out he'd been by the old man, but that wasn't over yet. Get right out and come in by another door. Make Clarence, Scylla, and the lot of 'em quite happy always. Play round his way and their way for ever. *And I'll give you leave to play till doomsday.* Not mother. Too late to do that. Sort of the old man's prisoner. Just thinking of that made him feel ill and want Clarence. Felix reached his finale.

"You've confused me very successfully, and you can put up with what I've become."

Scylla saw that Carston had had enough, and felt stifled and alone. Clarence returned in agony up the doubling wood-path, not the straight. Ross withdrew into his picture, and Carston hung on tight to a thought: 'We've all got to get out of here for a bit.'

Chapter XVIII

"TIRED," SAID Scylla, changing her dress, and leaving that to stare out at the wood— "Tired of your wretched beauty, your rearrangements of light on a leaf."

"Bored," said Picus, who had gone to meet Clarence and missed him. And he meant sad. And Clarence, giving Nanna a hand skinning the rabbits he had shot, looked at his bloody hands: "I suppose I've got a broken heart and these wretched feelings come in through the holes."

"Alone," said Felix, "when I've got away it'll be the same."

Only Ross embraced his solitude, thought of the shape of each thing he drew, until the earth seemed one growing stillness, of innumerable separate tranquillities, for ever moving, for ever at rest.

Unfortunately the members of the house-party were not behaving like that. An organic view of Felix, for instance? He damned the scene—knew that he had handled it without imagination. Besides, the boy should be wearing his "youth's gay livery" before a livelier audience than hills and the sea.

And there was more coming through than Picus's wiles, life opening like the unfolding of a scene. An endless screen of coromandel lacquer, the design travelling with it, fold in, fold out. Enough for Ross to know that there was design and seize the detail, a man content with the tangible, piece by piece, to whom no single object was dumb. He thought of the brickness of a brick until he seemed aware of it throughout, not side after side or two or three, but each crumb of its body, and each crumb reduced to its molecular construction, until the brick ceased to be a cube and could as easily be reformed again.

And the only prayer to which he condescended was that Scylla would keep her head since there were hysterics about; then left the studio and joined the party now slowly regathering on the lawn. All but Felix. Carston did not know how to greet Picus, not it seemed in any disgrace, and telling them a story about a parson's wife.

"So she knitted me a check sweater, and I had a pain. And I lay flat on the grass, and told a curate and another curate to play chess on my back. And I found a caterpillar and made them make love."

"They don't," said Ross, "it's the butterflies."

"These did. And the first curate said check with the white bishop, and I stopped enjoying it, and hunched up and went in to get my tea, and there was a party, and I stopped thinking."

"When do you do your thinking?"

"Never."

Scylla said: "I wish you had, before you let this morning's business be sprung on us. What did you do it for?"

They all waited for his answer. It came.

"Mind your own business." Like a rude boy. And then: "It was my mother who was driven to death."

"That's nothing to do with it," said Ross.—"Pawn your father's collection. Throw it into the sea, but don't—"

"Don't what?" said Picus.

Felix came out.

"Here's what's left of your bloody book. Nanna took it off the fire." Ross opened it with kind hands not afraid of char-black and turned the middle pages the fire had not curled up. He stared.

"Look at this." The book was open at a full-page photograph of the cup. Underneath was written—*Plate* 17. *Early English altar-vessel. From the collection of Christopher Tracy, Esq.*

While the cup was fetched from its drawer and passed from hand to hand, Carston appreciated Picus's blissful look, untouched by relieved anxiety, not too elated or even too absorbed.

"Picus," said Ross, "in common decency tell us what you know.

"Now that I've been asked, listen. I took the cup. Mother and I used to pretend with it. Not this time, but when I came back to Tollerdown last spring. The well was brimming and I took it out to get a drink, and it slipped through my fingers like a fish. It couldn't be got out then, and I didn't want Clarence to fuss. He didn't know. Once it was gone, I wondered what it was, and I this time told my father that I hadn't seen it lately, and something he said put me on to that book. So I left it to see what would happen. And Felix fished it out with Clarence's spear. It may have come from India. The whore who killed my mother may have used it. It suited the old man to palm it off as a church vessel and to tell you it was a poison-cup. He's lived in India long enough, and his best friend is an arch-deacon. That's all I know. Oh yes, I curled up behind an ant-hill on Hangar's ridge Carston shied at. And I stuck the cup in his room to teach him that ants don't bite, and give him something else to think about. Oh yes, I made love to Scylla because she is a darling, and usually I'm afraid of women. And—"

"Hold up—" said Ross.

It was a great blessing that the old man had done the lying. Put untruth away in a far corner. Far corners are more difficult to get at. But what they needed then was Picus's brightness restored.

Carston said: "It seems to me that your father's story was a lie because he wanted the book back."

"Trust Nanna," said Scylla, blissfully, "she wouldn't have the kitchen fire put out."

"The kitchen fire, mark you," said Felix, suddenly interested again.

Hesia is an old goddess—I think she had a name written under her altar not even the Romans might know. And in her case, their lives, the sap of their bodies was nourished at Nanna's fire. There the sea bubbled in butter, the meat dripped its red juice, birds split into white shreds. Round it the lettuces sparkled, the roots under the wood boiled, old herbs scented the place, wine dripped in like dew, and Nanna was perhaps the only person unequivocally loved.

The wailing that went up round her: "Nanna, I'm hungry." "Nanna, I've got a cold." "Nanna, I've blistered my heel." "Nanna, where are the buttons on my white waistcoat?" Nanna who liked cigarettes and silk stockings and no device for saving labour, her hair tied up like an old gipsy, and her tongue free. She had got them round this corner. All the same, a lie is harder to run to earth three counties away.

"We are left where we began," said Felix, "with the Thoroughly Rum."

Also, as Carston noticed, with the thoroughly boring. The adventure of the cup had happened. It had been complicated, violent, inconclusive. Now it would be too much trouble to take trouble for more trouble. For a new series of untruths or "stubborn, irreductible" facts. Not much chance of them, and difficult to get. Three counties away. As though they had been in a room together, and something had passed through that had left too raw traces for all its invisibility, had left them alone with private griefs and memories quickened. Which, if it came again, would enter by a different door. Picus, stirred by the story of his mother, victim of victorian social stupidities in an age less agreeable and more remote than that which produced mass-cups, and complicated biographies of public characters like Huon of Bordeaux, son of Julius Caeser, and Morgan le Fay.

They were tired of it, as he saw, till another door opened. This, when his own interest for the first time was really aroused. The business was more or less out in the open. News. A story. He wanted to find out exactly what Mr. Tracy had been up to. If they were prepared to leave it alone until something else happened, he was not; anticipating a dateless, glorious moment when he would appear before them with the story complete. Hand them the finished psychology of old Mr. Tracy. A new philosophy: a fortune: the cup of the Sanc-Grail. No intention of leaving now.

Then a sound that was almost "service" rose in his thought. Not public or personal or progressive, or in relation to the "hard-eyed men of the Y.M.C.A." Not even for results; there might be no results. As the conception grew, fortifying like a cup of wine *à point*, he saw an approach to Scylla, without reference to possession or to her reaction. What she did not have with these unemployed condottieri her peers. What he must do for her, and she was no spoilt american bitch.

Immediately, he stepped into another world, their world and his own. At its largest, airiest and freest. He had never been there before. He had always been there. He would always be there, never the same apprehensive, gifted, rootless man. Reckoning without his hosts, he urged another slice of cake on her, and suggested that it might be his turn to fetch the evening fish.

"We'll go together," she said. "A walk will do me good."

Chapter XIX

IT WAS PERCEPTIBLY cooler, stale-cool, uneasy air-threads stirring in the straight wood drive. No sun since three o'clock, but a glaring grey gauze overhead. Outside the wood, below the little cliff, a small scoop of bay protected the fisherman's boats. From the edge they could have stepped on to the roof of his hut, whose tarred shingles were frosted with salt. Set on a ledge out of storms' reach, brambles padded it from the cliff's side, and it was reached down wooden balks, steep-set and built into the clay. It surprised Carston to see the egg-blue and peacock water changed to the colour of a gun-barrel. Little wind, but the sea was twitching, slapping against the rocks; the colours inland, neither light-veiled or shining, but off a new palette.

Scylla was staring out to sea, and her head lifted in profile made her look at the sky, where it seemed as if some mathematical monster had risen out of the west. For where the sun was turning down-Channel, a ball glared, surrounded by ranks of rose bars, and out from these clouds radiated that reached over to the eastern heavens, across whose spokes strayed loose flakes dipped in every variety of flame, the triangles of empty sky stained all the greens between primrose and jade.

"Herring sky," she said.

"What does that mean?"

She laughed with a confident joy he understood the first time.

"South-west wind. Listen!" He heard his heart beating, a hair in his ear, and a trans-finite length away, the stirring that had made uneasy the sea.

"A big storm," she said, turning on him eyes full of an

animal's pleasure. Round the point where the day before he arrived they had played at Aphrodites, a boat came dipping back, the bowsprit dancing and dripping, where over the deep-travelling reef the sea had begun to coil under and over.

"Harris is back in time. We're in for it. No more fish." A note in her brain about the fish problem. More too freshly killed meat. Picus and Felix on the subject. Then the only good poem a bad poet ever wrote, anticipating jazz:

"When descends on the Atlantic
The gigantic
Storm-wind of the equinox."

He took her hands and they rocked, saying with her:

"From Bermuda's reefs and edges
Of sunken ledges
On some far-off bright Azore
From Bahama and the dashing
Silver-flashing
Surges of San Salvador."

Fallen into nature with her. For the first time in his life. Good old Gulf Stream.

Harris the fisherman had downed his main-sheet, flung out an anchor and was rushing a dinghy to shore.

"Take your fish, Madame Taverner, it's the last you'll see. I've got my pots to get in."

"We'll help."

Two minutes later Carston was in a dinghy in a slightly resentful scoop of sea, and spent an ungrateful hour hauling up lobster-cages filled with kicking, pinching sea cardinals, ink blue; and the humanitarian protest came from Scylla when they were tossed into a cauldron bubbling on the stones, in an angle of the little secret cliff where England rose out of the harvested sea.

The wood was darkish, fearful and sad, until they saw

the windows shut and already lit, a fire leaping up made out of the driftwood he had helped haul up. Blue sparks and white and green, wind shifting about outside in the trees, until with a scream the up-Channel gale was loosed and they became creatures couched under a stone that quivered in the uproar and mounted to bed with candles streaming.

Carston lay in bed and heard above the thunder a gull repeating itself. "Ai, ai," it said, up somewhere in the tumbling sky, a little noise laid delicately upon the universal roar of air. The house was strong, he thought, its stone thrilling but not a window that rattled, tapped by their climbing roses.

There were pockets in the wind when he could hear the sea. A crash, then under-roar and scream of pebbles, the ravelled water dragged. A light-patch fell on his floor, a piece of the late moon racing apparently from a cloud whipped off her, and behind her a star or so, unhurried, observant and indifferent on a night when everything was out and about. He looked out to sea, surprised that it appeared no more than a bright silver lacquer, when water mountains should have been moving in.

Scylla alone wondered how the wood below Gault was bearing it, flooded with salt water, heaped with seaweed, the little stream choked with wrack.

Dark again in Carston's room. A rain-flaw drummed on the panes. Then with a shriek the wind sprang again. He could not hear the gull, but a few seconds later a crack and a long crash, knew it was a tree gone, and looking out in the next moon-interval, saw something altered in the outline of the wood. It disturbed him to think how hopeless the dawn would be, the 'dew silky' quiet changed for grey air, spray-salted on the lips. Would the others enjoy it? Would it blow the nonsense out of them? They might be house-bound for days. Oh, God! He was wondering how to prevent this when he fell asleep.

Chapter XX

BREAKFAST REASSURED HIM how far they minded the weather. They had been out and there was news, a tramp aground on Tunbarrow Ledges, and twenty-three drowned men laid out on tables in the parish room.

"A danish boat," said Scylla. "Does anyone here speak it?"

Carston did, but did not see that it was his duty to say so in order to assist what was left of the crew, who must have a consul somewhere. He bore it when Scylla took him out down the wood, quiet under a colonnade, until they came out and staggered against a wall of air.

The little bay disappointed him, packed with dull drift that choked the waves, a pocket for the storm's mess, and on the headland they found the sea racing, but not with the explosion he had imagined up the cliff's side.

"Tide's out." So that formless bright patch of moon was still pulling the sea about, holding it off the land. Then she led him carefully to the edge, and he saw a hole in the clay, blue, raw and dripping from a wave's mouth.

"That came out last night."

Still the sky travelled, torn cloud and blue enough for trousers, rain-flaws, and air ribbons. The wildness enervated him. The excitement was cerebral, all spectacle, a whip-up for the eyes and the salt-refreshed palate, the ears cut off from common sounds.

At lunch words crossed his wind-filled head like the gull's cry in the night. The well at the cottage on Tollerdown would be filling; floating corpses could be skimmed off: the vicar at Tunbarrow was reliable with the shipwrecked: Felix had gone over there.

While they relaxed over coffee, the boy came in, bare-headed, strapped into oilskins, pale, his cheeks burning with two red circles exercise would not account for.

"Eaten?" said his sister.

"I don't want to. I've seen them."

"Seen what?"

"Twenty-three dead men." They all reacted to the young voice horror and drama made unsteady.

"Singularly drowned with their wounds shewing—where the fish gnawed—"

"Haven't had time to be gnawed," said Ross. "Don't overdo it."

"I saw them till they had no significance whatever, because I saw death. I suppose you admit they're dead?"

"A death," said Ross, coldly, "you court yourself in the cutter year in, year out. We court. What about it?"

Felix swallowed, and stared right and left.

"Death's family party," he said. "I've seen it. Getting nearer home. Don't you know you're in league with that sort of thing? And that your shifts for getting away are hopeless—"

"What shifts?" said his sister. "Ease up, boy, stop running round in circles. I didn't drown them."

He addressed himself to her:

"Your love affairs—what are they worth? and your famous strength that supports us? I know you're a strong woman, with your stunt of opening doors every sane person knows are better shut. I'm your brother and you'll not take me in. Twenty-three bodies, twenty-three pictures of death have taught me the worth of your tricks. And I don't flatter myself I shall do anything on my own. You've sucked me too dry for that—"

Carston saw her swing the crystal slung from her neck he knew the boy had given her.

"Dearie," said Picus, "let your back hair down, and be yourself."

"Go away," said Ross.

"Go and look for what you want where you think you'll

find it," she said. Temperately, ineffectually, the reserve shewing how she loved him.

Carston wanted to kick him. Clarence yawned. The boy took no notice. Carston thought: 'Ways of clearing the house. A full well at Tollerdown, and Biarritz the brighter by one cub.' Whose adieux were being made separately.

"And Clarence can nurse his fancy heart-break and Picus his second-rate chic. And Ross make his appetites serve his art, or whichever way round he does it. And Carston get kick out of being taken in by our fake aristocracy. And Nanna slave and tell you how wonderful you are. I'm going where there won't be any more fairy-stories, and my complexes can rot me or—"

"All right," said his sister, "we'll try not to overwork Nanna, or impose on Carston too much."

'Well, well,' thought the latter: 'the new type of child: Biarritz, bars. *What every little boy in a bar knows.* And how far had her love got Scylla?' His new-found confidence working easily in him, he smiled at Felix.

"'Portrait of the artist as young man,'" he said. "Good luck."

But the boy answered:

"D'you fancy my sister so much that you've learned her tricks? She is keeping them for someone else than me, that's all."

She wondered as she left the room, and for once ordered Nanna to iron his linen immediately, if his version of the truth was refreshing him, as any contact should. And, pitifully, how long it would last. And anxiously, what he would do. And, maliciously until she felt better what sort of a fool he would make of himself, what gaping mouth would snap him up.

So he lost her until he should come to look for her, Grail vanished, girl and all.

Incidentally, he settled which of the rest should go or stay. Next day, contrary to custom, the wind fell, and a torrent of soft mist packed in rain brimmed the land, refilled ceaselessly off the falling sea as it passed in over the hills. They could hear the water slowly thundering and not much else but their rather distressed voices. Carston alone had the serenity of plans. After he had persuaded Scylla to go up to London, Clarence said that he would go over to the cottage or the dust and damp would get in and annoy his young man. Picus had gone already, flitted off, the raining fog hiding him for a time. Carston meant the same landscape to swallow him on the trail of old Mr. Tracy. He asked Ross for his plans.

"Stay here and get on with things. I'll wait till you come back."

FELIX

FELIX BOLTED black and stormy to his hotel and emerged again into the gold light, fresh as roses. He crossed the river, and on the brink of the Champs-Élysées felt the rhythm of Paris begin to stir him and caress. A movement of tireless youth, each instant crystallized a century, illustrated by details small and intimate, grandiose or chic. His lost goodness returned, recomposed out of adoring attention, until like a polished bay, the Place de la Concorde opened before him. There the fragile Paris façades grouped themselves round the bronze ladies washing their faces, round a boy wandering out among the skimming taxis, in love.

He walked some way before he remembered that he had a rendezvous with a person as well as Paris, and turned back along the Rue de Rivoli, drowned in the evening sky. He had forgotten what he had left behind, novice at his first ceremony of mystery, he turned up the Rue Boissy d'Anglas and found himself indoors again.

His friend was with a band. Felix hated bands. No setting for him when he felt that he was not really there. He knew he had an inferiority complex, but there were too many draped legs and wrapped coats, and he might not have heard the last story, would have to pretend it had arrived stale from London. He would be found out, and no one would care how he loved Paris, or how much he knew about art. And with what was left of his generous simplicity, he did not count at all on his clothes which were the original of many replicas, or on his money, which was not borrowed.

Here was a different kind of loneliness. With his own generation, not as at home with the half-generation ahead. Loneliness all the same, self-imposed. In the french-american group he was a distinguishable figure. Boys fresh as roses in a shop-window, as picked and perfect. Only a close observer might have said that Felix was still on his bush. Or having left it, that his stalk was not down in the water.

How to pretend to be the devil you are afraid to be.

How to be a grand seigneur on nothing a year.

How to be yourself when you do not know that self, and are afraid to find out.

How to get tight when you don't do it regularly.

The café walls were black, filled with mirror panels squared with small red and gold lights. Like an old mirror that has a circle of miniature mirrors inlaid in its glass, the place reflected and repeated a great deal of what is going on in the world. And Felix, with his letter of introduction, could not pull it out, with his pass behind the scene over his heart, could not present it. He forgot the walk he had taken, fell back into the easy trick of disapproval, mask for longing to be a little king in that bright crowd. King over a french boy, pencilled like a persian miniature, discreet and gentle as a cat. Shut absolutely in his race, yet escaping it by an indescribable sweetness, a perfume of goodness uncorrupted by intelligence which would last—how long? Felix told himself that his complexion could not last long anyhow, and retired on a loud excuse to dust a little powder on his own fair nose and chin. Never be able to impress that boy, who was neither in authority or out, who wore his youth for a fairy-cloak which for Felix was a naked skin.

Nor the buddha-shaped musician from the Midi, loved for his wit, serving his turn with each of them in turn as though they were not there. Felix turned to the boy he had come to see, the adorable American who knew everybody. He wondered if he was after all another Carston. (Felix had underrated Carston, having no experience between the man from Boston and his friend from the Middle

West.) He was smarter than any Carston, brimmed up with sap and impudence, a boy who, if he had come from the moon, would have made his friends dream until he taught them not to. On whom, if Felix had known it, Scylla reckoned for vengeance. He was glad enough to see Felix, wear him for a night or so in his cap. Remember him as a spoiled, sweet girl remembers. Felix would have the money for several parties and was an authentic specimen. He would give him his turn.

They all spoke French better than he, who always wanted to do it too well, whose ear was not in tune. His next brandy went down, and as his brain quickened he heard a party being discussed for late that night. Would they ask him? How could he bear it if they didn't? In reality it did not occur to the Frenchmen that he would not want to go to Montmartre, and did not know how to take care of himself. Not that they were interested—the brandy mounted darkly—nobody was interested. Their pure speech hummed like a dynamo. He stretched himself insolently and spoke to a bulb-cheeked yellow-haired child there pursuing the career, and impressed by Felix's obvious need to do nothing of the sort.

The party began to discuss a well-known eccentric who had just left.

"Oh, that man—" said Felix, gladly. But his comments in pretentious French were too severe, and left the others in doubt whether he really knew him. Soon they were not listening, and he saw the Frenchwoman catch his friends's eye. Only the bulb-cheeked child was still attentive. Little *faux monnayeur,* fresh from his lycée, still rather ingenuous, he helped Felix along his transitions of envy, wonder, and fear.

A russian boy came in, tight in a merry circle of private intoxication, small, black, asiatic head in air. He sang:

> *"Si par hazard tu vois ma tante,*
> *Compliments de ma part."*

A baby-faced negro rolled his drum. The saxophone began to cough out variations, apparently played backwards, on *Dinah Lee.* His memory of the sweet tune pricked a bubble in the boy's petulance. He asked the Frenchwoman to dance, and moving easily with her, a little drunk, he began to bubble praise of Paris. When they got back, the little bar off the dancing-room was roaring with the love of life. In a frieze along the bar, in squares and fives and sixes round the scarlet tables were all the right people to play with. People of the world and the half-world, people who found the arts useful, and a fair number of people who were found useful by the arts. Eminent eccentrics, the very poor, the very rich, capital in wits or youth or looks or wit; diversity of creatures, young society in action, the motif of the time and the place repeated in the exit and entry of the pick of Paris' basketful of boys. It was Felix's party, too, if he could have forgotten himself, let himself go, torn up his silly little mask. Instead, he allowed himself to feel home-sick, looked timidly at his friend who had caught the eye of a princess, and was making her sure she was pleased to have caught his.

"Let's have a day in the country to-morrow. We might go to Versailles."

"All right, if we're up." The voice was soft and virile, touched with a brogue. No getting him to himself where everyone was out to be seen. In desperate need of a focus he gave up trying to understand French, and began to describe the people at his table to himself. He would never get to know them. Who ever gets to know the French? He might as well have something to remember. When he was a famous man, they'd wish they'd been nicer to him. There was the Frenchwoman in her man's coat, without make-up, half-boy, half great lady, level-eyed and low-voiced, incapable of pretention or any false gesture. Then the musician's chinese rotundity, the pouting lips, flat and amiable white hands, contradicted by a chin cleft like a Caesar's, and terribly intelligent eyes. Felix respected those eyes.

They had looked at him kindly, and he suspected pity, found himself caught with an emotion that was like pity when he looked at the third, the young Frenchman, because his beauty was "no stronger than a flower." Scented like one, too, out of a bottle Felix wanted the name of. —"But he's no brains," he said, "and they say he takes drugs. It's a pity." He nursed the idea that he could be happy nowhere. Was there any one else in the room who was alone? He looked around. Even two boys having a row at the bar were in contact. A swing door burst open. It was the Russian back again, if anything, tighter. Felix saw a glass of champagne beginning to slide on the top of the downy black head. Skull of a tibetan idol: mouth of a wicked baby. In the middle of the floor he lowered the glass, and began an on-the-spot Charleston. "Hey, hey," he shouted. Then a rune:

> *"O qu'il est beau, mon village,*
> *Mon Paris,*
> *Mon Paris."*

He shot through to the dancing-room. He was ugly. He had exquisite hands and feet. 'Probably a shop-assistant pretending to be a prince.' Felix's demon was on the spot. He came back again, carrying the glass now like a chalice, empty, and looking crossly into it. Felix burst out laughing.

"Excuse me," he said, "have another drink," and went with him to the bar.

"Enfin il s'amuse, le petit anglais," said the musician. Felix's friend frowned. Money spent on that demon would not last long. But Felix had sensed that here was another isolation, but not its quality, its brutal and innocent acceptance of things. But he was talkable-to, with his unmodulated French, his trick of sprawling sideways at the bar, his head pitched forward, laughing down at his feet.

ROSS

Ross finished the drawing of a plant that grew in whorls and spirals and tendrils and bracts. The naturalist had trained the painter. He copied it exactly. To-morrow he would do it differently, double it, halve it, add six to it, make a picture out of repetitions of a stalk.

It was very late. The hardly perceptible noise of his pencil was all he had for company. He went into the kitchen to look for bread and cheese. A candle was lit in a tin lantern, there was a fire-stain on the floor. Nanna, long in bed, had left her sewing.

There was an old woman and she sat spinning,
And still she sat and still she span, and still she wished for company.

He grinned at the old nurse's horror-story, went back to the studio and watered one of the shallow pans stuck with the seeds he had gathered tramping Europe. A bee-orchid had come up: an odd-scented herb from a pass on the Pyrenees: a rare lily was over. Whenever he touched it life grew. Plants and dogs and children. Eggs hatched. And men? They were there to make him laugh. If they found rest in him, he was indifferent as Nature, and in general as kind.

He loosened the earth pricked by a hairy spike, tossed a pebble away, opened a window. A bird disturbed brushed him without alarm. An owl sailed by, curved over at the house-corner and skimmed down the wood. A dark grey night, brimming with business. His portfolio under his arm for a picture-book, he went up to bed.

PICUS

On the same night Picus went out, also alone and in a clearing among trees. English yews, black and untidy with their shoots that are never young, a yard of rusty twig, old as a house-high lime or beech.

The space was diversified with the stone boxes of a country churchyard. Dressed for Piccadilly, Picus was lying face-down on his mother's grave, on turf not dew-sown, but rain-sodden, overlooked by a sugar-white marble angel carrying an urn. He was telling the stalks and the worms and a snail how he loved her, and resented her death, and was troubled by its mystery.

'Pretty mother, why did you do it?'

'Why did that tart matter?'

'What did you want me to do?'

'Why do I hate all women?'

Once Nanna had made him ill when he had heard her say: "What did Mrs. Tracy mean by drowning herself with Mr. Picus a boy, and his father taking his child to the inquest and saying it was suicide?"

And Scylla's answer: "People went in for sensibilities then." Blaming his mother. Now he'd see if she had any. He grasped the turf mound and tried to shake it. Get mother out and make her tell him what had really happened and that he must never make anyone suffer as she had suffered. That was like his father and he must never be like his father— The marble parody of a nymph went on offering him an urn. He tried to see if the lid would come off, but it was all in one meanly designed, badly chiselled piece. His father with his impeccable taste had stuck it up on purpose. Fattened on his son's hatred. Had used the cup to make him wicked. To lose him the people who comforted him. Would go on living forever. The wires of the rust tin flower-box caught his cuff. Rain water in it, and no flowers. Can't go daisy-hunting at midnight in the rain. That's all mother had, an empty tin box with the rain in it and no flowers. He did not count his six feet of young man flung there.

"You'd no business to go off and leave me like that. Gives me nothing to do but want you back. Just for a minute to tell me something: put kick into me again. Mummy, don't you see: you gave the old boy the game? You were so much prettier: might have stayed and seen me through. Now you've made me be a bitch."

He sat there weeping and considering how he had been a bitch and couldn't stop. Didn't know how to find old Clarence and Scylla again and love them and see that they loved him. Clarence now. One of his suspicions was that the change in Clarence was his fault. Why wasn't it entirely the man's own fault if he chose to go gaga and mope about like a frustrated hen? Funny. They used to call Clarence a bit too handsome, like a super-chorus-boy. Now you might say like a butler with a past. Tell him that. Now Felix beginning to act like a toad. Good old Carston. And great Ross. Hats off to Ross, doing nothing at all but what he had to. He remembered their old conviction that Ross had some sort of stable tip in invisible affairs. 'Won't tell. Says we can look at his pictures.'

'We should have been all right together, Scylla and I, and now the sight of her scares me stiff. Lovely and witty, and decent and passionate and kind. There's a figure that stands sentinel before her. I can't see its face. Not a chap you'd care to meet. If I looked at him, he'd go.'

'These things matter a devil of a lot, and they don't matter at all.'

'Scylla's a darling. Want my Scylla.'

'Mother, why can't I have Scylla?'

The angel went on holding the urn. He kicked the turf till a sod tore off. A glow-worm turned its back on him. By infinite degrees the green gem moved off.

'And for half a minute I thought that cup had come to light us up a bit.' He whistled *Waiting for the moon to rise.*

'And it was the old man after all!'

'And Carston shan't have Scylla if he does call the old man's bluff.'

He had the usual difficulty in extracting the glow-worm from the grass.

'Go and light up mummy's tomb.' He stuck it round the knob of the urn, where it fell off. He kicked the muffled earth that squelched, the tears pouring down, till he found a cache of pebbles under his heel and pelted the marble female in the thick dark, and then he had another idea, and with a handful in his pocket went across, round and over the graves, to a low, unlighted house, and tossed them up against a window. A head poked out:

"What's that?"

"Me."

"Come in, my dear boy, come in." An old man in a nightshirt opened his front-door and let him in.

WHEN WE WERE VERY YOUNG

While Felix was whirling down from Montmartre in a taxi with the boy friend and the Russian, all of them drunk. Different drunks. The boy friend roaring gay, the world forgiven because of midsummer Paris, crossed with his original irish love of a spree. He beamed, an arm round Felix, an arm round the Russian whom he usually detested.

"I've got a new crab."

"Let's go and christen it."

"What shall we call it?"

"Aloysius."

"Où allons-nous pour le baptême?" Felix suddenly pitched sideways, his forehead on the Russian's knees.

"I speak it a bit, Boris," he said. It was true. The American felt too jolly to be angry even at the unknown tongue. And Felix knew that he had found what he had come for, this slip out of Russia, a burning black pillar of congenial romance. Birth and ruin and exile, and a name not like green hills, but a wild, snow-crested tree. He would take Boris away. He would go back with Boris into Russia. He would take Boris home. He had found what he had come to find. Not the other one, who, after all, wasn't a gentleman. An awful, delicious fear that Boris could read his mind, had heard his last thought and was amused by its stupidity. While the American sobered up to be surprised at Felix, all his high and mighty airs melted before that notorious lost wolf-cub. God only knew what sort of a not bad sort originally, but finished by having to live on its wits. And Boris was a trifle embarrassed, observant, indifferent, and thoroughly enjoying himself. An evening after his own heart.

They were on the shore of the Place de la Concorde, this time an empty sea. The taxi raced across its grey glass, over the arc of a bridge, and began to thread old Paris like a furious shuttle.

"O bel! O gai!" whispered Felix, upright now between them, his dark blue eyes turned stars. Both admired him a little, nervously. Both profoundly hoped he'd enough money on him, the Russian because he had none, the American because he had no intention of spending any he had. And Felix saw Europe folk-wandering, and how out of the movements of the peoples he had found his companion, young and wicked, and in need and kind. Like a bow bent and relaxed, and strung with fresh arrows, his desires took purpose. At a ghastly little mixed bordel, he walked in like a prince come home.

MARY BUTTS

SCYLLA

She arrived in London at the time when all reasonable citizens are trying to leave it, and the place seems fuller than ever. Full of townspeople shewn up by the magnificence of summer, with children who appear brutalised from want of contact with things growing; where, in spite of every grit-weathered leaf, there is a pretence made that all is for the best inside the vast, roaring, fortuitous wilderness: that Epping Forest is the true green wood, and Southend virgin sea. If Paris is a lovely salon displayed for conversation, London is a lumber-room to be foraged for junk, rubbish, white elephants, treasure. Midsummer is not the time to do it.

Scylla walked through the green park, fresh from no substitute hills and the sea, and not in the least grateful for them. Yet with only contempt for the posters and pretence that represented the Londoners' poor escape to the land. Her yellow lawn frock blew up over her knees, under her powdered arms and throat there was a faint gold patina of freckles. Her little neck-scarf flying out behind her, she walked like a nymph in a temper, blessing nothing she passed.

Something had been taken away from her. Not Picus or Felix, but what they had made her think about. Apples of Iduna the goddess, given her to feed the Aesir, without which she pined without dying. What happened to Iduna and her apples after? Loki, Saturday, had stolen them and shut her up in a giant's castle, and she had been waited on by elf-women, very pleasant in front, but round the back made out of hollow boards. Beastly hot day and no adventures. Business at grey offices in Lincoln's Inn. The only woman she really liked married to a boy she did not. She was going to dinner there.

She remembered that the woman, her friend Lydia,

had wanted once to marry Clarence. Might have married him until, one day, Clarence had made a scene: said that he could not leave Picus: that Picus needed him: had told Lydia that she did not love him: that it was a trick to get a husband: and had broken down badly after. Lydia had said nothing. And 'had never been quite the same since.' That said it exactly. Had probably married her slick young outsider to annoy Clarence. A real chorus-boy beauty with a spirit to match. She would dine there, in their pretentious flat, all shams. It pleased Lydia if her friends flattered her husband. Scylla knew that it might please her that evening if she shewed contempt.

So no sweet temper adorned her as she swung into the new sitting-room with its faked cabinets and painful majolicas, and saw Lydia in a too-short frock and a too-tight hair wave, and a too-pink make-up, reading the *Romaunt de la Rose*. A woman bred out of great stone castles for a life of power and danger, she looked a fool, stripped of what should have been on her, the formal setting that should have extended north, south, east, and west of her. Not necessarily castles. A bare table and a window stuffed with sacking might have suited her purpose, when the purpose was her own, not a stunt to please her husband, like a lion riding a bicycle at a fair.

Vexed deliberation marked the ivory forehead, her chief beauty. Her stockings were not drawn tight, and did not match. An intelligence made for children and learning and administration was adapting itself to marriage, with a gigolo, in a shaky business, in London, without capital, after the war. Would do it badly unless she broke him. Could not break him, he would twist and slip off.

A cathedral had better not turn mouse-trap, or a chalice a cocktail shaker. A ten-inch gun should not be trained on a mark that is not there.

And Scylla found that all she could do was laugh to see her friend so much in love.

And Lydia knew this. Also that Scylla had kept her freedom, was up to all their old amusements out in Europe, down in the South. Scylla saw Clarence continually and made fun of him. Might flirt with him, more curious things can happen, when her proper business was to marry too, and establish herself.

And both the young women knew that this meeting if inevitable was unfortunate, the end of a friendship from university to marriage. Lydia had made a dangerous one. God only knew where adventure would lead the other.

The husband came in. Knocked over his wife's book with a movie paper, and began to talk about himself. A row at the garage and how he had scored. Lydia frowned.

"Phil, Scylla is here." He kissed Scylla several times, while she stared up to see what the prettier woman could do with her eyes; while she was loathing him because he had taken her friend away from her. To use Lydia's practical brain and her unpractised love for her own little ends, to betray her, mishandle her, exploit her. And be dreadfully punished when Lydia recovered from her passion because he had laid familiar paws on her pride. Her heaven-born pride which might as easily move to hell. In a timeless instant she saw the woman Lydia would be, when she would punish her fancy-boy for being the slick little animal he was. And, during the transition, break both hearts.

I may become like that, too. A thought passing, passionate then dispassionate.

At lunch, on Philip's insistence, she praised the table-setting, who had adored Lydia for being the world's worst housekeeper. It was easier when Philip dropped the garage and making eyes, and shewed frank jealousy. He was really afraid of his wife's old friends, knew that he must detach her from them quickly. And Lydia revelled in his authority, her mind storing it up for later, for part of the interminable, intolerable score they would have to recite to one another.... In a house where there would be no children, nor any garden for forgiveness full of the other's favourite flowers.

Now Scylla minded this. Minded also that Philip had not even thought to approach her as his wife's friend. What was left her now but observation? She had had enough of grief. There was only her amusement left, the contrast between Lydia's naïve eroticism and her formidable wits: Philip's technique with her no more than the length of rope on which he had to hang himself. His method was to cut conversation, to interrupt whatever was said; and when he spoke, interrupt himself, so that there should never be any continuity. Perfectly sound. The quickest way to exasperate Scylla. He was reckoning that he could, not quite such a fool as these grand ladies thought him. Could shew them that not being a gentleman was worth something: give Lydia's lady friend something else to call him than a misplaced insect.

And Scylla no longer believed that her reserve of charity was an arsenal. She did not want Lydia if she could not tell her the story of the cup, draw on her learning, and on her instinct for tradition, which might have been created to meet the situation. Without that story her summer in the South was no story, and how often had Lydia been down with them in the wood? Philip once, had followed her there, uninvited, and found her singing them troubador songs. Had bawled jazz and almost dragged her away. Impulses cold, cruel, and insolent grew in Scylla, along with understanding perfecting itself.

A new aspect of the worst had arrived. They were already too accustomed to it. Had seen too many designs broken, whose assembly had been mysteries of harmony. Until they had forgotten unity, harvest ahead of vintage; forgotten that there could be any condition but emulation, advantage, and personal success. She despised herself because she had not the clean surgery to cut out memory and hope. As the story of the house could not be told without the wood, the house-party could not be described without the cup. As well talk politics to Picus as speak of the cup with Philip in the room.

"What happened down South?" said Lydia. "London makes me ache for it. I hear the waves turning over—don't interrupt, Phil—and the branches turning round in the wood." Scylla thought: 'Concentrate on Carston. Make him funny—with the fun left out.' Nothing that she said held together, who had Picus and under Gault to tell to the proper person to hear it, *soeur douce amie*. Lydia must know that because of Philip she could not tell. Lydia had refused to dine alone with her. Scylla did not know the stupid scene he had made when Lydia had tried to go, until he had made love to her, and snatched a promise she did not dare break.

Lydia knew and was not consoled. There might be news of Clarence. She was a jealous woman. Scylla had had Clarence to herself: had looked up at Philip, smiling. Already she knew what she had married, what they would become. Soon she would not be with Scylla's people, or even in their world. And Scylla stayed in and walked out of it so airily. Soft, bitter, little laps of far-seeing. The quickest thing to do was hate, before it was taken out of her in sorrow. Hadn't Scylla come to triumph? Her husband's delicious voice and vulgar accent enchanted and fretted her. His words and the beauty of his wrist as he lit Scylla's cigarette. How could she keep him? And keep him Phil? Be sure of him and improve him? Possible or impossible, it was not her job. Who should have been advising Scylla, correcting and fortifying her.

Exasperated, the lion's paw fell, claws astretch.

What follows can be as well represented operatically—it began:

Philip: (recitative) "Lydia and I are often thinking of you, Scylla—and I'm sure you won't take us up wrong."

Lydia: "We were both thinking if it is quite the thing for you to be there alone with all those men!"
Scylla: (song) "Felix is my chaperone, chaperone," etc.
Philip and Lydia: (duet) "In the end it does not do, does not do,
People know you for that kind of woman."
Scylla: "What sort of a woman?"
Philip and Lydia: (recit.) "We feel it since we married. It does not do, it does not do, to go against society."
Philip: "I've seen a good deal of the world, you know—perhaps not quite the same society as yours, but—"
Philip, Lydia and Scylla: (trio) "People say—"
"What do they say?"
"You know the things they say."
"What have they said?"
"We'd rather not tell you and go into details."
"Go into details!"
"You're doing it for MY GOOD."
Philip and Lydia: (duet) "Of course we are, of course we are.
We wouldn't hurt your feelings,
BUT—"
Philip: "I'm so fond of you, Scylla."
Lydia: "We're so fond of you, Scylla.
BUT—
We've found it out, we've found it out.
The world has reason on its side."
Scylla: (solo) "What is the world?
Lydia's world was my world,
And I don't know Philip's world.
What reason has the world got, anyhow?"
Philip and Lydia: (anthem) "IT DOES NOT DO.
IT DOES NOT DO."
Philip and Scylla: (duet) "What good do these men do to you?"
"What good do I do them?"

Philip and Lydia: (quick recitative) "But can't you consider that every one thinks that you sleep with each other in turn?"

Philip, Lydia and Scylla: (trio) "Including my brother?"

"Now, Scylla, be decent!"

"I am learning behaviour from you."

"You're so young,
So attractive—"

"I am several years older than you."

Lydia: "You were always a baby."

Philip: "And always the lady."

Philip really said that, and when Scylla giggled, the string that tied them burned through and snapped. She remembered Picus at home: under Gault. A cup in a well: in a house. Out of India: in a book out of no man's land.

A shore like that, my dear,
Lies where no man will steer,
No maiden-land.

Most men steer there, and away before they have properly landed. 'Land me where my friend and her fancy-man are waiting to bite.' She noticed how they hunted a single line as a double technique—Lydia wanting to find out, Philip to defame. It infuriated her that she should be hurt.

Lydia was saying:

"I am awfully fond of those boys, Scylla, but they're *mal vus.*"

"What is that?" (Don't defend.)

"Well, you know—"

"No, I don't. Try again."

Lydia did:

"Why did you break up so soon? You said Felix had gone to Paris and you don't seem to know about the others. Where's Clarence?"

If she knew even that, she would have something to keep the old heart-break company.

Philip was saying:

"Scylla, why don't you marry Clarence: People say he's a beauty, and it's time you picked up a husband—"

"She wouldn't," said Lydia,—"despises Clarence. But she can't go on like this."

"Go on like WHAT?" Philip answered her.

"You know what people say about a set with no real men in it."

"What is a REAL MAN?"

"They don't amount to anything, and you know it. I've seen the world in my little way, and that sort don't count. I think I've got Lydia out of that kind of thing. We mean to make a good business of things as we find them. Can't finnick about with white hands, old standards, and fancy words these days. Don't mean to, do we? And we shan't get into quite the messes we might find if you asked us down South. Perhaps that's why you don't. And, honestly, I don't know if I'd let Lydia go—"

"If you mean that you'd find Ross having an affair with Nanna, you can go and look."

Philip went on:

"You know we don't mean that. If you'll excuse me, but Lydia said the other day that you're getting to think of nothing but sex—"

Insolent little cub. She had a last look at Lydia, twisting her wedding-ring.

"Of course, I am," she said. "I know something about it. Very naturally, now. I've been trying to tell you. We have all separated now because (not my brother, of course) we can't decide which one of them shall marry me, and we've run away to think; I can't make up my mind. Not Ross, or Picus. But I've decided not to look outside our set."

She saw the blood rising in Lydia's face. Not a blush, a tide to the brain.

'Now I've done it. I've lied. I've hurt her. Considering my present relations with Clarence—'

Lydia was saying:

"I don't know. There is something fatal about your life, Scylla." She noticed that it excited Philip to think of her desired.

A gulf had opened between them, on whose widening edge they shouted brutal farewells. They were telling her that her brother had given dishonoured cheques: that Picus had syphilis: Carston blackmailed: Ross was a satyr and a stunt painter. And Philip that Clarence had shewn cowardice at the front. Then his wife turned on him a look of insanity, and Scylla saw a tiny thread of blood run out of her nostril. A posy stood in Felix's wedding-present, a bowl of flint glass. Philip dashed the water of it on her forehead, and held the sweet scented names to her nose. Lydia struggled up and the bowl was knocked out of his hands and splintered. Scylla had to force herself to laugh, and not to say: 'It's a camp story I told you: invented it, spite for spite.' "I'm going," she said.

Lydia cried: "Is that all that happened?"

Again she almost meant to say 'No, it's a long business. I came here to ask what you thought.' Then was damned if she would.

She said: "What's the good of my staying here? We shall all be back there soon. I'll ask about the syphilis and the satyriasis. Does one put a notice in the papers about Felix's cheques? Shall I tell Clarence to let you know how he escaped court-martial in spite of his seven wounds?"

CARSTON

He was struggling with the branch line of a remote english railway. He got to a place where people changed, and was in the mood to bear with the proceedings of another century.

He had plenty of them before he reached the village called Tambourne. Plenty of fine old women in black-beaded bodices, one button always missing where the strain came over the breasts. Plenty of young live-stock being shifted up and down the line. Plenty of the porters' family party. Plenty of a plate of macaroons locked alone in a glass box in a deserted refreshment room.

Plenty of superb trees, and white nettle-scented dust. At the inn called the Star at Tambourne, plenty of regret for Nanna's fine darned linen and china tea. A night of stars and bats came very slowly. Once out of the wood and away from his relations he asked himself why in Christ's name he had come to see old Mr. Tracy. An ancient of days was living a stroll away from him at Tambourne House. He fetched the cup from his suit-case and put it on the red baize parlour table, a dumb circle of pale green. Why couldn't the thing speak? Just once. Dumb was the word for it. He got rather tight all by himself, but without inspiration. He would have to go and call, have to go call. All up that yellow drive by himself.

LYDIA

She was alone next morning. Philip had gone out to meet a Jew whose favour they were nursing. She had refused, felt she no longer cared if he mismanaged it. She had not spoken since an hour after Scylla had left, and in that hour they had said worse things to each other than they had said to her. But Philip, who had almost cried with fear, in the morning was not dissatisfied. One does not leave the gutter without a few knocks. He had his own plans, his own adventure. Hoped from his heart Scylla was marrying the man. That would get them out of his way for good.

Lydia sat at her writing-table, without her mask, either of love or make-up. Her head, still disfigured, did not belong to this age. She wrote:

> *My dear Clarence,*
>
> *How are you all?*
>
> *Scylla is up and dined last night. She seemed very well and a little mysterious. I understood, though I may have got it quite wrong, that you're thinking of marrying each other.*
>
> *Please let Phil and me know if it's true. It almost hurts one's feelings not to be the first to wish you luck.*
>
> *No chance of getting away until Phil has pulled off some more business, and then he wants to go to Eastbourne!*

She went out herself and posted it to Tollerdown.

Once, down South, one of the boys had called Scylla "bird-alone." They had all asked for names. Picus had been cat-by-himself. Felix, *l'oeuf sur le toit.* Ross, bird-catcher. They had quarrelled a little that morning, and she had not been pleased when Ross had said, grinning: "If Scylla's the bird, one might call you 'wolf-alone'."

FELIX

Felix sobbed in the taxi: "Can't you see we are all damned." And that love and death were one.

They had considerably enlivened the cabaret, a sentimental infamy, its men and girls drunker than the clients. Among their slobbering, rapacious familiarity, the three appeared like drunk young gods. And Felix, a young king receiving his subjects, was courtly to the fawning, swarming band of both sexes in changed clothes. Proud of his companions, unconscious that he was paying for the party, he did not know that Boris owed money there, how he balanced the chance of being dunned with his worth as conductor of a rich client, and hoped that his debt would be put on to Felix's bill. A thing he would not arrange. He had not yet come to that.

Round their table moved the herd of painted animals, Felix's subjects, their tongues parting their lips for what they might get out of the flower-skinned, sapphire-eyed boy, who looked at nothing but Boris. Black briar-rose, he called him, who saw Felix an absurd young splendour. Felix noticed him strange, observant, a moon-baby. Not how the infant was putting two and two together. Nor would he have cared, lifted above any complex of the shopkeeper to be paid in any kind of thanks.

It was the American, later, who developed an intoxicated conscience about Felix when, in the taxi, romantic metaphysics and song gave way to hysteria. He cuffed him roughly into place. Unfortunately, Felix's head broke a window, and all he did was lean out and cry: "I want to suffer as you have suffered, Boris— Police! police!"

The taxi slowed round a corner. He was bleeding from a cut. Boris alone kept his wits. Withdrew Felix's head delicately from the hole in the glass, shouted in Russian at the chauffeur he had picked. Felix had become merely a thing to get home. They pulled up at the Foyot and got him out. Out but not up. The American retrieved the silk hat rolling on the stones: while Boris extracted three hundred francs, taxi, window money and useful change for the next day.

Then came the pilgrimage to which they were hardly equal, in the liftless, ancient barrack, their support to each other physical not moral, an age of social hatred lived through as they hoisted Felix upstairs and round corners, indifferent to his cries that he must *faire pipi,* followed by the concierge jangling the key. Ages of dissimilarity between the American, sudden flower of strength and looks, and the russian-tartar brat of family, to whom neurasthenia had become a habit.

They dumped Felix on the bed. Boris sponged away

the blood, and got off the clothes that would hurt. The blood sickened the other and made him fretful. He gave an odd exhibition of nerves. Boris soothed him and they stumbled downstairs. In the street he said: "I have a little money. Let's go on." The American refused. Boris circled a little on the pavement, and, finding himself alone, drifted off to his little hotel, and slept face-downwards in his only convincing suit.

CLARENCE

At the cottage on Tollerdown, Clarence began a call to order. He had stayed on a night with Ross, the last of them to scatter.

The cottage was indistinguishable from the white, flint-casing chalk rock out of which it was made. God knows when built, its walls sagged in a broken angle with the down-slope. Placed at the mouth of a quarry, he lived naked as could be after his late smothering in trees. A single mountain-ash at the quarry-mouth raised its scarlet against the hot white cutting and the burnt gold grass. From the door a path of glassy flints ran to the cliff's edge, and joined the valley track. At the angle the cliff broke sheer. Four hundred feet below the sea murmured and tumbled on a beach of round yellow stones. Clarence had set the flint path, chipped and cemented them for a touch of construction in an air-haunted land. A place where no sane man would live. But there was generally water in the well-shaft, and just then a blood-mist of poppies on the stony earth, cultivated to just that level. With an ache that he did not understand was for Versailles, Clarence had swung in.

Inside there was not the mess men are expected to make for themselves. A little art and craft, a little cubism, a little chic, made interesting by one of Picus's amusements, models of all sorts of ships.

A viking-boat was a dragon on the sail, a shield-wall along the sides. An Armada-ship, the Virgin all aboard. A lovely proa. A greek galley, and, the first thing Clarence saw, Picus's card at the mast with "A present for Scylla" on it.

Now where did Picus find out how to do them? A family mystery. History did not exist for him. He hated the sea. And that black open boat might have come out of an egg hatched at Salamis.

In the living-room, panelled, and painted a flat jade green, Clarence plumped the scarlet cushions, making everything gay; while in the kitchen, the shepherd's wife set the water running in the cobble channels, skinned rabbits, polished the blue plates. The particular master was back. Long ago, before she'd married the shepherd, and had ten children and lost but three and taken up with the soldiers before he died and his brother had come along, 'twas the same name, and they'd a disease in common, and she'd still be walking over to the camp at Chard, and though she'd lost her teeth, and the better part of her speech, the lads would be over themselves with beer in their pockets, she'd been kitchenmaid at one of the country houses.

She could not read or write, and her time must have been different from ours. Mr. Picus gave her port of an evening, but the one she felt about was Ross. This singular *fille de joie,* over fifty, toothless, palateless, type of disreputable peasant hag, when she knew he was in the land, would stand out on the turf and watch for him. Gobble at Clarence, cooking meticulously the food he would not let her touch: ask if Mr. Ross would be coming over. Scylla terrified her. Nanna laughed at her and was called ma'am.

Clarence strode out, collarless, in riding breeches, to draw water. He looked down into the well, dark fern-ringed tranquillity, round which had happened such a singular little event.

He drew one bucket after another, and sluiced them

over his body, branded with shrapnel and bullet and bayonet thrust.

A vast, delicate strength, not used, not properly understood, piteously alone against the white rock and wash of the blue-wrinkled sea. A scarlet coat in a palace and some gold lace on his shoulders would have fitted him better, watched only as he was by a gasping, furtive old woman behind the kitchen panes. If the other had been there, he would have shewn affectation, talked about his nakedness and her. While Ross and Picus would have skipped through the house and chaffed her if they had noticed her at all. Such was Clarence's audience, with a scattering of poppies, a house huddled against the ground, and below the aphrodite sea.

Indoors he preened and poked everywhere, exceedingly afraid of the coming night. Then he would be alone, the shepherd's wife off at her mincing trudge to her hovel, where occasionally was heard the roar of a carouse. Ross might have joined it and been the life and soul of the party, or lain out sea and star sailing.

Clarence, by himself, was simply and terribly afraid. Not of individuals, but of a menace that walked hand in hand with night, joined with the fear natural in remote places to a man not intuitively tuned. First he told himself that everything would not be ready for Picus, and he would scold him: then that Picus's scenes were a disgrace. Then that Picus was never coming back. Then that it was Scylla who would not let him come back. A rage got him by the throat, shook him, crawled over him. By the time it was night, he was incoherent, and half a dozen times started over the hill to walk seventy miles inland to Tambourne where Picus might be. It was not his humour that checked him, but fear of the vast spaces under the star-blazing sky. The stars were not his friends. The Pleiades may have been weeping uselessly for him. When he lifted his eyes up the hills, he averted them. Rough, barrow-haunted places. He shuddered and turned back.

Only candle-light in the cottage, in the silvered sconces on the jade-blue walls. Casket he had made for Picus, hung with brilliant xviiith century paintings of birds. That woman had done it, the slender, cousinly bitch. Once he had thought of dropping the handkerchief at her, and few he'd ever done it to had said no. His extreme vanity had never surmounted the transition from his boy's beauty, which Ross had taken as a matter of course.

'Introvert, introvert' said his mind, full of fashionable fads. Then his torture came on him again as the huge night swept on, and even his fear of it was forgotten in the grinding and tearing of his frustration and desolation and rage against Scylla, until for all human purposes he was mad. In other surroundings it would have been a bad break-down, needing work, praise, new loves, above all admiration. Here, a pebble-throw from a gulf of air, it was ruin for one who in camps and cities and a classic personal relation had been heroic.

The story of the cup, now become a horror, came in. That his reason was not overset was because he took the hollow greek ship with "A present for Scylla" on it, and broke it to splinters.

Next morning he had not slept and sat staring when Lydia's letter came. A horrible fit of laughing frightened the shepherd's wife. She ran home like a half-plucked hen, while Clarence with affected deliberation for some unknown frightful audience took pen and paper and wrote in his exquisite hand.

He told Lydia that it was not so, and in a few lines conveyed such a loathing of Scylla that Lydia half saw the truth, and nearly went to find her. But Philip found the letter amusing, and she did not go.

The levelling afternoon sun that came in through the cottage door found Clarence drawing Scylla, on huge sheets of paper pinned to the walls. In charcoal, obscenely and savagely contorted, and with little darts made of fine nibs and empty cartridge-cases he pierced the bodies of his paper martyrs. Then he tore them down, finding no content in it, so that ragged strips of paper covered the floor, the silver divan, and the cushions bright as fresh blood.

Perhaps he was the man who had suffered most from the disbelief and disuse of all forms of religion. Bred a Catholic, he had left the church and the question superciliously, uneasily. Incapable of Ross's and Scylla's faith that there was a faith, with all its pains and invisibility, unquestioned as air. A religion externalised by a powerful discipline might have upheld him, but all that he had then was a suspicion that this was the punishment of a neglected set of gods.

The hour came when the light began to shew up the earth in relief, with a distinctiveness almost monstrous, like a drug reverie. A little freshness blew in off the water, a cloud or so travelled, teaspoonfuls of fire-dipped cream. Spent with pain, his fear of the night returned.

MR. TRACY

Carston spent the next morning thinking about old Mr. Tracy, or, more exactly, how he would hate to walk up his drive. In his country he would have faced a dozen of them, but he had been out early to scout and had seen the house up a much-too-long-yellow avenue between high clipped shrubs. Unsympathetic. Like a long neck into a trap.

At half-past twelve he had an idea. At two o'clock precisely he had passed the lodge. At two minutes past he saw old Mr. Tracy leave his front door and halt, turning as he walked, to speak to someone within. Two seconds later he saw a neat painted gate in the laurel wall, the entrance of a tunnel. One second later he was mastering the latch, and had disappeared from sight.

We will follow him, as earlier writers say so prettily, as he commences trespasser, in hiding from the approaching master of the house.

He followed the tunnel about ten yards, where it led him on to a wood-path parallel with the drive, whose principal feature was a pavement of enormous roots. He listened to the crisp sound of Mr. Tracy's boots, waited till he had passed, tripped over the roots, slipped down the tunnel again, and reached the house as though nothing had happened. He was ashamed until he noticed that it was a sound instinct that had made him avoid the old man in open.

Half an hour later he was in the library. He heard: "So you want to buy that mischief-making cup for an antiquarian friend in the States? And you want its pedigree? I can write you out the particulars, of course. My name counts for something, but I imagine that I was sufficiently precise last time we met."

"No, sir," said Carston, "you were not. I have its photograph in the book that wasn't burned as thoroughly as you might have wished. There it's described as a mass-vessel, early english, from your collection. Now, I don't give a damn which it is, but it can't be that and a poison-cup. And before I write out a cheque I want to know which."

"But, in any case, Mr. Carston, while we are speaking of money, I imagine that any cheque should be made out to me."

"No, sir. I and three other persons heard you confirm your son's gift of it to Miss Taverner." (His reputation as a collector's at stake. It can't be two things at once)— "As to a second opinion, I expect your British Museum could give us that."

"I admit," said Mr. Tracy, "that it is probably a mass-cup. In my horror of loose feeling I preferred to suggest any origin, however grim or far-fetched, than that my relatives should abandon themselves to superstition."

This might have sounded noble, but Carston kept on. 'Bit of bunk: what has he been up to? That's what I'm not to find out.' He said:

"It seems to me that you've exchanged a fine, mysterious, almost sacred fable for a sordid, even brutal, personal invention. Facts are what I'm here for."

'What I won't get, not the ones that matter.'

"You can be satisfied that in all probability the photograph describes it correctly. An early Church vessel, its shape suggests a chalice, with the setting lost. If so, it might well have been part of a crusader's loot. Incidentally, since its probable origin greatly enhances its value, you might do well to stick to my earlier suggestion, the last part of which is no more than simple fact—"

"Cool!" Carston gasped. Cucumbers and icebergs.

"—Or is to be part of the price for Scylla Taverner's hypothetical virginity?" Carston thought:

'If I start losing my temper, it is he who will find things out. He chose blind-man's bluff. We must play until we needn't.' At the same time conviction came to him that they would find out nothing. His direct attack was obvious, useless, unfruitful.

"I have nothing to say, but that I buy nothing with my eyes shut. And what I've come to get is your reasons for supposing it a Church vessel—" Vain repetition. Not even taken the wind out of the old man's sails. Sailing serenely on: through a weak position: through fraud.

"You shall have them, Mr. Carston, to-night. Signed on my authority. You are staying at the Star?"

IN AND OUT

On his way down the drive Carston knew what you did. In Trollope, in cases of spiritual difficulty, you consulted the vicar. Whether it turned out well depended on whether you found a good vicar or a bad. The landlord directed him. His way led through the churchyard. He noticed a staring white monument, and read on it the name of Picus's mother.

"Old devil to bury her like that and keep it clean." In the flagged hall, he walked up a ribbon of green matting, and saw at the end Picus playing with a blind cord.

"Tracy," he said, "I've been trying to clear this up."

"Any luck?"

"None. Have you a good vicar?"

"I left the churchyard at two in the morning, and said 'It's me,' and I've been here since. Sick of night and mist walking. I've told him. Come in."

* * * * *

Felix woke, rolled over in a flood of gold-spangled dust to find himself lapped in faultless health and spirits. Paris' morning surprise for her children, last night's debauch innocent as a game of kiss-in-the-ring. Last night's resolution clarified and unimpaired. He had Boris to find and explain to him what he had meant. Claim his own. He shaved his hardly perceptible beard, whistling an air from *Louise*. Paris was waiting for him, had given him the day, now in mid-morning, which would only be begun by night.

He ran through his pockets. Boris's address was lost. There were names of unknowns, scrawled on the cabaret cards, not the shred off a bill he remembered, the splendid name scrawled in sucked purple pencil— He rushed out to find his earlier boy friend.

"My dear Felix, how should I know? Those boys sleep anywhere. You might try the quays. You'll see him about again some night."

"I don't mean to wait—I've got to find him, if I go to the police."

"Well, I shouldn't do that— They probably know too much about him." Then, incautiously—"He's probably pretty sick after last night. They say his lungs are going."

Curiously, that fanned Felix. The older boy for the first time liked him well. Wondered if by any chance he saw in his eyes what "one would fain call master." It was odd.

"He used to live somewhere in the nest of hotels round the Rue Buonaparte."

"Good," said Felix. "I'll try them, one by one."

* * * * *

Boris woke up. The young head, a little brutal and afraid in sleep, on waking lost those expressions. "Comme j'ai fait la bombe hier," rubbing his eyes like a baby. A sixth-floor room in a cheap hotel in old Paris has no romantic quality. It was as much as Boris could do to rise nightly like some sort of phoenix out of the ashes of old clothes, torn socks, and russian newspapers. A miserably recognisable room, in a bitter world now burning under the sun-cracked roof, with no room in it for penniless, palace-reared brats. No excuse for the room either. A shameless, shameful pity of disorder, and want not above the trickery. Only on the lavabo shelf there was some sort of order, and a glass full of brushes for the bright white teeth.

What sort of boy was the english boy? Half Boris's nature was curious, the other—it was a nature profoundly divided—had no interest. The indifference lay beneath, the under-waters of the stream that ran in and out, up so many curious creeks, round islands not fixed yet on any map.

His interest was chiefly whether the boy would be good for a few nights of Boris's necessities; some food, unlimited drink, no sympathy, but a kind of companionship. Charm was what he liked, who had it for sole asset. Someone to laugh with. He would have laughed if he could have seen Felix, followed by the taxi he was too impatient to jump in and out of, entering and leaving shabby door after shabby door. He lay on his back and dodged the flies. He was very tired after four years of Paris. Four actual years, but he had never been able to calculate more than a day ahead, which must set ordinary time going differently. Also, what time had he in the sense of future, a bloody curtain between him and his land, his torn roots not fed by the transplanting? Over two hundred francs (the compatriot chauffeur had been merciful) of the english boy's money stuffed away. It might also have startled him had he seen Felix a door nearer, a door further off. One hundred and fifty francs to pacify the old *vache* in the bureau below. If misery had turned the key on him, what of it? Get the second best shoes out of the cobblers. Forget till the money was gone, and in the next spell of rain take cold and go about sore-throated and aching. Till it was time to drink again. Drink to forget. Forget what did not matter. Yet if a fly brushed his caste dignity, he would rage childishly, and laugh and forgive and not forget.

Felix pitched into his room, his heart almost preceding him. Drew himself up and said languidly: "All right after last night?" Poverty that amazed him and he pitied, for a moment dismissing romance for sense.

"Get up and we'll lunch. I'm not in Paris for long. I want you to come away with me."

"Where?" said Boris.

"To my people in England."

"I've always wanted to see England," he said—"we like the english best of all races."

Russians do not gush, and he was arranging his shame about the room; the shirt he had worn last night all he had on him, and his feet grimy and no slippers, and how to turn himself into a desirable object with Felix there; and how to get his clothes out with the bill not paid if he was really going away; and how they couldn't make Felix a cocktail, and would probably refuse to send up so much as a bottle of Vichy; and how soon or if it would be safe to tell Felix about it. And if Felix was really a bore or not. And, suddenly, how bad it was to have to think like that.

And Felix, brimmed with grace, said:

"This was just to tell you. Meet me at the Foyot in an hour."

* * * * *

In another room, in another hotel, in a chaos of elegant poverty, Scylla answered the telephone bell. Philip's voice said:

"What made you let on you were engaged to Clarence the other night? He doesn't seem to think so. Like to hear his letter?"

She was ready for that, through the occasional sense that one has lived through an event before it arrives.

"What's that? I said nothing of the sort. If Lydia likes to think such rubbish. She must have written him one of her letters."

The voice changed:

"I wish you hadn't told her whatever you meant like that. She's been upset."

"Well, she might have married him herself once," and rang off and sat still. This would not do. If their alliance was not to break up, she must get the idea out of Clarence's head. Played into Clarence's hands, she had: to finish her with Picus: give Clarence the game. Subtle-minded, he would know how to bitch things more than they were already bitched. All to bitch Lydia for bitching her. God, what a world! So much for Sanc-Grail cups and maidens. She felt positively superstitious over her own experiences. Then suffered under what seemed, after all, an unfair lack of grace. Then saw the cottage on Tollerdown, a desolation with something in it that raved. Translated it into possibility of annoyance, petty insult, even tragedy. Playing the Freud game, the name rose "Philoctetes." Just the sort of rôle Clarence would pick and play badly. Did Philoctetes play well before he found his Sophocles? Oh! damn analogies. Better go down at once, make at worst an armed peace, and give him something else to think about.

A telegram:

"Arriving shortly with Russian ill to live with us."

Nothing like Felix for letting you know. And Carston had gone to Tambourne with a plan. Picus might be there. Felix was coming back. All roads lay south again. Sleep at Starn that night and go over to Tollerdown in the morning. Have it out with Clarence. Might seduce Clarence and shut his mouth that way. Then to Tambourne and Carston's news.

With serene courage, for she was uneasy, she made her preparations.

* * * * *

Picus introduced Carston to english ecclesiastical life. At last there would be something that he had been led to expect. The old man in his library looked and spoke right.

Picus said:

"I've told him all about it. He's had the devil in his parish."

"Well," said the vicar, "I'll go so far as to say that during the course of our long association, your father has illustrated my picture of hell. And, as usual, any heavenly landscape has been all around and so unobserved." He examined the cup.

"I cannot tell you anything. A piece of worn jade, this time, for the question mark to the question we can none of us answer."

"What is the question?" said Carston.

"Our old friend. Whether a true picture of the real is shewn by our senses alone."

"Can't we leave it that we don't know?"

"Then the picture we have becomes more and more unintelligible."

"I don't know. All I can say is that I've never been so bothered, never behaved so like a skunk, never so nearly fell dead in my tracks till I got down here and began to think about such things. It's unfashionable now, you know—"

"Naturally," said the second old man, so peaceful, so cordially, with such disinterestedness, with such interest. It was going to be a singular ecclesiastic this time. Old Mr. Tracy turned saint. Carston gave up trying to cut providence.

"Can you give us your professional view?" he said.

"My dear man, Picus comes here to be consoled for a grievance because he has given his heart away twice, and doesn't know from which victim to ask it back. You ask my professional advice about this business of the cup; not only for its history, but on the spiritual upsets following its arrival. Here it is: say the seven penitential psalms: go carefully through your failings before man and God: communicate to-morrow at eight: come to matins and sing: attend to my sermon. In the evening sing the Magnificat and remember that when I dismiss you with the prayer *Lighten our Darkness,* I am saying the last word I know. (I suggest a day's devotions because I am sure you have not done any for a long time.) Add to them the lovely sobriety of our church and our liturgy, the splendour of midsummer filtered through old glass on cold stone. That is as far as I can go in my profession, which, like the ancient mysteries, depends largely on what you bring to it. My hope is that some day somebody will bring something. In your case, Mr. Carston, clean hands and a pure heart I'll be bound. I administer formulæ and recall memories—that work and still live. In what lies the scientific triumph but that its formulæ work?"

No one on earth before had told Carston that he had

a pure heart and clean hands. He was startled, touched, nearly cried, and said:

"But we're both in love with Scylla Taverner."

The second old man said:

"Well, I dare say she can do with two fine young men in love with her. She's had no soft life, with her batch of demons."

"He means," said Picus, "that I got off with her and he didn't."

"I hope," said the second old man, "that I'm being asked for my unprofessional opinion."

"We're telling you," said Picus. Carston's courage jumped. He'd been told he had clean hands and a pure heart. Now that it had been pointed out, he saw that it was true.

"Why are you so spiteful about me, Tracy? How do you think you'll get the best out of a man if you fool him, and show you despise him and give your sweetheart away before him?"

"Everyone goes to bed with me," said Picus—"always."

"Now that's a new thing to sulk about," said the vicar. "I am very useless. I cannot tell you about the cup. I cannot judge which of you does or should or could love Picus best. Or Clarence. Or you. His father will probably tell us as much truth as he finds convenient. But when I think of that sensitive, frustrated, pain-racked man who has given his life for you, Picus, alone on Tollerdown, in the fairy-house he made for you—I judge no man. And I do not think it just for you, with your temperament to have the responsibility."

"Nor," said Picus, passionately, "do I."

"Nor," said the second old man, "why Scylla should be your leader and your neglected toy. Nor why you who all wish Felix well should have become his poison. In this business there are no easy answers, and we are left with our honour to lighten us."

Picus said: "Lighten what?"

"This story as I see it," said the second old man, "is true Sanc-Grail. The cup may have been an ash-tray in a Cairo club. But it seems to me that you are having something like a ritual. A find, illumination, doubt, and division, collective and then dispersed. A land enchanted and disenchanted with the rapidity of a cinema. Adventures. *Danger and awe and love.* What has Felix found in Paris that brings him home so quick? Our virtues we keep to serve these emergencies. Our virtue to induce them."

"M'yes," said Picus, —"but there ought to be sharper detail. It was Clarence's spear that started me."

Carston said: "It is true. It has happened like that." He was in a state of consciousness unique to him. Not vision, but wonder become a state, an impregnation of being: that excited and held him in absolute rest. An expectancy more real than the old furniture, the two men with him, the shallow stream that tore past the window, water whistling to itself, a running trap for light.

More than an approach to wonder. Wonder was the answer, and familiar objects out of their categories. He also saw Picus without prejudice, and loved him.

A flock of telegrams was brought in. Carston opened his, brought in from the Star.

"Going to Tollerdown then home come along Felix arriving sick Russian live with us."

"Whoops, my dear," said Picus.

The vicar opened two:

"Coming south take care of us Scylla."

"Is Picus with you? Clarence."

"The grail knights are gathering, it seems. This only I see clearly. Either this is a curiously coincidental hash, or we are taking part in events, only part of which are happening on the earth we see. Meanwhile, I approve the spacious dust-bin into which you throw most things, and have seen everything thrown."

"Then you believe there is a moral search?" said Carston, ignoring what paralleled with his wonder.

"I do. Even unprofessionally. As valid and as open to revision as research in the electromagnetic field. Practically I advise you to stick to your tastes as gentlemen and your love of art. You're so damnably proud and fastidious you'll do that anyhow."

"Felix," said Carston, eloquently, "I really couldn't do justice to the way that boy behaved. The way he treated his sister; has and will again."

"He seems to be arriving from Paris on an orgy of tending the sick."

"Feeding the hungry," said Picus. "I know Russians. I wonder what we're in for?"

The second old man said:

"I'll take him off your hands if he is any good. The young are getting worth watching again."

Carston said:

"I wish the cup could be disposed of."

"I'll go over to the Star," said Picus, "and wait for my father's idea of convincing you. I've a lech on the boots."

When they were alone, Carston said with an effort:

"My intentions are very sincere towards Scylla Taverner."

"I think they are. So are his. I'll marry her to either of you with a psalm of joy if it works out that way. But you do realise that your relation with her will not be the same as hers with Picus? Young men think sex is all the same, or at best a sacred or profane love, when it's as varied as art."

They chatted. Picus brought back a letter with a black seal.

Cup found in the vestry in the church of St. Hilary-under-Llyn sometime in July 1881. *Given me by the rector, the rev. John Norris, as it could not be identified as church property. Believed by me, on the authority of* (a string of names followed), *to be a cup of the rare but occasionally found chalices of the Keltic church.*

"The Llyn is on the Welsh marches," said the vicar, "and the man's dead."

Carston said:

"Then we get nowhere."

"Nowhere. Only in ghost-stories, and those not the best, do you get anywhere that way."

"But what are we going to do with the damned thing? It can't lie about the house like a green eye that doesn't wink. The man's dead. Suppose the authorities stick by Mr. Tracy. Or don't? This has been a fool's errand—"

"I have an idea," said the vicar. "Take it back to Toller-down and replace it where you found it. If the next drought sends it up in a suspicious manner, well and good. It seems to like wells. And truth, if she prefers not to talk, can return to one."

Carston said: "I like that."

"Good," said Picus, "learn it to be a toad." Both prayed he would add—"I'll be off with it and look up Clarence."

Not at all.

"I'm not ready yet. Someone had better take it and fetch him. And Scylla. He gets ideas in his head when he's alone there. Carston, you started travelling about with the thing. Go and drop it and bring them back. There's a train to-morrow that starts at six."

CLARENCE and SCYLLA

Scylla slept at Starn. She overslept. A terrific heat had sprung up, and made her feel that there was danger in approaching the hills.

Neither Ross nor Clarence had been seen at Starn, only Nanna had driven in on the baker's cart to conduct her favourite campaign about the quality of preserving sugar.

"She just wouldn't listen to me, ma'am. All she 'ud say was that she wouldn't have you or your raspberries poisoned by what I'd sent." The grocer's wife told her.

So Nanna was making jam. Felix was partial, especially to raspberry jam. Russians put it in their tea. It was after lunch that she discovered that there was not a car to be had, and also took a lift off the baker down the valley to Tollerdown. She bumped and swayed over the flint-dressed road, the white dust powdering her, the overwhelming sun bearing her down, until the driver pulled up at the valley's end, an earshot from the sea, under the hill.

Vast its burnt gold desert shoulder rose beside her, the ribbon path bleached and crumbling. She went up. Struggle with fire and earth and steepness upset her physically: her arms were red, her neck beaded with sweat, her chemise stuck to her skin. Poor nymphs of Artemis. What complexion could stand it? That was why they were painted hunting in woods. Half-way up she sank on a stone and fanned herself with her hat. Remembered another walk, to Starn. She feared that Clarence had seen her, was sulking inside instead of coming to meet her. That was sad. She remembered how once in London she had come to him straight back from Spain, and he had lifted her up and carried her over the threshold, so glad he had been to see her.

Clarence had not seen her. Unshaved, half-dressed, he was trying to torture the body of Picus, the statue he had done of him in clay. He had dragged it out against the quarry wall and pierced it with arrows of sharpened wood, feathered from a gull he had shot overnight.

Scylla found the door open and went softly in.

"Clarence, I've come all this way. Can I have tea?"

He heard the low voice, thought of the gull crying. She saw the bird's half-plucked body, bloody on the floor, and that there were papers torn in strips and little darts. She turned over a fold and saw her own body, and her cry was more like the gull. Bird-alone in the lonely room. Except for a ghost called Clarence, everything was empty. She thought:

'Run away: Can't: Where to? It's all empty, and my

knees shake. And I'm curious. Curious and furious and only my body is afraid.'

Clarence wanted to be sure about the bird. He came in slowly, dazed with violence and grief. Bad conscience and fear of making a fool of himself nagged his blazing obsession. He saw Scylla at the door in silhouette, her scarf fluttering off the back of her neck, sweat-darkened curls appliquéd on her forehead, her hat thrown familiarly on a chair, her mouth open.

"Come and look," he said, and with the fingers of one hand dug into her collar-bone, led her through the kitchen into the half-circle of quarry behind.

She saw Picus in greenish clay, pricked with white feathers. Clarence had made him exactly as he was, a body she had known, for which hers ached.

"You see," he said, "I only had what I'd made of him to do it to."

There was an arrow through his throat, and his head had not fallen forward.

"You're going down the well, where the cup came—"

"Why, Clarence?"

"Best place for you, my fancy-girl. If there's enough water, you'll drown. If there isn't, and I don't think there is, you'll break every bone in your body."

She could run like a lapwing, but he could run fast. She was strong as a tree-cat, but he could tear her in two.

"I came to bring you to Picus. He does not want you to be alone on Tollerdown. He is at Tambourne. Lydia sent you a silly letter because" (get his vanity if you can) "she is so in love with you that she's mad."

"And so are you, it seems. Gods! I'm a lucky chap. Unfortunately, Picus doesn't join the harem. He doesn't like me any more.

"Going to marry me, are you? You shall in a way. I mean to follow you down the well."

"Picus is at Tambourne, waiting for you."

"In time he will be here again. My body will fetch him."

"You are the most beautiful man in the world, but you won't be when they get you up out of the well."

He took her other shoulder in his fingers, thrusting them into the muscle-hollow under her neck, hurting her. She forgot him exacting, petulant; remembered him long before, beautiful, merry, inventive, good. And cruel now. Stupid cruelty. Cruelty frightened her. She lied:

"Clarence, I am going to marry Carston—I teased Lydia—" He turned her towards the well.

"There will be one less of you bitches to come into our lives."

"We bear you, and I am no stronger in your hands than that bird. Why did you shoot a gull? It isn't done." Time seemed very precious. Only a thimbleful left. The well very near. The sun turning a little away from them.

"Woodpecker," she shrieked, and flung Clarence off, and ran to the statue. She had been so careful not to say that name, and now saw Clarence hurrying to her, the mournful crazy mask splitting, the mouth turning up, the eyes shooting death at her. And Picus, pierced with arrows, smiled down his sweet equivocation. She heard: "That'll do better." He had a cord round his waist. He had cattle-ranched once: that was his lariat. She ran once round the statue. A second later he had thrown her, picked her up half-stunned and tied her against Picus. A black flint had cut her head, a patch of blood began to soak through the moon-fair hair.

Clarence walked back and stood by the kitchen door, fitting an arrow to the string. It ripped the skin on her shoulder and entered the clay. She saw another fly towards her and notch her forearm. Another, and there was a tearing pain below her left breast.

Three instants of pain, set in one of fear. Like a great jewel. Clarence stood by the kitchen door, sharpening an indifferent arrow. She made a supreme effort: not to scream much: not to betray herself. Then a moment of absolute contempt of Clarence. Then of pain. Then, as if she were looking out of a window, into a state, a *clarté* the other side of forgiveness. Not by that route. She fainted.

CARSTON and CLARENCE

Carston's day had been a penance. A train had landed him some time in mid-morning at a place called Chard. Picus had said that it was nearer Tollerdown than Starn, but no one there had heard of the place. The station lay in no immediate relation to the village. The inn was fusty and unsympathetic. The heat atrocious. A day for no sane man to tramp while the sun was high. Miles across another bend of the heath where Picus had lost him, the down-banks rose, aery turf walls, solid as flesh and blood. One of them was Tollerdown. He held up a passing motorist, who was kind. He gave him a lift down a white road sprung like an arrow across the moor that filled the lowlands like a dark dragon's wing.

At the foot of the turf, he set Carston down. "Go up the track," he said, "and make towards the sea. If it's not this shoulder, it's the one that follows it." Carston mounted, into silence, on to height. He had never been so well in his life, could not have stood that if he had not been so well. Never had his heart been so touched. Could he stand that?

He mounted, past the trees, the copses, the gorse patches, on to the last crest of raw grass. The earth and the sea extended in a perfect circle round him. He had only to follow the hill's spine, and drop half-way into the valley to strike the cottage before he walked over into the sea. Like a man who has been given a heavy treasure that he has not looked at and must carry home, he walked on.

Bear your burden in the heat of the day, he sang, who had been in great request at parties for his bawdy repertory.

His track ran through five barrows. By one was a crook-backed angry thorn. A bad patch. He passed it, glad to have left them behind, keeping his face towards the sea. Interlude this day alone, in a train. On a hill. Find a cottage on a shelf. Console its inhabitant. Bring him a cup to pop down a well. Fetch him away. You could make a ballad about it. About a mile more to go. *One more river to cross.* The turf turned over in what was almost a cliff. He was not on Tollerdown. Picus and the man in the car had said two hills. This one dropped into a narrow neck. The great bank he could now see rising on the other side, that was Tollerdown. He cursed, slid down the break-neck path, over a wall of unmortared stone bound with bramble that ripped his clothes; across a field, ploughed and deserted, its furrows baked to iron. Over a gate crested with barbed wire, whose rusty thorns drew blood from his knee. Sprinted down a sparkling grit road, met cattle and an angry dog. Hurry, hurry, he did not know why. Get this over. Hanging about an eternity he'd been, up in the air. Now for people and the end of the cup. A baker's cart passed him on the road, directed him, and he found himself mounting again by the way Scylla had come. Stopped at the open cottage door, knocked, waited, went in. He saw the bird. The torn papers. He went through.

He saw Clarence, slowly and awkwardly trying to re-string the bow, and the lovely nightmare, Scylla hanging bound to the stake of her love. His reason had vanished. Returned, abnormally clear. A madman and the girl probably dead. No gun. Behind them a gulf to the sea. Was I made a man for this? *Lighten our darkness.*

Play-act. He pulled out the cup. It had kept its jade-coolness. He shewed it to Clarence.

"Just got here. Picus wants it put back in the well, and you to come to Tambourne. See? Sent me." He took his arm: "Put it in yourself. He said you were to. Drop it in. Feel how cool it is. Wants to get back to where it came—into water. He'll be wretched if you don't."

Clarence staggered a little, moving towards the well.

"My head's not cool," he said. "Hurts like hell. The boy wants it dropped in. I can't see why I should attend to all his fancies."

Carston tried not to look at Scylla, not let him turn. Clarence's step shambled a little, his head dropped.

"I'm not to do it. Only you."

"All right. Here goes." Plop went a noise a very long way below them. Clarence covered his eyes with his hands.

"Dear man, it was decent of you to come. Such a way and the country strange to you. Hope you had a car. D'you mind if I go in for a bit and fix you up some tea?" Carston guided him carefully, back turned from what was out there in the sun, into the house-shadow, into the studio.

"I'll make tea. You lie down a bit." He was thinking how to lock him in, when the young man dropped, moaning that his head hurt, and that something was trying to get out through his eyes. Carston hoped it might be the tears he'd cry when he knew what he'd done. He had always liked Clarence, disliked that his affection should have turned to horror. He even put a cushion under his head. Then snatched up a knife in the kitchen, rushed out and cut Scylla free, and carried her on to the sitting-room couch. Then followed a time when time indefinitely suspended and extended itself. Attempts to withdraw the wood that pierced her, to stop the blood, to revive her, sustain her, dreading her consciousness and her unconsciouness alike. Listen to Clarence moaning, listen for him moving. He had not found a key to lock him in. Try to find a revolver without leaving Scylla, and later not to fall over the gun he had laid across the table at full cock. At one time he wondered if he should pitch Clarence over the cliff while he went for a doctor, and went nearly mad as the light failed, for he saw her coming back to her right mind alone, and the ghost of the man who had injured her crawling up the cliff-face to go on with his dream out of the flesh, and two ghosts, not one, would carry on, the torturing and the tortured.

* * * * *

An immensely long shadow flung back was travelling the hills. As the sun slipped incandescent into a crescent of far cliff, Carston heard outside whistling, liquid notes of everything that has wings. He remembered, 'Like Mozart.' Thought it might be death, coming sweetly for Scylla, as Picus walked into the house.

He saw Carston glaring, feeling for the gun, heard him say:

"You sent her to this. You laid this trap for her. You drove him mad—"

He answered:

"If that were so, should I have sent you? Should I have come myself? Whisht man, let's look." Passing, he put the gun at safe, and Carston saw him lay Scylla's body across his knees, open the chemise he had slit up and re-tied with a scarf.

"Scylla, you silly bitch, wake up. Man, I know all about wounds. Side glanced off a rib, the rest's nothing."

"All but our cruelty to her. I've not been that."

"No, you've not. Less than us. Yes, call it my fault. I can be sane. Where's Clarence?"

"In the studio, not quite conscious. I can't find the key."

"He'll do. Scylla's quite comfy here. Go and make her some tea. Stiff whisky for us. Clarence had a bad head wound. With that and the sun, and my bitchery— Where's the cup?"

"In the well. I made him put it down. Said it was your orders. Then he collapsed."

"Where did this happen?"

"At the back. Go and look."

Picus went out into the quarry and looked at the statue of himself. Spots of Scylla's blood, blackening in the dying light. None of his own. He took an axe from the woodpile and knocked the image of himself to a stump. Carston heard the dry pieces falling, the patter of dust.

* * * * *

Scylla stirred and sat up. Two cups of tea pressed to her lips met and clicked together.

"I can't drink out of two cups at once." Carston withdrew his. She drank.

"Is it Picus?" she said, feeling for their hands.

Carston said:

"Is there nowhere in this hell-forsaken country where we can get a doctor?"

"She doesn't need one," said Picus—"only us. No, love, I won't go away. We're going to sleep here. Hush, love. I've got to do magic and make you well. Better magic than at Gault."

"What's happened to Clarence?"

"We've put him in the studio. His head's all wrong. To-morrow he won't remember about this."

"He isn't coming back? Picus, I don't know how. Lydia wrote an idiot letter. I just came in. Not to be beastly, but to try—" She began to cry a great deal. Carston stayed with her. Picus went to the studio alone.

Soon he came back with an armful of bedding. He laid it on the floor.

"He's asleep. He will sleep."

"What are we going to do?" cried Carston, at exhaustion's breaking point.

"Sleep. We shall all sleep. Where we are, round her. Cover her over. Put a drink for her in the night. Finish the whisky. So. We shall all sleep. You at the foot. I at the side. On this side, love, or you'll lie on the cut in your hair.

"Shoes off, Carston. We shall need our feet to-morrow.

"Door open, and perhaps a rabbit will come in.

"Sleep, man, sleep. We must. Scylla, that's a fat star winking. Clarence is locked in. Had a turn like this before, and thought he was a nun."

Carston heard a giggle.

Of course, if Picus said a rabbit would come in. If Scylla wanted a rabbit to come in. . . .

* * * * *

The shepherd's wife sat up on a heap of rag quilts. The thatch bore down over a window sunk in the rubble wall, the panes wood-squared, double-fastened with paint, the ledge filled by a tropical green geranium, flowerless, filtering the light. The shepherd snored.

"Get up!" she squealed, and kicked him. "I be going across to the house."

A little later the old trollop left the rustic slum, and was crossing the hill's dewy shoulder in the delicate light. The day before she had been afraid to go; but in the night, encouraged by a bottle of whisky, she had seen Mr. Ross in a dream.

Clarence had built the studio out into the quarry at the back. She looked in first at its window and saw him sleeping there. Always out and about early he was. Picus had left the key outside in the lock. She went in. Clarence woke. There was a pain in his brain that felt like a nut. Before there had been a worm in the nut, but that had gone to sleep. He had felt the nut before. In a day or so there would not even be a nut, certainly not what went before the nut, the worm boring and making a wild pain that made a wild dream, on the edge of whose memory he was living.

"You're early," he said—"Get some tea." And I'm in my clothes. "And mind you put it in with the teaspoon."

He went to the well to sluice himself and saw his statue in bits. Looked up for a rock-fall from the quarry, which was impossible. Found bits of wood and feathers sticking in the clay and strode back to the kitchen. Heard her clacking that indeed she didn't know, and that the living-room door was locked.

He went round to the front, to the open door, saw where a hare had made her forme. Looked in and saw, still sleeping, Picus, Carston, Scylla. He shook his friend's shoulder gently:

"Hi, boy, what's happened?" Picus woke at a touch, pointed outside and rose silently.

"Who's taken my statue outside and smashed it?"

"Come out with me. Out and down a bit. A boat's in. Down at the Lobster Pot they'll fry us fish."

"But I'm not shaved. Can Carston fix up some breakfast for Scylla? Does he know the old woman can't? What's happened, lad? You look like a wet Sunday. Headache again?"

"No. Only you must come on."

He dropped sharply down the hill, Clarence behind him. He felt his mouth twist into a sneer. Clarence the kindly host, the country-gentleman making the best of a cottage and lack of retainers. Then that contempt was unjust. The unfamiliar concept of justice and injustice stuck and was accepted.

Then that punishment was on him. He had to operate on Clarence, not prick and bewilder. Had to undo his arts, his graces, his wit. Clarence's first protection would be to turn on him. A man of perverse and subtle mind, he would be quick to distort to save himself. Making me think.

Then at the Lobster Pot he acquired immediately tea, butter, bread, jam, and the first batch of the landlady's personal fish.

"Damned hungry," said Clarence, helping him to the one small real sole.

Ouf. Why did Clarence look so lovingly at him, when for the first time on record he threw it back on to his plate?

He did not like being hurt. The others were more used to being hurt. Now that he had to hurt, he did not want to. (A reaction impossible to Carston, for whose race sadism is not fun but a serious expression.)

Ow. How much he cared for Clarence, for sport and adventure and work shared. More than them all. Except Scylla. Because that love was shot through with something like an arrow and the feather of a bird. The blood on her white shoulder, the rose feet and feather of a bird.

Ai. His breath came on different sighs. *One more river to cross.* To be sure that he did not act, in this, in any way like his father. That understood, he left his desperate network of light and dark and gave himself up: neither to Clarence, nor to fear: but to a space full of clear forms and veritable issues. What he must do in order not to be any way like his father. Was that to give himself to Scylla? He had met her on his path. So. The bird's thought darted into a song:

So every way the wind blows this sweetie goes in the South.

While Clarence saw an assurance like maturity drawing itself in the set of the head and the subtle mouth.

Picus looked for a moment out to sea, and began:

"What have you been doing the last three days, since I went off to Tambourne?"

"Stayed on with Ross a bit. Walked over. Got the place shined up."

"It must have been pretty hot?"

"The sun bored like worms into your head."

"What happened then?"

"There was lots to do, but I found the nights, short as they are, damned long. When it isn't dark and it's going to get dark and you listen out. You know. But in places like this you can never tell what day which happened."

"What was yesterday like?"

Clarence screwed round, ever so little equivocally.

"I sort of remember that something rather miserable happened in the morning. Might have been a letter." And quickly—"But I can't account at all for the statue being in bits. I know you'll say it doesn't matter what happens to my work, but Ross liked it. You said you liked it yourself—"

"Looksey," said Picus, tenderly—"you've got to know, you know. You went off the deep-end again."

"You mean I smashed it myself?"

"No. I did a bit. I mean I broke it. I felt I had to."

Clarence listened gravely, his eyes still altering their angle.

"Well, if you thought it bad, that's that. But you've taken so much of my life, do you think you should do in my work, also?"

"It wasn't for that. You've forgotten about yesterday. You said something miserable happened, and it did." (Now are his eyes shifting memory or madness?) "Remember when you thought you were a nun? This time you must have thought you were Apollo, or a roman official with an early christian. There was some story in town, and Lydia sent you a letter. And Scylla came down here on purpose to clear it up and fetch you along. She found you shooting at me, and you tied her up and shot her. Carston came over and probably saved her life. I followed, and by then you'd got through your fit and were asleep. She isn't badly hurt. That's what happened. Why I brought you down here. And you can kick me for my fantasies and tempers. Half the blame's on me." Is this going to release me? Have I been looking for that? *This sweetie goes?*

"It's another of your stories," Clarence said.

"Go up and see."

"Excuse to put me in an asylum. I get you."

"Balls, man. The old man at Tambourne, the vicar, I mean c'd explain. Tell us what we could do."

"His orders aren't even valid."

"Don't know what you mean. Go and see. You tied her

with the lariat. You shot a gull to wing your arrows. There's one struck her shoulder and her side. After Carston had cut her down, I smashed myself up with the axe. Sort of apology."

"Did I really shoot a gull?"

"You shot her till she fainted."

"Did I drag your statue out and shoot you?"

"Picked me out carefully."

"It was the best thing I've done, but I haven't hurt you, boy?"

"You threw Scylla. She cut her head on a stone. Carston took an arrow out below her left breast. She was pinned to me by her shoulder—"

"Getting kick out of it, aren't you?"

"Go and see."

"And face that dumb fool Carston."

"Look at Scylla."

"Where's the cup?"

"You put it in the well."

Silence, while Picus watched the bright, brown close-set eyes turn this way and that. Never into his eyes. Never out to sea. Over his shoulder, at the fish-bones, into his cup.

"It's a clever way of breaking things up. You say that you came later?"

"An hour. You were lying in the studio. You were saying something about worms and time and cups. I think you know, that you actually *did* a dream."

His simplicity amazed Clarence: made him thoughtful.

"I am sure that you're letting Carston take you in. You're simple sometimes, bless you. You weren't there. He found me a bit off my head and I went in and fell asleep. As a matter of fact, I don't remember yesterday.

"I'm going up. You might stay and see if that net we broke is mended and follow. I even think you believe this, but it is more likely to be some revenge of Carston's—"

It was suggested to him, fretfully and quite unjustly,

that Carston could neither improvise a bow and arrows, throw a leaded cord, or hit a sitting haystack. And it was painful on their present undertaking to see Clarence stride off to clear up the affair. Picus fidgeted about the beach and threw unsuccessful ducks and drakes. One suddenly skimmed out. So much for that.

And every way the wind blows this sweetie goes in the South.

* * * * *

Clarence followed him full of anger, full of breakfast up the hill. Then, as he climbed and felt the strengthening sun, of a kind of catchy fear. The nut was shrinking. How was he to persuade Carston that they had not been entertained by a sadist? The business faintly excited him. With each step he felt the sun's menace. He wanted to be alone under the cool thatch and whittle at a mazer he was making to hold punch at parties. A present for Scylla.

The night before Carston had thrown out the half-plucked gull over the cliff. It had caught on a bush, and almost at the door Clarence saw the torn white rags. He stood a long time while the dew dried.

"I suppose I thought she was the bird." The whole memory came back. The nut in his head dissolved like a drop of wax. His skull filled with pure memory.

The figure he had cut with his excuses. How save his reputation for sanity? With Picus. With all of them?

What does one do when one has done a thing like that?

How act a repentance unfelt as yet, only betrayal by time, chance, magic, interfering friends, offending gods?

The gull, held on a twig by a pinion-feather, loosened, balanced a second, and vanished over the cliff.

"I must follow," he said, "now."

The sun had thrown his shadow to the threshold. Carston saw it and said nothing, afraid, helping Scylla to splash in water smoky with most of her host's scents, combing the blood out of her hair. Sweet to have her safe and look after her. Then he heard her say, "There's Clarence." She had seen him at the cliff's edge. Carston held that he waited to be seen, but in truth he had forgotten Carston and Scylla. Carefully looking not down but out to sea. Taking a last pull at memories there.

Of Picus. Of the band he had grown up with. Of war, whose issues he had found too simple. Of their spiritual adventure he had not been equal to. Of the fool he had made of himself. The revenge his death would be. Not stay to be called Judas. *And bring our souls to His high city.*

He took a step to the edge. Scylla jumped off the divan, and with her hand at her side, ran out to him.

"Clarence, come in."

She had hold of him as he had held her.

"What'r'you doing out in your chemise?"

"You know. Come in."

"Get me," she said to Carston, "a wooden bowl in the studio, and a green baize roll of tools." She lay down again. Clarence paced about once or twice, and sat down beside her.

"There's going to be an awful party over at the house. Felix is bringing home a Russian."

He said:

"I'm not mad. No need to go on like that. I remember. The bird made me."

"Did you think I was it?"

"No. There was a letter, and the sun and you know my head."

Look," she said, and pulled off the handkerchief that tied her shoulder—"and my head is cut and my side. It was partly my fault that Lydia wrote to you. Go on carving while we talk."

He did as she told him. Carston watched them. Like an idyll: a young lover making a present for his sweetheart, sitting on her bed. A harrow of wild geese with their necks out at flight. A border of fish.

"It ought to be set. Can you work in silver, Clarence? We might melt down that atrocious salver—"

Insufferable to be hushed like this. He preferred Carston glaring at him, wondering if he should get the gun. Picus came in.

"D'you know now?"

"Yes. And I'm not fool enough to imagine that there's any apology or excuse. Or forgiveness that isn't from duty or impulse. You can have Scylla."

"I knew you'd take it wrong," said Picus. "We're not talking about beds and we know who we'll sleep with. What you ought to know is—"

"Look here," said Carston. "You've had a touch of the sun. We'll grant that. Scylla has a fool female friend in London, fool enough to be in love with you. Wrote you a spiteful letter you lap up. Scylla comes down to explain it and comfort your feelings, and you try to kill her by torture. I know you were mad. If you don't pull yourself together and try and face it, everyone will know you were mad; for you'll do it again outside your home circle. The world won't make delicate excuses for you, you spoilt, hysterical, self-pitying, self-centred, uninventive, incompetent son of a bitch."

"Not uninventive," said Scylla, "but you'd better try something else."

"I'm taking you over to Tambourne right away. We'll start now, and you can wait at the inn while I get a car. The old parson there is the company you need. You can come back to Gault, if they want you, when you've got your senses back."

Picus nodded. "We are all for you, Carston."

"All of us," said Scylla.

"Don't say," he answered, "That if I stay here much

longer, I shall be one of you. Because I never shall, and I don't want to be."

"Our house is your house," said Scylla.

"Besides," said Picus, "did you ever enjoy a summer more?"

"Hasn't it been better than a movie? Leave Clarence at Tambourne and come over and look at Felix's find."

In his heart he knew he would not. Though there was continuity in this adventure, a circle like the design on Clarence's mazer, a ring near to a magic ring, he knew that nothing would induce him to go back to that poverty and pride, cant and candour, raw flesh and velvet; into that dateless, shiftless, shifting, stable and unstable Heartbreak House. Not for a bit. Off to Paris on his own folk-adventure. In his last moments with them, looking at Clarence's bowl, he saw the changes in things.

There had been an apple once. There had been an apple tree. When it gave no more apples, it had made fire, and a slice of its trunk had become a bowl cut out into birds. The bowl unless it was turned into fire again, would stop growing and last for ever. Things that came out of time, and were stopped; could be made over into another sort of time.

Clarence sat silent, a tear or so falling, shame and anger mounting. Once away, he would leave Carston; would not go to Tambourne. He would go to Tambourne because he must have somewhere to hide. The old parson might have comfort for him while Picus was with Scylla, and she enjoyed the reward of warriors. She and Picus alone together, playing at happy warriors.

If there was nothing for him at Tambourne, there would still be Picus's father, a fine story to pick over together.

He said:

"Perhaps you'll send my clothes. We must go before

mid-day. I shouldn't like Carston to have a repetition before he gets me to Tambourne."

And bring our souls to His high city.

He took Scylla's hand, remained a moment in her embrace. Carston followed him down the hill.

* * * * *

That afternoon cloud flecks flew over and the wind freshened. Ross and Nanna left the house scented with boiling sugar and took a walk down to the sea. He listened to a comparative history of her jam-making and a sketch of her intentions about the vegetable marrows with the interest he gave to each man on his subject alike. From the cliff above the fisherman's hut they saw a ketch running before the south wind, straight for the bay.

"A french boat," he said, "they're running her in too close to the reef." The old nurse shaded her eyes.

"It's Mr. Felix steering. In a hurry he is as usual. It's a nice way to bring his friend home." Silence. A Russian brought over in a fishing-smack: in a hurry. The ketch made the channel (where the bluff hid it from the coastguards' telescopes and the sooner the better), and Ross saw Felix and a sailor drop into a dinghy and pull fast for shore. In the stern sat another. They went down to the water's edge to meet them. A few strokes out, Felix sprang thigh deep in the weed and dragged up the boat till her keel scraped the rocks. He embraced Ross, turned and gave the boy a hand to spring to shore.

"Ross, this is Boris."

"But what made you come this way?"

He thought that he was looking at something at the same time old and young. A youth he understood. An age he did not. Also that it was worn and tired and sick. And that Felix's eyes were like dark-blue coals, his step certain, his voice without petulance.

"I had no papers," said Boris.

"We got into a row," said Felix, "the police raided a café, and we did a bolt. We ran straight into two men up a back street and sent them spinning. One was hurt. Then I saw that it was no good, especially for Boris, and got a car to the coast. Paid up those chaps to bring us and cut back. There's a third man below to replace Boris in case we were seen from the shore."

Not bad for Felix. Ross looked again at what he had brought, standing on the tide-mark, his back to the water, the ooze soaking his poor shoes. The sailors landed two suit-cases.

"See here," he said, "and excuse us. D'you mean you have no papers and no papers you can show—?"

"He's a White," cried Felix, "and he lost them."

Boris said: "That is exactly so."

"And you're not running dope, or away from any crime worth mentioning?"

"On my honour, no— I need a holiday and your cousin was good enough—"

Ross saw that, so far as it went, this was true. The vistas opening were more oblique. He had only to look at that head in its sea-wide aureole, the high forehead and temple-thinned black hair, the slanted cheekbones, and observant green eyes. From the remote east. Out of the sea. Lovely, ugly, helpless, high-born thing. Whipcord and ice and worn out. Wangle him papers in London.

"Boris, our stranger," he said. "Our nurse."

Boris kissed her hand. They climbed the little cliff path. At the top he began to look around him.

Out at sea, it had been land, earth under his feet after a night and day's pitching. Land: an interesting new place. Another people who might have no use for him. Why should they? No longer in doubt, soon there would be food and a bath and fresh linen and bed, he took a look at England. He saw a line of treeless hills, a puzzle of fields; under his feet a pattern of sweet herbs. An arrow of wood they entered, into a tunnel of light where birds broke cover, green even under the feet. A house where the windows were doors and stood open, in front of which a yucca, taller than a man, had opened its single flower-spike. Over the house, a hill turned wall. Into a room where air and bees whispered, honey smelt and the sea. And something he remembered: the smell of fruit bubbling in copper pans, in a kitchen—a child with his nurse—in a country-house, in Russia, in a pine forest.

Death of Felicity Taverner

Chapter I

A YOUNG MAN who had arrived uninvited from France lay under the green slate roof of the verandah perfecting the idea he had suggested to his hosts, that, if he had not come, they would have sent for him. He had not had to walk the ten miles from Starn to their remote house above the sea. A cart had given him a lift along the lanes. He still smelt of dust and crushed nettles. And already the brother and sister and the sister's husband were reinstating him—their minds making delicate interior adjustments to excuse their weakness—into his position as a cherished family curse. Scylla, his hostess, did it best. "He is our ring of Polycrates," she had cried out suddenly in the hour of spiritual angularity just after he had appeared. "We are infinitely well-off here." "Polycrates exactly," said Felix, her brother. "It didn't end there." Still, after that, the situation had run more easily; for with a certain kind of english person a classical allusion has the weight and function of a text. Instantly their minds had gone out to sea: Samos; the Thalassocrats; and their eyes had sought it from where they stood, beside a very old stone house, built under a green down, set with its lawn deep in the base of a triangular wood, stream-bisected, which ran down to a blunt nose of cliff and a ledge of rock to the sea. Terrible cliffs, airy, bird-trodden, flanked their quiet land-cup and its easy promontory of worn gold stone. The turf hills backed it, a chess-board of fields filled it. Round one side curved a village of extraordinary beauty. On the other, two miles off, sprang their wood. Centuries ago, their house had been built there—in the most ancient part of the wood within sound of the sea.

There was no road between the village and their wood,

only three paths. The easy ribbon along the little cliff, the field-path half way up to the hills, and the third—the first ever made by man—the green road along the down top. Past five kings' barrows on your right, and on your left seventeen geographical cows. On that road a light car could bump itself quietly along the top of the world and down a flint slope to the gate outside the wood and the dark path to the house.

The land's way is important in this story, because its people will be continually running to and fro by hill or shore or field—from the house in the wood to another house, a little above the village across the cup. A house not like their house, the wood's jewel, but a more familiar elegance, built in the eighteenth not the sixteenth century, out of the same grey stone. A house that was now shut-up and blind; its jade shutters bolted, its roses run to suckers, its fountains dry. It had belonged to their cousin, Felicity Taverner, who was dead. Her death was still a kind of death to the three of them, to whose family the two houses in the hollow land belonged—to Felix Taverner and to Scylla, his sister; whose husband, Picus Tracy, came from a variation of the same stock and the same country a hundred bee-miles inland. It was now spring, but the thought of their cousin's death in the past winter remained like a small tide mounting and retreating, reversing the usual formula for death. They wore no mourning for her, but there was a stain under Scylla's eyes as though a dead violet had brushed them, and her light hair flung back from her white forehead sometimes hung raggedly, as though combed by fingers trying to tear thoughts out of the brain. She loved her cousin; did not know if it had been suicide which had left her, bloody and dusty, beside the road, under a rock where the Lower Corniche rises above Villefranche.

After the first shock, she had not been sorry to see Boris—the uninvited, cast-off-at-intervals, sprung-of-a-murdered-Russian-and-a-Upas-tree discovery of Felix.

Whom they had fed and loved, and by whom they had been selected to bear all things and endure all things. His reasonable behaviour would last a week at most, and then the lurid extravaganza would begin again. But any distraction would be a diversion, for the men were taking their loss in two varieties of silence; her husband reduced to nothing but inconsequent monosyllables or ways to match; her brother pretending that it did not matter, either the event or the reasons for it. Boris's sensibility and curiosity would help them. There was always an oblique help in Boris, as incalculable but as certain as the monstrosities of behaviour by which his friends paid for his love.

She went into the house to see to his comfort and propitiate their old nurse, and found her already propitiated, her darning egg stretched over one of his socks. And Boris was there before her, perched on a corner of the kitchen table, waving a spoon and praising the existence and the nature of her jam.

Before dinner the spring night turned suddenly cold, but before they had time to realise it, Boris had a great fire alight. Green sparks leapt from a drift-log out of a fire-wall of pale gold. Nanna had alchemised food into a dinner. Boris added a russian dish. Picus had risen, his thin skull cobwebbed, up the cellar stair, with good wine that only God could have preserved there till then. After dinner, with his familiarity which did not offend, Boris took the tallest wax candles and filled every wall sconce and rubbed silver candlestick. So they sat before the fire, in light all down the long room. The shutters were bolted across the french windows. From nowhere could the night come in.

An hour before dinner Scylla had walked in with Boris down the wood-path, towards the sea. There under the high tree-talk he had said: "You have had a trouble here. I saw it in the french papers." She had repeated that her cousin was dead. "You never met, did you?" Then: "Let us try and talk about it after dinner. We have been too silent about it. After dinner, listen to us. Make us speak."

After dinner they were silent, but aware of something like a thread of renewed well-being stirring in their veins, and pleasure because of the lights. When Felix asked: "What are we to *do*?" Scylla answered: "Tell Boris." And since she told stories well, it was left to her to tell him.

She began slowly, knowing that they had none of them yet arranged such facts as they knew into a version of the truth. She smiled: Boris as a truth-elicitor, a mould into which a series of events, full of omissions and each distinct and white-hot with their charge of emotion, could be poured. Presently the mould would be broken and leave them with a death in its proportions. Felicity's torn and strewn members collected; laid out; laid in state. For them to assuage themselves with offerings. This done, let the earth take her; do what it liked with her; make her serviceable for its coarse business under the soil. (But she'd been cremated.) Scylla laughed. Anyhow, she must have her requiem: give occasion for a good story, and so to her survivors some peace, since ballads were no longer within man's capacity. In their house-saga, her story well-told would keep her memory brighter than earth's freshest grass. The first recital should have her for rhapsodist. Felix later should write it, the family's professional chronicler. She began:

"You must know, Boris, that Felicity was my first cousin, and so kin to Picus. Tracys have married Taverners before. (Remember also that I shall have to try round and say a great many things that are not true until I start a truth.) So, I'll call her a fool. A fool because life had given her everything, yet when you'd admitted her every beauty, grace and gift, you knew that something had been left out, like some secretion we haven't yet isolated or named, and whose lack made each of her qualities ineffective—" She hesitated.

"This dish without the salt," said Boris.

"I could have said that before if I'd meant it"—rather

tartly—"you've got to endure it while I get this story straight. If I'd said 'without salt,' you'd have taken her for a lovely fool. She was not. She was adorable. If a crystal became a white narcissus, you'd have something like her. She walked, laughed, prayed to Mozart. She was dis-interested and without pretension. Yet she knew when she had been, even when she would be, abused. Accepted it—just as in the Middle Ages she would have worn a hair shirt under a white shift and a dress stiff with gold. Her choice of objects—of possessions—was perfect, and her virtue—for she was most men's friend and very few's lover—had the same passion and detachment. If she was poor, and she generally was, she could make and mend and cook potatoes, with or without butter; but once out in the world it seemed as though great houses had been built to display her."

"But," cried Boris, "you are describing not a fool but a saint."

"She was a fool," said Felix slowly, "or how would this have happened to her?"

"But I hear it as a story of someone the Gods loved and took young."

Then he saw Scylla's face and the nails drawing blood from the palms of her hands. He saw Picus, her husband, look at her, the ray that passed between them. And that, though Scylla did not look at him, her fingers relaxed.

"I'll withdraw 'fool.' Only with her wit she must have known that persons of her quality have the whole brutishness of our society against them. They can only save themselves by planting their feet hard into some patch of earth. Clean earth, and suppose it's muddy, it grips better. But Felicity seemed always to be perched up an almond tree or a pear, shaking down petals for blessings on the unjust and the just. If you protested, she said that Nature did that. *'Like the sweet apple.'* Oh, she was always off, robbing some heavenly orchard and sharing the spoil. Only it seemed that a warning went with her, like a cream-dipped-in-coal thunder-cloud, that fat menace that sits along the horizon and means that the weather will break."

Scylla paused, knowing that the men were on the look-out for the bias proper to a female cat. Must allow for it and ignore it in her search for the story's truth; endure it until its finding justified her.

—"One of the greatest poems says at the end:

Or if virtue feeble were
Heaven itself would stoop to her.

Boris, even I know how curiously and actually that is true. Enough—if our age would allow it—to justify talk of miracles. Only it seemed as though—as though—Felicity of all people—in the end had been left out. Almost everyone we know is worth less than she was; you, *mon ami,* and I; and outside our range, the rough stuff of the earth and its scoundrels even. And I've seen heaven's ambulance rush after them. While she seemed left alone to do first-aid on herself. Who never thought of herself. I watched it for years: called it a mystery."

"You are speaking about a woman who was a miracle herself," said Boris.

"I think I am. But that raises questions. Don't you see, I tried to get out of it by calling her a fool, who had all heaven's weapons and wouldn't or couldn't use them. Don't you see, we shall go mad if we can't account for the awful luck which left her dead at thirty-three with all our loves at her service?"

"But she is back in Paradise now," said Boris.

Felix said: "Your virtue-level, Scylla, is about what the world will stand. If it's properly bullied. And that's only because of the patch of mud you talk about, and carry round with you; stick your feet in when you're up against it; sacrifice a pair of socks. Like a praying carpet. Now cut out the mystery and tell Boris what happened."

Boris nodded. She began again:

"Family-life. What can't you say about family-life? To-day it's considered no more than the forcing-bed for the Oedipus complex. While our national variety either works exceedingly well, or it is the most brutal thing alive. An english family gets born, and if they don't happen to like each other, the young are handed over, without benefit of counsel, to a judge, jury, prison, executioner of its parents and itself, disguised under a sentimental conception of family love. Oh, it makes us hardy; drives us out to Ispahan or to suicide; on to the streets or to the Mountains of the Moon....

"Well, Felicity's mother is our aunt, a Taverner only by marriage. She was her only daughter and her mother didn't happen to like her. Old Aunt Julia is a notable dowager and an infernal bully. I've been watching her lately. Once her activities had to be diluted with a strong dose of sentiment; lately she's reversed gears, become as acid a cynic as she was once a sentimentalist. In both cases, alternate statements of the original bitch. You'd think that she'd have bullied Felicity until she'd married her off. Not a bit. Somehow Felicity managed to elude her, and when, very rarely, elusion failed, you saw for an instant another Felicity, which was like.... Think if the crescent moon showed you its teeth.

"Anyone but a limpet or a practising criminal would have quarrelled with Aunt Julia, but that situation was hopeless. Aunt Julia had borne this creature: couldn't break her: couldn't (suppose she had tried) teach her sense; wouldn't conciliate, but could wound and torture and bleed her to death. Chiefly about nothing. Or about her friends. Yet her mother to-day has her house full of people we should not tolerate and Felicity omit to notice.

"Think then of a mother a bully, with several sons whose docility and whose sex got them off comparatively scot-free. A woman in love with power, who got it in so strong a dose that in justice to her I believe she would have feared it if she had understood. Only she became persuaded that it was her duty to punish Felicity. And Felicity, who could do all things for some people, had no 'hands' with the Great Crested Dowager of our family. Anymore than Aunt Julia wanted a Lesser Spotted Debutante under her wing. Felicity who had 'hands' with elderly scientists and young men it was worth misunderstanding to help; and with tapettes and concierges and lost princesses, could find no formula for her mother. When Aunt Julia was young, things ought to have happened to her, and they didn't. Married to my uncle, who loved a female skeleton in a barrow more than any properly covered bones in bed, she had no young practice in love. Can anything make up for that? Then to have Felicity for daughter, growing up in one of our intervals of freedom—"

"Besides," said Felix, "she was distinctly chaste."

"That's what I mean. To have your own daughter turn up her nose at what you hadn't dared do; or refused to please God. When Felicity started an affair, it was somehow outside the rules, regular or irregular."

"You can imagine how much her mother stood for it," said Felix.

"And I've seen her," said his sister, "with the same look that Saint Catherine of Siena had in ecstasy."

"By Sodoma," said Felix, "exactly."

Boris spoke: "Is it that you mean to say that your aunt murdered her?"

"If you like. Infanticide *à la mode*."

"We've not got to that yet, if she did," said Felix's sister. Boris went on:

"Your priest who I love so. I asked him when he was teaching me English to let me hear some of your eloquence, your rhetoric. At first he did not seem to understand. Then he read to me out of Shakespeare and out of Byron. Then some of your prayers. They delighted me. One of them said you were 'to set your affections on things above, not on things of earth,' and told me particularly to do that because there was no danger that I should do it too much. I thought that adorable. Afterwards he said that to a very few people it might become a sin, because we know something of how to live on earth but not at all how to live in heaven. Was not that your cousin's . . . ?"

"Miscalculation," said Scylla suddenly. "No. And if I called her a fool, it was because she so often shamed me. And if it's true that heaven didn't rush up with the help it gives any malignant child, then she had comfort too rare for us to notice. Or else it wanted her back. . . ."

"If it did," said Felix, "the last thing she wanted was a return to our father's house. With all her star-and-petal talk, she put early death into the same category as wrinkles."

Said Boris: "What was she afraid of?"

There was silence, acute with attention and appreciation of Boris. Then Picus expressed himself, in words for once.

"Now you've asked, it was like this. She was afraid of going without things any more. Not the heavenly treasures, but things like cut glass and jade and the first flowers and fruits. And of how the way having no money hands you over to vile people, virtuosos in the art of being vile. There was a man once who sowed dragons' teeth. I don't know what Felicity sowed, but there came up vile bodies with a beard and a bill and a voice you go on hearing in your sleep."

Boris shivered. Picus added casually: "That took murder off her mother's hands. Her idea was that her daughter had done wrong not to live on the stuff that isn't butter and had gone to hell besides." His wife looked at him with troubled and adoring love.

"We're on the track now," she said. "A mob is ordering itself into a ballet." She leaned staring over the fire; sat back, her fingers raking her hair.

"After Picus's lead, the story is clearer. And intolerable."

Felix acknowledged again Picus's intelligence, a man

who usually never opened his mouth except for an irrelevance or for some finally condensed statement. Was his sister right, and Picus sometimes inspired? To the world he assumed their marriage to be one of convenience and divorce imminent. In reality he feared that he might at any moment become an uncle. Would hate to watch Scylla's figure spoilt. A glance reassured him. Hill-walking had built her up like a light tree; while all winter long Picus's arms seemed to have moulded her as much as the summer's long wave-tumbling and the caresses of the sea. He saw her eyes burn with the intelligence Picus had quickened and the wordless quiet play between lover and lover. Suppose then, he thought, that it was true that they loved each other, assume the improbable, original unoriginality; one had to admit that their variety gave an illusion of strangeness and beauty, as though it had never happened before. Suppose then that true love was like art, and no more original, and each time as unique.

Picus and Scylla were of the generation before the war; Felix of the half generation after it. And at the bottom of that dry gulf between half a generation there are corpses, who did not notice the gulf was there. He saw Boris too, approving of them. Felix thought of his relations with Boris and their uneasiness. All should have gone well with them, but after the start, it was as if they were both playing at a game of which neither knew the rules, or if there were rules. Not only because Boris was a pest, and one that fell chiefly on the just, the unjust recognising it at sight; but because Boris seemed also to have the key to some private disreputable paradise where Felix could not go in.

Meanwhile, at Picus's word, Scylla was about to reduce a hideous chaos to a tragic cosmos. Their blood-link made him aware that her imagination was tuning-in. She sat back from the fire, grave, attentive, about to give them their cousin's Lycidas.

"Yet once more, O ye laurels, and once more
Ye myrtles brown with ivy never sere."

He heard the drums and flutes of that opening: of that poem about a drowned curate and shepherds more respectable than Theocritus and english rivers in mourning, by which Milton arrived at the same universe as the Fifth Symphony or the Ninth.

"This is her story: I mean one version of it," she said. "You must know, Boris, how poor Felicity was. We are poor, but we make something and we shall inherit; and not one of the three of us will go off on an orgy without knowing that it will not quite ruin us. Also we can make and mend; and Nanna, who had meant to spend a tranquil old age with Felicity, chose to stay and care for never less than three of us. So, not an eggshell is wasted, and I haven't to think about it. What I mean is that we have just enough: Felicity just not enough. Which makes you reckless." Boris nodded.

"We had this house left to us and Felicity the one across the valley. It was let from time to time to people we did not like. So you did not see it when you were here before. It is rather too perfect: a museum-piece. Complete early Eighteenth Century Bijou Residence, once the Property of a Young Lady, Killed by a Broken Heart. Yes: that will do for the present. The salon has an alabaster chimney piece, italian, with little amoretti *'in terms of learned and exquisite fantasy.'* Honey-pale and gay like the house.

"D'you understand, Boris? A house can be gay and tragic. This one can catch the sea-roar and turn it into peals of laughter. No, I know nothing about the history of her house. A cadet of ours built it, to park a widowed mother there or an aunt. Only somehow it is over-charged with sensibility: has the vapours and pouts at you."

"It's the house *Haunters and Haunted* happened in," said Felix.

"(Our best ghost-story, Boris. No. I can't stop and tell

it. *No.* Yours are always about vampires, a pleasing thought but limited. We don't have them here.) I must finish Felicity's house, it's important.

"It needed to be kept-up and it asked to be lived-up to. You see it is an *objet d'art.* Round quicksilver mirrors set in ebony on the panels of an octagonal room. Some painted with birds, or with diminishing glasses in their glass. Curtains and coverings of old *toile de Jouy,* and some royal brocades. Cupboards with glass doors sunk in the walls. And a small shallow stair that mounts as delicately as an empire train. So take back *Haunters and Haunted,* Felix. That house was square and grim.

"Like so many things in her life, her exquisite house wasn't much good to her. Goodness only knows what snob-ghost lived in it, but it snubbed her. On summer evenings she would run here across the fields."

"So she did," said Felix uneasily, whose love was not yet of the painstaking kind and who shirked the irrevocable.

"Leaving family affection out, it was to get her feet attached again to earth—to the mud-patch. She said once that all the hoops and crinolines worn in that house made her feel she must go up like a balloon. *This* house anchored her. It does not stir to find you, but it never turns any, or hardly any, creature away."

Here Picus muttered something about "nor live nor dead, nor fox nor rabbit" which essentially unfriendly combination he did not explain.

"And it was like Felicity that she would not let her house down. Perfect it was and had a right to be. But it's a *poule de luxe:* eats money and paints its face."

"Who lives in it now?"

"She died intestate and with no children. It goes back to her brother, Adrian. (I suppose you know when she *did* die—last winter, four months ago.) There never was a divorce." Two voices intoned the following tune: "that ghastly man she married—"

Boris noted the caste-feeling assert itself.

"He was a Russian, Nicholas Kralin, son of a political exile, long before your Revolution. For believing in Tolstoy, or something. No, not your sort. A proletarian-idealist. A very thorough one he must have been to have had that wolf for son. Tolstoy found the way to heaven blocked by the books he would not go on writing. So he was left to drive men to God over the rough. With every morning a footman for remembrancer: *'Monsieur le comte, votre charrue est à la porte.'*"

Boris nodded, agreeably serious for once.

"It is right," he said, "to be a great noble or a great artist or a great saint. But they cost each what they cost. And this disciple. Had he jewish blood?"

"Not officially. But his son is not *arriviste,* but by reaction, a wolf. A wolf that tried to turn house-dog, and became neither dog nor wolf."

Picus asked: "Does a man become a castrato for his voice's sake and then never sing again? Or feed the flies on the arsenic he bought for his wife's tea?"

His voice died away, and then continued clearly: "—And this not out of idiocy or fear, or by mistake, or for any reason. Except for no reason at all. For the what's-its-name—virtuosity of Unreason. Which is a God. Nick Kralin's answer is that there's no answer. If you asked him the meaning of meaning, he'd answer 'no meaning at all.'"

Felix broke in: "Yes, and with a pretty copy of nice english diffidence. And in some ghastly way make you feel he was in the know: that if your poor intellect was worth it, he'd just make it clear to you the jolly little secret he and Meaning have between them, that there is no meaning to anything at all."

"Was he very gifted at metaphysics?" asked Boris, anxiously.

"Mercifully not," said Scylla, "a top-heavy mushroom on a rickety stalk. Both full of maggots. Superficial, scientific pornographist. All for style, nothing for content.

The usual camp. What more could he be if meaning's meaning's meaningless? I'm sorry for him now, who's become a eunuch of the kingdom of nothing's sake. Yet, when he was young, he had an air, a quality, which made people ask if he had genius. Also, he was very beautiful. He had the pleasantest speaking-voice."

"Where does one arrange him in the world?"

"In Snob-cultivated Society. Assembles with impeccable perverse taste a number of *objets d'art.* Has been psycho-analysed out of any pleasure in anything. Or so he thinks. Felicity fell in love with him when he was young: married him: helped him. (He acquired his money later.) Ran away from him. Believed that she had discovered some frightful secret. Called it the Grey Thing, but it was what Felix meant about meaning. And Un-reason which Picus said is a God. That man is sure that he has the inside dope on the ultimate senselessness of everything. And is content."

She paused: the story paused. Then Felix said: "You were so busy, Scylla, high-hatting him, that you were never all round the man."

"I know," she said, "I may have been frightened, too. Go on with him yourself."

"Well," said Felix, "the 'grey thing' was Felicity having the vapours. It's a real horror. Kralin's no ordinary pessimist. None of that russian gloom so conspicuously absent in Boris. Our Boris's reaction to the unpropitious is to run amok."

Explanations, admissions, excuses followed.

Felix went on: "She used to run over here to find us, at any hour, if anything grey happened to the weather. She was afraid of the sea-mist. Panic-fear. Or of one of those cold summer days after rain when the hay lies down in swathes struck a sort of silver-slug colour. And I remember one iron frost when the sky came down on our heads, and sent her out bare-headed. I'd even had a feeling she was coming, and had gone out to the edge of the wood and noticed when I saw her, running like a lapwing over the open grass, that there was grey under her eyes and no red on her cheeks. And when old Marshallsea came here one night and told us about the drowned ghost that comes up from the cove clung on to by something—"twas a grey corpse with a grey, greasy trail of weed come up out of a grey tide,' I thought she'd faint."

"I've watched the cove for it for years," said Scylla. "There's nothing there."

"I never said there was. But there's a something, a quality you can call grey about Nick Kralin, a grey that repeats itself. So grey frightened her." Picus spoke: "You can get a first in Greats or fly round inside the crater of Vesuvius, but what you depend on for your private life is your degree in witch-doctoring. How much you can smell-out the propitious from the unpropitious."

Boris, who had been following attentively, seemed to agree.

"Suppose what you call 'the grey thing' is the same power that made our Revolution distinct from other revolutions. For it is." They nodded.

—"It was your priest again who suggested that to me. And not because the Bolsheviki were against the Church. The French were that, but they invented the Marseillaise, and for one who did not believe, there were a hundred who thought 'Liberty, Fraternity, Equality' were three new names of God. Suppose then that your cousin believed at first that she was embracing a beautiful young lover who had genius, and found that she was being embraced by a *comprimé* of—" There was sweat on the high, round forehead.

"Of the demon who gave your sword of justice to the Tcheka to handle," said Scylla. "Will that do?"

"Or," said Felix, "as though you had gone to sleep on your marriage-bed to wake up with an octopus in a tank."

"Fool that I've been," said Scylla. "Felix, I hand over our house-saga to you."

"No," said Felix, kindly: "only Felicity was rather my affair. She really was what people call humble; had an inferiority complex about us because there was nothing particular she could do. I used to point out that to love and be lovely was a whole-time job."

Blind with her own humiliation, Scylla covered her eyes. Then turned to Boris.

"I know it was an obscene evasion when I called her a fool."

"A woman would," said he kindly.

"In my heart I felt myself inferior before her. That made me impatient."

"Wonders of the complex," said Felix, "and this isn't the time for them. Here's her photograph, Boris. What d'you make of it?"

Then it occurred to all three that Boris might easily have met her in Paris. He looked at it quickly:

"She is what I said at the beginning—a woman who came out of Paradise; and if she left it, it was to look for people who could not find their way in. She was on earth *'pour faire aimé l'amour.'* The world did not want to and it killed her. But what happened to her just before? And when Picus spoke about money?"—

There was silence again, while Scylla prepared the next sequence, and the room had its turn. Instead of four voices, the fire spoke, the voice of flames disintegrating salted wood into the quiet fall of light ash. The crack of old panels responding to heat, and behind them the ground-scratch of mice. A door in the kitchen quarters opened and shut. Nanna's feet and the maid's mounted the stair. The heavy shutters bolted-out the interminable conversations of the trees. Behind these incidental breaks, the pulse of the long room in the delicate candle-light beat in time with the house and the wood. In time with its own time, a pace inaudible, yet sensible to each. Felix had said that a sonata could be written on the room's tempo, whose finale should be a demonstration of relativity.

Then the long room took advantage of their silence, and its shadowless walls seemed to move each in its own direction to some uncharted place. Happy lovers, asleep together, sometimes imagine their bed sails out, indifferent to walls, and visits those countries which lie east of the sun, west of the moon. In this second silence the walls left them behind, preoccupied with Felicity's passion and death; aware only that something was happening to the place where they sat, to describe which the comparisons of poets have been used to obscure reality. So that a literal description passes, even among poets, for metaphor, as when Wordsworth said: "as if to make the strong wind visible"; "as if" discounting what he had to say, who had seen the wind, and not dared say so.

So the four observed the four walls set at right angles, on the march, and not interfering with one other. A perception not easy to discuss for lack of terms. It had happened before, and after history had been ransacked for analogies, Felix had supplied them with Alice running with the Red Queen on the squares: Picus with a story of John Buchan's about a man who died of finding out what space is really like, and in it quotes a dream of trains passing without collision on crossed rails.

Felix ended the silence: "Ready to go on, Scylla? The walls' parade is getting on my nerves." They were ready for her voice with its human stresses, pauses and climaxes, for research into a story in known terms.

She began again:

"The meaning of money is that it determines the route, not the goal, of things. You can get on with it or without it, but you will get on differently. And so are modified yourself. The other Taverner boys were pushed into professions, out into the world. They are younger than Felicity, and they have nothing to do with this story.

"There was her younger brother, Adrian, and he has, I think."

"I've met him," said Boris.

"Everyone has. And you know in any country the position of the favourite son. Mrs. Taverner held the purse-strings, but she gave a lot to him. Well, about six months before she died, Felicity thought that he'd realised something about her. At least he came to see her, after she had been struggling to live on nothing for a long time, and said that she was his darling and that he would put her affairs right."

"Wrote it as well, I think," said Felix.

"At any rate there was a promise that there should be an end of pinching and uncertainty and window-shopping and waking up and dawn-staring because there was a man coming about a bill. Felicity was not a bad manager, an exquisite one and quite careful; only she was not born an economist. It was proper for her to have room to flower in. While her candour and timidity both loathed debts; felt them a dishonour. She had none of the technique some people learn of how to live on what they owe, in which you, Boris, are a talented amateur. I said *amateur*.

"But Felicity was helpless. While her mother always implied and often said that since cheap shoes were all she could afford, they were what she ought to wear. And that she neither could do or would. Aunt Julia will wear any kind of shoe with a Lanvin dress.

"It did not seem just to Felicity. While it hurt her that a mother could be like that. To this part of the story there is an under-song you have heard before: *'Felicity had not "hands" with her mother.'* Aunt Julia thought that she ought to make it up with Nick Kralin: or marry again: or get some work. Felicity shuddered at Kralin: didn't want to marry again: didn't know any 'work.' Could not convey to her mother any notion of what she was.

"Her occupation was to be lovely and exquisite and kind. And to adorn that bitch of a house. To learn things and never to show them off. It was her business to understand things and to love. (What better business is there?)

But what ice could that cut with old Mrs. Taverner? 'Who could object to Jane, her understanding excellent, her manners captivating, her mind improved?' While her mother saw her a scandalous piece, whose generosities reproached her meanness, whose failures justified her common sense. For it is now time to say that she gave a victorian dowager something to put up with; she did not gild the pill or sweeten it, or, if you like, justify herself by any conspicuous success. Mind you, she would have had success, ordinary social success, if they had helped her; would have made a present of it to her mother, since it was her nature to give people what they asked. Only it mattered nothing to Aunt Julia that everybody loved her, and everything that they exploited her; and that her poverty kept her out of the houses she could have visited. Even made her run away from such people who could have protected her and adored.

"Instead she hid. Ran away, if you like. Here, out on wild nights with the shepherds at lambing time. Or in Paris, Boris, comforting people like you.

"Also she was piteously shy; her first reaction that insane sense of her unworthiness; and an adorable, poetic and often quite cynical admiration for persons as they were, or according to their kind.

"Her Paris-place—she even gave them up just before she died—was like a dutch interior. There she would sit and read and embroider; and hungry boys would come, hopeless, and she would feed them, and climb some tree in Paradise and shake down a petal-storm over them. Some of the petals stuck: some shook them off as they got outside: some kept a few in their cigarette cases and showed them with a leer. But not many. I know even french dowagers would send their sons to her, knowing they would come to no harm, pick up some fine English, and even sometimes come away with a momentary enthusiasm for virtue.

"Those mothers shrugged their shoulders, of course. I heard one sum it up: the pity and the inexplicable madness of it that such a woman should be alone: heard wish her a convenable husband and then a salon worthy of her.

"That impressed me. It was so exactly what Felicity ought to have had."

Felix spoke: "That is what she had come to see; it was that that she wanted: that she needed. She told me."

"Do you get it clear, Boris, these preliminaries?"

"Perfectly."

Scylla continued:

"Can you bear it if I go on? It is you who will make us remember everything. Remember that I have to be counsel for both sides. If I had to show you that Adrian and Aunt Julia were the cause of Felicity's death, I have to show you that I think neither knew what they were doing: and that her mother may even have thought that she was doing the right thing. Aunt Julia is the type that has always to believe that she is doing the right thing.

"Above all, you are not to go away and tell the world that her mother and her brother murdered Felicity—if it should be true that she was driven to throw herself before that car on the Lower Corniche. Still less that they hired a chauffeur-assassin. It was that, ignorantly, they had weakened her hold on life. Aldous Huxley writes of the enormous biologic pressure under which man lives in order to go on living. We are not lobsters to throw out a new claw. And I do not know if the destruction of the will is really possible. There was very little wrong with her health. She had got very thin and she slept badly, but it was bills that woke her. Mrs. Taverner paid some of them, but her alternative was to have bills or ask Mrs. Taverner to pay them. I don't know which I would choose for a death-sentence on sleep. One has known my aunt to do generous things; but never a generous thing generously. So Felicity lay hid in Paris where she had once played with Alastair. I'm afraid to think of her there, crouched like a hare in its forme, dead-still, only her eyes glancing with fear. 'Feet of a faun' and gone to no greenwood.

"There must have been fierce economics: her maid sent away: no flowers, or fresh gloves, or new books. And her place took a faded air, smelt of Paris dust, whose scent is unique, almost a perfume, sweet, and most demoralising. While her hands must have coarsened, though they had learned how a floor is waxed, or kitchen tiles washed red, or a bath white. This went on happening after Adrian's visit and his promise to her, and she was waiting for it to come true.

"Why didn't we help? God forgive us. Picus and I were getting married and away in Greece on mule-back. Quarantined too on Scyros by a plague scare. We didn't know that the year before she hadn't even found a tenant for here. Felix was turning an equivocal penny leading an american party on a search for culture, of various sorts, in North Africa. Culture for cash and surprises thrown in. An un-rest cure. We had never heard from her after she had so adorned our wedding that Picus almost changed wives.

"Felix saw her once, I think."

"Yes, I did—" the young man cried out— "I could not tell you, but I'll tell you now what I saw—"

Remorse to-day is a rare emotion. They evaded it, Scylla, Boris, Picus.

—"It was on my way south, to pick up those art-lechers. I stepped off in Paris and went to see her. Found her door unlatched and walked in. Found her in the far room, with the shutters closed, in the half dark. I remember her dress was white on a black divan, and she'd a candle beside her, because, I suppose, the electric light was cut off.

"She lay on her back, and her arms were restless. I thought she was asleep. Sat down to wait. She'd neither been asleep, nor heard me. Sat up suddenly, and you're right, Scylla, about her eyes. They were red too, round and bright. She didn't see me: drew up her knees; staring, staring. Stared round and saw me and smiled.

"I said: 'Been asleep?' 'No,' she said, like a truthful kid. She'd frightened me, and I suppose I shouted at her to tell me what had happened. She shivered, and if you'll believe it, she stammered that she mustn't be shouted at any more to-day."

"*Son amant l'avait trompé sans doute,*" said Boris, nervous, it seemed, at Felix's emotion.

The walls were in their place again: the shining room charged-up with pain.

"She told me she had been lying still, waiting until the day should be over, when her brother had walked in. Hadn't expected him, or known that he was in Paris. Had charged in on her, and it was like a storm, she said. Sounded more like slops from a top window. 'He told me,' she said, 'when I threw him a cushion, not to waste civility on him: not to think that he didn't know that all I wanted was money from him. That money was all I was out for from him and from mother, money to spend on my fancy-men.

"'After that he said what hurt even more: that there was no such thing as disinterested action or sentiment: the only decent thing was to admit it; and that all I did was to add hypocrisy to the most sordid, shameless, above all profitless desire for cash. But I needn't think I'd deceived him or my angel-mother. They knew me through and through.

"'Then, he asked, where had my idealism got me? What had it brought me? How much longer would I have the face to pretend that clean hands and a pure heart were worth it? Besides, I'd lost them. They're a fancy for the rich.' Then she put out her hands. 'If you believe in what were called the Signatures, Felix, it made me afraid when my brother said that. I'd been sewing a great deal, and my needle had pitted the skin of my forefinger into shreds and my hands weren't very clean. I couldn't answer him.

I can't tell you the violence of him: how he paced about. Flung himself up and down again: let out his voice. I knew how quiet and detached I ought to have been. Only, by a cowardice I shall pay for, I felt shouted-down. It hurt my body, the pure sound of him as much as the sense. I couldn't breathe right. I loved him so. And because I've been for a long time strained and tired, I could not forget how easily he could have taken all that out of my life. Let alone what he had promised me.

"'And in some awful, false way he made me ashamed. Like that poem "He must be wicked to deserve such pain."' —This was what she told me about Adrian and his promises.

"I suppose I deserve never to forget how she said it.

"What did I do? Oh, I took her out and she danced so lightly and laughed so sweetly, that she made it quite convenient for me to forget. I paid a few bills, and swore I'd see Adrian and put the fear of God if I couldn't the love of man into him when I got back. And when I got back, she was dead."

Felix was not crying. It was Boris who wept. There was something that checked Scylla's apology for causing him pain.

A wretched silence followed, brimming the room, making the warm comfort comfortless. Dostoievsky's dreadful insistence on the reality of the comfortless seemed to have come in with them to rest. To be truth.

Scylla began again: "I'm glad that you're here, Boris, to be told this. I've somehow got from you a double image of her. One like a cameo, cut delicately, and then another, a terrible duplicate, over life-size, Io, Hathor or some such divine simplification—out of the Book of the Dead. Do you see what I mean?" Felix did.

"Io and Hathor were both cows," said Picus. "Who wore the moon. And one came to Prometheus."

"That was part of the worst of it," said Felix: "Felicity never found a Prometheus."

"I'm not so sure. There was Alastair."

"His number was Philoctetes."

Boris, who owed his Philoctetes to Gide, considered it an inappropriate moment for a display of classical erudition. His small, emerald torch-point flashed again about the piled, distorted shadows his friends evoked.

"Can you make a summary of this now, or is there more to tell?"

"There must be a great deal more, Boris, that happened. That is what we have to find out. All we have done is to try to begin to understand her. To tell each of us what we know, until we may—and then, I am not very sanguine—find out the truth."

To a silent Boris, whose eyes could not keep still, Scylla said again:

"We know now that she was a woman made for a particular kind of love, a love that the world at present has particularly no use for. Recognises no God with her for priestess.

"It was as good as any art to her. *'In whom alone love lives again'* and all that. And all we've said is the sugar of her story, not the honey. She was beginning to see what she had to do. I suppose it was Alastair who made her see. She'd seen the world going to its present senseless devil, anaemic with stupidity and spite, and she had meant to do something about it. Until, and I mean it, she was killed. She'd become more dangerous than she knew.

"As you can be made sick with bad painting, so was she by bad loving. If Boris thinks that a woman like that must play Chopin and have a foot like a tea-leaf or look like a boy in the wrong pants, he can think something else. She wasn't sentimental, she was passionate. She had also what made her 'genial,' she gave to each relation its appropriate love. If beds were trumps, she was in one like a pearl in a shell. Or, and when she was at her rarest, she could turn all passionate feeling from its concentration on the person into the discovery of its relations with ideas and actions, unsuspected until her imagination linked them, set them to music."

"She called that her suicide-cure," said Felix.

"And I've heard her say," said Picus, "and this is my way of saying it; that there are people who read-up the Poor Law and people who read Pindar: people, usually the same people, who never go to bed and people who never get up; people who have contraceptive delirium and people who spawn like fish. Any fool could do either, but that life began when you could do both. What she never found out was that immediately you understand that, you become over life-size. Which is what the world cannot forgive, and only finally adores."

"Is that size then not strength?" said Boris.

"Her humility destroyed her," said Scylla. "She did not know her own power —her own discovery."

"Is there anything more to tell?" said Boris. "Did not one of you see her again after Felix left her on his way south?" Their silence answered him.

"Let us think about it a little more, Boris. There are three people to bear witness against her: her mother, Adrian and Nick Kralin. They must know some things that we don't know. Aunt Julia's anger had been maturing since her birth. The duration of Adrian's I do not know at all. For once he loved her. While Aunt Julia's conscience was the old-fashioned kind; to hate her daughter she must be justified; to be justified, she must create a legend about her. The world passionately resents freedom in others—freedom of genius or beauty or madness or crime—it's all one to our teeming sphere. Still, she could not have been happy about her child's state, and here the legend came in. For her, Felicity's life was wholly composed of the excesses she would have liked to have enjoyed, who had sacrificed her *jus saturnalia* to God. That since then God has changed his mind for every boy and girl, did not excuse Felicity. So the legend had it that Felicity in Paris reeled nightly from Montmartre to Montparnasse, and in the taxi home was at least kissed. And it was to most peoples' interest to keep the legend green; women who were jealous of her; men who had not found her light. Kralin, too, had his revenge to consider: Adrian as well could not have been proud of himself."

Felix broke in:—

—"D'you know, I believe the legend became a mania in that house. Before I saw her in Paris for the last time, I went down to see Aunt Julia. Found her with Kralin, both as thick as thieves. Then Adrian came in, a bit flushed and restless. Had some story about his sister, when she must have been trying to make him understand that she was hard put to it for food, that she'd been seen down at Biarritz with some chic notorieties who happen to detest Adrian.

"Now that sort of accusation is the hardest thing on earth to disprove. I knew that Felicity had met those people, but that she'd no more been to Biarritz with them than she'd been to the moon. I said so. Saw that they were furious, both ways: that she had been to Biarritz, and equally that she had not been to Biarritz, and when I told them she'd never left Paris and that she needed help. For I'd seen her there casually already, before the time I've told you. Only I had not believed that Adrian would promise everything and do nothing.

"Then they cross-questioned me, until even my male mind noticed they were ravening after garbage. So I tied them down, or tried to, to the fact that she hardly knew the people, and hadn't been to Biarritz for years. Faked a guarantee that I hadn't got. Their defence was pretty poor. Only Kralin was dangerous. About the scruples of an emotional alligator. It was odd. As though everything was all of a tremble in that serene room along the terrace at Pharrs. I was shaking and you'd excuse the teaspoons, but not the chairs and the cabinets and the pictures on the walls.

"Then I saw Kralin's cleverness. A true story might

have been easier for me to handle. Also that they could turn on me, and say I was in love with her.

"They did. Well you know the fool that makes you feel. Till then I hadn't noticed it—not the way they would think of it. I was going to stop, when—well, I thought of Felicity, and that, if she was right, I must not mind making a fool of myself for love's sake. So I told Kralin I wished we'd been of an age, and I'd have given her a better show than he had. Played the snob-stuff too."

Felix's popularity, a fluctuating quality, ran up to a degree unparalleled.

—"All of a sudden, I went dog-tired. More than tired, and had a ghastly feeling—the ghastliest of all—that it was just no good. The Devil had got his trap set first. You know those future hunches."

The silence that followed was an empty one of fatigue.

"To end it," said Scylla, "after Felix saw her for the last time, we came back but not by way of Paris. Raced back here, to finish our honeymoon in our own place. She was in our minds, as if she had come, running up-channel to meet us, and along the top of the downs. When we went to the Dancing Rocks, she landed there, and the sea kindly reproduced Boticelli's wave-curl edge. She walked up the wood with us and quickened it: she stayed with us. She was how I have tried to describe her to you, everywhere, so that the hills were her body laid-down, and 'Felicity' was said, over and over again, in each bud and leaf. She made it as though she were a third with us. Think of a shape of bright darkness, blowing out flowers."

"I'm glad," said Picus, " that you liked your honeymoon. I did too." Then it ran through the silence between them that he and Scylla were accompanied still.

"That is no part of the story," said Scylla. "I said it partly for our excuse. Boris knows how in ancient tragedy a brother 'off' may be hacking his sister in pieces to a chorus about birds."

No one knew better than she that moral justifications

were as wasted on Boris as on the weather. They had been enjoying themselves, and that, for him, was enough.

"We came back to our senses and to London soon after Christmas. Felicity, though she'd given up the flat, was still in Paris, hiding, waiting, holding on. Still believing in her mother and in Adrian's promise. Until she must have gone south suddenly—and died there. And other things that we do not know must have happened by then. And we must learn them.

"God knows why she didn't write," Felix said. "All I know about that is from a man who saw her, but who didn't see much. And what he saw suggests that something abominable may have happened to her. Something that may again have got round, twisted, to her people: usual talk about a disgraceful love-affair. —Believe it or not, but I mean it when I say that I thought she'd have written if she'd wanted me."

Felix's cry of pain brought his sister to him as a bird might drive its way home through a storm.

"This is where I'd have you all admit her imperfection. It was solely that her pride had got out of hand. She knew that she had us. More than one of the gods have scolded her that she, our lover, wouldn't use Felix's love."

Then Boris spoke:

"It is possible that this time she had done something that she would not want you, of all people, to know. Suppose," he went on, a tiny smile tight on his lips, "that this time it was true. Neither a 'potin' nor a distortion nor an invention."

Scylla found herself roused from an agonised meditation to give Boris more than her reason's attention: to listen to him with the backs of her ears. Felix said soberly:

"I think you'll understand, but I don't think it would have mattered with me. Not if it had been shady, disgraceful even, foul."

"He's right, Boris," said Scylla, "and we seem back again at the pride that took the wrong turning."

Boris did not answer. All that she could have explained was that she was aware of the backs of her ears; or the bones of her skull, in the state called intuitive, her mind working too fast for its process to be followed. A state allied to fear: to excitement: even to awe. And there went with it a re-relating of the time-sense, as of speed eaten by speed. She had kept note of such times in the past; made a scrupulous examination of them. So far it seemed that if given sufficient rein and a certain form of detachment and control, those moments led to results not otherwise obtainable, a short-cut to reason's slow re-construction of events. Nor did they seem liable, as with reasoning, to become invalid at the entrance of a new fact.

Meanwhile the backs of her ears told her that Boris knew, or guessed something, something at once foolish and intolerable. And that their enquiry and the working of their grief's slow passion had touched the nerves of slav cruelty in him.

Was he going to tell them? No. Not yet.

He had been in Paris part of that time. There were friends, gossips, various threads and all untrustworthy between Felicity and him. Were the others thinking the same thing? (They were.) She tried a direct attack.

"Boris, you were about Paris. Did you hear a rumour of any sort? You did not know her, but are you sure that you heard nothing? (Never mind our feelings . . .)"

It seemed as though Boris did not dare to hesitate.

"I do not like to say, because the memory, if it is a memory, is so indistinct. Only it may have been that I heard a story of an Englishwoman, who might be your cousin, in alliance with a man of great promise and charm. Of a sudden, brutal break. That he left her for no reason that was known."

To Scylla his story was an admission. A grim thought occurred to them all, that Boris might have separated their cousin from her lover. For devilry or innocently or for fun? That was why he had let them talk. He had been curious: thought himself secure. Their ignorance had been too much for his vanity. Conviction seized on them. Yet by trusting such guess-work, they might do him great wrong. None of them wished, they even feared, to do him wrong. Yet each was prepared to chance it.

Accuse him? The brother and sister were on fire when Picus said:

"Enough of it for to-night. Let's go to bed," the rare note in his easy voice that made them obey him.

Chapter II

ALL NIGHT the earth and the heavens followed their usual arrangements. Stars passed: an immense tide went out. The Dancing Rocks lay naked, a single gull hung over them. A silent sea raced back with the sun, its wave turn-over small, delicate and comfortless. The most glorious of all stars hung above the sun's threshold and went out. An hour later the sun governed the earth again, mist-chasing, flower-opening, bird-rousing, ghost-driving, spirit-shepherding back out of the various gates of sleep.

Nanna first opened to him the dining-room's terrace doors. The pain of the room had cried out to her as she came in; also its shameful look as of a stage-set in disuse. She counted candle-ends and fretted at the waste, but her real preoccupation was with fear for her children. She had come down first into a dark room, stale with dead smoke and cold ashes and wax shrouds. Out of these some grief seemed to have made itself a body, and some evil doing, which would declare itself and Miss Felicity's death not over yet. For the Bible told her that "there is nothing hid that shall not be made known," and her good sense that the world was not made to spare Miss Scylla or Mr. Felix. Any more than she trusted Mr. Boris, not from the day two years back when she'd seen him land, come up there at their feet out of the sea. Love them he might, but his loving wasn't their loving. You might as well expect a cat to care for you the same as men care, or your horse or your dog. And suppose they knew that, did they know that there was danger when a man of his sort loves? He couldn't help it, she knew. But it made her think of Miss Felicity and Mr. Kralin. Foreigners both, she understood, from the same part. And it didn't matter that one was from the great gentry and the other from goodness knew where. While Mr. Boris was pretty, Mr. Boris was witty as they used to sing . . . she knew how he'd get round her in her kitchen . . . give him what he wanted to please her children and because of his family out there being murdered. Yes, and for his pretty ways too.

Lend him out of her savings though. Not she. Any more than she'd tell Miss Scylla he'd asked her.

So the old nurse ran on, while under her eye the maid drove out the night. But even when the rugs, after a tea-leaf massage and a sun-bath on the dew-heavy grass, were replaced, when pillars of new wax stood in the sconces and a pyramid of dry sticks had been built in the grate, she felt none of the housewife's satisfaction. Though the wood's scent and voice were now everywhere, something had come in during the night which could not be driven out; that Mr. Boris had brought with him across the sea. A bitter thing for them to know. Truth was well enough, but Miss Felicity was dead; and suppose Miss Scylla was with child and didn't know it. Shaking a duster, she found herself taking a few steps down the grass path to the gate of the wood. Was it the truth coming to take revenge for Miss Felicity? It seemed to her that it would need a lot of it to do it, and that she didn't see how. Meanwhile, that there was no comfort about the house, nor was likely to be until Mr. Boris had done his worst.

They'll have to get over it, my lambs. Let's hope whatever's coming is worth it to them.

So they awoke to a morning whose pleasant prospect ran counter to the abominations of man. With shameful ingratitude they came down to spring's best effort, birds triumphant and new birds; that year's hatching out of coloured eggs, cup-held, plume-warmed, sung-to, worm-fed; and now out, a feather in spring's cap, wing-trying, learning to sing.

For once in their lives they had no use for it, nor at

breakfast for the sea's small fish-harvest, and Boris's offering, a rare tea, was drunk ungratefully. Certainly they had smoked too much: from their symptoms they might have drunk too much; conscious and ashamed of discontent at the matchless weather saluting them. There it was for their pleasure and adoration, and where was Felicity?

And each carried their grief in a separate picture, a tiny image of what might have happened to Felicity. Felix as though he heard a light engine-sound which meant that a car had bumped its way across the turf. He ran out and saw that it was Felicity, in the jade and silver coupé she had wanted so childishly and so much. She had come back to them and it was all over. Adrian had kept his promise. And she had brought no more pain with her. The car meant that it was gone for ever. Scylla saw her in winter, in a room where she was going to give a party, in a dress the colour of the lights through a rose. An admirable *femme de chambre* was arranging winter's rarest things to eat, with strawberries Felix had taught his cousin how to build in pyramids, backed against splendid wines. Rings of jade and crystal slid up and down her arms. The woman was looking at her mistress with pride. And so as to be there early and speak with her alone, a young man, superb, adorable, had just passed the concierge's *loge*.

While Picus, without the least sensuality, saw her before her mirror, just out of her bath. In a room which was to serve beauty and nothing else. There in a shift, sea-green, incorruptible, she was making herself lovely for love. It was all rather like the best american advertisements and they knew it; irritated as though they had given her a cheap funeral. Until Scylla told herself that they were past that cant of the intellect which denies the loveliness of pleasant things.

The silence of their pain returned to them. Felix went out with his sister across the lawn into the wood. His arm round her shoulder, he muttered to her at last:

"Can't someone be born—someone has got to be born—who will make *'On Heaven'* true? A God that's no blind man. A God that's our father? *'Because she was very tall and quaint. And gold like a quattrocento saint.'* There was a car in that. It must be true. And the place they found where they could love each other. Wherever your fancy is . . ."

Then out loud, petulant and fierce, "Are Adrian and Aunt Julia to have the last word?"

* * * * *

Against his doctor's orders (he was his own doctor), Boris was undergoing a katharisis. It had happened to him before in England, with the Taverners, that he had not been quite able to follow his instincts and extract profit out of bad to worse. He slipped off down the wood to bathe, stripped on the Dancing Rocks, crossed the reef, white as a birch-tree walking, the smallest wind moving in his black curled hair. While he genuinely admired the view and his own addition to it, he tried not to listen to a small gong in his head, dinning insistently that curiosity killed the cat and that for once he wasn't sorry if it did; glad and ashamed and indignant that his emotions were about to betray him. And what was it that had betrayed him before, made him cross the sea to visit the Taverners with a present of china tea, when he had lately helped kill their cousin? There was virtue still in Boris. He was not old enough to have become quite bad. At that moment, the eastern-slav tincture in his blood dyed all the rest. He was there, in their house, in their hearts: eating their salt after helping to destroy one of them. At very least, it was bad magic. He winced as though the stones' worn gold burned his feet. Every superstition in him dictated a penance. "You made them talk. You must speak now." What a position for a man, as he considered himself, of breeding.

He turned back again to the cliff's root, as though he did not dare enter that pure sea. He dressed and scrambled up its crumbling path. He wanted to hide, and where in that open country? He feared the wood.

He was in the state in which he usually got into serious mischief, when Scylla met him, kicking his heels on a stone stile; and he was not sorry when she swept him off with her on a round of village errands and a long walk to a distant inn for lunch. They tramped in the growing heat, side by side, silent.

Boris felt the sweat start out between his shoulder-blades, as lightly and wearily, shoulder to shoulder, they mounted a precipice of flint-sewn chalk just above the village. There he nearly made his confession: checked himself. Scylla was looking up towards some building, hardly aware of him. Looking at Felicity's house. He thought of the rehearsal with her once they had passed it, prelude to a full confession, after dinner, before them all. Only it was just not quite the right moment for him to make the adjustments necessary to suit this scheme to his vanity, his actor's sense that repetitions are stale; his vision of Scylla's smile when he repeated to her husband and her brother a story that she had already heard. He could hear her voice: "*Boris, comme c'est déjà bien travaillé.*" That would not do. He knew too well what their sense of plain-dealing would expect. He began to resent as never before what these people had done for him. Was he not being forced to behave as they would wish him to be? And how many men, from rarities like Boris to the workman who cuts his wife's, his children's and then his own throat, do it with the cry: "Why couldn't they leave me in peace to be what I am?" Scylla moved fast beside him, innocently staring. The road to the down top rose straight up into the sky. Right before them was the church, enclosed in immense trees; beside it the vicarage: on the other side, in a line with them, Felicity's house.

"There she lived," said Scylla, coldly. "And she is not buried there. Bead wreaths on a box in a marble chest of drawers in the south."

Boris licked his lips with pleasure at the house. Built of grey stone, on the façade there were wreaths of stone fruit, and above the door twin fish, the Taverner arms between them on a raised panel of stone. Then he saw what he took to be a green marble rope enclosing the whole device.

"Look again," said Scylla. Then he saw that it was a snake with its tale in its mouth. A curious addition to the lovely sobriety of wreaths and fruit. Odder than fish for mantling.

"No," she said, "we don't know who put a snake for frame round our arms. Or why there should be fish. Heraldic fancy roams usually in the direction of sea-weed. There's an intention in it that no one knows. One of the question marks about this house. Like the pavement in the hall, black marble and white, diamond-squared, round a centre mosaic. First a wreath of green marble; then, what would you expect? Cupid and Psyche? Cupid or Psyche? A head of Moses? Marcus Aurelius? Alpha and Omega? A local view? Not a bit of it. A set of stars. But no known constellation or patch of the sky. If you know your heavens, there is something almost improper about it. As though there the choice lay between formal star-dots or the Zodiac."

She went on, speaking to herself:

"About 1700 our family took a turn; before Nature happened, Rousseau, Swedenborg, Blake. Before Voltaire. I can't describe what happened, but Felix is wrenched by it."

She called herself back. She had brought Boris with her to confront him with Felicity's house. A house that they suspected. She cursed their family indolence, content to accept its intuitive speciality, without scrutiny or analysis, once it seemed justified. Suppose Felicity had died to make them look into it, until knowledge made them acquainted with their gift? For if they did, she more than half suspected that an account of their perception might be the means to an incalculable enlargement of human power.

On no account must she say a word to Boris about it. Extension of that kind of capacity would make Boris dangerous—more dangerous than he was.

At the gate, it was piteous to see the rank lawn, and the Cupid, from whose hands a water-plume should have mounted to play with the wind, bound in the sucker of a fierce rambler, the teeth and claws of a rose. A fresh one was fastening on the slight flanks. She told Boris the name of an old flower run to seed in the border. He took no notice of her. There was something of the wolf about his attention.

"There is someone in the house," he said.

The door opened and a young woman came out. The kind least tolerated of all strangers in that land. Out-of-town by rapid transit from its slums; young, heavy-haunched and over breasted, wearing a terrible parody of country clothes. Her mouth expressed discontent, her brown onyx eyes stared about with mistrust. Bored to extinction she seemed, to exasperation; one hand on her hip, rocking on ill-balanced heels. The kind that only a tincture of fear keeps from tantrums which are like running amok. From behind the house a girl of the same sort joined her, dragging her feet along the path. In the lane, Scylla and Boris observed them, standing beneath a tree.

The pair of them kicked their heels, their arms linked. Come to a village, God at the moment seemed to know why, grave and still under the spring-chorus, dimly aware of Nature's enormous, satiric eye on them. Had the order rested with Scylla, she would have had them driven into the bull-field and left. With the high peremptory voice that Boris secretly feared, she was about to speak to them, when the door of the house opened, and there came out Felicity's husband, Nick Kralin.

He had brought his harem down: that was evident. She told Boris. Nick Kralin, who knew her only too well by sight, saw also that he was no more than an exhibit. ("Adrian must have let it to him.") The widower passed between the two women and came through the gate. No hand-shaking. Boris was observant. These people's people had peddled fairings at the back-door of his château. You could not tell it in the man; he had quite a distinguished air. He might have been an exquisite lad. No, he would not insult him to please Scylla. He could hardly afford to. The family went sometimes too far. In private, an indication of the difference between their ranks would be sufficient. He heard her say to him:

"Are you introducing Felicity's *remplaçantes*?"

Kralin looked as embarrassed as any decent man.

"Hardly yet, Scylla. We motored over. I have taken the house, and wanted to see if it was in order. Didn't like to bother you."

"We should have been glad."

"That would be perfect then, if you would. I only remembered that grilling field-walk. And the bull."

"Wouldn't it be as well if Nanna saw to it?"

"Of course it would. I didn't know you were here yet. We're leaving. I had hoped to be back the day after tomorrow, for good. Alone probably."

He strode back into the house. A man's walk. The women nudged him as he passed. Scylla sat down on a stone by the wall, beating the dust with her stick. Through the half-closed door came sounds of girlish curiosity and squeals and Kralin's low voice turned brusque. He came back almost at once, and gave Scylla a bunch of bright steel keys on a ring.

"They're in duplicate. I've kept mine if you don't mind." A slip. Why should she?

"Why should I? But I think that Nanna has a third set that Felicity gave her. Anyhow she'll have the place in perfect order."

"I know she will. Thank Nanna. I'll thank her myself when I get back."

That was well done. Without insistence he would still have them consider him part of their family. Only, was it just perceptible that he was uneasy that Nanna should have another bunch of keys? As Boris took the heavy ring from Scylla, he said:

"They are, I think, the surest. The locksmith came over and refitted."

Her assent was earnest and polite.

"If you are going into Starn, can I drive you there? I've my car here. I could take you in now and come back for the others."

"We are only going half way, to Stone End, but it would spare you a climb, Boris." Then she introduced them. The ex-husband of Felicity Taverner shot Boris a look; the smile of introduction showed for a second superb teeth. Quickly calculating possiblities, Boris slipped into the car. Kralin shot them up-hill and down into the further valley by a road of dreadful curves, like a demon charged with a convoy he hopes can be damned. The wind parted Scylla's hair into pale ribbons. Boris saw her eyes and her skin, flint and chalk pale. Kralin set them down beside a grass-patch in the centre of a village, beside a stone where one would have expected a cross. For some minutes the thunder and shriek of his car-sound marked his return up the long hill which now lay between them and the sea.

Chapter III

THEY FELT CUT-OFF in the valley, pickled in spring smells, undiluted by salt from off the sea. Over a beer outside the inn Scylla questioned herself. Nothing but the inability to kill them without killing himself had induced Nick Kralin to land them there. A point she had realised from the start and he had realised on the first angle of the hill. So they were there, intact at the village of Stone End, rather than in hell. Which he had considered to be their joint address. Or only hers? Or Boris's? Kralin was often in Paris. Had he met him before? What *did* Kralin know?

He had not been pleased to know that Nanna had a third set of keys. It was necessary to consider this separately. It might be that he was looking for something in the house. Something then that he had not found, otherwise he could conceal it or destroy it. Or was it simple dislike of contact with them? During that crazy shoot up-hill and down, had he shown something of the quality his wife had called the "grey thing"? Or had it been plain human rage? What reason had he to feel that against her cousin, there on her lawful occasion, and scrupulously polite? Nothing in reason, unless he believed her to be condoning some atrocity that Boris had done to his wife. Which was unlikely. (But was she?) She looked again at Boris. Suppose it had been Boris he had wanted to kill. But whatever Boris had done, and whatever version of the truth he was arranging to tell them, Kralin was more responsible than he for Felicity's death. An infinite degree more responsible, an irrevocable, unforgivable responsibility. A volition measured against a caprice. It would be that. And, whatever he had done, they would all of them forgive Boris quicker than Nick Kralin. For reasons that would bear a fair amount of scrutiny. For Boris would be sorry once he had understood; not for long, but passionately. While there was an equal certainty about Kralin, he might even suffer for what he had done; but never would he be sorry. It was there began that "grey thing" which had made his wife afraid. Made a bad wife of her too, and excused her, even to her own gentle conscience. Of course, the "grey thing," whatever it was, was more than the inability to say "sorry" and to mean it. She paused again. What more was implied? What goes on in the secret places of a heart incapable even *de s'incliner devant Dieu*? It would mean a man persuaded that there is no such thing as good. Oh, God! How far would the death of one young woman bring them? Five people at least glancing over "the most fearful depths of the spirit." Nor likely to be let off at that. Boris's part seemed suddenly become unimportant, a thing to be got out of the way.

She drew deeply at the scent-charged air, whose taste was like an opiate.

"Boris, what did you do to Felicity, in Paris, during those last months?"

Boris had had time to make up his mind, suggest himself into belief in his rearrangements. He turned to her—his gesture a superb compound of relief, remorse, passionate candour and bewilderment touched with curiosity; confidence and perfect penitence. Against which Scylla had to brace herself. Against such bravura how dull truth seemed, and difficult of access. Never had the bottom of a well seemed less attractive. She must hear him first. She could go down later. He began:

"By the end of last night I was already uneasy. It was that I felt more than sorrow for your sorrow. In bed I could not sleep, and when I slept, there were dreams—"

Scylla had a recollection of untroubled snores.

"It came back to me at dawn, with the birds. But more when I went down to the rocks where the sea dances, as you say, a ballet with each tide. That is so. I remembered all that had happened there. How we played long ago in Paris, and how not you but your lovely cousin got the apple. I did not agree." Under his lashes he took a look at her and went on quickly:

"It is a good thing that we are alone together, Scylla, now. I had just remembered it all, seen it all, and had to run up off those rocks like a man under a curse. You know me. I am the kind of man who when the intolerable happens has so great a wish to run away—to lie."

She heard herself saying coarsely:

"Cut the cackle, Boris. What did you do in Paris that helped kill Felicity off? And don't stop to register feelings. Have mercy on us. We know you are less to blame than Kralin." Boris thought her indelicate. Only since it was essential to humour her, he salted the dish with a pinch more truth.

"It was like this. I have a very old friend, an Englishman for whom I have had an affection for years. While always we have been separated: I am so poor, and they will only let Red Russians into England. Always we wrote: always it was intended that in the Midi we should share a little house.

"At last he came to Paris, and I had to look for him. At last I met him by hazard, and I saw that his ideas were changed. He was charming and sad, and I could see troubled. Then I heard that he was with a beautiful lady. That she was your cousin, at that time, I did not know. I suffered too. I did not see them together. I was alone. Then one night I met him, walking on the quays. There I asked him if he meant to marry and *ranger* himself. Suddenly he told me that he did not know what he wanted to do. Your cousin—the lady—was too good for him, and there would have to be a divorce. Then I understood that he must not get drunk again if he was to marry her; not never get drunk, but drunk as I used to get."

"You mean that you went off together and did."

"I told him," said Boris gravely, "that she was right, and how the sobriety I had learned from you had saved more than my life—" Her sigh might have conveyed a sudden regret.

—"There was also something else that he said. I do not know it all, but one part of it was that he might lose some money that was to come to him from an old lady, who did not wish him to marry anyone. So he did not know what he wanted to do. It was an exquisite night, and the river like an enchanted serpent from the *Mille et une Nuits*. I was with my friend again. He is a man of genius, and such charms that he has always had everything given to him. That means that he thinks that the world is his only; and that if you do good, you do it as a woman puts colour on her face to increase her beauty. What we call honour means no more to him than that."

"Name, please, of this beauty. Gigolo, I take it, by profession."

"No, I tell you that he has genius. And he is a gentleman. Already he had made *fausse route* as I had."

"What's his name? D'you suppose it will take us long to find out?"

"T'chiquo. You will surely have heard that name for him." She had not, and it is a poor position not to know the *petit nom* you are supposed to know. And it was good fun to watch how Boris made the tiny advantage serviceable.

"*Ma chère amie,* now begins what I am not able to forgive myself. Of course, since you do not know him, you will think worse of me, but at least you know what I am like. There was a little 'dancing' on that quay. They were kind to us. I do not pretend that we did not get drunk. Only I was astonished that it took so little to make T'chiquo drunk ... not drunk only, but altogether drunk ... wrongly drunk." Engagingly. "Now I used to get drunk. He had not been like that before, and I was troubled. For he might have been mad . . . and became helpless, and in such a way that he became a bore. You will say that this does not matter. Only it explains—"

"What?"

"What I have to tell you. For a long time I listened to him; then I understood." (At that moment, faith justified itself.) "You will know what I am trying to say: how T'chiquo told me what he would not have told if he had not been drunk. How because of me his will had become in two: how all the time I was at least as dear to him as Felicity, and because of her there could not be that house in the Midi. She would not have it, because she said that I would make him drunk again. I, who have not drunk as I used to since I promised you—" He could not judge how he was affecting her. A bad sign.

"Scylla, you must not be unjust to me. Scylla! I tell you that I tried to send him back to her. And he would not leave me. He said he was not good enough for her, and I believed that. I found that he would be afraid to go back to her at that hour, drunk. Nor could I take him to her, did I then know where she lived? And can you not see that I thought she must be stupid."

"So you took him back to his hotel?"

"Into a taxi. It went off, and we did not know where to tell it to stop. Rain came on. We were in the country. It was very dark. The man was cruel. He wanted his money all the way back into Paris. We hid behind a tree.

—"It was one of the long straight roads with a canal beside it. When T'chiquo got out and we woke up, we had to walk along it in our 'smokings' in the rain." (No, he did not see that a ten days' interval, during which Felicity had had no word of her lover, could so long after be established.)

—"It was when we got back to Paris that the old lady arrived, and from her I understood that your cousin would neither marry him, nor tell him to go away. I swear to you that in those days he had no one he could be sure of but me. And is it not you who have taught me to stand by my friends?"

"So?"

"The old lady—I admit that by old ladies I am sure always of being loved—sent us down together to the country. There he wrote music. I have the score. To play it to you was a great reason that I came. He was to write and ask Felicity to join us. I do not know if he did. She did not come. What could I do?"

Silence. He had finished. Not so badly. Except a timetable evasion, not an event that had not actually occurred. No sign from Scylla. It exasperated him, these peoples' minds slow-working and slow response. For good or bad, who wants to wait?

But wait as long as she liked, where would she find—not contradiction, mercifully it did not need that—but his tale's amplification? A part of Boris's nature which he valued and despised could now equip him with a sense of injured innocence. A touch of caution, of finesse, warned him not to show it. With a little helpless laugh, he hid his face in his arms.

For once, Scylla made no attempt to believe him, was content to wait until whatever Errinys who was on his track should arrive and take the situation in hand. From indolence, from charity, it was easier for her to assume all men innocent, and the greatest rarity in Nature a lie. This time, without judgment, without shock or even the least pain, she admired his story and dismissed it. Dismissed too much. Said nothing. Boris understood.

At that moment they heard a shriek repeated, far-off and high-up and knew that Nick Kralin's car was threading the hill road on its second race back. And though there were now two of his fancy-women in it, he hardly seemed to drive less furiously. The inn lay a little off the highroad. Neither of them were too nice to cross and observe him from behind a hedge-rose screen. Not known for an insane driver, he showed the village no mercy. The women were packed behind him, and when the dust settled, they saw that an orange cat had been sacrificed, the white dust drinking up its blood freely.

They returned slowly, not by the road, but by diagonal field-paths that mounted the downs, to the base of the green hill earth-works above their house. When the path gave out, they attacked the hill-flank direct, glad of a lynchett to stick their toes in. By midsummer it would have been as easy to walk up glass. Before they reached the top and the sight of the sea, the wood and their house, she said:

"Don't you know us well enough to tell us the truth, without arranging it to excuse you?"

Time, place and sentence uniting one perfect want of tact. Even so, if Boris had not blistered his heel and wanted his tea, his growing unhappiness might have prostrated him. Instead irritation of body cancelled discomfort of soul. If that was all she thought of his beautiful story. . . .

A watcher from the village below would have seen two forms the distance had reduced to the size of tea-leaves, moving perpendicularly up the bare green. Had his curiosity held out, he would then have seen them stop, and the two leaves unite, but in an agitated manner, not as though joined by an embrace. A moment later, he would have seen one tea-leaf, still stationary, but waving itself about. Then suppose he had believed them to be tea-leaves, he might have said that tea-leaf A had swallowed tea-leaf B. This conclusion might have led him away from tea-leaves to the remoter speculations of human thought. The truth being that leaf B was now invisible because Boris had knocked Scylla down.

Women of her sort are not used to being hit by men. It makes them angry and not in the least afraid. She shammed dead an instant, from surprise, and then because the sky she watched under her lids seemed a most delicate and restful blue. Meanwhile, tea-leaf A would still have been seen, stationary but unquiet. The watcher might have suspected this to be a digestive process instead of an offer, shouted back, to walk away at once until it reached Starn, and never see leaf B or leaves C, D and X again. An offer it began to fulfil. For raising her arms to pillow her head, "you had better go now," Scylla had said.

The watcher from Stone End might have lost interest in leaf A returning alone, unless he had remained to see his theory contradicted by the sight of leaf B, perpendicular and on its way again alone. To collect further data, he would have had to wait for leaf A's return to the village.

This, except for the error about tea-leaves, was what Nick Kralin saw from his seat at the porch of the inn, where he had returned, having put his lady friends into the train at Starn.

He too had changed his plans. Once more he was a lusty bachelor. He had taken his dead wife's house on a short lease, and had brought down a selection of her possible successors. The house had instantly shown them out; instantly made two fine wenches loathsome to him. Once rid of them, he had to return to it alone. He had met Scylla and knew that the house across the fields was full of Felicity's kin, and that she had seen the women he had brought. He had seen the young man she had with her, and that he came of the race who carried dislike of his to its logical conclusion. He detested Scylla and everyone over at that house. What had he heard about their pet, Boris Polteratsky? He would tell them what he had heard about him; might see them turn him out.

No doubt which keys they would use, now, that to right himself over the women, he had put the house into their hands to clean. Not that it mattered. He had had time to put away something which they would look for and must not find. On his way back from Starn, at Stone End, without petrol and without garage, his engine had given out, left him neither on nor off the spot. Though the inn was kind, he was in no easy temper as he watched the tea-leaves, which had looked to him like tea-leaves on the hill.

Nor had he identified them with Scylla or with Boris, until nearly half an hour later he identified leaf A crossing a near field, on the easiest step that ever the spring-grass sprang up behind uncrushed. Already he had tried to sneer at feet so small they should have made the height unstable. It would not suit his plans for Boris to tell them that he had come back. If he saw Boris alone, he might want to hurt him. That would not do either.

He took himself off. The shed where his car had been dragged would hide him also. A small dirty window let him look out onto the village's curious green. Certain houses bordered by a white track round a patch of grass whose outline defied geometry. In whose centre, and not exactly there, there was nothing but a stone. And the grass about it and the track round the grass were a four-sided figure of peculiar shape; and the stone which, as Felix said, looked as if it had stopped there on its way to Stonehenge, by virtue of some strangeness of form, stayed in the mind as a thing out of its class. "*On no account touch this stone: yours sincerely J. Patten.*" Kralin remembered that story and Felicity reading it aloud: his disgust, impatience: the others' pleasure and Felix's staring eyes. The sticky cobwebs about the window stuck to his fingers. For an instant the Jew-about-town admitted that country life allowed for the invention of such fancies.

Boris had not yet appeared out of the lane, sunk between the curled hedges, that rose into the green at the furthest point from its stone. Waiting for him, Kralin had time to observe the houses man had built round a shape which seemed as if it had been dictated by a stone.

The place was not a period-gem like the Taverner's village over the hill. There Felicity's house was called the New House, and on the cliffs stood a Martello tower, built to discourage Napoleon, called Taverner's Folly; and there was a nasty story about that. In comparison, Stone End was a patchwork. It might be as old in parts but without unity; nor was it the english labourer who mattered there, nor the speed of the plough nor the silver fruit of the sea; not the country house nor the kingdom of the birds; not lobsters or fleeces or bees, or what goes on in the woods. Only a large, naked, pale-grey stone. There was the inn beside him, dun plaster laid over some dateless rock. With its porch and garden, it stood out, while the other houses seemed to have shrunk back. At the far end, at right angles to it, the ground descended suddenly into the valley, and a long, white rose-hung farm had chosen to follow the earth downhill. Suppose it more than one room thick, the further side must be reached by steps; while its thatch hung down and savage plants shut the small window-eyes beneath it. *"An eyebrow of flowers"*—Felicity's words he had done his best to sneer out of her.

At right angles to the farm and by the lane where he must watch for Boris, stood a narrow house made in the one century in which England had forgotten how to build. A flat roof with a parapet, a flagstaff and no flag. Blank, black windows and a basement with railings and up to the door five neat steps. A fanciless fancy. Outside the railings a laburnum hung out its branches loaded with gold rain.

Set there in protest or in alliance with the stone?

Next it a façade, between towers, a grey-stone-shell whose pierced windows let through the day from a row on the further side, and a distortion of trees and light. An ancient house, almost a ruin, shut-up. Quite in the Taverner's style. He saw above the door a splendid, glossy hand of ivy covering the shield of an extinct family. Another Felicity-flight. Why in hell had he taken her house, in her land? Here he had learned how to dislike her: how to hurt her: watched her try to get him to cancel her hurt. Calculated the time needed for her to despair. The way she had run off, first with, then later without a row with him, reminded him of animals supposed to know a cure for snake-bite. Results inconclusive in her case. Sometimes she would come back muddy, torn and red with tears. Sometimes just quite well. Occasionally—it was that he had feared and hated in her—transparent, glorified, a dew on her no cloud had condensed. What business had a woman's body, blood-driven engine for secretion and excretion, to play such tricks? Dead, she was at her tricks again, making him dance to her tune. Eyelash of flowers and a shoot of ivy closing the eyes of old fame. There were images in his mind—learned out of the cursed mythology they had sucked in with their milk, and he could never get right. Was this their secret—how to make love and put it to sleep and where to find its eyes?

He twitched with impatience. Ivy in growth is ivy, and lobster lobster, and man man. Lobster turns into man and man into lobster. *Nothing could be more mysterious.* As though God had said, "*Be Yourself*" to the whole creation: who had obeyed him. Had man? Kralin did not know and would not have cared, did not the question sometimes nag at him. Was he himself? He did not know, or if he had a self to know. In that ignorance and his assured indifference lay his satisfaction, his strength and a fear. If man's test is the attainment of biologic security, he would pass. Very comfortably established. Besides—it was when his meditation reached this that there came a look into his face no man so far has been able to name; while, whatever his shapely hands were doing, a finger lay against his increasing nose, and through the snigger which replaced his rare frank laugh, you caught a word of his secret. The reason for his reason. Which reason was—and at such moments he had the power to convince—that there was no reason; no meaning to meaning: that not only is man incapable of conceiving truth, but the truth is that there is no truth for him to conceive.

Men like that can have great fun with young women in love.

Chapter IV

At that moment tea-leaf A appeared. Not like a tea-leaf, of such distinct identity as to suggest to Kralin that here was an almost unique work of Nature and it was laughing at him. Under the laburnum tree Boris looked up, took hold of a branch and shook down a gold storm over himself. Twitched his shoulders and crossed delicately in the full sunlight towards the inn. Kralin's eyes, two almonds of grey jelly, watched him through the dim glass.

Real *bouleversement* had driven Boris back to Stone End in the direction of Starn. Starn he did not intend to reach. He had no money. Suppose he wired from there and Scylla had a black eye, they might send it. Enough to get back to Paris third class. Then his own particular "*Jésus la Caille*" might grow impatient at his perfectly genuine stock-in-trade as White Russian in distress. While if his plan came off and he managed somehow to remain in England, his little *voyou* was to have followed him as valet. While, as it turned out, on the second day he had knocked his hostess down, and was suspected of having played even more part than he had in her cousin's equivocal death. How should he have known that he would come upon them in mourning? That they would ask him questions and scrutinise his answers? That he would lose his temper and be told to go? Impenitent, the spring-walk had run the irritation out of him. Play in the valley with some setter puppies in a cottage garden had set him perfectly free, and as he ran up the hill to the village, he had commended himself to his god. Invited that god to put the affair right, and see to his quick return to the Taverners.

To give the god time to start, he sat down at ease

outside the inn. Kralin saw that he had been maladroit. For unless he waited till nightfall in the shed or Boris drank himself blind, he could not avoid meeting him. At dusk he had been promised a mechanic when the men returned from the fields. The woman at the inn had found Boris a deck chair, three cushions, lemons, a syphon and gin. Was he to walk out of the shed in full view of him and then six miles to Starn? Abandon his car? Kralin watched him sink, further and further into his ease, into sleep. Detested him for a son of the morning. Where was he going? A question that was being asked on the other side of the hill.

"Yes," said Scylla, "but I saw it coming and I fell soft. My head sang, so I lay low and looked at the sky: into the blueness of blue. Let him agitate himself. Told him to go back to Paris.... Yes, he may have got as far as Starn."

"Or," said Felix, "as Stone End. And suppose Kralin is still about?" A moment of happy contemplation followed. Two men who would be equally too much for each other. Nor did it occur to any of them that Boris need not come back, who was their offering to luck, to fate—which would probably not be accepted—their indulgence of their humour and of their love of daring, who was once also a god.

She listened: Picus was leading the birds' dusk chorus from the wood. As he crossed to the house, Felix answered, fitting words to his tune:

"And the worst of it is, we like it
We like it
We like it.
And the worst of it is . . ."

Her husband came in and stood over her like a tall bird. She ran two fingers up under the sleeve of his coat, over cool skin, over fine bones which did not match his powerful hands.

"We're waiting again—is it for Boris? Or for Kralin?"

He did not answer.

"There is no waiting for Boris," said Felix. "He's there. Suppose they've met, suppose there's been a row. Boris wouldn't come between Kralin and what he means to do."

"What is that?"

"What we're afraid of."

Nanna came in to light up. They did not know if their fear was for the coming event or for their ignorance of it.

* * * * *

By the time the evening arrived, softly and in full splendour at Stone End, Boris's god had given him no reason to transfer his faith. After the necessary rest, before he had time to get drunk, during a cat-nap, Kralin had found the shed finally intolerable; and as Boris's eyes had opened, had turned the corner of the hedgerow towards Starn. It was ten minutes later that the woman at the inn told him that the gentleman who had married Miss Felicity Taverner, who had died, had been there; and though he had been seeing after his motor car in the shed, she would not like to say where he had gone now. Boris giggled and explained that it was probably to the devil, with a picture of the sort of devil. His odd, good English worked a marvel of conviction. Nick Kralin, striding resentfully into Starn, might have turned back had he known in what fire his goose was being roasted alive. Yet suppose he had, suppose for a moment that he had found at Stone End not Boris but a miracle of grace. Suppose he had been told the story of his wife, not Boris's version but the true story, the whole story, if Boris had known it to tell. Told him with humility, with candour; suppose on the road two holes in the dust, and sharp flints marking where the boyard had knelt to the Jew. Boris might have profited by such a reversal of emotion, the situation nothing. For Kralin governed his soul by refusing to admit even immediate truth under any passionate form, to whom the soul's nakedness was no more than one of a series of masks. So Boris wasted no virtue on confessions. It ran more quickly in him unspent. His idea at the moment was that, if he owed reparation to the dead, what better could he do than prepare a nemesis for Nick Kralin? He went out and found his car, and quickly and deftly put it out of local or immediate repair. Through the open door of the shed there was no one for his witness but the stone. Then back over the hill to the house and the wood and the sea. To the people who, after all, he loved best. He told himself that he would alter the proportions of his conduct, be serviceable to them, tell them the truth. It was best so. *Entendu.* He had even paid with his last shilling for what he had drunk.

Which way home? He had had enough of the long field diagonal. By the road he might meet Kralin or might not get a lift. No. The man had seen him asleep and must have run back to Starn. Why? It was more than obvious—the man had a worse conscience than anyone else.

On the road, however, his god gave out. There was no lift. In the south of England there are few severer hills, and not even a cart overtook him. While, near the top, hungry, at nightfall, he tried an amateur's short cut. It was not a success. Crossing the stone walls, the thorned lashes that bind them cut off shreds of cloth and skin. Loose stones fell out and hit the delicate bones of his legs. On the down-crest he could not strike the green road. He had struggled up an earth-wall to the down top, at dusk, into sea and wind cries that were almost inaudible, and like the coming of another power which was to take over the world. He began to whistle piteously, and saw the sky suddenly pricked, one after the other, with cold stars. Prelude to more punishment? He lay down upon the coarse grey grasses and gave it up. He counted the stars. One had a cruel shape and there was too much night. He was a black slip patched with white under the stars, who would soon vanish.

He lay there and wept, quiet tears; until Felix stumbled over him, swore at him, embraced him; shouted to Picus that he had found him. Picus bent down over him and grinned. So they brought him home, and nothing more was said that night.

Chapter V

NEXT MORNING Felix and Scylla went over to Felicity's house. The night before they had decided among themselves that Kralin's permission to Nanna to put it in order was a free gift, that it would give them time and opportunity to go over the place for themselves. Once there they could do the only thing that had occurred to them, look for their cousin's papers, for diaries, letters which might tell them more about her death. The more they thought of it, the more the idea pleased them. It was, at least, something to do. It seemed certain also that they would find them there. They remembered that she had given up her Paris flat, sent home all its smaller contents before she had gone south to die.

They said nothing to Boris about it. They would deal with him later, after dinner; who had perhaps no more than one clear day before Kralin came back.

So the morning found Felix and Scylla alone, in a room with eight sides to it, Felicity's bedroom, the most exquisite cell in that house. Cell of a queen bee, forme where a hare had lain trembling, its octagon panelled in white wood, each wall set with a round quicksilver glass to diminish and repeat. A glass chandelier hung from the ceiling; from the wall sconce above the divan where she had slept hung a cluster of glass grapes. The fire screen was a sheet of framed glass. On a round table lacquered sea blue was a glass fish. The whole room was in terms of glass, transparency or reflection. The carpet they moved on noiselessly was sea-cool like the table, and the curtains and the cover of the low bed. There, as they knew now, love had lain waiting, lain bleeding. Her pretty things still lay about; she might appear at any instant, by any of the eight panel slips.

In one of the windows an old flawed pane distorted the country outside. Through it she might swim in, from the fair land where wolves had hunted her.

"It makes me think," said Scylla, "of a fairy-story I've forgotten, except that there was a glass room in it where a blue bird-prince lay wounded and was found by a princess. Was there ever a prince here? Did one ever sleep on the bed? Not Kralin. I think I remember it was to his room that she went."

Felix found himself composing "Those Blue Bird Blues," until he opened a window and at once let in plain bird-song and the noise of carpet-beating. Nanna was hard at it, getting ready her nursling's house—for Kralin. They had had a day to find out her secrets, if she had left them there; discover her papers, select from them, destroy them. To loose the memory of her and to preserve it, but to keep rather than to destroy.

They began with her bureau, of ivory and black wood. Open, it showed the pillar drawers of its recess, whose sides were lined with mirror very dirty and old.

"Someone has been at it before us," said Felix, and pointed to scratches round the outer lock as though made by a wire.

It was then that they began to enjoy themselves; at that point their cousin's death became a detective story of high merit and entirely their own. There in a ghost's last hiding-place, on the supposition that it would please the ghost.

"Take every paper you can find," said Scylla; "relock, and we'll read them over at the house." Felix nodded; preparing for himself a piece of wire in case of necessity also.

If he had not presumed so many secret drawers, they would have been a shorter time about it. As he tapped, she ran through the books on the shelf by the divan. Ovid on the transformations of heroes and heroines; Ronsard and Phantastes. The Moon Endureth and the Testament of Creseyde; Les Enfants Terribles. These for *livres de chevet.*

She held each out and shook them; bumped them together and no secret slip fell out, and only one bill. "For riveting one cut glass jug: 10/6." Unreceipted. Then Felix found out that one glass wall of the cabinet's interior was made to slip aside, and behind it there was a door to which there was no key. With his wire he went to ground with it until it seemed that most of a large young man was disappearing into the cabinet's recess. Scylla found the key in the standish, fastened to seven blue slips off a jay's wing, tied in a fan. It was empty. So was every other drawer—of letters; but neither of them would admit discouragement.

"Put everything we've found on the table," said her brother, "and see what they tell us." So Scylla arranged them: the jay-feather posy, a handful of red rose leaves, paper dry; a ring of grey jade, two anonymous keys, a bundle of orange sticks, a rouge pot, a box of nibs, four french stamps, a bar of green sealing-wax, a bar of black; one drawing pin; a sock of the gayest pattern and the softest wool trodden into huge holes. Three curtain rings, an amber cigarette-holder, once a thin gold trumpet, now in half, with a tooth-bitten hole at its mouth. Half a french card-pack, a domino, a cribbage-peg, a spellican, a draught piece, two chess men and a halfpenny to play shove ha'penny. A pin, a safety-pin, a needle, a darning-needle. A ball, a reel, a card, a skein, of wool, of silk, of cotton. A coat button, a trouser button, a shirt button, a boot button; made of bone, of brass, of shell, of wood. Pinned together in a colour-sequence, a green rag of cloth, of linen, of velvet, of muslin, of canvas, of lawn. Inside the blue-bound blotter there was a sheaf of clipped papers. Hope for a moment. Then, a recipe for iced oranges, for corn-beef hash, for rouge; for and against constipation, weight, sleep; a french *ordonnance* for what sickness they could not determine. "Death probably," said Felix, and laughed unhappily. Nine gilt and five china beads, two jet beads, eleven silver beads, seven marble beads, fourteen ivory beads, eighty-seven glass beads, seventeen carnelian beads, thirty-one coral beads, two beads of wood. A box of tonquin beans of repellant similarity and dissimilarity.

"I shall go mad," said Felix. Scylla poured the crystal beads into the pocket of her coat.

"These may as well go back with us," she said.

* * * * *

Over the hill also nothing that had been expected happened. While the brother and sister were drawing blank at the house, Picus had gone over prepared to meet Kralin and to cope with him; and there found that he had no more than some mislaid washing to deal with and a discontented Boris. From the woman at the inn they heard of the abandoned car and the retreat on Starn, that the car had been dragged away by a lorry and nothing more seen of the gentleman who had been Miss Felicity's husband. After an hour or so of silent male idling, the butcher carried them back, with the washing and such news as there was, over the hill.

Nor until late that night did they ask Boris for his story, the true truth of what he had done, of what he knew. Enough that even he had learned that lies were not the only specific, that truth has, not only its virtues but its utilities; that by supplying it, he would bless, not only them but himself. While Boris also was curious, wanted to know more, if only that his share would be forgotten in the enormities disclosed—preferably of Nick Kralin.

He knew that they had not found what they wanted in Felicity's house, a house now aired and opened, polished and put away for others' use. They sat together, as before, in their own house, in the long dining-room, after dinner again and lit by candles and wood. They were waiting for Boris to begin, who began by bolting an interesting hare. He asked them what they would say if he told them that Kralin was a Red agent. There was a chorus of reluctant denial. His father had been a Christian kind of anarchist; he had been naturalised; his son did not know one kind of politics from another. Then Scylla stopped:

"Boris does not mean that," she said.

Boris saw that he must make an effort, drag a difficult meaning out of his instincts, his blind flair for the curious number of beans which in this case made five. Knowledge in one *"Born to see strange sights, Things invisible."* They spoke in English for the old nurse to hear.

"You do not think much of my morality, yet you do not doubt of my affection for you. And it is that which has protected our relations with each other." Unqualified assent to this. —"Nor does it annoy you that part of my tenderness is based on what I call old-fashioned in your quality. It was some time before I learned that it was not a thing *demodée*—it was the great thing you taught me—that what you follow is not old or new, of the last century or the next, that it is a virtue not affected by fashion. —I am still often angry when you make me appear without it. But at least I salute it in you—"

His grin saved them from embarrassment. While experience assured them that they would not be troubled long with Boris's pieties.

—"So you will not be angry when I compare even the worst things I have done with greater wickedness; with people we know even—"

Comparisons were being made hastily; a series recalled of Boris's appalling acts. Which were forgiven him. Why? Because of some power of love that he had? Partly. They gave it up. Anyhow, he had been forced into an admission of virtue.

"Carry on," they said. He went on:

"There is a kind of ambience around us here—or wherever you are—that I cannot explain. As if we were all inside a magic ring. You do not ask me to change myself, yet, it seems that I am changed—"

They agreed. Besides "ambience" had it. Race apart,

class apart, tastes apart, he was their own kind. Yet Boris was a bad man.

He sat back, the russian boy, and for the first time they saw an air of power about him.

"Think of the world, my friends, that is, outside our world. For, living here, nature repeats to you what you are yourselves. There are worlds enough, but one that is outside you, outside this place, killed your cousin, Felicity. A world that is like Nick Kralin."

"We know that, but not what it is. Go on."

"No, you do not know what it is—or the nature, the taste of it. What your cousin learned when she spoke of the 'grey thing.'"

"We know enough to recognise it when we meet it. And keep clear. It is *not* like anything in her mother or in Adrian."

"'Le Kralinism,' I have called it. Like pockets of poisoned air, it is everywhere now. And the time has come when you have not been able to ignore it—" Scylla said slowly:

"When you called Kralin a Red agent, I take it you did not mean propaganda."

"I mean propaganda of what he is. Of 'le Kralinism.'"

(How did Boris live when he was away from them? Slept all day and ran about Paris all night. And ran into—?)

"Now I will tell you what really happened in Paris. I went out many nights—apart from the escapade of which I told you—with them both. There I saw what they did not see—people hating that they should love."

"People generally do," said Scylla.

"Yes, but it was more than that. I do not know how to explain. It is active. People practising how to kill what they do not like. Their ill-will *works*. And among certain people I know of in Paris, they know how to *make* it work. This they do for fun, or under some compulsion; or an order.

How can I convince you? It was as if it had been decided on that she was to be crucified.

—"You will want to ask questions, and I should have to tell you stories all night to answer them. Different stories, like beads strung on one thread. But they did it. She is dead—not the only one who is dead. And he I told you of has found a café in Toulon where there is a drink that kills. He sits and stares at the stale water of the harbour. Sometimes when he is drunk he sees her, coming lightly across where the sun pours on the white stones. Then he plays a grand drunk game that he is sober. —It is not a new story. Old as can be. Only now no one seems to see any reason why it should not happen like that. There is no effective protest. Not from her friends. Not from her brother. A little from me, perhaps, and my conduct left to be desired. And if there are people to protest against it, they have only old reasons in a dull way. Or, if they feel passionately, they have not skill or wit to put power into their passion. Or else they are so alone and unhelped that they die of pure pain. It was not that Felicity killed herself. To me she had been killed already. (You say that she was driving the car alone. If it had not been like that the chauffeur might have been made to do it. That is not impossible.) Only your cousin was composed of imagination as well as love. She had seen 'le Kralinism' naked. Had she not had it to sleep with, a young wife?

—"Why do you all pretend that you are not crying? Be angry with me. Ask me why I played Kralin's game, and how. We did run away together, T'chiquo and I. As I told you, Scylla. But that did not matter. Men run away like that for their amusements. I knew that she was wise enough to let us run and laugh at that. But though I did not know that he did not write to her, I knew that 'le Kralinism' had bitten into him, and I did nothing. I, who knew enough to know that they were the condemned and that the grey web had been thrown over them. I let myself be its instrument. I suppose if I had Judas's sensibility I would hang myself. But again it is true that at the time I did not know how much I knew."

Nanna was sitting with them, as she often did. To the torrent of hard clear words a listener might have heard an accompaniment of tears, four cryings, from two women and two men. The words stopped; the crying went on. What is more curious than tears? A sensation in the mind, one spot of consciousness illuminated, a vibration there like a plucked string, plucked and replucked. A storm of blindness and one point of intolerable light. The result in each case a trickle of warm salt water, attended quickly by the ridiculous—a leak sprung from the nose. The salt-flood brings temporary relief. The images that formed in the tension before it fade. As the pictures in their minds—Aphrodite-in-hiding in a room with eight walls, or a ghost on light-sandalled feet crossing sun-white harbour stones.

Meanwhile a number of hands shuffled and groped for handkerchiefs. Boris had his arms round Nanna, whose old servant's patience mourned less openly than they the child she had nursed.

It then occurred to them all that though Boris had been illuminating and even truthful—that is to say a miracle had been thrown in—they did not know very much more about what had actually happened. Scylla said:

"What was the real name of this man she loved?" He told them. Picus whistled, his bird call, Mozart-whistler through the impediment of a last sob.

"He ought to have been what she wanted if she could have got rid of Kralin."

"Once you begin to find out things," said Felix faintly, "there is no end to the things you begin to find out. But if he's gone to pot, he won't be able to help us."

A tranquillity of suffering fell upon them. Outside the fair night hung like a winged face over the sea.

* * * * *

Next morning, the farm boy who brought the milk told Nanna that the gentleman who had been Miss Felicity's husband had come back to live in her house. This was quick work. It had all been quick work. One day Boris had arrived, and on the next Kralin had come and Boris nearly gone; and on the same evening Kralin had been driven away and Boris returned. Next day there had been no Kralin, and the house open to them. The day after, Kralin was back, and the house closed to them for ever.

They had not examined the assumption that in Felicity's house there was something for them to discover, for them to preserve. Something which Kralin had come to destroy or put to his own use. After Boris's night-speech, they were impatient to know more, and did not know what more would come their way, exasperated at a time which seemed to crawl between intervals of violence.

Chapter VI

IN THE SAME part of the country, ten miles inland, north of the sea and the Taverner houses, over their hill and the long valley which held Stone End and Starn at its mouth—north of Starn hills and the great heath, a large blue Daimler, reeking of prosperity, drew up before a house. A house, this time, not of grey stone, but of stucco, with sashed windows and doric candle pillars; set with its lawn and its gravel sweep in a ring of polished evergreens, laurel and rhododendron, pointed with arbutus and laurustinus. All dark, shiny and green, clipped and banked with firs, a melancholy place and neat. Adrian Taverner sniffed at it. His mother reasoned with him:

"It isn't for long," she said, "and it's as well for us to be down here. You said so yourself."

Her son said it was like a public lavatory run away into the country for a treat. His mother—Scylla's Aunt Julia, mother of Felicity Taverner lately dead, evaded this. A country-woman by instinct, what she missed was the spring green. Inside the house, she retired to organise it with her cook and her London servants; while Adrian toured the rooms for victorian relics, of which there were many, and some very modish indeed.

He was like his cousin, Felix Taverner, and he was not like. That is to say, they had the same looks and did the same things—the town things—but on a different rhythm. He was not at all like Scylla and detested her, analysed his dislike for her in terms at once gross and affected—until it was pointed out to him that even such reactions were a symptom, and so remained in a dumb dislike at the thought or the presence of her. While Scylla, who, except in relation to Felicity had forgotten all about him, did not know that he was not able to forget her.

The presence of the mother and the son in the far south was sudden, and their affair a delicate one. The younger Taverners did not quite realise yet, nor Picus Tracy, that, on a pretence of wishing to be again where he and his wife had lived on their marriage, Kralin had rented the house from Adrian for some months. Nor anything of the proposal he had made them, once the agreement had been signed, that he proposed to stay on there indefinitely, to buy the house from them, refusing to take their first "No" for an answer. In fact it seemed to these Taverners that there would be no getting rid of him. Aware that there must be something behind this, they had come down to negotiate. Felicity's small house was a treasure, set by itself in a patchwork of what was left of their once wide estate. If Kralin would pay high, it might be worth their while to part with it. For this it was necessary to nurse Kralin, court him, and eventually to intimidate him, if possible. They had none of Boris's magical estimate of him, nor did they understand him. They had come down to a house they had taken, not too near and not too far, to keep an eye on him and on a possibly profitable deal. It was a natural occupation for both mother and son, a tribal hunting for a stock by no means played out, used to its own way and to war, and to getting what it wanted out of war.

Kralin was perfectly aware of their intentions, which were as strictly dishonourable as his own. Mrs. Taverner had called on him after Felicity's death, at the beginning of his insistence about the house, and arch, stately and sweet, had made it clear that he was still one of the family. Still one? More perhaps than he had been before. A common sorrow united them; which, a little later in the interview, began to appear quite openly as a joint relief. Even Kralin had been surprised before he smiled, giving rein for once to his faculty for appreciation. He had taken his time, secured his tenancy, had not haggled over rent or committed himself as to the ultimate price, and had only just taken possession of the house again. Now a further idea had come over him, a "fancy chaste and noble" to surprise his mother-in-law. Though he, in his turn, was ignorant that they had taken the dower house at Pharrs to settle the matter with him once and for all.

But for his car's mysterious breakdown at Stone End—Boris's fun—it seemed to Kralin that so far nothing undue had happened. It had been tiresome to find the cousins at their house and have to accept their help; but before he had let them in, he had done what he had to do there. The young women had been a gesture. He had sent them back. The russian boy he had dismissed as an embarrassment, possibly of psychopathic origin; one he would examine later should he meet him, so that it should not trouble him again. He did not see him as a possible enemy or as a possible friend of his dead wife. On whom he had a perfect revenge to consummate. On reflection it seemed that it was just as well for her cousins to be there. There might be an experiment to be tried out on them also.

Efficiently he controlled himself. Not with pleasure, to whom neither wife nor kinsfolk had significance, nor the ancient land nor the spring. No meaning and no delight that he must not immediately destroy by an examination which, though he called it scientific, was actually obscene. This was part of the alchemy he had, a curious formula for the philosopher's stone.

So the next days found them all settled, at the points of a tall triangle, its apex in the north with old Mrs. Taverner and her son; ten miles separating it from its narrow base, the mile and a half of valley between the two Taverner houses, set in their trees upon the sun-worked bases of the chalk downs, the sea laid out before them.

Three days passed at the house in the wood, days of recovery, of silence about their dead cousin, of Boris's pranks. Ten watchful eyes were kept on the other house.

Nanna, of course, had sources of information denied to them. It was clear, for instance, that Kralin must be there alone, or he would have taken in more milk. Some relics of his father's anarchist snobbery had brought him there servantless, and even prevented him asking for village help. This had annoyed the archaic settlement which lay below the house. Women who had known Miss Felicity and had worked for her wanted to know what he meant by it, wanted to see how he was bearing it, and food for speculation had been stopped at its source. After the fifth day, however, Nanna, troubled for the exquisite order she had left, was relieved when he sent for a woman to come in every day; insisting, and this was taken to show proper feeling, that she should be someone who had served his wife.

"Mrs. Cobb," said Nanna, "and she's no slattern, but a terrible one for gossip."

There was little gossip that came across. He had some shocking pictures hung up, slept in the room where his lady had been; and when he wrote, threw ink about on the carpet. Said he didn't mind what he ate, took no pleasure in his meals and was mighty particular what you did. Sober a gentleman as she'd met, but "it didn't seem to do him any good, what he'd take and what he'd not take."

"Just Kralin," said the Taverners, "going on as he used to do."

So two more days passed, while much was digested and nothing said. They had learned silence, the brother and the sister, to whom silence did not come naturally, whose nature was expressed in terms of enthusiasm and passion; to whom silence had once meant suffering, who had wanted daylight everywhere. Daylight and draughts, whose pleasure it was to ride on a flood tide. Too much silence imposed from without could make them ill, Felix especially; and Picus's capacity for reserve troubled his wife to distraction. It was not until they had found out that silence is a most effective part of courage that they endured it and practised it.

For Boris, the effort he had made to satisfy them was quite enough to be going on with. He did not actually resent what they had imposed on him, no more than a man might who had been baptised against his better judgment into a new faith. And it was their turn now to be sympathetic. He took Felix for long walks, and told him about the perplexities he had left behind in Paris; to which the very young man gave ideal solutions which could not possibly be put into use. Felix was getting an education in how not to live, and how, in spite of it all, a great number of people do live. A lesson, too, in the destruction of an order of society, which happened to have earned to be destroyed. A lesson also in the slav temperament, in folk-movement, an acquaintance uncannily sharp for one at second-hand. And it was the measure of Felix's quality and his progress in virtue that the sharing of Boris's saga steadied him, become now so far less petulant than he had been before his cousin's death. So much could be learned from Boris, and there was one thing that coloured all the rest, an experience which came with a colour and tang to it like poetry, unexpectedly, in little shocks. It was this strangeness, this poet's quality in him, that lay at the bottom of their loyalty to Boris, who set no great value on the quality—or even the fact—of his love.

It was the sixth day, and the brother and sister were beginning to say out loud that it was time for something to happen again, when Boris went out for a walk by himself. He did not return to tea, he did not return to dinner. They began to speculate, but incorrectly, on what had happened to him.

Many hours before, Boris had been seen by other people, walking under a lattice of air green and leaf green, and air and leaf gold, up an avenue of old trees in young leaf, that led to a celebrated ruin outside Starn. Mrs. Taverner had gone over with Adrian to pay it her annual visit of inspection and respect; pilgrimage to a shrine, of a hunter to his totem, there was a ritual quality about these visits, very pleasing because proper to her. Adrian had gone with her, principally in order that she should not play. She could not endure it not to have him with her, but she would have liked to be allowed to enjoy herself. If Adrian sulked, she would return, unhappy; but occasionally he would break down and be gracious. Then they were really happy, the mother and the son. So, on this as on all occasions, she kept an old weather-eye open for anything that might prove a distraction for him.

A great deal about Adrian Taverner—though finally inexplicable and as mysterious as anything else, could be indicated in known terms by saying that he was one of the numberless young men who can neither live with their mothers nor without them. And Mrs. Taverner, innocent of psychology and avid of power, was not averse to this; too ignorant to understand its dangers, even when she suffered by them, which she often did. Or was it ignorance? Is there not a worse answer than that? Anyhow, two people were unhappy, who, not spiritless or ungifted, had a capacity for their kind of joy; two people often wounded the other, who might have blessed. Two people had each worn the other out of his proper shape, become like two trees interlocked, each of a different kind, neither strong enough to strangle the other.

So, that day, as always, the mother was on the look-out for a diversion for her son which would leave her to enjoy Starn's ruins, and a recent discovery after a fall of masonry of coins and bones. While it was a point of Adrian's honour to look a gift distraction in the mouth, a petulance which had kept him young, but the wrong kind of young; which made "old boy," if any of his friends had been vulgar enough to call him that, unpleasantly apt. Up to that time, he had criticised his way through the world, finding fault with things with which he was only too akin, and which his mother still loved, was wise enough to love still, but not for want of being told, in season and out, of their worthlessness, and how all true judgment consists in cutting away your own roots. Yet it is dangerous to throw away your mana-objects, let alone exhaust your personal mana. It is much more fatal than throwing away your tabus. Adrian thought that he had disembarrassed himself of mana-object and taboo, which was not true; and made a very troubled creature of him, who was making a wilderness of his life, and had too much wits to call it peace.

So Mrs. Taverner, who wanted her tea and was not certain if she would be allowed to have it, was getting desperate. They had gone back to their car and were sitting in it, beginning to argue, when she saw a male creature, moving between the trees, on a step which seemed to have sprung down to earth out of the sky.

"Look at that young man," she said, trying to distract her son, "how well he walks." Adding to his furious annoyance a quotation to the effect that he trod some kind of heather "like a buck in spring," and "looked like a lance" held firmly over the left shoulder. This would have ruined it, if Adrian had not seen him too, wondered what a body so strange and so desirable was doing there. He saw the little chalk-pale head with its close black curls, the eyes which were clear green, smudged on the under socket, the tartar-pitched cheek-bones, the elegant height, the candid smile, the wolf-flash of the teeth—took it all in. As Boris took them all in, did not hesitate a second, came up to the car and asked the way to the ruins in French.

Five minutes later, Mrs. Taverner drove away thankfully to her tea, leaving Adrian to take the young man round; who, left to himself with a stranger, explained with science and enthusiasm the antiquities of his native land.

An hour later, he was standing Boris a drink at Starn, and had heard where he came from and who he was.

Adrian and his mother's war against Kralin was barely open yet, nor had they reckoned on the Taverner cousins, whom they rarely saw. It might be as well not to discount them, and for that to encourage this young man. So thought Mrs. Taverner, but Adrian was Felix's cousin, a rather older Felix, with a mother, and some minute sap-gland left out of him. Boris amused and interested him. Boris was his cousins' friend. It might be amusing to supplant those cousins. More disillusioned than they and with more imagination, Boris, for his part, took Adrian's measure at a glance.

"The best thing for us to do," said Mrs. Taverner to Boris, "is to run you home with us to dinner, and then take you back to the top of your hill. There is no road to the house, and this car is too heavy for the turf; but you can find your way, can't you, on a clear night?"

Boris was enchanted. These people, so much more of the world he had lost than their cousins, went to his senses, and even at the start to his wits. Babbling with appreciation, spilling his charm out before them, he went back with them to the white house in the dark bushes. Out of the spring.

There he found everything that he understood as the *comme il faut.* Not of novelty, but of memory. This was a sober variation of how life ought to be lived. Here was the right formality, just enough. There was none at the Taverners, who were poor, who hurried over ritual through poverty, ritual not *décor,* because they were poor, because their essential attention was on other things, learning and thinking, pre-occupations with sport and nature and art. They wanted to live and know. These people wanted nothing so exhausting. It escaped Boris's notice that they were much less happy people, let alone less good. Or even agreeable. And Adrian, who had got Boris taped also, was elaborately free with drinks. In fact, it practically escaped his notice that these two were the mother and brother of Felicity Taverner, as he made himself handsome at Adrian's dressing-table, and ran downstairs to say charming things to his mother. He did it so well that he wished her kinsmen could see him. It was that which recalled them to his attention, made him wonder why he was not feeling quite so happy; until he began to remember too much, and packed his thoughts away, burying them on a system of his own with all things he resented. For he did resent it, and very sharply, that it might, in the future, be disloyal for him to be there.

At dinner Mrs. Taverner very properly set herself to find out what she wanted to know, which was, principally, the relations between her niece and nephew and Nick Kralin. How much Boris was in their confidence; how much he would talk. Now it is true about human beings that, with very few exceptions, when they are under an obligation, it gives them pleasure to convey something to the discredit of their benefactors. (It is part of the larger question that "*la mediocrité croit toujours se grandir en rebaissant la mérite.*") Boris was too bad a character quite for mediocrity, but the instinct was there; and he did not quite understand Mrs. Taverner's traps. Or, if he did, he did not care. If he excused himself, it was to say that there was no harm in seeing all round a question, and useful for Scylla to have a friend in the enemy's camp. In the end Mrs. Taverner gathered: that they were at civil daggers drawn with Nick Kralin, daggers which were not likely to return to their sheaths: that Scylla had her daughter's crystal beads: that none of them had been able to find any papers of hers, though they had been anxious about them, had even looked for them on their own responsibility. (Kralin, she remembered, seemed to have been curious there also.) That Felix had been in love with his cousin and knew something—here Boris was elaborately vague—to Adrian's discredit with regard to his sister. It did not disconcert the old woman in the least, roused her instincts, sharpened her appetite for battle. She was delighted with Boris, having no experience of his type. Adrian liked and despised him, who saw nothing but what was amusing or ignoble in any man.

It was a happy young man, not in the least bit thoughtful, who plunged back under the bright stars, over the hill.

No one had waited up for him, but doors are not locked at night in that country. There was a tray laid with food. He was eating a little of it, busy with pleasures past and pleasures to come, when he heard steps on the stairs. Felix came down, and when he heard what Boris had been doing, he showed interest, no pleasure whatever, developing into excitement; and Boris, who had not his story arranged, felt at a loss, most unfairly on the defensive and misunderstood. It seemed to do no good to repeat that Adrian Taverner was a "*charmant garçon,*" and his mother a "*grande dame véritable.*" It did not please. The first was a lie, the second an impertinence. He had enough sense to retreat to bed, and Felix not to rouse the house. The youngest Taverner lay awake, listening to the passion-laden stirring of the Sacred Wood, intelligible, unintelligible, their lives' tune:

Wind thou art blind,
Yet still thou wanderest the lily-seed to find.

Chapter VII

S*upreme is the genius loci.*" Next morning Boris awoke to a world that was the whole of such comfort and salvation as he had known since he became a man. Pure, perfect and kind, "*mysterious, beautiful.*" From the instant of waking, it came into his room, displayed itself to him. And he felt at once, as was most natural, that he wanted nothing of the sort. He wanted, he wanted—what he wanted was an indefinite saturation in the life of old Mrs. Taverner and her son. Ten years of repression had been loosed in one evening. This place, for all its utter detachment, appeared to his mind as something that had its eye on him. And hadn't his host an axe to grind, if it was only about his soul? Then he remembered that he had an appointment that day with Adrian Taverner in Starn.

It was because of the *genius loci* that at breakfast he lied about that; told a transparent tale about an american tourist he had also met; answered their questions without intelligence; made them, though he did not see it, blush for him. Then he tried to pick a light quarrel which would hurt them, and flung out of the house on his ten mile walk to the enemy's camp.

"Good riddance," said Felix. And then—"we're too sensitive by half."

"We are," said his sister. "Let's use it. Why have those two got him so cheap?" Picus said:

"What did you suppose he'd do?" And when pressed began to tell them in verse about persons who

> "*share the feast and view deceased, immaculate,*
> *well-bred,*

Who question all and leave the hall with fragments of the dead."

"If it wasn't us," said Felix, "what would you say had happened?"

It became suddenly easier at this, easier to look at, and then apparent that Mrs. Taverner must have come down, for reasons as yet unknown, to keep an eye on Kralin. While what Boris had told them and what he had not told them, instead of bewildering, helped, and cautious surmise became a delight. Once less personal, the affair became clearer, and once clearer, amusing. They had stepped out of the circle of Boris's power, who had often been prisoned in it, for fine reasons as well as foolish. The trick of detachment worked its old miracle; they were no longer angry with him; understood the repression and the reaction. Until they felt so cheerful about it that Felix suggested that they should go over and call on Nick Kralin.

* * * * *

Kralin lay on Felicity Taverner's bed, on his back on the sea-blue cover, stiff with silver threads. Not as a young man lies and relaxes or waits with impatience. He was not at ease or attentive for who should come to him there. About the room his gear overlaid his dead wife's, properties of a man whose interests were all cerebral, in the abstractions we have made for our convenience out of life. Formulæ about things, means for discussing them, not ways even for acting on them directly. There were books on psychology, but principally on the oddities of human behaviour and the curiosities of sex, and what young children may be thinking about. Books of theory like the "Decay of the West." There was a typewriter, a row of pipes and a pair of leather slippers, very worn and strong, and a dressing-gown of undyed wool. The man's touch; yet it seemed forced. A piece of protective disguise? But Kralin was in no way effeminate. It was perhaps that his things wore an air of openness, of un-secrecy, who was neither an open nor an innocent man. The illusion of candour was everywhere, flannel pyjamas sticking out from under the blue bolster, and seven steel razors which Felicity had given him in a shagreen case. And he would apologise for its lovely lacquer, in which any man would have been delighted; which he appreciated as much as any man. So he superimposed himself upon the eight-walled room, roughly against its delicacies, not put away but pushed back, and somehow accentuated. Books of ferocious reasoning, pipe-dottel and mud from heavy shoes. While there hung along the walls a series of etching by Rops, rather extreme examples of the specialities of that master, beautifully framed; an evidence of correct taste and sufficient wealth. While, as though wax had been poured and set over it, his attractive body was thickening. No more than that, and not evenly, round the waist and thighs and lower part of the cheeks, ageing the mouth, and filling out the thought-furrow which had divided the forehead between the eyes in youth. Lying-down, he had the air of a content man who did not relish his peace; a thoughtful man who expected no solution from thought; a chaste man from choice, whom the choice irritated; a sensitive man who wounded his own sensibility in order to display a stoicism he did not consider in any way admirable or necessary. A voluptuous man who could not yield himself to pleasure; a cruel man who could be exceedingly kind—to cats or people, without caring the least for either people or cats. A man who would say "no" on instinct, and if forced into saying "yes"—and to his own advantage, would deny the profit. A man who, though conventionally respectful of other men's freedom, had a pleasure, the only pleasure which ran in him too strong to be denied, to thwart it, to see its not-fulfilment, to bring it to his Nothing. Again, a man so indifferent to moral interests that men's acts seemed to him no more than arrangements, pieces on a board without even the significance of a game or a technique; to be judged, if they could be judged, without even the aesthetic excuse, like the formal arrangements of a work of art. Yet, with his impeccable taste, he had no delight in art. With health and wits, intelligence, security, learning and his significant luck, he had no delight in anything. In one thing alone he took pleasure, in the desert which can be made and is called peace. Into that he poured his sensuality, his creative desire, so that, where there had been a garden, there should be a solitude—with a few bones about. This he admitted to himself, without an attempt either to justify or to condemn, who had disciplined himself out of elation. Who felt no remorse. Who had no belief in discipline. Or fear of the elation he denied to himself.

Because there was nothing vulgar about him, there had grown in him a dry terrible power. Awful, it had mounted and spread, fused between his pairs of opposites. It was his formula of Not-Being which prevented that: Not-Being, Un-Meaning, Un-Doing, not with war or fury, but—find the linch-pin, the key-stone. Take it out softly and the arch will crumble, the wheel fall out. Nodens, God of the Abyss.

It was no common spite that had brought him south to a house he did not want. In a cheap cardboard attaché case beside him were his wife's papers, whose finding had made the place essential to him from the start; which he had found in the first hours of his arrival—but not in her bureau, which had cost him as well as Felix some trouble; before he had seen Scylla or Boris. So abstract was his imagination, that it had hardly occurred to him that they would try to keep her papers from him, what it meant to them to have been fore-stalled, and by him. Yet he had fore-stalled them knowingly. In the same way, there was no richness of satisfaction in his un-making and superimposing upon his dead wife's room. Nor was it in the least unintentional. It was the appropriate, the necessary undoing of what had been made beautiful, of what had been made out of love, for love. A god could not have acted more in accordance with its divine will; only a demon could have taken less delight.

To anyone else on earth it would seem incomprehensible that there was no raw revenge in what he was about to do, in what he had come to the house in the south to ascertain and to act upon. The situation he saw before him was full of the abstract measure of perfection his nature demanded. He would win on the swings and on the roundabouts—with the joy of negotiation for a valuable piece of property thrown in. One of the chemically pure pleasures that he permitted to himself.

He got up whistling, serene in his evil version of the magical secret, his poise of a winged worm hovering over a world displaying itself in antitheses, as Felix came to the door.

Chapter VIII

AFTER THE MORNING conversation Felix had gone over to visit him alone, across the valley, spring-hot and noisy with life. It had rained in the night, and the morning was one when the spring comes whiffling, and the underground, up-stem, down-leaf race is audible almost to sight and ear, and wholly to some nerve which is unconnected with ear or eye. That unheard sound is strange, a continuous cry or like the exultation of some bird of sustained song; like a deep breath or a shout that never stops, and of an intensity which would be unbearable if we were ever fully aware of it. Felix was too old and not old enough to understand how in order to be part of it he must relax and give himself to it again. While his senses enjoyed it, piece by piece, and all his vigorous body, his spirit was in a fret, about Felicity and Boris and his aunt and the man he was going to see, and what he must say, and what he must find out and what he might find out.

Kralin opened the door and received him very pleasantly. (It was one of the Taverner simplicities that they warmed to friendliness.) He did not take him into Felicity's room, told him to thank Scylla, and that Nanna had left the place in flawless order and gave him a pound note for her. Then he asked him if he had seen his aunt yet, and admitted that it mitigated his widowhood to be in his late wife's house. Told Felix that he intended to settle there, though there might be difficulties with his mother-in-law, suggesting that in his dealings with the country people he would need help. Also how he wished to restore the garden, and not raise the ghost of Felicity with geraniums and lobelias, which as a Londoner was as far as his vocabulary, if not his imagination, went.

While Felix, quite politely, showed perfectly that he disliked and distrusted him, that he had come over to find out anything that he could to his discredit and was not clever enough either to succeed or to hide his intention. Knew his own awkwardness and stumbled over it. We all know these painful dislocations. Then Kralin played-up and was a little shy too, until Felix began suddenly to feel—not sick, but uneasy and strange, as though nerves in him were being uncovered, which once exposed would hurt horribly, with a new pain, go on hurting all the rest of his life with a pain that had not been felt before. There would be a new agony let loose in the world. This was a new agony being let loose in the world. This *was* all nonsense. Then, that he must get away very quickly.

Kralin did not attempt to keep him, but faintly smiling saw him to the door.

When Felix had turned down the lane, out of sight of the house, he began to run, forcing himself—or being forced—beyond his pace, who was built for long-distance, not sprinting. But what he wanted was wings.

Winded, he pulled up. He was out in the open valley, on the path across it that led back to his house. He had run through a primrose-sown lane under immense oaks all in freshest leaf, out onto the new-bladed turf under the downs. Straight through mild cows and sheep who stared and scattered, through a copse in whose heart flowed a sheet of wild mustard, whose scent is that of gold, if gold were alive, or flame, if flame were not a hurried, eating thing. He had snatched extra breaths of it, but it had not stopped him, driven by the storm of an unexperienced fear. He was not now on a spear-bright square, where later the corn would set to partners with the wind. All his life he had known that long cornfield, the years when his mouth had been level with its ears, the years he had risen over it, foot by foot, which in harvest now stood to his waist. He knew it, red and purple under plough and harrow, gull-pecked and shadowed. He knew it stripped and emptied and gathered together into high bowed assemblies of itself. Then the cornfield held him, as tree and flower had not been able to do; made him wait for an instant. He crossed it, slowing down in spirit.

Once home again, he explained his failure, which they had expected, for which they were prepared; then tried to explain his fear; and they were not surprised at that. For the first, Kralin would see through them anyhow (even if there were nothing to see through); while the danger a year or so before would have been to Felix's self-esteem, against whose wounds he would have re-acted atrociously. But Felix was changing, what old guardians of youth called "hardening-out." By contact with the world, by quiet out of it—which was making his land endurable to him again, and more than endurable, blessed—he was beginning to find his own measure for life. He was saying:

"I spilt the beans—so far as showing our estimate of him. I couldn't help it. Then I found I had to run away and I ran. I found I knew suddenly what Felicity knew about the 'grey thing.' Not what it *is*. But I shall. We all shall." Then, more soberly: "What is it in that man that turns you up?"

"What we've got to find out, for it's what killed Felicity. And it will do the same to every felicity it finds. *C'est son métier.*"

"It had a shot at me to-day, whatever it is. It comes on you suddenly. And on top it was comic. With his books on the poet's suppressed wishes and how the complex sees it through." It occurred to them that Boris, who had hardly heard of fashionable psychology, nor the joke-screen we keep between it and ourselves, had been able to say more interesting things about it than they had. So Kralin represented a new variety of man, did he, and with aims that were essentially destructive? No life. Un-Doing, Not-Making. Not a child of wrath and tempest and resurrection, but oblique and gentle, so that impulse should fail like a falling leaf, and will do no more steering. Something like that. And not to serve his own turn even, though it should do so, it must. Man cannot detach himself so easily from his own will. They were in very queer country. *Childe Roland to the Dark Tower Came.* In the tower was an evil will that was also not-will, and because it *was* will, will and imagination and able to look steadily at antitheses, exceedingly strong.

"It was as though," said Felix, "a little white worm living inside his heart, poked out its head at me. That amused him politely, and I ran. And I didn't get my wits back till I was lost again, outside in the wind and the sun."

"But," said Picus, "Boris will want to know why Adrian should consent to sell him the house and have him down here at all."

* * * * *

It happened that Boris was asking this, as he lunched with Adrian at Starn.

"Have the house?" said Adrian. "Not unless he likes to pay three times what it is worth. That's why we're down here. He says he hates dealing through lawyers in a family matter, and my mother imagines that he has something up his sleeve. Or else that he wants to keep in with us, and we may make a good deal of money out of that simple ambition." He noticed that the last didn't satisfy Boris, who was saying: "Have it your own way" to himself; who for all his avid need of Adrian, thought him stupid.

It was then that Adrian gave him a message from his mother to take over the hills; how she had hardly seen Scylla since her marriage, and could she come over to their house for lunch, and would they ask Kralin? She would write to him, of course, but if they could all meet there, she had some business to discuss.

A message Boris gave them late that night, very pleased with himself and only a little discontented that they did not seem discontented with him.

"Have them all over at once. Find out what's up. If Kralin gets the house, we can settle down and watch him." At the back of Scylla's mind was a belief that the wild serene land would be too much for him, either change him or drive him away. Felix's mind ran on strange visitors who might come there—a touch of "Sapper" sophisticated, not observed, and when noticed, repudiated with horror. Until he laughed at himself.

Picus Tracy went down to the shore and repaired a boat, until the smack, smack of the short sea and the smell of tar did something to him, what the use of his hands and the stilling of his senses also helped to do, making him aware in another version of the way his wife was aware, of the turn of the event. The "awareness" always came one way, when, unless he took care to correct it, such things as "right" and "left," "before" and "after" became interchangeable, and he would say "yesterday" when he meant "to-morrow," and it was as if there was no difference between them. Confusing for others, but all right for him, because he acted as though he were living in both at once. Which he felt he was, but not *what* it felt like. So that afternoon the hours passed in a "now" inclusive of "after" and "before." Or altogether outside them, for his "now" was not what is commonly meant by "now." When he noticed he was in it, he did not enjoy that state.

He looked up from the beach up the short cliff, and saw Kralin watching him. The two young men looked up and down at each other. Then Kralin sprang down the cliff-path and said that it was years since they had met. Picus agreed, and with his vague bright courtesy indicated a seat on an empty lobster pot. Kralin sat down on it and watched him at work.

"When I settle here for good," he said, "I must ask you people to teach me how to sail a boat." Picus indicated that he had better not ask him, who had a gift for being sick, without warning, at any moment of danger or decision. He went on working. Nicholas Kralin sat on and watched him, until Picus asked him if he would not find it a lonely place in which to live. People give curious answers to that standard politeness. Picus, a connoisseur in his way in human futilities, wondered which one he would get. But Kralin answered by telling him several things that he did not know: that the land surrounding their land, lying on the boundaries of several old estates within its half circle of hills and the sea, was very much of it for sale. In patches, here, there and everywhere, which by judicious purchase could be made to link-up: that he proposed Felicity's house for a personal nucleus, putting his capital into a field here and a field there. He would then build a hotel and a row of bungalows along the low cliff, light the sea lane and drain it. One of the least-known places in England, he would then advertise it. The village, perfect as a single unit of antique building, would do half of the publicity for him. The bathing was the difficulty. He would have to find a place for people who could not swim. In ten years' time he supposed that he would be buying the Taverners out—at their own price.

Picus listened to this, and all that he was sure that he felt was a pain somewhere deep in the middle of his inside. He heard Kralin telling him about a golf-course, and where the garages and the parking-ground could be. As he listened he could hear at the same time a long cry, a wail, a lamentation from outside that never stopped. A mourning somewhere in creation that the freshest earth there is should lose its maidenhood, become handled and subservient to man, to the men who would follow Nick Kralin. "Felicity is dead, and her land is to die too." He could hear his wife say that. There was a wound going through his long thin body. His feet and her feet and her brother's would walk on knives always after this. He found, as he cocked his head on one side to listen to Kralin, that he was staring very hard at his exceedingly powerful hands.

"You're sure," he said, "that they'll sell?" ('What were

they given me for? To fight with.' "Not then," said his distorted time sense gone into reverse, when another man would have said "Not yet.") Kralin waived the question serenely:

"I got your note asking me to lunch. I'll be over to-morrow and meet them there with you. Now I'll stop wasting your time." He said that wistfully, as a man who knows he is not liked, and wishes to be asked back to tea. It was then that he noticed for the first time Picus's hands, that they were atrociously strong for a man of his bird-like air and delicate height, not an inhuman man, but as if he knew a delicate tune only very rare birds sing. The hands now lay idle. A tool had fallen into the sand. For an instant Kralin was almost uneasy, until he saw him feel for a cigarette. He went away, and then Picus knew why Felix had run. He was feeling odd too, because as Kralin had been humble with Felix, he had been wistful with him. He put away his tools in the boat-house and walked home alone up the path through the Sacred Wood, up from the sea. Many years ago it had been pebbled, with the polished, colour-taking sea-moulded eggs of local marble, a tender fancy of victorian gardeners in that part of the south. Now moss almost covered them, and rarely swept twig and leaf; while the centre was trodden back to its earth, clay in this case, and bound with roots, their ridges polished down to the core of the wood. On the blackest night they had each learned where not to stumble, an exercise when they were children in disaster and pride. Yet, on his way back, Picus tripped and fell flying, and lay for more than a moment, face-down, spread-out, the young light dappling his body. He got up, bewildered like a man who has been knocked down in his own house. Once there, he said nothing whatever about what Kralin had told him.

Chapter IX

ALL THE NEXT morning Picus watched the house being put into a state for the reception of old Mrs. Taverner. Not for Adrian, whom they would willingly have fed on boiled limpets, but for his mother. It is necessary to human nature that the more it dislikes and distrusts, the more it must find a formula for showing off. Elaborate rudeness will do. Or a last revenge of hate may be accompanied by a parade of hospitality and all possible splendour. Picus went down to the cellar, whose size for what they could afford to keep in it reminded him of the man who put a cathedral on the mouse. Felix took a bicycle and went over to Starn for ice, ice which melted in the carrier and did duty for a water-cart, all the miles of white velvet dust to the top of their hill. Stern-faced, Nanna and Scylla worked over the house. Unfortunately, Mrs. Taverner's wedding-present had been changed for something else, and Adrian's pendant was officially at the jeweller's for repairs. Would he be too refined to understand? Too rich if he wasn't or too stupid. Or spiteful enough? They were doubtful, and Picus, chased from the cellar for wine, to the shore for lobsters, to the kitchen-garden for salad, to the bathroom to wash, wished he had never married, and was in pain all the time because of what he knew; what Kralin had said, which the others did not know; which he had not told them, and in knowledge of which he was living. In which he had no business to be living, for it hadn't happened yet. Would it happen? Was the spoiling of their land a horror already begotten? Was time quick with it? It felt so to his perception, but he could not be sure. Out of the two cards or three, the one that might be drawn. He brushed his fine hair over his thin skull and disliked the processes of living, each one of which he knew how to handle, expert in the almost lost art of enjoying himself—as distinct from having a good time.

Downstairs he found a stern young goddess, looking at the dining-room table, her head on one side. With her was a sybil, ancient, prophetic, and he heard that if Mrs. Taverner found anything wrong with that, some doom known only to old women who had nursed her children would fall on her. Scylla gave Picus the same look she had given to the table setting, critical, ruthless, of one who is making the very worst do for the very best. He heard himself included in her "Nanna, I suppose this will have to do," and went and hid in the dark library, where it was a house-understanding that no one spoke to anyone else. Felix came in and ignored it with a tirade on the hollowness of family life, rather in his earlier manner. Picus wished life would stop, every form of life; and a few minutes later heard the steps of Adrian and Mrs. Taverner on the path out of the wood.

For her husband's brother's children Mrs. Taverner felt neither respect, interest nor love; for Picus, son of old Mr. Tracy, her true nephew, her brother's son, she would have felt a great deal, if Picus, from the hour he had first screamed at her in his cradle, had ever let her get within affection's distance of him. The rude, elusive child had become the exceedingly remote young man, yet she thought about him—old woman of her tribe—and sincerely pitied him his marriage with Scylla. Easy to account for her doubts on the cousinship, but—her sons apart—what she disliked was Taverners. Taverners, speculative, high-minded, secretive through over sensibility, whose instincts ran a little counter to their judgment, with their intellectual passions, their fastidious courage, their white heats. Their "moody haughty minds, essentially religious"—she had not the least idea what they were about. Any more than she understood their capacity for love and self-giving they were at pains to hide, whose instinct was to exploit it with the rest of the world. Nor their overstrained horror of the pretentious, who had no objection to extremes of family advertisement. Their world, for all its country similarities was one of which she knew nothing and imagined the worst. Boris happened to be the only one of their friends who appealed to her—a gentleman this time, and a wolf-cub of romantic misfortune; but Mrs. Taverner was quite shrewd enough to know that the bizarre was not her hunting-ground, nor the exotic her pack. It was different for Adrian, but Adrian, she noticed, was an odd mixture of interest about Boris tinged with contempt.

She came in to lunch with one intention, not to leave until she had made matters clear with Nick Kralin; make the best bargain with him, put him in his place; saucing the dish with a few Taverner scalps. It was not that she was nothing but an ill-natured woman. It went deeper than that. For one thing she was not a person to examine and correct the instinct which makes men—and women especially—desire the abasement—not too serious and not public—of the family into which they have married. Often they feel that they have given more than they have got (in Mrs. Taverner's case most unfairly, left a widow early and exceedingly well-provided for out of Taverner wealth). But everything that was not her own, she grudged to others in imagination, who, once it became hers, could be generous. Even with Adrian she was trying to trade his possession of his sister's house with him against his debts.

At lunch it was Scylla's mild ambition to prevent her aunt from feeling mistress of the situation. She did it rather well, the old woman thought, inadequately backed up by Felix, who shared his sister's desire to exaggeration, and was young enough still to be rude. While Picus, who was unhappy, was only polite. Kralin, if possible more civil, said very little, and it was Boris who took the situation in hand. One of those people who are able to forget that part of their audience have heard their stories before, he entertained the mother and son, at the same time provoking Kralin to almost visible dislike.

The exasperated feast went on, false for the givers of it. Emotions like these did not suit the house in the Sacred Wood. "It's the worst of her that she makes people like us behave like people like that." Scylla sighed, and wondered when it would be over, and they could get back to their own lives, learning and thinking and loving, and being out of doors, to the great work she and Felix had planned. What was the power in her aunt to make it all look contemptible? The exquisite but rather too spare arrangement of the table, the plain delicate food—Mrs. Taverner could better both by opening her mouth to give an order. While of what was unpurchasable in them and untouchable she did not know the existence. Scylla sat back while they finished their tart, of the youngest rhubarb and Nanna's special crust, said a prayer over the coffee, and then everything about her but her body went out of the room, arrow-quick, on a flight to a place she did not know, across pain. Would they never be rid of them, rid of the world that was not their world; rid of the living, rid even of the dead, even of Felicity's ghost? Then the thought: 'This won't do. Our business is to bring order, proportion, light into what is happening. That where there has been falsehood and muddle, there shall be knowing and clearness, conception for misconception. That is how life is handled. Get on with it.' Then: 'I don't want to any more. Felicity died because it was too much for her. And it's too much for me.' Her flight began like that, but instantly she was away in a faint world of travelling images, flying fast like sand, through dirty clouds to nowhere. Through nowhere, then into something burning-cold or ice-hot that she knew for Nick Kralin's mind, and whirled back from it into her version of the horror which had possessed the others. She found herself pouring out the coffee and hearing her aunt say:

"I hear from Monsieur Polteratsky that you found our poor Felicity's crystals over at the house."

Scylla had not forgotten them, had every intention of keeping them; because they were beautiful, because they were particularly like the dead, because she did not want Kralin or Adrian or Adrian's mother to have them. Felix stepped into the breach:

"I gave them to her, Aunt. Now she is dead, I want my sister to wear them." This was not true. The only thing they had been sure about was that the beads had not been a present either from her family or from Kralin.

"Indeed," said Mrs. Taverner, "I remember them. They are exactly like a string that belonged to your Aunt Jean. I believe she gave them to her."

"You can write to the jeweller and ask," said Felix, a shade too haughtily; but as Mrs. Taverner had invented her sister as the giver as much as they had invented themselves, it passed, until Kralin said quietly:

"I don't want them, Scylla."

Everyone was thinking that they had not an idea where Felicity had got them, everyone that is but Kralin. Brother and sister registered hauteur. Picus had the tact not to laugh.

Mrs. Taverner finished her coffee: "Never mind the beads just now. I have really come over—to see you, of course, but to talk to Nicholas about the house. In spite of our dreadful loss—I might even say because of it—there is no reason why we should not—" she nearly said "be friends"; judged that to be going too far and added "consult each other's wishes." (Now that Felicity is dead. Was that one of her wishes?) Her hosts looked stonily at her.

They got up from the table, dispersed to re-collect in the long salon where the family assembled its works of art. Nucleus of a new collection, who had each that instinct and fair luck. Adrian was irritated and impressed, Kralin was amused, who also understood such things and could afford better. To Mrs. Taverner they were suspect, as symbolic of some new form of the indecent, which she called decadent.

The french windows were open, and carried in on light airs, the sun put out the small fire, making it look like paint. She sat upright on a spanish gilt settee of extraordinary discomfort, strategically ill-placed, since it left her head in the light. Kralin, deprecating, took a tall chair opposite, with wings that threw a double shadow onto his face.

"Would you rather we left you?" said Scylla.

"Why should you? Unless Nicholas wishes. I have only to tell him the price we are asking for the house, and he can tell us, now or later, if it suits him to pay it." She turned the folds of her hard, old, painted face to the sun. They had heard it all before, and how many times must Adrian have heard his mother saying what she wanted, what was due to her, what she meant to have. What she usually got.

They seated themselves. Adrian looked round, bored; bored and sulky and not sure of himself, neither sufficiently interested nor aloof; cynical at his mother's parade of authority and ashamed, yet subject to it. His cousins knew that he was as much her prisoner, as certainly mutilated by her as any eastern prince with hands cut off, led by a cord through his tongue. For which knowledge he could never forgive them, to whom contact with his mother was like the hunting of big game. So the son looked away, the nephew stared. At twenty-five, Felix's jaw was hardening, his rings of hair, retracting a little, threw his tall forehead into relief. He was ready for a spectacle, and to speak a piece of his mind. While the niece was wondering how to keep her brother quiet, unless or until her aunt went too far and gave excuse to one of those climaxes of indignation and denunciation in which Felix excelled. Boris, who ought to have left them, was immovable with curiosity, curiosity and caution and a kind of loyalty and a kind of mistrust. Whatever the Taverners were going to talk about they should not give him away, or give themselves away either if he could help it, however much they were provoked. Bad conscience, for they were incapable of trying to discredit him. But to Boris his bad conscience was their fault. Only Picus Tracy, shadowy beside the ancient curtains printed with birds, was in pure pain. Without joy of battle, or the consciousness of *durée,* the being and becoming of life, on which the others were travelling like a wave-crest, he was alone, in a quiet pool of that evil which would be served out for them in transit, drop by drop, whose waters would pour off them as they poured on. Or so it seemed to him. Only he had it for what it was. All of it. All the time. And when had he asked for that, whose life was in laughter and pure sensations the delights of the ear and eye and skin, as far away from human evil as from the intellectual love of God? His instincts had been sufficient for him, because they were fine, and he fastidious and subtle. Taverners were not subtle, or only laboriously, on technique. They were deep and direct, lovers of truth, and their simplicity different from his distilled perception. He saw himself, explaining all this to himself, making it into intellectual seeing for the first time, and shook as though at the pains of a new birth. "So this is marriage," said his merry devil. Then "She is my aunt too"; and he thought of his evil father and then of Nick Kralin.

Mrs. Taverner began again:

"You must understand, Nicholas, I don't want to be unkind, and I quite understand why you would want Felicity's house. There were faults on both sides, as I know only too well; but I do want you to understand that you are asking us to make a great sacrifice in suggesting that we should part with it at all. Of course you don't know how our estates lie. Felix owns this house and land up to the foot of the downs and the strip of wood down to the sea. Scylla no land at all, though it would belong to her should he never leave an heir, and he, very wisely and rightly, allows her and Picus to make their home with him. But his property stops on the side of the wood that looks over the fields. We own nothing more till we come to you. What was Felicity's house is the only other piece here that belongs to us; with not much land, as you must know, though the high orchard behind it commands the whole valley. But over the hills, towards Stone End, we still own some. And it has always been my plan, by judicious buying, to try and link up the estate again. Of course, I know that the piece you want is really my son's, but he has come to an arrangement with me about it, and he so dislikes talking business. —So you see that what you are really doing is asking me to part with family land, when my object is to re-acquire it. As a business man, you must know how valuable a security it is these days."

Aunt Julia's bibful. Variations on a theme familiar to her family since childhood. She went on:

"And as you all know—and I'm sure that if Nicholas doesn't, he'll understand now—that my great desire has been, apart from the benefit to my family which can be got by good farming, to keep this exquisite part of the earth in the hands of people who will never let it be spoiled. It would break all our hearts to think of it vulgarised by bungalows, or by the sort of people who might come here. Certainly would, if they knew anything about it, and there was land to be had."

Picus, who had been upright till this, so light on his feet that his standing gave no impression that he was not at ease, whose sitting down was more like a movement poised for flight, caught at the curtains and slipped heavily into the window-seat. How much would the man pay? Probably a great deal to have so much power over them. Scylla was saying:

"It's always been a fear of ours, Nick, lest anything should happen, lest anything could happen to this—this bit of England." So she said, and what she meant was to the flawless, clean and blessed, mana and tabu earth;

strictly of their flesh, whose birds and beasts and eggs and fish, and fruit and leaf and air and water had nourished their bodies, "composed their beauties"; whose pattern was repeated in them, the stuff of a country made into man.

"Quite," said Nick Kralin. Mrs. Taverner now felt that she had her family on her side on an issue there could be no two opinions about. She went on:

"So I don't feel justified in asking less than ten thousand pounds for the house and garden as it stands, and that price is in consideration of our kinship." There was silence. As price it was fantastic. She went on:

"I'm sorry, my dear boy, but you see, we can't take less. I've my family to consider. My late husband would turn in his grave at the idea of my selling it at all." Silence for the entry of Uncle Henry's ghost. Listen for the grave turning. Kralin looked up innocently.

—"But don't answer me now. Go back to the house and think it over. But don't try offering me a penny less, for I won't take it. And don't think you can try and get at Adrian either. It's practically my property now." Her claws were out. They even felt for Kralin. Was an old bully any better than a young—? What *was* Kralin? They thought of Felicity on her path between this cruel power and that. Path down the cul-de-sac, to the blind well, to the dead end that was her grave. While Boris noticed that a woman like that would have no scruples about bullying a man like him; tyranny which might be more disagreeable than the Taverners'. Filed it for reflection.

"No," said Kralin. "I don't know that I need go home. I think we might finish it now." He looked up, coyly: "You see, *Maman*—now you will listen to this, won't you—" (She made a movement of haughty assent)— "I'm very anxious myself that there should be some sort of lasting memorial to my wife. In fact, I even feel I must do it myself. I mean I could do it, if Scylla and Felix would help me. Now I've got all her papers—she kept diaries, you know; and sorted all her correspondence into packets, tied with the appropriately-coloured ribbon—" He sniggered, deprecating with thrust-out hands.

"I'm proposing to issue them with a preface, in a limited edition to subscribers. I know a man who does that sort of thing, who'd jump at it. And in her house there is just the right atmosphere for the selecting and editing I must do. So you see?"

So he had got them. The faultless instinct that had sent them searching, ineffective.

"What papers?" said old Mrs. Taverner. "Her private letters? I don't quite understand."

"Yes," said Kralin, patiently: "her letters from her friends, and some by her which she must have asked for back. And her diaries and comments on people and on herself. It might become quite a classic of its kind." He waited. Mrs. Taverner spoke again:

"I can't at the moment quite see any objection. You would be on your honour, of course, not to publish anything which would offend her family. I can't imagine there would be much sale for such a book. You don't think so yourself, or you wouldn't propose a limited edition. But what has that to do with the house?"

They heard a sigh from Picus. A bubble had broken in his mind and let out understanding. Kralin was speaking again:

"You'll see in a minute. I don't think its sale would be as small as that. In these days of psychoanalysis, it might be very widely read. It would have to be a book people subscribe for because it is so very frank. It's that which makes it interesting, of course. Felicity had the art of telling the truth as she saw it. And she was—shall we say—an erotic expert. Of course, we are not the people who think of these things as indecent; but you know what the British Public can be like. James Douglas and the smut-hands. As for the letters to her, I expect I shall have to find out about the law, if the writers are still alive. Initials and asterisks, I expect, will be all I shall be allowed. Or we may come to terms."

"You mean," said Mrs. Taverner, slowly, "that there are things among my late daughter's papers that all the world might not see?"

"If you like to put it that way, Aunt Julia." He spoke with a touch of friendly impatience. "I doubt it, from that point of view, whether even her family 'ought to see' them. They are, I assure you, wonderfully frank and impassioned. That's why I think they might become a classic, an erotic classic. After my editing." He smiled, adding—"And incidentally, you may be quite sure that her death was an accident, not suicide. She would hardly have left such papers about if she had meant to kill herself."

"What *do* you mean?" said Mrs. Taverner, her hauteur turning a little shrill, glancing with rising fury at Scylla.

"Yes, what d'you mean?" said Scylla, slowly. All three turned towards him, staring.

"You see my point of view?" he said. "I am a man without prejudices. It seems to me that my wife's papers contain so much valuable material, throw so many lights on the ultimate psychology of our behaviour, that the fact that I was married to her ought not to influence me. After all, if I were to take that point of view, I might complain of the treatment I have received. I don't propose to. I have many most charming recollections of her. While, if it occurs to any one to blame me, I have *my* answer in this little memorial that I propose."

Mrs. Taverner did not understand. The others did at once, without analysis, by pure impression, as though they were made of hot wax to take the seal of Nick Kralin. Picus sighed again, but more easily. The bubble had burst now. He was less alone. They knew, his wife and her brother and her brother's friend. Adrian Taverner knew too. His first thought was pleasure. His mother was not getting her own way. Picus glanced at him, saw an avid spiteful look forming round the corners of his mouth. Mrs. Taverner said:

"I don't think any of her papers ought to be published if there is anything in them to bring discredit on our family. And I do not see in the least what all this has got to do with the house."

"What we mean is," said Scylla, "that now we know what your game is, we'll see what can be done on this earth to stop you." Kralin shrugged his shoulders slightly.

"I see you realise the position, Scylla. But if you feel like that about it—and you probably knew what Felicity was like better than I ever did—we can come to an arrangement. I am quite ready, Aunt Julia, to return you your daughter's papers in exchange for the house." Mrs. Taverner stared, as what served her for light broke on her; and nearly shouted at him:

"The house in exchange for my daughter's papers. Never on your life. The impudence of you! After what you've told us, we can go to law about it."

"This is blackmail," said Felix. Kralin deprecated:

"It is, if you like. But the position is one which makes one quite sure that you will not go to law. You see, *Maman,* I have Felicity's reputation—your family's reputation, if you like, to do what I chose with. Do try and understand. But I am quite willing to exchange it, to hand you over those writings in exchange for the house."

Mrs. Taverner understood now blindly, as an angry old animal understands a challenge to fight. And she accepted it hardly for her daughter's fame, in some part for her family honour, for her thwarted authority, furiously. Women like that, whose strength is based on their emotional violence, are apt to lose their judgment in a moment of crisis. Discharge of emotion being all that matters to them, they will rush alike an enemy and friend—sometimes more on friend than enemy—frantic to give an instant exhibition of power. There are men like that, but not usually so dangerous or so silly. She forgot that the Taverners must be on her side, forgot common blood and common generosity. There was something fatal about it. She began:

"What's all this? What is it you've the impudence to think you'll try and get out of me? I believe you're all in it together. You, Felix! I've heard it said that you were in love with her. I hope you'll like it when your silly indecent letters come out in print. It would be what you deserve. Give him the house, indeed, to save you! And you, Scylla, stealing her beads and pretending your brother gave them to you. I'm sick of you all. You're going to advertise yourself through your poor wretched cousin."

"Aunt," said Picus, "you mustn't make a fool of yourself now." Kralin nodded at him, intelligently, saying to no one in particular, "*But think of the money I save.*" Felix and Scylla sat close to one another, like people under torture, whom torture has taken by surprise, who have not remembered to scream. What Kralin had in his mind to do about Felicity, pointed, underscored, somehow made septic by what the old woman had said. Scylla said at last:

"I wouldn't take this man's side too quickly if I were you, Aunt Julia. He means what he says."

"And I mean what I say."—

"A moment," said Picus. "Aunt, when you say things like that, you are fouling your own nest. This isn't the time."

"I don't care what you say, Picus. I believe they are all rotters; that they're all in it together. Anyhow he shan't have the house."

"It's 'publish and be damned' then, is it?" said Kralin with his weary smile: "And don't misunderstand. Felix and Scylla figure, quite creditably, but prominently, very prominently. What she has to say about him and Clarence Lake will interest Picus. And about his father—that's your brother, isn't it?" Picus said:

"He means that there is plenty about you, Aunt."

"About me." She was one of the people who use the echo of the last person's speech for springboard.

"Plenty," said Nick Kralin. "Material for a practically complete study of the Electra-complex."

"That means you murdered Uncle Henry," said Felix, "and she knew it."

"I don't know what you are talking about. Do you suggest that *I* let this man have *my* house because he chooses to print some beastliness my daughter chose to write about me?"

"*My* house," said Adrian Taverner, softly, and tried to catch Kralin's eye.

"None of us are proposing anything yet," said Scylla. "We are only trying to make you see what Kralin means."

"What Kralin means! Thank you. I know that he's a blackmailer, and there's a law for that. And that you're all in it with him, and there's a law for you too." Kralin shook his head:

"You're quite wrong there, *Maman.* They've nothing to do with me. They're all on your side; they can't help it. Only they can't do anything, that's all." Boris, who was sitting rather behind them, leant over Felix's shoulder:

"But why," he said, "does he not ask for money? Why should he want that house?" Kralin staged a yawn:

"Picus can tell you what I told him yesterday."

"Tell us yourself," said Scylla, after a glance at her husband. "We are hardly here to save you the embarrassments of explanation."

Kralin regretted that confidence. If Picus had asked him to tea the day before, he would not have made it. It had been a bad move. Still, without hesitation, he explained.

Mrs. Taverner sat listening. Her wits were coming back. Her rage against her family had been the destructive, intensive rage, nourished in this case by its impotence. Impotence of an old woman against the young, the strong, mindless, universal, insufficiently examined, insufficiently understood passion. Even though her daughter had made her escape by death, it had been an escape; and if Adrian had remained, in her heart she despised him for it. In the destruction of her daughter's fame there was even a pleasure hidden; while as for disclosures about herself, they were something she could ignore, who did not fully understand what it was that Kralin could do. But the threat to their countryside was a plain issue, clear to her, touching less that was savage in her and all that was generous.

"Oh," she said, simply: "not content with having driven my daughter to her death, he wants to destroy our land also."

"The temptation," said Kralin, "is too much. You people talk about poverty and high taxation when you've got a gold-mine, above your ground, not under it. And your wretched peasants here lead such repressed lives. They're all—except one or two of the old ones—for something which would brighten things up, and bring a bit of money into the place. To show you I'm really a philanthropist, I'm thinking of running a cinema—at a loss—with all the new sex films."

It was no time to think of sheep or stars, or of the ghost in the cove or of York and Lancaster roses; of barrows or badgers or bee-pastures. Other words forced themselves, ringing, into Scylla's head: remembrance of:

that twice-battered god of Palestine,
And mooned Ashtaroth
Heaven's queen and mother both
Now sits not girt with tapers' lofty shine.
The Lybic Hammon shrinks his horn
In vain the Tyrian maids their wounded Thammuz
mourn.

That was what was really happening. Kralin was saying:

"The links will run along the side of the wood, Felix. You'll make a bit on lost balls."

They were now more stupefied than old Mrs. Taverner, to whom his alternatives were suddenly clear, with whom lay the choice. It was now for her to say which she would keep, her daughter's fame or her land's. Drawing closer and closer to each other, her kinsmen sat without speaking.

Mrs. Taverner had sprung at her decision. She did not care a rap about Felicity, published in a dirty book only nasty-minded people, not her friends, would read. Adrian might make difficulties, but she could deal with Adrian. It was the land, the land that mattered. She would never have sold it for such a purpose—there she was utterly sincere—while as for giving away any part of it— This horrible young man had gone too far. Thank God there was no child. Now she knew, she could buy up all that was for sale, as fast as she could. She saw that the others could not help being with her there, while it annoyed her to think that she had better not have scolded them, to whose nature apology was a kind of self-violation. She turned to Kralin.

"It does not seem to concern us, Mr. Kralin, what you choose to publish about your relations with your wife. But it is quite another question to give you our land to spoil. You may do anything you like, but you will not do that. While if you publish anything immoral or impertinent, there is a legal remedy. I think that my people here will all agree with me."

"What we agree about will come later," said Felix.

"Then that is all we have to say. Scylla my dear, will you ask him to go?" Scylla got up. They all got up but the old woman, and her son, trying to look non-committal and bored. Kralin rose and said pleasantly:

"Well, if I can't have Felicity's house for a nucleus, I suppose I can't. I shall be there for another two months. Rent paid in advance, you know. I can get on with my memoir there. And I'll see you all get presentation copies.

And special terms when I build my Hydro. *Au revoir, Maman, au revoir* to you all."

The delicately panelled door of the long room shut behind him, and he passed before their eyes again through the windows, crossing the terrace, on his way to the path to the east out of the wood.

"Well," said Mrs. Taverner into a cold silence. "Did you ever hear anything so monstrous?" Silence. —"But you surely agree with me that it would be infamous to let him spoil our land?"

"Yes," said Scylla, "we agree about that."

Mrs. Taverner took the plunge. These pride-ridden children were sulky with her. Perhaps she had been hasty.

"On thinking it over I feel sure that you had no part in what that infamous young man proposed. I take back what I said. Scylla can keep Felicity's beads. While I'm sure Felix's love was generous and disinterested."

"Be quiet," said Felix, "about that."

"Don't talk of us," said Scylla, wearily; unyielding, with the ungenerosity born of long experience and memory of Felicity. Mrs. Taverner felt sincerely hurt. What was the good of an apology to be sniffed at like a piece of poisoned meat?

"I'm sorry. I can't say more than that. And is this the moment to be quarrelling among ourselves?" Still no response to her harsh voice saying this. Then Boris leaned forward and spoke sweetly:

"If it is permitted to me to say anything, may I felicitate Madame Taverner on her choice? You see—" He had turned their eyes on him, pair by pair; his voice was a little tune—"the choice she has made is in all ways the just one. He can now, as was said, 'publish and be damned.' But he can do that anyway."

"You mean," said Felix, "that if my aunt, in memory of Felicity, had sold him the land"—

"In exchange for some papers. Yes. And an agreement. Papers. He will have copies. Others that you know nothing of. An agreement. *And* his imagination. He would have got round it—if only in speech. Or taken a chance with your laws." They nodded at him. Mrs. Taverner got up.

"I am going home," she said, "to telephone my solicitors to invest all my spare capital in every acre of land round here. Felix, are you in a position to help me in any way? We must all meet later. If I were you, I shouldn't quarrel too much with him, not yet, not more than you need. Keep an eye across the valley on Mr. Kralin. Coming, Adrian?"

As Felix said later: "Out she flew."

Chapter X

IT WAS NEXT day, and Boris was on his way to Starn to meet Adrian. He sat on a stone stile, reflecting. Perched like a gay gracious bird, his little head up, his green oblique eyes turned to the sky's unattainable blue, he reviewed the situation. It brimmed with possibilities, a sea of trouble in which it should be possible for a man of ability, and especially of Boris's ability, to boil his own egg.

The first thing that had to be done, even if he had to do it, was to prevent his high-minded English friends from losing their sense of proportion and making fools of themselves by quarrelling too violently with Kralin, and ineffectually with their aunt. For, among other things, Boris desired to see them through. It would help him to help them, and besides he was curious. Particularly he was curious about Kralin. That man was no more than half a Russian—more than half a Jew—he was sure of it. Boris had a quite different race-tradition, and quite different ideas about Jews. And he was sure that there was a great deal more going on behind that young man's activities than any Taverner could suspect. He thought: 'If I deliver them, I am sure of this—that they will never forget. Perhaps they will never understand, but they will never be what is called ungrateful to me. On the other hand—' "The other hand" was that loyalty to them was going to make it difficult for him to go his own way, develop, in both their interests, his relations with Adrian Taverner and his mother. His Taverners were in a rage, a rage they had very little under control, with both of them. The old woman's brutality, and disloyalty to them before Kralin, had ripped open old wounds and the memory of Felicity's agony. While against Adrian they seemed to have a feeling, an instinct, a reaction, that Boris did not understand. What if he were treacherous, a sensualist? What of it? A coward? A bad brother? Why did his dear friends want people to go about being so good? Valiant and disinterested, men of honour, men of heart and head? Excellent when people are, but it so rarely happens, and only under certain conditions, and obviously only with certain people. Really the Taverners were carrying rather far their demand for virtue when they were annoyed at not finding it in Adrian. A man who wanted to be let alone and amuse himself and attend to his connoisseurship, by which his family would ultimately be enhanced and enriched. Boris, famished for *décor* and setting, was nourishing the hope that a chance and one appropriate to him had come his way at last; that Adrian, properly handled, would take him into his business. Then—it was a good dream—he would spend his days looking for the things he loved, which would at least have passed through his hands. Until, one day—here he dropped off the stile, and strode along across the fields at the thought of it—somewhere, in a back street or a remote farm, he would find the Treasure. A T'ang Bhoddisat, a Fragonnard, a jewel,

Made for some fair queen's head,
Some fair great queen long dead;

an ikon from the Porphyry Chamber, the pearls of Ivan the Terrible's boy-friend. A game he played with Felix, who had the same dream. Not with Adrian, who found and bought with prudent business sense, with moderate, not fanciful, fortune.

And when he had found it, he would, if necessary, steal it. (So would Felix, but his dream ended with a fifty-fifty cheque to the victim.) And stolen, he would sell it; and live for the rest of his life, theoretically, on what it had done for him. Free and free and free again for ever. A slave, to Boris, was a man who is aware of the existence of economic pressure; and to him the question was simple, that it is not possible to demand of the son of boyards in distress the honesty, industry and adaptability which is asked of a slave. Which, on his definition, is asked of the majority of humanity. The courage, cunning, cruelty of an outlaw—yes. Qualities he was not particularly asked to use on his english visits, but he was quite prepared for their exercise. Meanwhile, he utterly refused to quarrel with Adrian Taverner.

He had told the others this. His final words had been: "Listen to me. I will be your liaison officer. It will serve all our advantages. This is no time for small dignity."

"Go and boil your egg, Boris," Scylla had said, bitterly: "of course we know that you must look after yourself. The world is too filthy for us, that's all. No, we aren't calling you disloyal, but can't you see that if Aunt Julia is out against Kralin, it is no more than a falling-out among thieves. Those three people, and what they are, and what it is that drives them, killed Felicity. Felicity is being killed again. Her mother hates her fame as she did her beauty. Can't you see her triumph? Her property will be augmented and her power. With revenge on her child thrown in. That's what she has done."

"Of course," said Boris, irritated and with no tact to spare.

"What we have to do," said Felix, "is to leave it to her to save the place, while we save Felicity. I don't see how, but it's got to be done. Can't you understand, Boris, our aunt would *like* Kralin to do what he intends to do?"

"But if in those papers there are letters which will compromise her?"

"She doesn't believe it. She doesn't understand what it means. Nor what Kralin can invent and spread about. She has *no* imagination. She thinks her brutal illiterate letters are those of a mother, who is also head of a family, reigning over a set of ungrateful morons, who all *owe* her something. It's a mania with her sort of woman to imagine everyone is in her debt."

Scylla said passionately, "The kind of person who has never found out that to ask for gratitude is not only the way to lose it, but to lose, instantly, all right to it." Boris shrugged his shoulders.

"You will only be able to do less than you should, if you let her know what you know about her. And does it not occur to you that there is Adrian to watch?" It was explained to him that their only reaction to Adrian was to kick him where it would hurt most.

"When"—Boris was more and more impatient with them—"it is actually his house?"

"D'you mean," said Felix, "that he'd get behind with Kralin and sell it?"

"Yes. *Sell.* In exchange—if he is what you say he is—a free hand, with Kralin, over his sister's papers. It does not seem to have occurred to you the possibilities of intrigue in this affair."

"The house, not as a gift, but cheap. And the papers?" They mused. It was then that Boris left them.

The Taverners were not stupid, but english family life has come to such a pass, that it was outside their nervous strength to put aside old wrongs, go for exactly what they wanted, act from their race-solidarity, which is the strength of persistent strains and families with power. It was not a question of will. They knew what they ought to do, and that their aunt, who had a bully's weakness, was finally manageable—if anyone had ever been found with sufficient magnanimity or sufficient detachment to handle her; induce her to understand what she did not wish to understand, do what seemed to her of no advantage to do. Cynics had achieved this in the past, feathered their nests out of hers with no profit but to themselves. But she had made her own suffer too much, until they were past comprehension, forgiveness, or even the necessary tact; people the ignorant violence of her manner had made afraid. They knew that they should go to her, praise her, be genial with her, make it easy for her to understand. By a tactful use of family sentiment and fear of effective scandal, it should be possible to rouse her to every danger inherent in Nick Kralin. She had the position, the wealth, the long habit of authority, which had not yet come, through the drag of their poverty, to its full flower in them. It is often a tragedy for women of her kind that they are left to the mercy of the interested or to their own mercy; that in all their lives they meet no one who has the chance, the courage or the character to possess them and put them to their full and valuable use. The Taverners could not do it, their imaginations rehearsing in advance her incredulity, her stupidity, her lewd suppositions, her sentimentalities, her sneers. There is no more fatal habit than to anticipate someone's future behaviour from disagreeable memories of the past. They knew that, and were not proud of themselves, shrugged their shoulders at Boris, and piqued themselves on their indifference to his plans. At the same time, they envied Boris his realism, even Adrian his egotism. To such a state of shattered morale can one power-abusing head of a family reduce its cadets.

Arrived at Starn, Boris was investigating how far that egoism went. He had come to know the room well, the dining-room of the Star at Starn. Admirable food and art furniture, windows onto a ravishing garden and a thrust-up shoulder of down. With his head propped on his cool slim hands, he listened to Adrian. A connoisseur of hands, he observed his, that they were well-made, but large, fleshy and pink for the display of rings, several of which Boris would have liked transferred. Adrian Taverner was developing his point of view.

"I don't know if you knew my sister."

"A little," said Boris, wary.

"It was the same when we were children. I don't suppose you'll understand. You had either to do what she wanted, or make her cry. I admit it was often fun doing what she wanted, but it was just as much fun—when it wasn't too easy—to make her cry. Until, I suppose, it became more fun always to make her cry. More fun and easier, just not too easy. You know. And one could always put things right later by doing something she liked, and she'd forget all about the crying and play like mad."

"By the way, I'd no idea Felix was in love with her." Boris was non-committal.

"I suppose he's told you I was a bad brother. But did I ask to have her for a sister? Why should a tiresome cliché be synonymous with simple truth? People seem to forget that you can no more choose who your parents will have as well as you, than you can choose them."

"Mine," Boris said, "are dead."

"That makes a difference, as they say."

There was a perfunctory pause,

"But, my dear, if you wish to preserve an affectionate interest, you know, as well as I do, that the grave has its points." The talk went on, guided by Boris, until with his candid voice, his direct glance and lightly veiled smile, he asked:

"I wonder what there is to be found in those papers that he has got hold of, your Kralin."

Adrian brightened: "Quite sufficiently shame-making, I'm sure, to stimulate even my curiosity." Then to Boris's joy, he began the following confidence: That the house was entirely his in point of law; that he had promised to trade it with his mother, ostensibly in discharge of his debts. Those debts were really all fakes, but what he wanted was capital to finance a really important purchase in tapestries, far beyond his means, and not immediately resaleable. The kind of maturing investment of great ultimate value that his mother had been stupid about. It was implied that Boris was not so stupid, who, trying to appear as intelligent as possible, looked a little mad. As can happen to the cleverest faces.

Adrian's plan was this, and it included the death of at least three birds with one stone. His mother was busy, trying to buy up land to forestall Kralin. That would safeguard that. He would go to Kralin, get as good a price for the house as he could, plus permission to go on with the papers if he were allowed to play too. If Kralin's comments and the letters from Mrs. Taverner were startling enough, he would put no difficulties in the way of publication. Kralin was almost sure to accept this, for who could help him better than Adrian, with scandal? While, if his sister had really said exactly what she meant, he would be in a position to restrain him. With only the house, Kralin could not do much harm to the land; with its price in Adrian's pocket, he hoped to detach himself finally from his mother. By the publication of the papers to pay off several scores against her. What did Boris think of that?

Boris sat, like a king on a fence, or a god whose head faces two ways, clapping his heels for joy. This was the sort of thing he had been expecting. He applauded, he approved, he embroidered the project. Twisting Adrian Taverner round his little finger, they set out together to call on Kralin.

Two young men—is this a speciality of our age?—can go off on deadly business in the spirit of a boyish prank. They laughed in Adrian's two-seater all the way over the downs to Felicity's house from Starn. Laughed at innocent things, a new song, a new "camp." Among other things, Adrian was a collector in snob-degrees. So was Boris, who, exquisitely tuned, exchanged follies with such radiant lightness, that passing countrymen looked at him and were inclined to bless his bright face.

"You'd better come in, darling," said Adrian, at the door. Kralin opened it and welcomed them with a politeness that seemed to have become a little deferential, making them more uneasy than any hostility or any triumph.

These three young gentlemen went indoors, into the manly disorder of the sitting-room. Adrian began:

"As the actual owner of this place, which I assure you I am at perfect liberty to dispose of as I wish, I thought it best to come over and see you myself. You must not take my mother too seriously. None of us do." Kralin smiled. Adrian developed his plan.

It was Boris's opinion that there are no cool hands like english hands. He had also thought, as he laughed his way over from Starn, that it would never have occurred to him to trade on his sister's reputation. Still less on his mother's. While even his Taverners would not see it quite like that. Their concern was with the individual, their passionate desire was to preserve the memory of Felicity, not because she was their cousin, but because of the person that she was herself. While little thought of her family, none for their kinship or her age restrained them about their aunt. At Adrian, now that he had squeezed the amusement out of him, Boris was almost horrified. Was he of the same stuff as Kralin? Infinitely more stupid in his egotism than Kralin, who had passed through his own personality. Where to? Boris forgot all about Adrian, setting himself to watch this man.

He was agreeing to what Adrian proposed, easily, attentively, like a good man of affairs. Not committing himself, but encouraging the man who would bargain with him. He had Adrian's measure at once. Left Boris out. One thing at a time. Until across his easy dealing there came an awareness of that young man. An awareness of something it was his natural destiny to destroy. Not for his personal satisfaction and no questions to be asked. "I am, that there may be no more of him," would have been the answer. "It does not matter to me, but I am to destroy that." Kralin did not quite like this. It seemed an order, and he, who had no conception of obedience except to his personal decision, must know from whence it had come. Interrogating his sub-conscious, he was annoyed, until it occurred to him that a great many young men of Boris's kind have been dying lately, within the last three decades, half a world-generation, a nation-full or so. Then he thought that he knew. It was because in the past, as he had known so well that the knowledge had put itself away, his people had suffered at this man's people's hands. It must be that. He adjusted himself, satisfied by the analysis. Boris was suddenly aware of the same thing. His surprise had horror in it, as of a man meeting his race-tragedy face to face, in terms of one man or two; or as lover and lover came upon themselves, walking to meet themselves, hand in hand, in a wood. He had a moment of horror, from which he came out, very quiet. Then a daimon spoke to him:

"Now that you know; do not think, do not feel. Keep very still." He thought it was his guardian-angel. Whatever it was, he would obey it. He saw Kralin move to open a drawer in a bureau, unlock it discreetly, and bring out the commonest kind of cardboard attaché case, with tin locks, and the initials "F.T. Bona Roba" scrawled on it fancifully with a red-hot poker.

"Excuse me," he said, "I find literary allusion a release. Here they are." There were manuscript books bound in french batique, there were letters on many kinds and qualities of paper, tied with ribbons whose knots had been sealed.

"These," he went on, picking up a packet of heavy grey paper with a black ribbon and a pendant of wax, "are from your mother, Taverner." He threw them over. Adrian pulled the knot.

"The references to them and the drafts of some of the replicas are in these books. My index will give the places." He consulted some slips, wrote for a few moments and pushed one over to Adrian. Boris read over his shoulder, struggling with the written word that was not in his own tongue. Both were a little puzzled. Why were they shown these? The letters were just like Mrs. Taverner, scolding and insisting, with less drama than usual, who had not the use of her pen. Insensible letters, full of accusations, the words trivial and heavy. Letters of an unfriendly mother to a scolded child, uncuddled, not mothered, a target for waning against waxing life, for an old woman against a young, for brute power against a tender spirit. For one kind of knowledge against another.

"My mother's usual style," said Adrian, not trying to hide his disappointment: "about nothing in particular. Things my sister needed and she didn't mean her to have."

"Ah," said Kralin, "wait. It appears, as you will see from some notes Felicity made, that what they chiefly refer to is some sort of claim she had on your family estate. I'm not sure yet whether it was legal or wholly moral; though it might have been the former, if she had known what to do about it. Something quite considerable, at least enough to have given her what she wanted. When she died without a child, she was worth very little and this house reverted to you. But as her husband I should be entitled to my share of whatever it is. You know that, of course?"

Adrian said amiably: "You have been busy." Kralin took no notice:

"You see this letter from your mother, 'prying into our family affairs. Let me tell you that no respectable lawyer would ever hear of such a claim.' 'You ought to be very thankful you inherited anything.' Very non-committal all through. But—" He looked closely now at Adrian, nodding at him. "What inclines me on the whole to think that the claim was only a moral one is this: Felicity knew. —(It pleased her mother to dislike her very largely because, if you follow me, she knew that she knew it.)— You, Adrian—there is not the least doubt of it, she had all the proofs—are not your father's son." Adrian Taverner just saved the pause from becoming silence:

"Indeed," he said. "What a relief. I never could stand Taverners. But who was he, and how do you make it all out?"

"Your sister knew all about it, as I will show you in a moment."

"But this is fascinating," said Adrian. "My mind is racing through such a series of possibilities. To which of the

Older Married Set shall I be singing *'Now I have to call him Father'*? I suppose you mean to say that Felicity tried to hold-up my mother with the news. Ravishing, but why not me?"

Boris spoke, not quite conscious of his intentions: "It would seem, surely, that she did not tell you, did not perhaps claim this money, because she did not wish to injure you, Adrian."

"Misguided woman!"

"It seems," said Kralin, "though not quite conclusively, that before he died, Mr. Taverner came to know about this. He either altered or intended to alter his will. (If he did, I should imagine that your mother managed to suppress it.) While, on thinking it over, I find I am in doubt again as to Felicity's death. It all turns on this. If she expected to die—that is if she killed herself—would she have left us *all* these papers to be found? About her family, yes; but about herself? She was hardly an exhibitionist. It's a question for very nice judgment." And for the first time, Boris saw his supple hands playing together, in a way that was not like his earlier deference.

"It seems to me," said Adrian, "that one only orders a coffin to let several cats out of it. I feel quite giddy. I'm sure, Kralin, you'll excuse us and postpone the rest of our conversation for a few days. I must go home and find out who my father really was. (Oh, I'm sure you know, but I'd sooner have it straight from the stable, so to speak.)"

They left the house. The afternoon was spoiling, clouds running up from the west. Boris wanted to get back at once across the valley to the Taverners, but Adrian would not let him go. He rushed the car back to Stone End, where they ordered drinks. Adrian was silent. Suddenly he leaned over the inn table and burst into furious tears, repeating:

"Damn the woman, damn her. D'you suppose I'd have let her take me in all these years if I'd known?" Boris deprecated, less from sympathy than from boredom and strain. He had had enough of Adrian for the moment. At Kralin's he had admired his nerve. He wanted to get away and think it over. Adrian wanted to tell him everything his mother had made him feel and endure. Adrian wanted to be sure which stick to beat her with. Adrian wanted to hear all about it. Adrian wanted to find his father. Adrian wanted to cry in his mother's arms. Adrian wanted to get drunk. Boris had to give his opinion on almost endless series of paternal possibilities, before he got Adrian into his car, and mistrusting his driving, went home alone on foot.

Chapter XI

THE TAVERNERS were not specially glad to see him, who had been out with their cousin all day and a good part of the night. Boris made up a long moral sentence, to their intense surprise, about ingratitude, and then refused to speak until he was fed. But after he had eaten, he had his reward.

* * * * *

Their moral temperature had been rising all day, the natural steadying after shock of characters accustomed to adventure and strain. But at the story of their aunt their feelings underwent an extraordinary release, their judgment of her mellowing at once into greater charity and some facetiousness. So Aunt Julia had been passionate once. Victorian women did not do these things out of levity or temper or sheer absence of mind. It was the kindest interpretation, characteristic of them, whose hearts had not grown cold; though the charity was really Scylla's. Felix revised his version later; and no one ever knew what Picus, her blood-kinsman, thought.

"This will take the stiffening out of her," they said, feeling as though they were being revenged, devouring what Boris had to tell them, praising him. Even Adrian, it was agreed, had shown style. Until Scylla said:

"It seems to me that it is only the villains within this piece who, up to now, have anything to be proud of. Kralin has shown himself flawless, a master in his vileness; and Aunt Julia has kept her character if she lost it once. Even Adrian only went to pieces with you." They did not add what they were thinking, that Boris, their pest, had played nobly.

"You see what I mean? It is our turn now. Up to us, who are friends and lovers, to put up as good a show."

"Meaning?" said Picus.

"What we have come to mean since this began. Felicity's fame preserved. The making her illustrious can come later. That's our secret. We've got to fight now for her name."

"Before and over and above that," said Felix, "we've got to fight Nick Kralin. The thing is getting bigger. We began with Felicity dead, and how much we minded it, and how we wanted to find out about her death. And then we became determined to keep her memory bright. Now we know that she was, in some way, killed; and that there are people who aren't satisfied with that, but will have her remembered falsely. That's how things stand now. Boris, how much did you read over there for yourself, how much were you only told?"

"I read all that I could, over Adrian's shoulder. I even held a journal in my hand, and there was a page—I saw it was an important page—loose." He laid a paper before them. "It was all I could bring you. I snatched it when they turned away." A shiver of pain-sharpened memory went through them at the sight of her hand. Felix read:

"To think that Adrian and I are only half-brother and sister. (Unless I'm in it, too.) Half a brother, but a whole sister, I think. Or I would have been if he'd let me. And I knew his father, too. We had a game when I was little called Treasure Hunts, when we chose what we wanted out of the past and made up the adventures we had in finding it. That began my History. I chose once Cleopatra's Needle, because I thought it was a needle. And there was the sword, Joyeuse—"

They said, as though they had been practising it together for weeks:

"Now, who was he?"

"Kralin knows," said Boris. "Adrian was intelligent enough not to let him tell."

Scylla repeated, passionately:

"Our end is plain enough, for once. We have to be for honour what they are for dishonour; for truth what they are for lies; for charity what they are for spite; for loveliness what they are for filth. And be their equals in wits and courage."

"Let's start," said Felix. Picus assented. Boris looked at them, frowning.

A release that felt like a glory came about them, as though separate and converging paths of light lay to be walked on at their feet. It was, at that moment, as though all that Kralin had done was to open a door onto a stadium set for the players of the sacred game. On which field he had his place also. They also felt that they understood a great many things which had previously happened to man. At Eleusis an initiation, the appearance and disappearance of the Sanc-Grail, the meaning of the Waste Land. The splendour was full of joy and the divine sense of danger, and hope and the love of daring were powers of pleasure, not of temptation or fear. They knew, too, that they would find their way, and were without desire to coax God for success. Boris watched their faces and did not understand, face to face with a power that he did not share. It was he who brought them back, but without a sense of loss, to earth.

"One thing is necessary," he said. "I had better go and stay with Adrian. I must be known to be in his company, not yours."

"Nanna," said Scylla, "shall have the story of an unbecoming row to tell. Kralin's maid will hear of it. So will he."

"The next thing," said Boris, "it is wholly necessary for you to know more what is in your cousin's papers, and on what exactly he intends to defame her. If I am with Adrian, I think I can manage that."

"D'you know," said Felix slowly, "I have an idea. I don't believe her love-affairs matter a row of pins. Kralin's worked it out this way. There may be erotics for sauce, but he's incapable, psychologically, of seeing that she was *not* the same sort of person as himself. He'll read or put into her draft letters to her mother and to Adrian nothing but a series of threats to expose them, if they don't help her. That she was unsuccessful—and with such a pull—because they didn't help her, won't matter to him. He'll twist it round or invent what he wants. But his 'Portrait of My Dead Wife' and his introduction of the 'Electra Complex' will be a picture of a blackmailer. You'll see. It's going to work out like that."

His sister said:

"Won't it sound thin?"

"Thin as Picus's hair, but people will believe it. Three-quarters of our darling friends and all the psychology crowd. Until it reaches the world. Kralin'll understand scientific publicity, and he writes well, you know. Hate is good for the style. And it's his habit to be thorough."

"I don't think," said Picus, "that he hates." And he smiled a terrible smile like the man in the french romance, who had come looking for a woman *who must have passed this way, for I see a corpse.*

"We must not let him," said Scylla, "give us the creeps." Boris took his own plunge into the affair's abyss. It had just occurred to him as relative to the whole situation that Kralin and he were partly of the same race. He put it differently:

"Kralin is a Jew. Now I have always refused to be prejudiced about them. At our château—"

"And now the golden rule," said Picus, "is broken." Boris did not laugh, and was not vexed at being laughed at. Then it occurred to them that he had his memories.

* * * * *

Adrian Taverner had returned home that night to the house set in laurels on the moor. Under a moon *like a dying lady* the night air had torn past him, ribbons of cold parted on his right and left cheeks. Slowly the elation of drink ran down and its release. He felt his tear-stiffened eyelids, the exhaustion in his throat. He had meant to go into his mother, but the house seemed so shut, so put away to sleep. He was deadly tired, and part of his mind told him that it would be more prudent to wait.

On waking, his reaction was the usual one, that this could not have happened, that the day before he had been dropped into another kind of life and pulled out again. He felt that he could not see Boris, and knew that somehow he would have to see Boris. A great deal of Boris. It was outside his choice now what he would see of Boris. After what he and Boris had done together, it would be like that. Reflections of a young man, who piqued himself on disembarrassing himself of persons likely to become a nuisance. A self-indulgent man, he was badly shaken, and not yet quite conscious of his hurts.

At breakfast he saw that his mother ate very little, and that her face was sagging and old.

"I have bad news for us, Adrian. Yesterday, as you know, I spent with the various agents. And the up-shot of it is that Kralin already has an option on every piece of the valley land that there is for sale. I can offer a larger price, but that would be what he wants. We should be ruined before we had bought the land, which we don't need at the price that he would run up. Look at this surveyor's map. He had it all worked out before." She spoke in candid distress. Troubled and grave and anxious for her son's help. A generous pre-occupation with the beauty of England was the largest thing about her, a passion for and some knowledge also of its antiquities and local characteristics, especially in her own land, in the south. There her energies and habits of domination had found a serviceable outlet. More than one valley and cliff she had kept unbuilt on, because of her many a stream ran pure, many a copse endured. Not through her did the public house lose its licence. The "wicked old woman" did not "feel well-bred," not in that way. "Let them walk, if their cars won't take them," had been her last word, when extension of road facilities had been up before the County Council, on which she sat, a scourge to its committees, who had Surveyor and Architect beneath her feet.

Adrian listened. He shared her dislikes on the matter, not her enthusiasm; caring less for threatened beauty, but loathing the people who marred it. Then what she told him and the memory of all that had happened at Kralin's met and fused, and he saw what was before them. "I saw Kralin yesterday," he said. "Mother, why did you never tell me that I—" ('"am not my father's son"? Too silly. How does one say these things?') —"that I had a different father from the others?" ('Was I the only one?')

"Who told you such a thing," she began, raising her voice.

"I went over to Kralin's yesterday. It is plain enough from Felicity's papers. I have no objections, I assure you, but I should like to know who it was."

Mrs. Taverner did not speak. Her mouth was open. She did not shut it. She held on to the edge of the table with both hands, her mouth falling a little, her breath just audible.

"Let's cut the protests, Mother, and tell me about it. You owe me that." About a minute later, she said suddenly:

"Yes, I fought for you all right."

"Who was he?" He wanted to add: "don't you know?" And was too frightened, not too ashamed.

"I prefer not to tell you." Adrian knew that tone and laughed at it for the first time.

"You needn't. I shall know soon enough. So will everyone." The old woman said, almost sadly:

"He is dead. I find it hard to understand sometimes how you can be his son."

"Well," said Adrian, "I suppose you're sure I'm the one. Or are we a Harleian Miscellany? If it had been Felicity, it would have explained a lot.... Mother, don't. I don't mind in the least." Mrs. Taverner said in a voice of extraordinary bitterness:

"He used to talk as though he wished she had been his." Then she drew herself up slowly into the chair. Now that it was inevitable, she accepted what had happened; as though she had told it to Adrian herself; as long before she had rehearsed it.

"My son, I would like you to try and see how it could have happened. I was married when I was very young. Your stepfather—as I suppose I must say—misunderstood him. For months I was left alone, all the years of my marriage. Not even because he trusted me, but because he was too indifferent to think whether he trusted me or not. Women, as I think you ought to know, can put up with anything but indifference. He was a better person than I. I suppose people would say that his mind was set on higher things. But I couldn't understand the way he laughed about them as well. All I had was you children to see after and the estate. Then the man who was your father came to live near us, and he cared for what happened to me. He didn't see through me. And it may be a wicked thing to say, but I was a better woman those years. It was he who showed me how to do things for the land. And you, my youngest son, were his."

"Did—what *are* we to call him—the man you married—find out?"

"Yes," she said in a low voice, and then it occurred to Adrian that this might be painful to her, and that if it were she was doing it rather well.

—"Just before he died."

"Changed his will?" (All this time a part of Adrian wanted to fling himself down and howl, with his head on her lap. He suppressed it. This was his chance and he knew it.) Mrs. Taverner hesitated a second, then answered him almost sweetly, in a voice which in youth would have been charged with all that is appealing and evokes protection in men.

"He said he was going to, but I persuaded him not to. I went down on my knees to him, that he should not injure you who were innocent. Besides, it was too late."

"You mean he died?"

"Yes, but I doubt if any lawyer would have acted for him in the state he was, at the last moment, like that—" In a voice of incredible bitterness, she added—"Changing his will for the benefit of his daughter—" By this she had made it clear to Adrian that she had still something to hide. He reflected.

"That is the story we must stick to," he said. Formidable and unscrupulous woman. He was free of her now, or he never would be.

"Stick to? What do you mean?"

"Yes. Everyone is going to hear about this. Kralin has an option on us as he has on the land. But you haven't told me. What did I get out of my real father for this?" Mrs. Taverner looked steadily at her son.

"It was a strange thing. I have always wondered at it very much. Lovely boy though you were, he never liked you. He always said you had no heart. No, it was—I suppose I might as well tell you it all. It was Felicity that he cared about. He did not leave very much, but he wanted the money he left to me for you divided between you both."

"Did he?"

"Why should I? She was no daughter of his."

"She seems to have been pretty popular with your two husbands. What surprises me is that she didn't blow the gaff."

Extraordinary was the contempt with which his mother answered:

"I suppose she hadn't the courage."

"Well, she didn't," said Adrian, thoughtfully.

"Do what?"

"Give you away. Any more than you gave her the money my father intended her to have. I admit that if I'd known it, I'd have done something. And, by the way, who was he?" Mrs. Taverner recovered herself.

"You can ask Kralin."

"I certainly shall, since we are sold to him."

"Yes," said his mother. "What are we going to do about that?"

It is a tribute to her immense vitality that she passed on to this, refusing to be overcome, as she had always refused; preparing, as she had always done, to do what must be done; helped by the sang-froid of old age, which has, after all, the least to lose.

"Who," she asked, "knows about this, yet?"

"Only me and Polteratsky. He was with me."

"And ran off to tell your cousins, I suppose."

"He stayed with me for some time. I was upset. I think—" Adrian reflected. Boris wanted things neither Taverners nor Tracys over the hills could give.

—"I think on the whole it might have been some one worse than that young man." The telephone bell rang. Adrian answered it and returned to his mother.

"That was him, speaking from Starn. I gather there has been a row. We were seen calling on Kralin, he says, and they asked questions. He says he refused to tell, and doesn't feel that he can stay there now any longer. We might do worse than ask him over here. At least he'd be less likely to talk." Mrs. Taverner felt the reluctance of a victorian-bred woman to meeting a man who knew such things about her, but with her strength of mind she put it away.

"I told him to hold on. Shall we fix it? I can talk to him when he comes. He wants me to be useful to him." She agreed. An hour later their car brought him to the house.

* * * * *

Boris descended happily at the plaster-candle porch. This was going according to programme. He ran indoors, into the room where Mrs. Taverner was sitting, came in quietly, dropped down on one knee and with respectful tenderness kissed her hand. That got it over. Mrs. Taverner liked it. In a confusion that was somehow delightful, a blessed release, she found herself almost in tears.

"Boris, you must help us," she said.

"As if you were my own mother," he said, "whom they killed." It was then that she did cry a little.

After lunch he walked in the garden, in consultation with Adrian and told how his honourable reticence had made it impossible to stay with his cousins. Adrian then told him about Kralin's option on the land. The two young gentlemen sought for what was best to do and did not find it.

Chapter XII

BORIS DISPOSED OF, Picus, Scylla and Felix sat down to the same consultation, over the hills. At tea-time a telegram came from him to tell them that Kralin was already in treaty for the land. Scylla said:

"There are things which must be tried, though they won't do any good. One of us must go and see Kralin again, and it had better be me, for he is said to like women. I'm the only one of us who has not spoken to him alone. When I have, it will round things off. At worst I can only find out that things are as bad as we think. At best I may discover something. No harm can come to me." Then they agreed, and walked with her to the inland edge of the wood.

"Good-bye, sweetheart," said Picus, and kissed her.

"Good-bye, my sister," said Felix, and held her close. Delicately dressed and made-up, she crossed the valley through the young corn's crystal spikes.

Kralin let her in, his excellent manners touched with that becoming shyness which made people attach the word "charming" to him. He took her into Felicity's room, because she must know it so well, and because it was delightful there. She curled herself back on the divan, her head on a silver cushion against the wall, displaying herself as was necessary. Her face was turned to the light. From there she saw the Rops, looked at them carefully, and then was careful not to look again. Kralin sat at the bureau they had once ransacked, so that again the shadow fell on him.

"Kralin," she began, "do you really mean to do all this?"

"Well, yes," he said, "I do."

"You will buy up this land in order to make money which you don't want out of the ruin of one of the fairest places on earth. And you will publish my cousin's paternity, make semi-scientific pornography of the life of his sister and your wife?"

"If you like to put it that way."

"Do you really want to?"

"'Want' isn't quite the word. As a practising psychologist, I am interested; as a man who likes to make money, who am rather good at making money, I see an opportunity too good to throw away." He spoke neatly, without hesitation, opening the interview like a game of chess.

—"Besides, I don't think you are quite fair. There is—or was—an 'or' between the two clauses."

"That is not true," said Scylla. "A farmer here has told me that you held an option on the land before ever you came to us. And even if you had struck a bargain with us for her papers, would that really prevent you from telling or writing what you know?" Kralin laughed this time, as pleasant a laugh as you could wish to hear.

"There is always the libel action." Scylla shook her head:

"Come off that; and you are far too intelligent to expect me to accept the reasons you give. If you aren't frank, you'll get one of your repressions. Kralin, you are out for your pleasure. Personal immediate pleasure, not abstract delight in scientific truth, or a business speculation which means a lot of hard work. Only very rare people get their pleasure out of the first, and as for the second, you've never been a business man."

"Perhaps I am a very rare person."

"I think you are." Looking at him, she noticed that already she was beginning to feel cold.

"I hold out. You want your fun. Revenge on Felicity. Revenge on her mother, and there I don't blame you. And if that includes a general vendetta on all Taverners, so much the better. And on anything they are or care about. Perfect. So many birds dead, and with only two stones."

"Quite so, but you misunderstand. All this effective stone-throwing and bird-killing is to me purely a by-product. Convenient, if you like, witty and amusing, but I do assure you, Scylla, not my aim." She managed to smile up at him, her eyes wide open, with the stare of a swift gentle animal before a deadly animal. A stare she managed to veil, to make provocative, inquisitive, anything but the look of a woman who has not even Zeus-of-the-Lost-Battle by her side.

"Go on, Kralin. Explain to me, then."

"You really should not think me an unmoral man because I like to reduce morals to their origins, to their exact meaning, to their social use. Clear them from their confusions, sentimentalities and inutilities. Especially I am interested in the way people will permit themselves what would ordinarily be considered crimes, if they had not given a moral re-christening to their actions. A sublimation is not necessarily an improvement. I am sure Felicity had very good reasons for leaving me, and told them very prettily to the rest of the world; but I am not concerned with that. What I should like to show is how her repressions with regard to her family made her capable of conduct which she would have called criminal, if she had not found another name for it. Yes, blackmail. It is not that her eroticism was so peculiar, generally too cerebral to be convenient for analysis; it was that with her nature, so apparently 'fine,' so '*exaltée,*' she should have persuaded herself to trade on the knowledge of Adrian's paternity." (*A generation that is learning to treat sex only too scientifically.* So Felix had guessed right.) She felt her cheeks begin to burn, saw Kralin admire the colour-tide. There had even been a touch of indignation—the moral kind—in his voice. She felt sick. Must not feel sick. Felt like a creature poised on some quivering wire over a pit of snakes.

('You will fall into the snake-pit. What will you do there? Sing like the saga-man? You won't be brave enough.')

"Prove it," she said. "Show me what you have read in her papers that makes this true."

"My dear Scylla, it is obvious. What else was it all about? They knew she knew. Their re-action, foolish perhaps but quite normal, was to make life as unpleasant for her as they could. I admit she was not the woman to do what she wanted very effectively. But after her accident—I ask you, Scylla, why shouldn't I clarify and continue what my wife began? Put it another way, and I should be avenging her."

How useful abstract statements are, to cover action. Into this distorted lucidity she had been dropped like a fowl trussed up. She must not stammer nor weep.

"Kralin," she said, "you know as well as I that the exact opposite is the truth—it was her life—or her death—that she would not use her knowledge, or do what, God help her innocence, she thought would injure Adrian, or her mother. Even on her she would not strike back. As to that—accident—what do we know about the strength of several evil wills? There were three against her if you count Adrian.—" How foolish is flat contradiction. She saw the beginning of polite ennui in his face.

"Anyhow, show me the papers so that I can judge."

"You can read my analysis of the Electra-complex, if you like."

"That is not the same thing."

"I think I have shown all the papers that I intend to for the present. I suppose it was your russian friend who told you about Adrian. He came with him. Then, I suppose, in an excess of family feeling, you turned him out of the house?"

She had made a slip from the start, who had to account for a supposed quarrel on Boris's reticence. This was easier going, mean and sharp and of the ways of the world, a condition of the game, which they, who could not win, must play to win.

"Boris Polteratsky? No, he was rather too discreet, that was all. It seemed to me that he preferred Adrian's friendship to ours. Later, we met Adrian in Starn and he told us himself."

That went down. Kralin nodded: "I should say that he was more of a temperament with Adrian than with you."

It was going easily again, the wire widened and slackened to a swing, an easy perch over the snake-pit. 'Swing in a wind off hell, south-country child. Be civil to your demon, deceive him if you can. *Love your enemies.* Had this case been provided for, even in God's mind? There was a man *who gave his enemy his plank and plunged aside to die.* Would we?' Then she noticed that hatred was not what she felt for Kralin, any more than it was love. What she felt was a cold awed thing; and with the awe a spirit was contending, cold and serviceable, to control the awe and teach her what she had to do. Like a person recovering from vertigo, she felt that now she could look again into the abyss.

"I think," she said, "that you're in Shakespeare, the man who made evil his good."

"My dear Scylla, what does evil mean?"

"What does good mean? That is what you can't tell me, for you don't know."

"Tell me, then," he said, coaxingly.

('I ought to be able to tell him. I ought to be able to say something. If I don't, I shall go away more afraid than when I came. Not only failure, but more fear. Good and evil. Good and evil. "*Good and evil are different, as their names imply. . . . But they are both aspects of my Lord. He is present in the one and absent in the other. . . . But his absence implies his presence, and therefore I have the right to say 'come.'*" Come, daimon, come. I have played as well as I know. I have been quiet. *There is nothing here that you can tell. That is what you have to say.*')

—"What is good? That is exactly what I cannot tell you, Kralin. Not because it is difficult, but because it is impossible. For since you do not know anything about it, it is as though you were blind to colours or to the art of painting, or insensible to the touch-difference between silk and stone, or glass and jade. But I'm sure, if it is any comfort to you, that you're a connoisseur in bad smells."

"Thanks," said Kralin, making a little face, "and cats like valerian, you know; and you like cats. But, I admit, these spiritual specialities are not in my line of business. While—" glancing at the Rops—"I've an eye for the *memento mori*."

"I must go," said Scylla. "You won't let me see her papers and judge for myself. That's a weak position, you know. You will hold Felicity's memory up to infamy. You will broadcast Adrian's birth and buy-up our land to destroy it. There never was an 'or' in it. A pretty complete job."

"That's it," he said, getting up. "You should go to Russia, Scylla. You're an intelligent woman, really, yet you are cramping your mind with stereotyped ideas."

"Yours aren't original. There have been blackmailers before." She could have sworn for a second that he looked hurt.

"There have been husbands who carried out their dead wives' wishes." She changed her tone quickly.

"As to Russia, after our departed friend, we've had enough of the place. Have you been there lately?" ('As I might ask if he had been to Paris.')

"I go there on and off."

"I suppose your politics are not those of our rather treacherous boy-friend." He shook his head.

"You should go there, if there is anything about me you want to understand."

"But you're a Jew, aren't you? Not a Slav."

He said, a little stiffly:

"Mixed."

She brought herself away from the house, intact, but as if bit by bit. She walked slowly down the garden path, reassembled herself in the lane, wished that she was out of sight, and could faint, so as to be in a state of not-knowing. Knew that the walk would steady her, that she must take it, that oblivion was not allowed; that when she got back they would have to get down to business, business that would include the understanding that things were as bad as they thought.

* * * * *

"This is wickedness," said Felix, "what are we going to do about it?" That is what they did not know, that no one knows to-day, for we have lost the habit of stating problems in moral terms. It is very awkward, reducing virtue to a state of emotions, without rules and without chart. Since their childhood, talk of sin to the Taverners would have been like an act of exhibitionism. Yet here it was, something that could not be excused or paraphrased or renamed. Charity would not cover it, or anger or disgust or a shrug. It was there, risen in their green pastures, writhing through their sun-pierced copses; and like the row of bungalows Kralin proposed, scurfing their hills. *The Lover calls on the Elemental Spirits to protect the Beloved.* They would call, but to what effect? What had they with which to meet Kralin?

—Heaven itself would stoop to her.

"Stoop, heaven," said Scylla, "for we have loved virtue. Whatever virtue is."

"Will it matter so much what is said of us," said Picus—"even of Felicity?"

"No," said Felix, "But the ruin of the land will unquiet her ghost and bring vileness that we cannot foresee. Multiplying vileness. Kralin will do it thoroughly. That has been his move, whether he knew it or not, behind the chances of his marriage."

"There is movement in this," said Scylla, "like a sound that has been waited for. The old stone waits for something at Stone End."

"Hush," said Picus. "It's no good our getting lost in that country."

"And what's the good of our observation, our Boris, our use of the world's tricks? We ought to be strong as death."

"We've got to be as strong as we are able to be, and see what comes of it. Kralin isn't God, Felix."

"I think," said his wife, "that what's wrong with us all is that we see God moving in Kralin, and nowhere else. We can see law moving in him and purpose, and most of the time we are blind to our own. Or we say, 'a poor little thing my piece of work and imagination. I daresay it's only a complex my desire for truth, for the intellectual love of God. I don't like to mention it, but I do think the beautiful is rather pretty, don't you know.' For fear of the bogey of rhetoric! While we've an angel's courage in our disbeliefs. Picus, you silent devil, isn't that true?"

"It's what I've been trying to say," said Picus, injured. He got up and began to straighten pictures on the walls; vanishing on his bird-step into the corridor, where they heard him sing:

"Dearly beloved brethren,
Isn't it a sin
When you peel potatoes
To throw away the skin?
The skins feed the pigs
And the pigs feed you.
Dearly beloved brethren
Isn't that true?"

But Scylla and Felix sat looking ahead, at the wall, as though it were not there, holding fast to each other's hands.

Chapter XIII

A WEEK BEFORE they had been living in a life that ran its course, alternating adventures of country and town. The double adventures of life out-of-doors, and life indoors, their life alone and their life as social animals, face to face with the weather and their work and themselves. Country-bred, they went to capital cities in the same way as their ancestors, for their amenities and for the people they would find there. To the country they returned, as head-hunters or sea-raiders, to examine spoil, but never as though their home could be anywhere else.

Three weeks before they had tumbled out of the train at Starn—stale with parties, high-speed transit and the excitements that private mourning no longer interferes with, into the spring. The week that followed had been a *sacre du printemps.* A rite that was like a bath, a purification, a becoming mana again, with which goes tabu. A separation for them from other people, from all that is inessential, a time to reject what they had experienced or make it their own; a taking-back, in a profound sense, into caste. They had begun to move at leisure, think quietly, speak only when they had something to say, enjoy each act of living. There Picus became a musician again and a gardener, a maker in wood and wax of the "phantasies of his peculiar thought": Felix, a bird-watcher and a naturalist. Scylla's passion, shared with the innocent man in the *Adventure of Miss Annie Spragg,* was—spending if necessary her life over it—to leave behind her the full chronicle of their part of England, tell its *historiê* with the candour and curiosity, the research and imagination and what to-day might pass for credulity of a parish Herodotus. There was material there, for ten miles round about them, which had not been touched; not only manor rolls and church registers or the traditions which get themselves tourist-books. She had access to sources, histories of houses, histories of families, to memories that were like visions, to visions which seemed to have to do with memory. To her the people talked, the young as well as the old; and there were times when the trees and stones and turf were not dumb, and she had their speech, and the ruins rose again and the sunk foundations, and copse and clearing and forest changed places, and went in and out and set to partners in their century-in, century-out dance. There were times, out on the high turf at sun-rise and set, when in the slanted light she saw their land as an exfoliation, not happening in our kind of time, a becoming of the perfected. She did not know how she knew, Kilmeny's daughter, only what it looked like—the speechless sight of it—her thread to the use of the historic imagination, Ariadne to no Minataur in the country of the Sanc Grail.

Into this life and land Boris had broken and been absorbed. Who was there to stand out against them in their own land? After Boris had come Kralin; after Kralin, what Kralin would bring. The timeless active life of lover and sister and brother had been changed—for something which seemed to them to be like the cold arms and legs and abstractions of machinery, an abstract of the cerebral life of towns. For the realities that held them in activity and in vision, realities of the blood and the nerves and the senses and what is meant by the spirit, was to be substituted contact with the chill, the purpose, the strength of a machine, and of the impure values begotten by the machine upon raw human nature and re-begotten by them in turn.

The Taverners were the kind of people who, if they have to choose, choose a boat and a library rather than a car and a club; cherry blossom before orchids, apples before tinned peaches, wine to whiskey, one dress from Chanel to six "from a shop." Who listen to jazz and Mozart, not to Massenet: who cannot endure imitations of anything: who do not tire of real things once they have got them home to play with. They knew what in relation to Chardin has been called "all the splendour and glory of matter." Like him, they were in love. "Could that exceptionally dark scullery really be packed with miracles of beauty?" Could that wall of loose stones have so rare a surface, or a bowl of eggs in the green light, filtered through the larder-window, glow like pearls? The polish on a horse's coat, the china-red lacquer of Adrian's car, two shots at a half-mirror, were to them surfaces as pleasant as petal or silk or fruit. A gull overhead, the sky's travelling cross, the treble howl of his note—what is the name for the satisfaction these things give? Like others of our age, they had re-discovered also the still-life, that, however it may get itself painted, it is not *nature mort,* but that each haphazard arrangement can be composed of formal perfections of shape and light—plates on a table, a basket of folded linen, a sea-scape off the beach in a glass dish. They knew that the twenty-four hours of the day and night are a cinema, an *actualité,* a continuous programme, whose hero is the sun and whose heroine the moon, whose play is the modification of light, whose "pathos" is sunset, with sunrise for epiphany.

Spending a great part of their lives in terms of these pleasures, they were rarely bored. With her house-keeping and adorning, her bees and boats and her love-making, Scylla's chronicle had grown, story of a site, of a name on a grave, the low-down—or for that matter—the high-up of a ghost, a family or a village; the story of what happened, or if not that, Aristotle's thing that would have happened, in the nation-breeding doings, plain or secret, of part of an english shire. There Picus grew his garden and enjoyed himself, whose chief art was that vanishing grace, lost by people who set out not to enjoy themselves, but to be amused. Then Felix watched his birds, with an attention human beings would have found wanting in tact, the first persistence he had shown, to whom impatience had once seemed a part of happiness. From the quiet that overtook him out of doors, they hoped for the development of his exquisite turn for observation—of life as it flew or swam or ran on four feet, or walked with a shell for house. Life that came up out of the ground, or flew in from the rim of the sky; life that mounted a few inches further each year, taller and taller into a man or a tree: life that spun for an hour in the air, a column of bright transparencies; that opened for a week in petals, soft as Felicity's skin, poised like her head; life that for ages lay on the hill-side, weathering, patined with the lichens' coloured leather, charged in some places with magic and always with wisdom. Science would come later, the machinery for handling his observations, but what was the explanation of the instrument that Felix was in himself, that just such and such phenomena should affect him and in such a way? All three loved as much, could observe some detail almost as well, but what was it that made the whole lucid to Felix, as if water, wind, air and earth-processes were all one thing, whose exterior workings were the signature of their nature, actual and invisible?

From this being and becoming they had been snatched; and there, in their own country, had been imposed on them the desires and purposes of Nick Kralin. About him and his evil they sensed something urban and mechanical, as of a large intricate machine in full use. Machines are ultimately a work of nature, since they are a work of man, the work of her cleverest animal, devising tools to meet his special needs. Only needs which are not always true needs, or the tool has not been adapted to the needs' best satisfaction, but become an object in itself. Tools and machines are not like thought or art or love. They do not exist for themselves, but to do something. Once they do not fit their proper use, or their use is an unwholesome one, they become a curse. For man does not always scrap them. Adoring their parts, he will see in their making, or in their makers, an end in itself. Hence the unparalleled faith shown to-day in the expert, forgetting that the man who knows all about one thing, may know nothing about anything else. This is particularly true of the applied sciences. Or, even more, since the concoction of poison gas is a wholly bad thing, there is no conceivable reason for perfecting its technique. But men to-day will perfect that technique, largely for the joy of doing it, fabricating a value and a need—how well one knows the process—by saying that, though it will never be used, it is still as well to know how to do it; that man has a right and a duty to have command over nature, so that knowledge of process must be followed for this and for its own sake.

And if Krupp meant his guns to kill,
Then Krupp must be a brute.

That was a song about it, fifty years ago. So it seemed to them that Kralin was derived in part from such values as these, a fabricated man. Not wholly, whose choice of evils must have had its springs deep in one of the natural orders, but who, on some such basis, had "arranged" himself, in the serene conviction of the town-bred that Nature is only here to listen to what he has to say about her.

It seemed to them also that in this situation they had been given a chance to make it glorious, and that they did not know how. What redeeming feature had it, or excuse for the exercise of courage and imagination? They could not hope so much as to preserve Felicity's memory, who had dreamed of making her illustrious. And before and behind and over-towering her memory was the threat to the land. The passion of the earlier hours was gone. Fatigue succeeded it and disgust and disquiet, endurance, but without ardour. This they knew was the hardest part of what they had to bear, but the knowledge hardly sweetened it. They sent a letter to Boris with what little Scylla had learned. Days passed, and they waited for news of him.

Chapter XIV

THE DAYS PASSED merrily for Boris at the house on the moor. The evergreens did not depress him, and from a ridge behind it, a moor-crest planted with pines in whose tops the wind made harp-sounds, he went to hide, to be placated by the sound of stringed instruments, to escape from Adrian and Mrs. Taverner, to meditate, not on the situation, but on whatever came into his head. Which is not the worst way of finding out what one wants to know. The sun drew russian smells out of the wood-sap and the needle-sap and the un-russian prospect. He would fling himself down there to stare over the moor. Away to the south, to the extreme horizon, it threw up a black surf, more pines, here and there, away to where the long green-shining downs rose between it and the sea.

One day, about a fortnight after his arrival, he found himself glad to be alone there. He did not fear his own company, nor was it usual for him to notice it, who was continually at a rehearsal—a re-mime necessary to him—of the hurried drama of his life. For thirteen years he had been scampering about Europe, born on the froth of a wave whose body was of blood. Up-sparkle and flash, tumble and leap in air, but the body of it blood, substance of the wave of russian emigration, folk-wandering in a hurry, not by choice, but by the argument of blood. He had begun by now to know a few important truths about that pilgrimage to no-where, not only the stock-phrases of his kind, but truths about himself and about the whole event. Court-page, young officer, he had been twenty-two when the real business had begun. Then there had been Petrograd, insanity and plots; then the long flight which had ended at Constantinople through Odessa. A dead father, a lost sister, a mother hiding in fear. Constantinople. Then a passage worked to Marseilles and his french odyssey; until two years ago Felix had discovered him; his shelter, his spring-board, his established refuge, but whose friendship and hospitality made its own demands. A refuge that could be a discipline, friendship that asked for no payment, that all the same cost something, and in a special coin—payment in Taverner values and standards. How he had resented this, resented it still; and this visit was the first on which he had doled them out, centime by centime, something in their own coin. His own he lavished on them, the change of his harsh bright devilries. And had he not asked now for their dirty work to do? In a way, too, he knew that he had the right of it. No man can really pay in spiritual cash that is not his own. His Taverners would not be content with that, asking him to part with some of his egotism, invest in a little common honesty, a little truth. Not for their sakes, but for virtue's. He had understood very well. It was a thing he could not really do. They were stupid to ask it of him. He could never do that, not for his own sake even, much less for theirs or for the idea of good. The thought of the demand drove him into a petulance that had madness behind it. One of his bad spells was coming to him. He sprang up from his pine bed as though the needles had turned into steel and pricked him. Memory for him was no mother of the muses, but a machine-gun for which he was target, each shot of its endless fire-belt telling on his bound body. Memories of how he had left Russia; dirty trains full of people in flight who had never been dirty before. (Scylla had a silly joke about the man who lost a day's shaving in the War and had never caught up.) Think of something silly and you're safe. For years now he had raised flight from machine-gun memory to a desperate art. Never in time, of course, but it was something to be able to get away after the first bullet-storm. That was why he drank, took cocaine, lied, cheated, throwing away what was at least a tradition of self-respect, as a man might throw his old father to the wolves. Dodging the memory-storm, he also dodged the poignant arts and the finer intimacies of love. Not always, but Felix had been the sole real exception. But even there with precaution, with cynicism, with defiance, with gestures sometimes as *voulu,* as deliberately grotesque, as Stavrogin's when he bit the General's ear.

That was the worst of his Taverners; they had led him into thought again, they and their land. For the life he had learned to live, towns were essential, and the country a menace, crouched waiting at the end of every pavement and every street. From every point of the earth's circumference it lay waiting for him, like an animal for a cub that has been torn out of its womb. What was town house or palace to the field and the forest-bred boy, to whom trees spoke and the air's blue flights, *autumn's wonder and winter's chill*? While there was no one who enjoyed a palace more, who had its conventions by inheritance. He knew what a palace was there for, how to serve it, how to get the most fun out of it, whose training had been to enjoy splendour. So thoroughly taught that he was incapable, as his Taverners approved, of pretension about it, or about any of the things which a boy of less birth would have displayed, bragged about or traded on—with Americans and other impressionables—(and who is not impressionable? Who does not want to know what the Queen has for tea?) Boris did not do that, assumed no rank or dignities; concealed those he had. Could not be brought to speak of his youth except to friends, or—and then impersonally—when he was very drunk. Let his walk speak for him, his hands and his feet.

He was on his feet now, panting a little, his eyes staring, uttering words in Russian and little cries. All because he saw a tree in front of him, standing away on the moor by itself, a tree that he had seen before. It was the same tree that he had seen when they had been turned out of a train, onto a countryside half under water, on a grey plain, at dusk. He and his sister, his father and his mother, on their flight east across Russia. They had woken up, sitting on foul boards, to a complete awareness of train-dirt. His sister, bleeding from a hæmorrhage, could hardly stand. Stunned past the sense of danger. They were all like that. They had nothing. Knew they had nothing. Nothing was the only thing they knew. Who had had everything. They each had a nothing, like a great corpse hung by a string that cut their dirty necks.

It was the same tree as the one which had stood there, a little way off the railway-track, on the plain. He was back there again where the train had stopped; and some way off up the line there were huts and people shouting. No lights. Their nothings hung down till they stumbled over them. His sister with tiny steps splashed into a puddle and stood still. She had his mother's arm round her. His angry father did not swear at them. The weight of his nothing had silenced even his cruel rage. It *was* the same tree. It had seen him now, and it was growing larger. It was coming to meet him. . . .

There by the train he had flung his nothing across his back, in order to do his best for his women and because he was still able to hate his cruel, stupid father, who would play a game of abjectness and low birth, and then let flash his selfish rage and habit of authority. Blind brute. Why could he not think of his wife and his daughter? Or his son, for that matter? He had looked at the buttons on his father's coat. Now he could see them again, round-plaited leather buttons of an old shooting-coat; and behind every one there was a space hollowed out and the shank replaced; and inside each one there was a jewel, a single stone, torn out of a necklace or a ring. Four down the front and three on each sleeve and one over each pocket. Coloured eyes. He had expected to see them burn through and betray them. Ever since then he had been afraid of single stones. He'd half-a-dozen himself the old man didn't know about. The old man who might run away and leave them at any minute. Another bullet tore through his breast, one that the memory-fire repeated constantly. He had shifted the weight of his nothing, he had kept an eye on his father that he should not run away. But then, for the first time, in sight of that tree—it was the one thing he saw, the one thing in the growing night—there came upon him hatred of his sister and his mother. Because with his youth leaping in him, it would have been easy for him to shift for himself. But because he must stay with them, help them, shift for them, they might all three die. (If they did, his father should go with them. He would see to that.) He was wary and attentive about death, his still unflawed youth strung like a tightened bow against it. What had he to do with these women? Did they care so much? Did they matter so much? The old man, their mate and their parent, was looking for a chance to abandon them. He spat again as he had spat at his father's back. Into that pit of the spirit he had sunk with his father. That is what happens in that kind of revolution—that the persecuted become base. Then he had seen his mother, her arm about his sister in the puddle, and heard her say:

"It does not matter, so long as we love each other enough." Ai, Ai. She had dissolved the grain of his evil thought then as she always did. He had given her his arm, and very slowly they had stumbled through the mud towards the huts. Past the tree, which seemed to turn and look at them, as it was looking at him now.

At the huts they were making enquiries, not very dangerous ones, as they were only among peasants at this end of the earth. There, also driven off the train, he had seen a man he had been at school with, still dressed in ragged elegance, teasing the men who were trying to find out whether or not to kill him:

"Son of the people! Son of the people yourself! Worker! What d'you suppose I am?" It was an ancient peasant who had answered, whose words had by some mystery passed for truth:

"Of course, he's a worker. He is a poor man like us. Look, he has only been able to buy a glass for one of his eyes." So the single eyeglass, whose *bravura* made Boris envious, had saved his life; as now the memory saved him, taking cover under the fun of it against the bullet-storm.

He moved up a few trees along the ridge. He sat down again and lit a cigarette. The tree had taken its place again in the landscape.

Like a man in whom some incurable malady recurs, he was not quite steady. That had been a bad turn. In his mind there was plenty of room, not for sins, but for the state of sin. Of which hatred of his mother was a symbol. It was more, it was bad luck. From the dreadful moment when he had been tempted to abandon her—(he had not abandoned her, left her in the Crimea with forged papers, in an obscurity whose misery was tempered by comparative safety)—he had felt that he had come under a curse. A curious outlook which made the fact of temptation significant, not its resistance. His father had finally left them all, landed up in prison and was now almost certainly dead, and Boris rejoiced at it. For his sister he had good reason to believe that one of the new officials had violated her, and that she had then killed herself. Anyhow, she was dead. But his belief in the curse was confirmed by what had happened to him later, explaining a gesture his friends noticed, by which when excited, he clutched at the base of his throat, as though feeling for a chain or a ribbon that was not there. There had been a ribbon once, because, before they parted, his mother had given him an ikon, an ancient one that was also a jewel, had hung it round his neck and told him never to take it off. Never to give it away or to sell it in whatever distress; still less never to lose it or allow it to be stolen. Good mother-magic. But in Constantinople, not six months later, he had gone out one night to get drunk. That was allowed them, the life of the russian exiles a saturnalia within a saturnalia in the life of that city, occupied then by Allied Armies, each on a national spree. He remembered the evening well, the scots officers, often beautiful to look at, who were exceedingly kind to him, with whom the party had begun. One of them had tried to take him home, but the minute devil-who-will-not-go-to-bed was already his familiar. Nor had he much of a bed to go to. He had run away, and the scots officer had run after him, and they had both nearly fallen into the Bosphorus. Then he had dodged away and the scots officer had given it up; and he had run into a Turk and danced round him, trying to recite the ninety-nine names of God; and got them wrong and tried the names of the eighty-eight ways of making love, and annoyed the Turk and made it up with the Turk, and they had gone off to a "dancing" together.

All he remembered after that was waking up on a seat in the gardens at Péra. It was winter and still dark, and as his hand went up to his throat to feel for the ikon, it was not there. Feeling down his body, he had mistaken the edge of a button for the jewel where it had slipped, and the horror of disappointment had done something to make him mad. In his waistcoat pocket he had found a packet of cocaine. Had he traded his jewel for that? He did not know. He could never remember what had happened at the "dancing." Nor could he ever forget. Nor be persuaded that his vital misfortune, something very like the ruin of his soul, had not begun that night. On that night something had been settled about him. Something that Felix could not undo, friends, food or fair surroundings. Something that made vice and dissipation equally a matter of no importance. There was one help—the usual one—not to think, to scurry through life to artificial oblivion. Again it was part of his resentment against his Taverners that they led him into experiences which were sincere. It was like a diet of fresh food to a connoisseur in tins. He had not, up to then, observed that his plans for getting amusing employment out of Adrian Taverner implied a partial acquiescence in what his own Taverners offered him. For years he had been trying to find a happy-go-lucky way to kill himself. Nothing but his pure blood and the scrupulous physical care of his up-bringing had kept him alive; his body's perfection, except for intervals of starvation, hardly touched. The disintegration worked in his spirit. It was already reaching his nerves, and it was curious to watch the effect of inward experience on a body that hardly of itself knew how to be ill.

Even Felix Taverner did not know that Boris said to himself: 'If I had not spoken to myself that day on the railway lines, and said "It's not my business to save my mother and my sister," I should be to-day *un homme sauvé*.' They knew about the loss of the ikon, not that to Boris it was the consequence of a thought beside a railway line, looking at a tree. Nor would they have understood it, because it is not understandable; an indecency of unreason, men, especially Englishmen, knew they had better leave alone. But, as Felix pointed out, it was no use saying that Boris ought not to be like that when Boris was like that. While a sound instinct told them not to probe too far, nor lose themselves in the insane, enchanted no-man's-land of the slav spirit.

Their Slav sat down again, propped his back against the rough purple bark of a fir. He was feeling a little better, as people do whose skeletons have done rattling, popped out and done their dance and gone back to their cupboard. His head was full of fairy-stories, and he was remembering the girl in the red shoes. She had stolen a loaf to spare those shoes, and now they would never come off her feet, nor she stop walking. While he remembered that she would never say: "Cut off my feet in the red shoes." Identifying himself with her, he approved. Stuck out his feet and admired his ankles. What was he going to think about now? The Taverners' troubles, and that person across the valley called Kralin? *A lapse of cuddles with cheese and nearly bats.* The haunting phrase repeated itself. And repeated. Repeated itself. Repeat and repeat and repeat and self and self and self....

The Taverners were expecting his help. He remembered this suddenly. It was a good thing for them that they did not know that, since he had left them to stay with their aunt, he had forgotten all about it. Not quite. The tune of their distresses had kept up a kind of disagreeable ground bass in his head. But what with his scheme to become Adrian's partner, and the tact necessary to insure that and handle Adrian's mother, and Adrian's cry-parties over which he called his illegitimacy and the agreeable life they otherwise led, he had left the complicated sufferings and vendettas over the hill to pass out of his imagination. Twinges of conscience had made him deal very grimly with their intrusion. He had written to Felix to borrow sweaters, riding things, shirts. Paid great attention to his toilette, which repaid him.

Now, sensitised and made vulnerable by memory and the sight of the tree, their situation returned to him; vague, but as though it were already a stage advanced, setting into a new form and ripening—and clarifying round the figure of Kralin.

It was his opinion that, however far the Taverners might regard him as a trial by God or an attention from the Devil, the Taverners had deserved Kralin. What on earth did a family of their sort, or the society they represented, mean by knowing such a man? He thought he knew the type, and that every nation had its variant of it, and that it was only in England that they are not suspect. The Taverners' answer to that would be that trust had evoked trust. This was childish to Boris. He was not anti-semitic; pogroms in theory he abhorred. But intimacy? Marriage? Felicity, unhappy in her home and in her youth, detested by her mother, had been deceived—by looks, glamour, and a chance of escape. That he could admit. But once undeceived, why had not her family got her out of it, if only for their own sakes? (Unless, of course, his Taverners were right, and they had considered her marriage the least compromising short-cut to her decease.) He saw the man spinning the kind of web round them that Boris's race for one had not taken the trouble to cut. And paid for the omission.

Before Boris's eyes, in the tender heat, the stretch of moor-country was coming to the new life proper to it, its salute to the sun as complex and exquisite as that of any greenwood, any pasture, any garden of flowers. Already there was bee-stirring, and a warming of tint; praise in obscure music, but praise. Spring having its way with England. A new shock went through him, not of pain, but of sudden awareness. Had he been allowing England to put him to sleep, setting back the clock for him that had struck the hours of hell? He sat forward. Whatever Kralin was, he sprang up before him for reminder. There, in this land. Kralin, whatever he was, a sculptured grave-stone, a ghost? A daimon pointing? A demon beckoning? While he had been playing around, breathing again, feeling again, sleeping again deep. Now Kralin was standing before him. Like the tree. In Russia the tree had been tall and lean, standing by itself. Able to move about, pass from there and travel from land to land. Kralin was like that tree. Risen up in England to remind Boris of what had been done to him; of what he had become because of what had been done to him. He was not to forget, who the Taverners would have over-laid with saving thoughts, with Scylla's loved word, *sôphrosynê*. He was the happy lad who had once stood up in the seat of his troika on its bird-rush across sparkling snow. He was the young officer in bright uniform on guard about an Empress. He was the ragged shadow helping two women in torn clothes, their feet wrapped in rags, into a stinking train. Teaching them names that were not their own. "*Adieu, adieu, mein klein garde offizier. Adieu, adieu.*" He was the laughing drunk *déclassé* in Constantinople, whom ordinary men still wished to help. He was the scamp of Paris Felix had stood before like a shield. He was the man who had begun to accept help, running away over the water to Felix's home for refuge, like a thief running away from his cross. He had even been making up his mind that his was a cross that might be lost. Until this vision of Kralin. Kralin, whom he now saw as a Red agent, as confidently as the newspaper-doped man recognises a little bearded man with a scowl carrying a bag of Moscow-labelled gold.

Boris understood little of the public events of his Revolution, perplexed by what had happened as any young gentleman not trained to politics might be. Scylla and Felix were far better informed. But certain things that he knew, he knew well. Something the Taverners could not know, that few Englishmen realise, the lives of people who may be called the under-tow of the world's tides. People of mixed or exiles' up-bringing; of fallen, uncertain or bastard origin; or of no fixed caste or situation. A world not necessarily criminal, though criminals are drawn from it; nor a world—as it sometimes poses—of thwarted talent or genius, though creative intelligences are found there. The untraditional part of humanity, poor materially, supplying the ordered ranks of societies with crooks, cranks, criminals, creators. For these are not always rebels or throw-outs at first-hand from the world groups. Discontent, protest, gifts, misfit or sheer bad character or sheer brilliance may run in families; and these, unless they inherit wealth or their women stop them, have a way of turning up in the under-tow. These are international waters, not properly charted, and little of any value is known or has been written about them to-day—though the picaresque novel, from the *Satyricon* down, is full of them. For their picture-making qualities are obvious, and their nature is that any fish can come out of them (including the fish whose chief ambition is to find the upper sea again and rejoin its shoal).

Russian emigration is making a world within this

world. Persons whose position in society has been taken away with their goods, and who lack the chance or the will to re-establish themselves. Slavs who have given in to the slav character. Boris, his short flat nose in the air, had been running about in it, curious, fatalistic and amused. To his Taverners it was a world for an occasional spree, suspicious of it and aware that it had nothing to do with the Bohemia of the arts where they were perfectly at home, to which it pleased them to think that they belonged.

Boris was now sure that Kralin came from there; could hear Felix place him. Assuming that he had made Felix understand, he could hear the Englishman say: "Son of a crank with no known history behind him but his crank. One of old Tolstoy's hangers-on. A son who doesn't follow in father's footsteps, or make a bee-line for the opposite camp. He was a pacifist of sorts in the War." Then Felix would add: "but isn't he the fish who finds his shoal again?" Then Boris would answer that it was not so, that Kralin was doing his own fishing with a hook to open up the gullet of his catch so that it could never close again. "Throats like ours, and that's why we're called poor fish?" Boris would agree with that, but all the same Felix would not quite have understood. He did not realise what Boris had learned, that there *are* people in the world with nothing to lose; with nothing to lose in the sense that a peasant has, a mechanic, a manufacturer, a landed gentleman, an actor or a parson; than Felix; than Boris had once had. Having nothing to lose—a nothing which includes an indifference in their inner selves—they are free to make things happen; bizarre or violent things, stupid or intelligent things; secret or open—with often an odd preference for the secret. Sober theories or experiments, delirious irresponsibilities, grotesque, monstrous, idealistic or savagely realistic things—anything is possible to persons whose isolation and liberty have freed themselves from common inhibitions. Boris did not think of it in these terms, but he sensed it, and with some of its implications.

Why smile—
When you've nothing to gain and plenty to lose:
Those community blues—?

A group chorus. Not the song the fish of the under-tow sing. Reverse the second line, and you have the majority of the men of Boris's Revolution—especially the men behind its scenes—the earth's majority of bad men and a few of its best. A rather large proportion of its brains. He would as soon join it as not, who had no fears of being drowned in the under-tow. (Not politically, that he would never do. Before that he would enter the Roman Church—as he sometimes thought of—and turn monk.) But there was another thing, that his Taverners spoke of and seemed to set store by—the fact of european civilisation. So much less conscious, so much less informed than they, he was beginning to see in his own way what they meant by it, the nature of the force that threatened it. So there were moments when he felt as if there was a terror about, a small iced wind, part of whose furtive body was blowing in from his own country, running in and out of Europe's cities, along back streets and the noble rooms of palaces; in and out the intricacies of a machine; about a factory, through a spring wood, across a heath. His fairy-tale mind saw Kralin as a man carrying that wind in a bag under his arm, as a sower carries seed; letting it out now and then in little draughts and puffs. Sometimes he saw him letting it out of his mouth like a breeze, like *putti* puffing in a picture; but then his face was not that of a fat boy angel, but awful. An unspeakable face, with cheeks drawn in, and his teeth sticking out below his lip.

Boris noticed that this morning he was finding solitude difficult. He decided to go back to the house and find Adrian and ask him a few questions. If Kralin were really some kind of political agent, the police—little use as Boris had for the police—might be questioned. But, instead, he found himself settling his back again against a fir-trunk, making up a song which went in English something like this:

'If Kralin is a man of that kind, everything that has been happening falls into its place, and the attack on my Taverners is not an isolated devilry, but part of a large plan.

'If Kralin is one of those men, the attack on the Taverners' honour and on their prestige becomes essentially more reasonable. Such elaborate acts, in mere private revenge, are rare.

'If Kralin is that kind of man, the attack on the land might also be part of a scheme. A great scheme, and so far more intelligent than château-burning.

'If Kralin is one of those men, he is doing very subtle work to discredit an english family; and if it is all part of something larger than that, he will not get tired of it. Private revenge becomes a bore.

'If Kralin is that kind of man, he is not among their fanatics. He is serving his own end as well. And having a cause and himself, himself and a cause, his power will be doubled.

'If Kralin is that kind of man, where is this to end? What is the plan behind the plan? The plan they have behind the plan in Russia also?

'Where do I, Boris Nicolaivitch, come in? There are the people my Taverners call mystics, who say that none of this is by chance, that an appropriate design runs through our lives, a pattern; that what happens on the great stage is played again on the small, as it is played in heaven and again in hell. They believe in something like this, and I think that it may be true.

'If Kralin is one of those men, he will think it necessary that I and Felix, Scylla, Picus, even Adrian and his mother, must be destroyed.

'If Kralin is that kind of man, I am face to face with a man who has destroyed my Russia. With the man who killed my father and my two brothers; with the man who made my sister kill herself.

'Also with the man who has made me what I am like. For I was not wicked once. I was not good, but there was a good person in me. That good they killed. Only my Taverners were sorry about it, and I can only laugh at them. But I am not laughing now, not even at myself. Those men killed the good that there was in noble Russia, and when they did not do it to our bodies, they did it to our souls. They will do it to the souls and bodies of the world, and first of Felix's world. For they have learned the attack which looks as though it were part of a different war about something else; and their move is like the knight's move in chess. I have seen this in Paris.

'If Kralin is that kind of man, I do not know what it is that I should do. If I were good and still Boris I should know, for I know now a great deal about it. But I am bad, and the worst of bad is that it does not know how to be good. My Taverners are good, but they are weak because they do not yet know enough, because their lives have been gracious—'

Then he began to laugh, on his feet now, striding between the trees; and against their harsh trunks it seemed as if there was, suddenly, a heavier bulk of manhood about him.

Chapter XV

INSIDE THE HOUSE on the moor, masked by Mrs. Taverner's habit of domineering, Adrian's cynicism and Boris's airy delight, Nemesis had taken possession. The Nemesis who is called "If," inserting itself into the phrases the mind speaks, rising to his mother's and even sometimes to Adrian's lips with a sigh. While Boris was meditating, pacing and reclining in fir-plantation, they were sitting on the verandah; looking onto the small, square lawn the shrubbery hedge surrounded, whose borders only seemed to send up flowers because they were made to, sulky, even in spring, like a child coerced.

It was in the dead hours between lunch and tea, the worst hours of the day, the only hours which really die on man of the day or the night. But half-past two to half-past four can, if they like, be intolerable. Too early and too late, harshly lit, too long and not long enough. Not for sleep, not for play, not for talk, they insist on work and are not friendly to it. The morning Mrs. Taverner had spent gardening. She gardened well, yet with the instinct of those who have "the green finger" she knew that the soil and the young roots and the small leaves were not responsive. Only the savage dark shrubs, striking into the earth with an animal's strength, flourished there. Outside, the heather was watching, the gorse and the bracken. If man the cultivator took his hands off that garden and his tools away, they would get in within a year. They had covered the garden-ground before and the ground where the house stood. It occurred to Mrs. Taverner that they wanted to have it again. It was the kind of thought she referred to as "unwholesome fancies," but to-day her imagination, deep as well as narrow, was seized. It was as though she could hear the fierce plants waiting; the uncurling bracken-fronds were snakes poised to strike, ready to glide in; the fire-scent of the gorse a smell of conquest, the camp-fire of the vegetable world.

After lunch she had given it up. Adrian joined her, who had spent the morning idling with grim thoughts. Some days before, his cousins had brought over clothes for Boris, and Boris had seen fit to disappear. His cousins had then taken Adrian for a walk, and told him some of the opinions they held about their aunt. The one thing they had seemed prepared to forgive her was Adrian's birth. While they had parted from him with some of the forgiveness which comes from speaking one's mind. Picus had not been with them. Adrian, finally and against his will, had been interested. Something in their attitude towards his sister had impressed him, made him begin almost to suffer.

Glancing up to catch his mood, his mother sighed and nearly shrank from him. But, on her morality, she must bear for a punishment both his moods and his coming desertion of her. Besides, it was possible that by that way she might not lose him. He had the habit of brutality with her, and she had drawn a certain pleasure from it. But she knew that the time-interval before them was going to do its worst.

So two people sat down together in whose minds was the same ghost. And out of the dark green ivory shrubs the ghost came, until it stood before them and looked at the small memory-ghost of itself each of them was nursing like a doll. As the true ghost passed, the flowers looked up, lawn daisies opened like white buttons, mother and son heard a blackbird give a sudden mellow shout.

"I suppose," said Adrian, "finding a worm would justify this afternoon to some people."

"The first brood," said his mother, "must be fledged and flown off."

"Ah, that accounts for it," said Adrian. "Or he's just pitched out the cuckoo's egg. Which is what I am."

"The hen sits on it; and anyhow I don't believe she'd let him."

"Very handsome of her. More than we'd do." Mrs. Taverner had a most literal mind.

"Your father would never—" Adrian gave his contemptuous sophisticated giggle:

"I didn't mean that. I was thinking we go the other way about it. Kick out your own off-spring for the cuckoo's sake." Her "What d'you mean?" had lost some of its assurance. —"Push out our own, while showing the cuckoo's every attention. I was thinking of Felicity." The ghost's eyes looked out under a frown. It watched Adrian.

"You know as well as I do that she went off and married that man of her own will."

"You know as well as I do that she was driven to it."

"How can you say that? She had her home, her friends, everything she wanted—" Adrian glanced at his own doll-ghost:

"Versicles and responses of an edwardian dowager. Cut it out. You know what a sensitive little fool she was. She didn't think it was much of a home when her friends came and you showed her what you thought of them, and presumed at once that they were vulgar or vicious or interested. Or both. Or all three. What you meant was not smart. They weren't. But they were a change for her; a new kind of person, people who were kind to her. When everything she cared about, the idiotic enthusiasms we all have, was called silly or affected or dirty at home—especially dirty—" Here he squeezed his doll a moment, as though to make memory articulate in a squeak:

"—I've an idea it was the last she hated most. You know, Mother, we always used to say in our simple childish phrase that you'd a mind one could make toast at. You have, you know. Like most women of your education. It was the way you were brought up. But when you don't see the point of a story, you're sure it's a dirty one. You've a set of verbal symbols, paraphrases for the things which are 'coarse' or 'improper,' and you use them in the voice of a nasty old priest telling a lavatory story. You must have been a queer bride, appallingly shocked, and appallingly curious. The two made a pretty amalgam by the time we were growing up. You think you are chaste and reticent, and quite broad-minded—so as to get on with me, but, Oh, Baby—! You're scared, you know, with a temperament that's gone bad on you—(Allow me to get this off my chest.). If it were done now, you'd go in for rescue-work. Beat the girls to make them tell you all about it. You should see the look in your eye when you hear of a young woman, married or not, having a romp in bed. While you simmer with jealousy. I hardly like to think of the time I've had to spend telling you about the complex and the repression, so you can't pretend not to understand. If my or your—I mean one of our fathers—had picked you out of the Gaiety chorus, instead of the refined victorian home you came from, you'd be quite human.—No, Mother, you're going to hear this."

She had been trained to listen to Adrian on sex, and with any amount of personal reference. Talk she enjoyed and feared. This time she found herself admitting that it might all be true. Her doll-ghost wouldn't squeak when she pinched it. The real ghost looked at them with trembling lips.

"—I admit I mightn't have seen all this about Felicity. It was Scylla who gave me more than a hint, the other day, when they brought over Boris's clothes. I'm no connoisseur in female virtue, but I see it now that my sister was the chastest maid that breathed. Which was exactly what you could not see. I knew that for a fact at the time, of course, but as Scylla explained—rather intelligently—her quality of purity was explained by you as your old favourite 'coarseness of mind.' It wasn't fear in her—as you thought it ought to be, or chill, or ignorance or abnormality, or the least indelicacy either. It was so rare as to be normal and exquisitely sane. *Prochaine Aphrodite,* if you like. She knew passion was coming to her, but in its own time. She hurried nothing, feared nothing, despised nothing. It was like a flower. Only not passive, not a vegetable love—" The ghost's lips quivered, smiling at its brother. A breeze sighed and spent itself on the grass at their feet.

"You got this rigmarole from Scylla?" said the mother of the ghost.

"From Scylla and from Felix. But what I can see, without Scylla and Felix, is that her kind of modesty must have got a nasty jar from you." There was something like regret, or at least defence, in her voice as she answered:

"I know I am grown more broad-minded since my children were young. But wasn't I right to protect my daughter from dangers she seemed to talk about with what I was taught to consider disgraceful knowledge, and to care nothing for?"

"You were, you know, because it wasn't like that. They weren't the real dangers. You didn't try to protect her from anything that mattered. Look at Kralin. While ignorance isn't even fashionable to-day. But do you remember that summer when we played *Comus,* and I was the first brother and she the sister? You wanted my best speech cut because it might put ideas into Felicity's head!"

"I admit I was foolish, but when I was her age I shouldn't have known what it meant. Only that it was something unpleasant." But Adrian was staring right through the ghost on the lawn and saying:

> *"And like a quiver'd nymph, with arrows keen,*
> *May trace huge forests, and unharbour'd heaths,*
> *Infamous hills and sandy perilous wilds,*
> *Where through the sacred rays of chastity,*
> *No savage fierce, bandit or mountaineer,*
> *Will dare to soil her virgin purity;—"*

He spoke coldly, but the contempt was gone out of his voice:

> *"—gods and men*
> *Fear'd her stern frown, and she was queen o' the*
> *woods.*
> *. . . So dear to heaven is saintly chastity,*
> *That when a soul is found sincerely so,*
> *A thousand liveried angels lackey her—*

"We've had that in the house. And it's dead."

"I don't want to hurt your feelings," said his mother, "but when Felix played your part next day, he did it much better." But Adrian did not seem to hear.

"It's a wonder," he said, "being what she was, that it didn't kill her off young, being told by you she was filthy, when she was clean. Still, we can none of us quite see what drove her into Kralin's arms."

"I believe that his attitude about the War had something to do with it." Adrian looked at her sharply.

"After a particularly vile scene with you here, I suppose?" (This had been Felix's supposition. None of them knew.) Mrs. Taverner did not answer.

"—Scylla said it may have been because he had an abstract mind; after I had been so cattish and you so female, and life full of chit-chat and scandal and talk about nothing but personalities. She said she wanted to warm him to life and wit and show him his perfection; being too young to know that you can't make your man over from what he is. And she reminded me when Kralin was young, how beautiful they looked together."

Mrs. Taverner still said nothing. Her own little ghost would not squeak. The night before the girl had gone away and got married to Kralin, its original had also kept silent; had stared at her mother as if she did not understand her mother's accusation. Who had said:

"Pretending not to know what I mean, Miss. I mean

to tell you in very plain language—the kind you prefer—what I mean. In the words the servants understand—" And when she had finished the girl had only said:

"What do you mean, Mother? You can't mean such a thing as that. You're my mother. You can't think that." (She had been too young to understand that the period in Mrs. Taverner's life made her irresponsible. When, later, she had thought of that, she had assumed that her mother had forgotten all about it.) But she had not, in fact, been quite able to forget.

The real ghost was still there, at whom the blackbird was still singing like mad. Adrian looked at the sun through a branch of cherry-blossom, on a discontented small tree, standing alone on the grass.

"—'Without cherry-blossom,'" he said. "Kralin wouldn't have love with it and you wanted it artificial, like the silk flowers they sell in the shops."

"No," said his mother, in her rare lowered voice—"only not wild."

A cloud moved across the sun. It was suddenly colder. A little air waved the cherry-branch at them. A poor tree, not body enough for the fair tall ghost the blackbird was shouting at to stay; who did not stay easily in a dark, poisoned garden, hollowed out of rank shrubbery, out of savage moor. Trying not to grow.

"I've half a mind," said Adrian, "to go to a séance in town. The kind where they guarantee a Direct Voice Manifestation. I presume that one is allowed to answer back. This place is somehow full of Felicity. How she'd have disliked it."

"I believe such things are irreligious when they aren't frauds."

"There are several things I want to find out."

"What things?"

"Well, I'd like to feel surer, I'd like to hear her say that it was all sheer accident. That nothing pushed her off against her will. Neither despair of us—nor anything. Nor malice. Unless," he added, "Kralin killed her." The mother shuddered:

"Don't say that. Isn't he doing enough?"

With a little weeping note the air pushed past them; surrounding them, touching them, all about their faces. Adrian moved fretfully. Mrs. Taverner shut her eyes. Opened them again and blinked quickly, because of the picture, the coloured cinema that had sprung to life under her lids. It was not one of the worst scenes between them, but a repeat of an old theme of childhood. There was Felicity, half grown-up, her legs delicate as a crane's. And she was telling the girl, and it was the kind of thing she told her constantly, that she had climbed over the wall in order that the gardeners might see her legs. Not the common maternal injunction at that date, that at no time might a gardener see legs; that the good gardener is pained, and that the bad gardener—and gardeners are chiefly bad—are moved by the sight of shins to unspeakable thoughts. In her attempts to dominate the child, she had reached a further stage which insisted that all such gestures were an invitation on the girl's part to "the lower orders" to "think." Nor did she—and this was where the fun began—spare the girl their thoughts. This was where she became eloquent, reading shame into the young bewilderment, untruth into the young dignity, immodesty into its laugh. It was dead now, the long-legged child. *A thousand liveried angels. . . . only daughter of Richard and Julia Taverner. Born at Pharrs. . . . Died at Villefranche-sur-Mer. . . . in the thirty-third year of her age . . .* "

Soon after his adolescence she had nipped the sweetness out of Adrian's boy's love for his sister. Derided it, clouded it with innuendo and suggestion; playing on the young man's insatiable taste for luxury and *chic,* his fear of certain forms of public opinion. Bribed him. As it usually happens, this was made easy for her both by her daughter's weakness and her strength. She could not bribe; she would not plead. She could only love. If Adrian had lifted his little finger, it would have been different; but at first she had not understood, then she had not been quite brave enough, and then too convinced he had actively rejected her, to fight. So fear and pride, reticence and an innocence that was sometimes fatuous, had driven her off, and on the light grass of her greenwood love was laid bleeding, and a fawn sobbed out its breath.

So Mrs. Taverner had had her way. She sat back in the garden chair, trying to find her ease. Told herself that she had had her way. Not, for once, that it had been God's way; not even that she had done it for the best, but grimly that it had been her way; admitting that it now seemed that there might have been a better way. While what chiefly concerned her was the way her son was going to take it now—with all the rest. Their situation was unbearable, so difficult also in its complications that they could only be aware of it, all the time, in detail. They could not think of it or deal with it as a whole. All she could think of then was how his sister's death would affect his relations with her. She looked at him again, sitting sideways in his chair, as ill at ease as she.

"What are you thinking of now, Adrian?" He had wanted to be asked this, in whose mind bitter sentences were shaping to be shot out to stick in his mother. He began to speak deliberately, simplifying his words:

"Oh, what it feels like to be blackmailed and a bastard."

"I've told you over and over again that you're not that. Your father—my husband, I mean—never repudiated you. He couldn't—"

"Yes, he died conveniently. But are we not both beginning to notice what it feels like to get what one wants—or what one has wanted? Felicity is well out of it. She has got the laugh over us now. And looks like getting any revenge she wanted—" The blackbird stopped in the middle of a note with his beak open.

"—This is our punishment. We have got what we

wanted. We have got her out of the way. And I for one should prefer the body of her now to any ghost."

His mother was thinking: "How well he speaks. In such clear sentences, not like his real father, nor like me. Like his cousin Felix, only better, of course." She was playing the old woman's game of "where did he get it from?"; whose life had held too few of the more normal excitements of that kind. But Adrian still did not mean to let her off.

"It seems obvious to me that the way we let her die, the way you, at least, wanted to be rid of her, has let—I don't know whether it would be in or out—a very unpleasant series of consequences. This business with Kralin isn't only unpleasant, it's damned dangerous. Hell alone knows where he intends to stop—" He stopped talking to the air, turned round on his mother, snatched the sprig of lad's love she had been pinching and smelling, and threw it away.

"—Felix's comment is that we've pulled the plug out of the bath that kept in the waters of life. Graceful sanitary metaphor, and there was another about the main-drain of evil pouring in. Charming of Felix, but there's too much truth about it for my taste." His mother said:

"I am beginning to wish now that we'd never interfered with her in the way we did."

"If you consider it, it would be pleasanter if we were all three sitting here, having our tea."

The blackbird gave an impatient clutter and flew off; perched again on the further side of the little lawn. Their ghost-dolls had fallen unnoticed under their chairs. The true ghost stood now a little further off, under the tree, beside the hedge, near the bird. It had been weeping. It was now watching the man and woman in the chairs; driven off as it had been driven before, in life. All hope gone and curiosity dawning, trying to smile at them and at itself.

"—Something tells me that without Kralin to point the

situation, it would be just as bad. He's called our attention to the pleasure of getting what we wanted. That's all. We now know a little more what an empty bore life can be. Just now I felt a kind even of physical emptiness about us—there had been a sort of presence before. While I don't believe, dead or alive, that my sister was ever bored. It is really one up to conventional morality. I've been a bad brother; you've been a bad mother. While what have we got out of it?" There was an echo of Felix in his slight vehemence.

"—Why don't they bring tea?" Then he tried again:

"—Conventionally bad. That's it. I never thought I was a young man of convention before. —Not originally or even thoroughly bad like Kralin. Now we've nothing in ourselves to allow us to deal with him. It is perhaps humiliating. Neither Scylla nor Felix expect us to be the least use. Nor does Picus. At least where Felicity is concerned."

"All they expect is for me to ruin myself buying-up the land because she chose to marry a scoundrel."

"There we go round again and round and round and round. Amusing, isn't it? You drove her into Kralin's arms. Together we three drove into her grave. Now Kralin, our hitherto-loyal partner, intends to drive us into ours. But what I am finding most painful is the way those two keep pointing out what might have been —"

"I suppose Felix imagines himself with a wife seven years older than himself."

"No. Agreeable as it is to be a spectator of human folly, I shouldn't say he does that. His idea seems to be, that like another Thérèse de l'Enfant Jésus with the nun left out, Felicity came down on earth to *faire aimé l'amour:*

> *In whom alone love lives again*
> *Is nursed and bred and brought up true.*

They think that when her destiny took a practical turn, it aroused, in unblest persons like Kralin and ourselves, a kind of inevitable wish to destroy her. They seem to think that in her papers would be found miraculous accounts of imaginative passion, courage, with a devotion to the service of love. A genius for love, victorious or not, in all its forms. They seemed to think that we wished to be rid of her because we represent—it's nice to be bracketed with Kralin—the opposite set of values. (Not that they seem to think that it absolves us of any blame.) They seem to think that we serve Kralin's purpose as he serves his own; and both of us an unknown master in Hell. They seem to think that Felicity died, as someone like Keats died, with some of her work done. That the story of it is written in her papers, which they proposed to get hold of and deal with before Kralin came down. These are the papers he must destroy. Whatever he publishes from them, however he distorts them, it's as much his business to destroy them as to edit and defame. They seem to think that it is equally their business to find some way, even now, to preserve her name and make it illustrious. Then there's the land. To them it is part of her—'part of her body' Felix said; and there Kralin has got them. While their final conclusion seems to be, though here, as Scylla says, the hope may be the bastard of the wish, that we've dug our own graves when we helped dig Felicity's.

"There Mother! You are *au courant* with opinion in the Younger Married Set. What they are actually going to do about it, I can't say. Probably nothing in the end. What can they do? My God, what is it we can do? While it is you we have to thank for saying all those years that you were trying to do your duty. My teeth on edge for the rest of my life, and Scylla and Felix aren't any too happy. Though I'd sooner be them now. Sooner be Felix—"

She hardly understood a word of this. Excepting that it meant that she was to blame. Which she could not admit; which she resented with the strangled bitterness that made her dangerous.

"You have learned your lesson very well off them. But at least you did not marry your cousin Scylla."

"I'm not so thankful for that as I used to be."

This was too much. Her hatred for powerful attractive young women came raving out of her.

"Scylla! That immoral calculating woman. You'd be wishing yourself dead. I've heard the most dreadful things said about her." Adrian giggled. Her voice stopped suddenly, as it rarely did on the congenial subject; and the coming words turned into an escape of angry breath, then a sigh.

A sense of immense futility came over them. Into the garden, now empty of bird or ghost, it poured, filling it instantly like a change of air. With it the fight went out of the old woman, the momentary understanding out of the young man. They saw the activities of their lives as those of insects, without the insect's self-preserving end. Looking into the boredom of it, Adrian turned white. With something like terror on their faces, fear they tried to mask with a sneer, the vilest of man's gestures, they ate their tea. Deliberately, as though here was a sole and certain pleasure. It was then that Boris joined them.

Chapter XVI

A WEEK AFTER this, Scylla walked over to meet Boris at Stone End. They sat once more outside the inn where Boris had played tricks on Kralin, from where six weeks before this adventure had begun. The place from where Kralin had seen them on the high downs as tea-leaves, and one tea-leaf knock the other down. Where Kralin had hidden from them in the barn. Where in the middle of the green there was a stone, lost on its way to Stonehenge, unsculptured, tilted a little to one side, its top rounded into something the shape of a sausage. Round the green and the stone were the houses that would not change either; the ancient rose-hung farm, eye-lashed with roof-ferns; the Tudor façade that was no more than a shell; the coy house at once coy and bleak with the laburnum, the basement and the flagstaff. As before, they sat outside the inn, in afternoon light now strengthening to summer, looking at the stone. Boris asked:

"D'où vient-il, ce pierre?" She considered, careful as one is with a foreigner, put all the facts before him:

"Stones like that—they are either left by a glacier and later they become a magic, and later still a curiosity, if they aren't broken up and built into a house. Or else they were brought here—God knows how—because they were wanted for a magic."

"From where a glacier had left them then, somewhere else?" This seemed to cover the ground.

"In either case they are generally said to be stones that an angel threw at the Devil, or the Devil at an angel."

"Outside my father's park there were five, which several angels threw at each other. That is like russian history—" They sat silent, looking at the stone. Tilted-up on end, it looked, even in that light, like a pale slug; going to nowhere, like a slug. Yet it had gathered no moss. Clean as if it had been scrubbed, she had always felt that she would rather not touch it.

"Why," said Boris, "are snails adorable, even to eat, and slugs, even to think about, disgusting?" She agreed, except about eating snails. They talked idly, feebly, about food. Looking at the stone. Then she noticed that the stone made you think. It stopped what you were thinking about and made you think of nothing. Then even the thought of nothing went out, like a candle when you "puff," and you were nowhere. She felt sleepy. She had come here to meet Boris, almost secretly because of Adrian. Felix and Picus were out in the boat. She must remember everything he had to say to tell them.

Her eyelids were slipping down like weights over her eyes. At Stone End were there any more stories about the stone? It wasn't a devil's nine-pin. Archaeologists did not connect it with sacrifice or the sun. It was a local stone, the wrong kind really for Stonehenge. Nobody carved their names on it. It wasn't a tryst. It was just there, and the real village dodged away from it along the valley. It was said, vaguely, to be unlucky. They said that it had brought about the ruin of the family who had lived in the tudor house. (Was Boris falling asleep, too?) Her eyes closed. Then she thought that just as some trees have character and personality, so also have rocks. If one has had time to know them, a very long time. Of course, a very much longer time than persons, and a longer time than trees. 'That old stone—silly—all stones are old—is a bad stone. I have known it all my life, and I have only just found it out. What is bad stone-nature? Not bad man-nature or tree-nature. That's the mistake. Bad stone-nature. What is it? I don't know, but my body feels it. Try it on Boris.'

—"Boris, is there something bad about that stone?" His voice also seemed to be coming back from a long flight of thought.

"I think that it knows something—that it has a bad secret about nothing. A bad nothing is what it knows." And then: "I call it Kralin's Stone." Scylla was saying to herself:

> *'Truth is the heart's desire;*
> *There is a stone instead of the heart's desire . . .*
> *. . . Be comforted.'*

They moved their chairs away from the door to have tea in the garden, out of sight of it.

Scylla was poised for this meeting with Boris like a gymnast on a trapeze. They had sent him over to Adrian and to Adrian's mother to have a friend—a friend who was also a spy—in the lesser of the enemies' camps. It had seemed a prudent thing to do and the right kind of intrigue, giving them at least the illusion of action. It excites passionate and idealistic people to play at *savoir faire.* For three weeks they had waited for his news, and there had been no news. Only requests for clothes, and the day they had taken them over, Boris had disappeared; and their only satisfaction had been the walk with Adrian, and what they had been able to tell him about himself, the praise they had made him listen to of Felicity, his sister. It had given them in retrospect very little pleasure. They had impressed Adrian, as his mother knew, but he had been clever enough not to let them see it. So, with that over-sensibility which was their curse, the symbol of their weakness, they had felt next day, not that they had spoken a part of the truth, but only that they had given themselves away to him. There is no petty suffering to match this. They writhed at the thought. But Adrian had taken them in.

If Adrian had taken them in, Boris had let them down. This they had feared, this they were prepared for, but with that turn of hopefulness which kept them young, they had hoped to have hope in Boris. He would be doing all he could for them; he would have forgotten all about them. Their minds swung from side to side. The last was nearly true, yet Scylla came to their meeting ready to hear and judge what he had to tell, like an athlete prepared for some supreme use of all the body's faculties.

Remembering to be feminine and not too feminine, remembering to have tact, she did not let her impatience leap at him. Talk about the stone had served for an opening, an opening that had chosen itself.

She poured out his tea, coarse tea which pulled you together, or might equally make you sick. Then she said:

"*Alors,* Boris, what has happened while you have been over on the moor?"

"*Très peu.* If you had not made it so very clear that the little quarrel we pretended was serious, I should have returned a week ago." She was furiously disappointed. Their three weeks had been spent in useless waiting, during which Kralin had gone away for ten days. (They had not seen him. Only a letter he had sent them, to say that he had gone to London to see his publisher, and that it would be useless for them in his absence to search the house.) Their minds had been turned on Boris, Boris who would not write, but would come when he had something to tell. While Picus had not dared to point out that, news or no news, Boris would only be certain to return when he was bored.

"*Que veux-tu*? I have done what you told me. I have watched them, only there was nothing to watch. I have amused myself. I have done, I think, what I wanted with Adrian. Would you grudge me that?" He was pettish. So was she, through frustration and suspense and tension relaxed in the wrong way. He pointed out to her that it was unworthy of her to show nervous strain. Unworthy and ungrateful, but women were like that. He begged her pardon for not having been able to create events. They spoke in French, and their words clattered like angry bird-noises. To his fury and alarm, she began to cry. He called her a bitch. She called him a gigolo, exploiting Adrian for his pleasure, instead of joining them in a holy war. The scene between the tea-leaves seemed about to repeat itself. Then she cried out that she had been unjust and that she took it back. He sprang up and strode about the torn rose-garden, with broken arbours in its hedges. She sat where she was, staring, a dreadful pain like a steel bubble in her breast, rising and sinking, a balanced agony, quite intolerable, of the body and mind. Then Boris did a thing he did not do. He came back and comforted her, more inexpertly, she thought, than any man had ever done, but from Boris a kind of queer miracle.

—"*Ma petite chérie.* We must not. It is what Kralin would have us do." A quick run-through of unworthy emotions had created understanding. Reconciled, they sat once more side by side. Then she said:

"But Adrian—hadn't he some plan of double-crossing everyone and selling the house to Kralin himself?"

"Yes, but he has done nothing."

"Does he know yet who his father was?"

"Yes. He has got it out of Madame Julia."

"*Well—*" But Boris had forgotten the name. Wild with impatience, she tried him with a dozen. It was hopeless. She would not believe that it was not cruelty—until Boris had the sense to swear that it should be repeated to him again that night.

—"But why—? They seem to have all gone dead. Why is it?" She saw that he paused to consider.

"I think that it is natural. They have had a great shock. To them now it is all, for the moment, the matter of Adrian's father. That was her secret that she kept. Now it is found out. And she did not tell him, Kralin told him. They are filled up with that, and the changes it will bring." It was well-observed. She began to forgive him.

"You mean that Adrian has to consider his mother—and his own life—all over again? Can you guess how it is shaping in his mind?"

"To me they seem like people who are partly paralysed. He takes small revenges on her all day long, but he does not know yet what will happen to him. And she is old. It is too much for them all at once."

Then Scylla settled down to listen to him. Slowly she pieced together how the time had passed. Felt how bad conscience was carrying its impure lamp, and memory throwing an acid ray over the house on the moor. She told Boris what they had been doing, the enquiries the had made among the estate agents, and the map Felix had drawn to show exactly what part of the downs and the valley Kralin intended to buy. He had bought nothing yet, but Felix's map of his intentions showed their world nearly all gone red, and for the names of old bee-pastures, the words "golf-links," "bungalows" and "shops."

"He was getting ready *before* Felicity died. This began when she had left England for the last time. You don't mean, do you, that in the excitement over Adrian's father, they'd forgotten about the land?"

"You must remember that Adrian does not care, and that he is not allowing her to think about anything but him."

"You are friends with him now, and it's as well; but I am going to show you the letter she wrote to us last week. It is characteristic. When we saw what the map really meant, Felix decided that whatever the cost he would buy the middle stretch of the shore, which would at least hinder Kralin's plans. *We* had plans for what we would do with it, something like Kipling's story about the Bloody Picknickers and Angélique the pig. (You must remember that these places were hardly on the market. It was Kralin who went round and offered a big price if they would sell.) It would be very hard for Felix to afford it, but worth it, he thought, and right for Felicity's sake. So he wrote to Aunt Julia, very civilly, and told her that he would go in with her for so much. But he got an answer, thanking him with that insolent coldness for which she is famous; and saying that if anything could be done, she preferred to do it herself. It is that kind of ungenerosity that rouses people against her. While if she is off her stroke now by having had a different father for Adrian, she may do nothing at all. D'you see?"

What Scylla thought malignant, Boris thought silly, and a consequence of giving women power. They went on talking, gently and eagerly to one another. Then Scylla said:

"How did you get away to-day?"

"I pretended I was going to see some Americans I had met in Starn. Adrian was lunching in Gulltown and he dropped me there. I said I might stay there to-night."

"Kralin should be back. Come and spend it with us."

"*Bien.*" They got up and walked out onto the green, past the stone. She said:

"Sad little war we're fighting."

"I see now that when our Revolution came it was like this. We fought of course, but we'd no chance. Europe wouldn't help us—"

"That doesn't explain why the Bolsheviks stayed in power. They might have seized power, but how did they keep it?" Boris did not know. Scylla did not know. They stood side by side, ash-fair waves and black tendrils of hair stirring on their temples, their eyes raised to the long green hill they must cross between them and the sea.

They went by the road, because the lower fields of the hill-path were down for corn, and the track invisible. To the right of them and to the left, the inland valley ran wide and shallow between the downs. A river of green, its length squared into strips, corn or roots or hay or pasture, patched with round trees or triangular roofs of grey luminous stone. But in spite of its field-squaring, the valley flowed between its windy banks, and the high downs' dim green. Flowed from Starn in the east, out of the sunrise, down to a bay in the west; flowed out into the sunset between Gault's vast cliffs and the green paws of the downs. Birds crossed the valley by air, men and cattle climbed by stony paths. There was one road down it and one road across, the road by which they were mounting, over one shoulder of its banks, to the open sea: to the two houses and their village; to Taverner-land. Not an exciting valley nor an enchanting; not a spectacle or a diversion; without nucleus or "a place to see." (Starn with its towers supplied that, and few people looked further.) In no way celebrated, without special mana, not like Taverner-land; but a river, a stream of life, in its small tide of men and its larger tide of beasts, in its wind and fruit and leaf and corn-flow. One of the streams of England, whose spring where it rises is the life-source of a people.

—"Kralin would make this also his kingdom?"

"He has precedent in England," said Scylla bitterly.

The hill road was very long, and whoever first chipped it out of chalk and flint, and slung its links across the high downs, the Romans had nothing to do with it. Near the crest, scarlet face turned to scarlet face.

"I am not," said Boris, " a snob, but it would be intolerable now if Kralin overtook us in his car."

Chapter XVII

OVER THE CREST, the wind met them, delicately off the fish-patterned sea. They drew aside from the road a little onto the grass, so that if anyone passed on the road they might see them and not be seen. A mile and more away the ribbon of the Sacred Wood widened at the top into its fan. Below them the chimneys of Felicity's house pointed grey fingers among the orchard tops. Below it the village wandered seawards. The Sacred Wood hid the Taverners' house, but the field-path that bound the two houses like a ribbon, was clear at that height.

"The links," said Scylla, "are to go in the middle of everything. The bull that Marshallsea, the farmer, keeps in the middle field, footpath or no footpath, will go. So will the hazel copse where you find the best small birds.

> *The willows, and the hazel-copses green,*
> *Shall now no more be seen—* That's a poem, Boris.
> . . . *As killing as the canker to the rose,*
> *Or taint-worm to the weanling herds that graze,*
> *Or frost to flowers, that their gay garlands wear,*
> *When first the white-thorn blows—* "

"*Comment?*" said Boris.

"A description of Kralin. Two fair specimens your land has sent to this oldest of the old part of oldest England." She laid her hand on his and he smiled.

"We must be the only Russians it has seen."

"There was another. A tale I heard from my father. About seventy years ago there was a wreck here, and another Russian was washed up. A passenger on a ship coming to England with furs, his own furs, to sell. There's a cottage not far from here with a rug in it, now worn and trimmed and declined and fallen to a bedroom mat, which came out of his cargo. Well, the vicar put him up, and they salvaged what they could, though everyone round about that winter was wearing furs. Then the vicar's wife fell in love with him. Went away with him to Russia, and years later, the Russian sent back her body to be buried in the churchyard. It was the same vicar, and he didn't know what to do about it, or how he was going to bury his own wife under the circumstances. The curate did it, I think. A year or so after that a russian son turned up, saying that he had come to fetch some furniture that had belonged to his mother. There was a new vicar by then, and they couldn't find any for him to take. But to quiet him down and get rid of him—it seemed that he upset the people very much—they told him to take something out of the vicarage. He chose a grandfather clock, and drove off with it in a fly, with its head sticking out of the window, ticking like mad and striking at the wrong times and nearly all the time. He took it out at Starn Station and stood it on the platform, and went off with it in the train; and that was the last that was seen of him. But the old station-master when I was a child remembered the clock."

The afternoon began to hint of evening, like a loved guest taking his leave, introducing delicately, confidently, his successor. With the turn of the tide, the sea, a mile away below them, called attention to itself. The light on it had changed, for the flashing diaper of light-scales, a plain of pure colour, a looking-glass for the sky. From one grey finger on Felicity's roof rose a question-mark of smoke.

—"That's the library fire. Kralin must be back." The slight coil that the wind broke as it rose above the tree-level, recalled them to themselves, to what was being done to them. For an hour they had been released from what they knew, climbing the hill, sitting on the top of their world, recalling old tales of its valleys. Nature has arranged this forgetfulness, but the recall is violent, as if the organism had only been rested for a sharper realisation of its pain.

"Ouf," said Scylla, adjusting herself to it. Boris stared. He was beginning to see more what this meant to them, not to their pride or their pockets or their ambitions, not even to their personal loyalties and affections. The death of Felicity Taverner—the double death, to the body and to the memory of her—that was terrible, it held much of the horror of life, but as if in a crystal, in miniature. Full of anguish, it was at the same time, a manageable tragedy, and so to be endured. But behind it lay the second attack, immeasurably the most formidable, the attack on their bodies, nerves, roots, the essence of their make-up, in the attack on their land. To begin with—where would they live with Kralin in possession? Alongside of him and his friends? Scylla was asking this, and in her voice there was exultation and anguish, not under strict control:

"It is awful to see it now, in one mode of the perfected. And to know what is to be done to it." Boris answered:

"I remember my sister a few nights before the Revolution began. It was very quiet of course in Petrograd, there were none of the great court assemblies, but she was going to a little party, almost her first one, of the great nobility. I was on leave and I took her. She wore pearl and silver shoes, and a little coronet of pearls and silver in her hair. She looked like a fairy-tree. Like you see them in Russia on winter nights. She is dead now, but I understand when you say it is the same here." She nodded; one of the unsatisfactory gestures which shows sympathy, when the imagination is running away as fast as it can from someone else's pain. She took up the burden.

"The links sprawl in the middle of everywhere. The road to the sea is tarred and widened and straightened. Along the shore there is a row of little bungalows, called High Jinks and Mon Repos. One side of the green is the parking ground, and on the other side, a terrace of seaside houses, shops below and flats above. The barn below Felicity's has the movies in it—he told me about that. He told the agents what he meant. They were most of them horrified on our account; could not understand why Adrian consented to sell. He is building a garage, so they tell me, with petrol pumps 'in sight of the old house.' Felicity's ghost can look out through the windows and look at that."—

A breeze shivered in the grass beside them, the short grass of the high places that springs out of the earth upright, with a kind of sturdy passion, as the ghost of Felicity Taverner trod their light crest, looking down into the sea-valley over her cousin's head.

—"By each midsummer it will be trodden, worn and a little shabby; by autumn, bare and patched and tired out. The rest of the year it will be trying to cleanse itself, and as it begins to get clean again, the people will come back. All summer the greasy papers of their meals will blow about, the torn newspapers and the tins. They will blow to the boundaries of the Sacred Wood and clog in its thorns. They will clot in the hollows, and the rats will nose in and out of them after scraps. Until the land gives it up; and horrible weeds that stink will grow on rubbish-heaps, and it gets the sullen, chained, savage look that comes over country-places once man comes to defile them. Look. It is exquisitely civilised now. For centuries it has been doing that to itself. It is a nucleus, capable now of perfect expansion in terms of itself. It is for us to apply the terms, not destroy the formula."

Boris nibbled pennywort leaves, squashy and saladish, growing between some stones. She nibbled too, for company, and the glow of evening began to adorn the land below them. As the shadows lengthened, it took the contours and moulded them into relief, and the slanting light showed the texture of each field, the character of each bush and tree. Felicity's ghost sat down beside her cousin, who moved a little, as though disturbed by an unaccountable breeze.

"It is nothing," she said; and Boris heard her begin to sing softly the letter song from *Figaro*.

Two men came towards them over the soundless turf, Adrian and Nick Kralin. The ghost left them.

Chapter XVIII

IT WAS BORIS who suggested first that he was surprised that Adrian should visit Kralin secretly. Adrian answered that he had supposed Boris to be visiting friends in Starn. Boris explained that they were ill, and that meeting Scylla there, they had made up their differences.

"When I saw Boris in Starn," she said, "I realised that we were too old friends to waste time on misunderstandings. To put things right, we came over here to wait for Picus and Felix, who are out in the boat. Are you—" she added, "coming to an arrangement of your own with Kralin?" All three ignored the man, until he said pleasantly:

"I think I'll be getting back now—to the house."

"Have you sold it to him, Adrian?" his cousin cried sharply. Adrian's plans had changed. He had gone over to Kralin's secretly, in several minds, but chiefly, as Scylla had gone herself, to find out if he really meant what he had said. No mystical perception of evil had seized on him. He had found Kralin a dirty piece of work, no doubt, but an interesting man; and instead of business, they had talked antiques. Nothing could have been further from their mood than to find two Parcae, under the shape of Scylla and Boris, sitting on a hill-top, looking down onto the roof of their house. Kralin said again:

"I suppose I can't ask you all three back to a dinner of sorts."

When he said that, a kind of grey blur moved across Scylla's eyes. For weeks she and those she loved best had been living in anticipation of what this man would do. They had had no respite, on whom the fullest knowledge lay. The power that feeds anger began to work in her to the last ounce of its strength. Her delicately-cut face became a mask of short harsh lines, her breathing altered, there was something menacing in the unconscious movements of her arms and her hands.

"You dare to ask us to eat with you?" Boris glanced at her. This was the Scylla that he feared, the Scylla that he knew he could not restrain. At that moment, from the west, two long shadows announced their bodies across the grass. Felix and Picus joined them.

"We saw you two up here through the glass. What is happening?"

"He has just asked us to eat with him, in Felicity's house—" Felix saw his sister's face and stood beside her. Spat openly. Picus frowned. Boris deprecated. Adrian shrugged his shoulders and hesitated, standing between Kralin and his kinsman.

"Go and feed with him, Adrian"—and her voice chilled even the men who loved her—"Go and eat with the blackmailer, your sister's murderer, the man who would sell the body of our land to the Jews." Kralin answered her softly:

"You seem to be demonstrating to me, Scylla, that hard words break no bones."

"But you will not leave here," said Felix, "till you have heard them. From me as well from my sister."

"You look," said Kralin, "as if it is only fear of the law that keeps you from going for me." To which Felix could only make the answer that he was not worth hanging for.

"I have called you by your right names," said Scylla, in the same short hushed voice. Their horrible impotence, impotence fallen on persons who had once made short work of people like Kralin, was strangling her, as it strangled them all. She made three steps toward him, ahead of her men. Kralin stepped back. She stumbled forward onto the grass. Felix gathered her in his arms, saying to Adrian—"Get out." Boris knelt down beside her and whispered in her ear. Got up slowly and turned to Adrian with his enchanting smile and led him a few paces off.

"It is better to leave them. It is they who suffer, they who despair." Then to Kralin who joined them:

"You see, Monsieur, it is not possible for me to accept any hospitality of yours."

"I suppose it has occurred to you," said Adrian, "that you will hardly find them genial as next-door-neighbors."

"I know, but is there anything like money with which to counter—or even persuade—difficult neighbours?" Adrian smiled uncertainly. Boris said amiably:

"That, Monsieur, sounds like the remark of a devil."

Picus, Scylla, Felix, were standing with their backs to them, looking out to sea. To this melodrama their impotence had driven them. Their arms were round her as if they were holding her up. Without looking back they walked away along the down-top, in the now level light, straight into the sun.

"Where, *mon ami*," said Boris, "is your car?"

"Outside the house." With his arm in Adrian's, Boris made off, east to the gate onto the road and the hill, then due south to Kralin's front-door. Kralin followed them just behind. There Boris turned.

"Now that we have made our little gesture, may we come in and eat with you?"

It occurred to Kralin to wonder why this young man should be taking it so easily. Yet it was reasonable to see why he should, why he should wish at least to keep *all* the Taverners as quiet as possible. Kralin guessed at his position. Too occupied with their own affairs, they might be too busy for his. But he had left his original Taverners very quickly to return with Adrian to his house. Probably Adrian Taverner was of more importance to him; but it had the air of a *volte-face*. He must have decided to follow Adrian's fortunes at all costs. Yet it did not quite fit. He would keep the tenth of an eye on him, the fraction of attention one gives to such side-issues. He had a stranglehold on the Taverners. He had nothing to hesitate about, and little to fear. Suppose the young man had come spying—? Let him, if he could afford the devotion that implied. What could he expect from people as poor as his Taverners? Kralin knew also that this might only be his cynicism making the easiest assumptions. Knew, allowed for it, and did not care. He would find out though about his family in Russia. The evening passed, and all that Boris said about their native land—to Adrian's surprise, who had heard a version of the truth—was that he had been too young to remember much about the Revolution; that his family was a Kadet branch, and that several of them had found employment under the new régime. He assumed Kralin's views to be in sympathy and asked no questions. Once he was seen to look pale, spoke of the fire's heat and went out into the garden in the dark. When he came back, Adrian said:

"When we go back to London, I hope Boris is coming in with me." And Boris had hoped that he would. An understanding was created; that no good could be done by discussing a painful matter—Boris deprecated at the idea before a stranger like himself—; that reflection might produce a better feeling; that Kralin might possibly modify his plans. He had no objection to this. Let them think that they might at least save their faces. So again they talked about acquaintances and about antiques. Kralin then told them that he had a friend in Paris with a taste for the *baroque,* and how when he had been in Spain he had found for him some pyxes of that period. Gilt tin trash, but decorative; they had painted over the signature of Christ on the plaque with more amusing symbols; and arranged for them to glitter along the dark furniture of the studio like altar-lights.

"How french," sighed Adrian.

"Did you know," said Kralin, "that there are such things as obscene ikons? I was given one the other day. A whole lot are being made cheap to be sent out to Russia. A friend of mine is doing them." He went to fetch it. It was the same subject as the ikon Boris had lost; and, as Kralin said, obscene. Boris—intermittently devout—surprised Adrian by saying amiably:

"It is for your campaign against superstition?" Kralin assented. Adrian as well as surprised was uncomfortable. Vile taste one would expect from Kralin, and he had not thought Boris capable of such control. He began to talk at once about removing the over-painting from ikons of the old schools.

Again Kralin did not know quite what to make of it. He had noticed Boris say something to himself when he recognised the subject of the ikon; saw that his eyes were looking through his surroundings, and then the nod he had made to himself as of some decision taken. He reflected and dismissed it all again, with the solution that this young *déclassé* had decided to make the best of things, and to try and get something out of him also. It would be as well to find out what that was.

"I am going over to Moscow shortly, but before I go, you must come and see me in London. You draw, don't you? I've a commission on my hands, illustrations from the Gospels for a People's Chapbook. What you might call a restatement of the story in terms of those ikons. In the traditional manner, but with a proletarian rendering. If you would care to do some sketches, it strikes me that your name might have propaganda value." Adrian fidgeted.

"I don't think you can expect Boris to be as sympathetic as that—" Boris shrugged his shoulders.

"Not quite perhaps. But one wants to live, my dear Adrian."

"I suppose," said Kralin, "that you are in touch with many of your émigrés. All sorts of propaganda is to be found there if it could be tapped. Napoleon showed us what could be done with royalist names. If you can think of anyone. We might meet in Paris also. You live there, don't you? I shall be there on my way back."

"My family," said Boris, "were exceedingly liberal. My

father used to say that changes were necessary and would happen. He has certainly lived to see them—" Adrian gasped. They got up to go. But this time it was Adrian's car that refused to move. They did things to it, while Kralin held a lamp that wavered and finally blew out. Adrian said that they would go to the inn. Kralin insisted that they should stay the night. Once indoors again, Boris astounded Adrian by refusing more than a final glass to drink.

An hour later, in their bedroom, alone with him, he said:

"Boris, what on earth do you mean? Even I do not understand why you should alter your whole family history to be *au mieux* with the worst enemy my family and your friends are ever likely to have. What do you think you'll get out of it?" Boris sat on the foot of his bed, looking, as he noticed, very wise and serene.

"What, my dear Adrian, do you?"

"With me it's different. I'm hanging about the man for my people's sake, for my dead sister's sake if you like. To find out what he really means, and how far he will go. To try and get round him if I can. It's my duty, I suppose. (If I have to sell him this house, it will be for both our advantages.) Someone has got to do this, and not hide in hysterics, like my cousins in that place of theirs they call enchanted, and I call a ghost parade." Boris nodded. Adrian resented his air of acceptance and indifference.

—"While considering *your* relations with them, do you think it quite decent for you to be here?"

"It is all right, *mon ami.* I want you to believe that I am doing it so that I may find out something. Something which may be useful to us all. Remember that we come from the same country. But to do what you all want, it is necessary that I play this *rôle.* Quite soon you will understand—"

"You want me to believe this, but I want to know if it is true. What is this plan?"

"I cannot explain yet. You will see. We could not think of anything, Scylla and I. We sat on the hill together, and then it came. It was I who saw it. Like a little baby born by her wild anger that I have brought home— But I must have a little more time to think." He giggled and sprang into bed.

—"Do not ask me any more now. To-morrow you will see. My English is all going, but let me instead ask you why your mother will not let Felix help her to buy the land." Adrian had need of new stories to fortify him against his mother. He listened to Boris, collecting material for a fresh scolding of her. The day had been long. The two young gentlemen fell asleep.

Chapter XIX

THE NEXT MORNING Boris went on puzzling a drowsy Adrian by being the first to get up. As he watched him dress it seemed that in his quick precise movements there was something of a soldier, and that his toilette that morning was one that a fastidious man might make before a campaign or even before a battle. When he was ready he came over to Adrian's bedside.

"Listen to me, *mon ami.* I cannot tell it to you all now, but I have found something out. Something for the discredit of this man, something that he has done. If we use it against him, it may give us power and save us. But as it is I who have found it out, it is better that I should tell him. So, do you make the car to march this morning, while I take him out and talk to him—" Adrian meditated on this as he in turn got up. Boris came back again, his shoes brushed with dew.

"You will do this for us, Adrian? You will leave him to me until mid-day?" Adrian said that he would. It was too early in the day to have opinions. After breakfast they found the car still immovable. Adrian said that he would go and find help in the village. Boris said to Kralin:

"Do you feel it is yet too early for us to go for a swim?"

"Yes," said Kralin, decidedly, and went on to explain how rocky the cove below the village was, and how necessary it was for him to find the best places.

—"I see I shall have to buy Cousin Taverner out. He has places of his own, the further side of the wood, along the coast."

"Come with me. I will show them to you. I know that they are all three going to Starn to-day." Adrian could hardly believe it when he saw them setting off together down the village road to the sea. Boris seemed to be talking all the time, and Kralin strode along beside his light step, glancing right and left, as a man does when he is placing where things should go.

Then it occurred to Adrian, left alone in the house, that it might be possible to find out where Kralin kept the papers. He knew the furniture of the house. It had an ancient safe, and he had seen Kralin use its key and knew that he carried it with him. By process of elimination he decided, in less than an hour, that his sister's papers must be inside. He left the house to see to his car.

Outside the morning passed with heavenly quickness. The moon had pulled the tide out early, a spring tide; and the great flood, the Channel wind had roughened, hung chafing, balanced on its turning-line. Travelling inland, the wind fell, and split up into little breezes and catches, dying against the huge wall of the downs, like another, invisible sea. They walked round the bay, and halted first on the Dancing Rocks, the squared spur of gold stone that ran out from the end of the Taverners' wood, smooth and flat, gently under the sea. Kralin said:

"Your Taverners are safe, I think. I shall hardly want to buy this off them to drown my visitors. They will need an alternative to a dive-off rock into dangerous currents or lying scorched and cooking in a tide-pool."

"Ah," said Boris, "but if you like I will show you their secret place. You will not know it, but round the point there is a small cove that the cliffs hide, and a perfect pool to swim in whether the tide is in or out. A place they would not show me. I found it. Perhaps your wife would not even show it to you. It is opposite a rock that makes an island, out there in the sea. The island has a cave, which you cannot see from this side, and a rock-path when the tide is out between it and the cave. Shall we go there? We can walk out to it now before the tide comes in."

"Pity," said Kralin, "it is really too far off."

"But when your houses reach all around the bay—

And you could cut a path to it direct through the wood. Allow me to show it to you, at least." The day was beautiful. Kralin assented.

He followed Boris round the coast. Between huge boulders they went, Boris leaping, Kralin stumbling and splashing through pools, until they came to a sheltered angle of the coast, and Boris sprang onto the round back of a boulder and called to Kralin to look. They had left the low shores of the Taverners' bay, above them were the downs, breaking off into the precipices of Gault cliffs. A trackless, sheep-wandered land, savage with thistles; bird-flown, sea-hammered, a desolation of loveliness whose "visible Pan" has not yet found its real name.

Kralin peered round a boulder and saw a tiny cove, and a little cascade, hung with ferns, not trickling down the rock-face, but undulating in a trembling scarf, and then running clear across a sand-arrow into the sea. A piece of pure pastoral, unvisited. And beside the sand there was a basin of rock, a swimming-pool, just as Boris had said. And from the swimming-pool a rock-track, flat as pavement, linked the place with a little island out in the great bay, under Gault.

"You see," said Boris, "*and* the little island. It has grass on it and birds. On the other side there is a cave. It is large and full of interest. If you really intend to possess yourself of this land, you must make your people go there and give them things to eat. And since it was I who showed it to you, I shall expect a commission." He laughed—his laugh which could not be thought of in the same breath as money—"Come with me, Monsieur Kralin, and we will see the cave." Kralin demurred.

—"No, but you must. You cannot see it from here. There is a sheltered place on the other side and one or two little trees. And the cave. Before the turn of the tide."

"I'm afraid it is too far to be of any use." But he let Boris lead him, across the causeway, to the island, towards the returning sea.

"Go first," said Boris. "What I have to show you must come to you as a surprise. When we arrive, keep to the left of the rock. He walked across after Kralin, following him quickly and once or twice he looked back, to the high empty land, to the untrodden beach. The eyes of man, if there had been any eyes, would have seen two men walking along a rock-path, at low tide, to an island in the sea. Two men, and then he might have rubbed his eyes, and asked if there was a third, or what was making the confused transparency, that the sea-sparkle and weed-dark showed through, as of a shadow threaded with brightness that followed them.

"Ai, Ai," a gull cried overhead. They reached the island. For some minutes there had been a stirring in the tide pools, their surface not yet broken, their cups not over-flown, but as if they were troubled from beneath. It was the first turn of the tide.

On the island, gulls were mewing like cats over some sea-scraps, débris from a ship. On the sea-face, cutting them off from sight of land, the cave opened its mouth. Caves are a fascination for the greater part of mankind, which is seized with a proper desire to explore them at once. But one of the instincts which had been left out of Kralin was the wish to visit caves. He peered in. Boris glanced for a second out to sea. There was a steamer on the horizon, a fishing-boat low down also, and they almost below the level of the sea.

"Isn't it generally under water?" asked Kralin, who knew almost as little as it is possible for a man to know of such places, hardly enough to judge the tide marks, not hiding his discontent. Without the slightest taste for anything he had been shown, he had been brought a very long, rough, empty way, by a man who probably wanted to get something out of him. People had often wanted to sell him things, but—it made him laugh—no one had ever before tried to sell him a cave. How pleased his Taverners would be with their friend. He had seen the place long ago from the cliffs. Then he remembered how one afternoon he had amused himself, when Felicity had wanted to take him to the island. He had come part of the way with her, and stopped half way and staged some sulks. Now some one was wanting him to buy her precious place. Well, he might see if anything could be made of it, with a motor-boat for excursions and a faked story of its history. Boris was saying:

"The tide does not come to the upper end. I have kept something inside to show you." They went further in, and Kralin noticed that by some action of the sea on a chalk out-crop, the cave's wet floor was paved with round pebbles which were white, very pure white; and in the pools as pure a green; and there were jelly-fish like red flowers. He appreciated the sight. Altogether the lighting was strange, and inside they were standing so low down that they could only see the wave-sparkles out to the horizon and not the sky. A connoisseur in sensations, he relished a fear that came to him—that where they were walking was really underneath the sea; that already it was creeping back on them; that in three hours they would be standing underneath the ocean, in the darkness of the roots of the rocks.

"Further on," cried Boris, mounting what looked like a wall, a partition between the place where they were and an inner cave. A very long, very dark cave, full of water up to the barrier and at the end, a patch of what looked like the beginning of more light, from what must be an opening, a lunette high up on the landward side of the rock.

"Up here," called Boris, and gave him his hand. The barrier that divided the caves was broader than it seemed, and ran in a path round one side of the inner cave, beside a pool of water that filled its floor, absolutely clear and still.

"You see," said Boris. "You see that light high up, far off at the end? You understand? That is a *siffleuse,* a blow hole. What a spectacle when the tide is high and the wind is driving the sea—" (Lesson he had learned from Scylla. Lesson that it had wearied him to learn. Lesson he had learned for this moment.) "When the tide is high it fills this cave and the other. Always it forces in more water and more. Till this cave can hold no more. And it bursts—bursts—out of that window at the end—bursts out of the island—in a spout of water and a voice that is like a bull. A little further—" Edging Kralin a few feet round the path by the side of the pool, he fell back a pace.

—"Look into the water, Kralin. It is flat, like glass, and you will see a man drowned." Kralin said, after staring at his own face:

"I see nothing."

"But you see yourself. That is what I have brought you here to see. *Bien.*" Instantly as he said it, Kralin understood. Why he had been brought there; what was to be done to him; what Boris was. In a single flash that was like an image, but shapeless—as a stone is shapeless. It made no difference that he heard himself told not to move, that Boris was covering him with Felix's automatic borrowed for practice with Adrian. He had not been trained in the kind of courage that is of use at such a time. He stared: "Felicit—" he said and swallowed, tasting his death.

"You know," said Boris. "It is good. It is enough. You are to die for what you have done; for what you were going to do. But I shall not die for making you die—" and with his whole strength he hit Kralin a blow on the jaw, knocking him backwards, so that his head struck a point of rock sticking out of the wall of the cave. He fell full length on the path. Boris knelt beside him, turned him over, considered the torn contusion at the back of his head. Examined his body attentively. He was not in the least dead. He rolled his body over into the pool, and when it had sunk, weighted its chest with some stones.

Then he withdrew to the outer cave; then carefully, from behind a rock, lest eyes should come and stare at him out of the sea, he considered the tide. It was coning in fast.

In an hour the caves would be awash. He had only to stay there and see that Kralin did not recover consciousness and struggle up before he was drowned. He was drowning now inside, stunned at the bottom of a sea-pool. He had feared for a moment lest he should die before he was drowned. There was very little more to do, but he must not be seen. "It is all over, Scylla, Felix, Picus. All over for you, *mes biens aimés.* Hush, Scylla, hush. You can forgive him if you like. Hush, Felicity, hush. Have you met his ghost yet? Are you afraid of his ghost? But is not this right? Ghost of Felicity, is not this what had to be? You know that, for we've felt you about us and you have not prevented us. One thing I have put right, who have not put many things right. If ghost meets ghost and he can torment you again, you know that no more of his harm can come to friends or lovers or islands or trees—" A little wave broke over his shoe— "It was stupid of you, Kralin." A flicker of water iced his ankle. He looked and saw the sea-floor dancing in on them. He went back into the inner cave. Kralin was lying on his back, as he had left him, his limbs spread out a little under the water. Then Boris remembered what he had forgotten to do, and that he must not return wet. He stripped, taking off his clothes carefully and laying them on his raincoat, he let himself down into the pool, deep as his waist, and searched Kralin's pockets for his keys. Found them in a pocket-book, laid them on his clothes and went through the papers. Replaced the case on the body with Kralin's cards and his ticket for the Reading Room of the British Museum. Kept some letters and seven pounds, ten shillings in notes. "The payment of the executioner," he said. Then he rolled the stones off his chest and dressed again. Went out of the cave and returned quickly to the shore by the causeway, now just awash. Once on shore, he left the little cove until he found a place where it was possible to climb the cliff. Mounted to the top and then stood about in view of all Nature, giving a perfect mime of a man looking anxiously up and down a dangerous coast for a friend who is out of sight. Along the cliff-top he made his way back to the Dancing Rocks, turned up through the narrow end of the Sacred Wood, along its green pebbled path to the house.

Chapter XX

HE HAD SENT a note to the Taverners early that morning. They were waiting for him. Their night had been an exhausting interlude. Scylla had lain in fever. Picus had sat up in bed watching her by the light of a candle, whose star-flame made their room seem enormous. Felix, also sleepless, had joined him. They had watched together, giving her to drink, and as she seemed not to hear them, talking in whispers. In spite of the windows wide open, the room seemed impenetrable by the spring night, to have become an organism in itself, a presence, full of secrets—and memories—not of their bridal-nights. They were shut inside this room become a thing, as if they were unborn organisms inside an egg. Scylla's fever mounted. The air seemed to grow hot, but not from the small fire Picus fed with dried bog-myrtle and scented sticks.

"I feel I am going to be hatched," Felix whispered, "and not out of the right egg or into the right nest." The hours passed and they dozed, Picus beside her, Felix across the foot of the bed. In turns they fed the fire and gave her to drink. With some re-action from anger or vision, she had been ill from the moment they had led her away along the hill. They did not know what Boris had said to her, hope of whose loyalty they had given up. With the light, Felix left them and they all three slept. Lover by lover, side by side. Once she had murmured to them: "It will be all right only if we love each other enough." And Picus had seen Felix weeping quietly.

After breakfast Boris's note came. In it he said what he had told Adrian, that they were to say nothing and to wait for him. Scylla had dressed and come downstairs and gone about the house with Nanna. And Nanna had given them all three things to do, as she had done when they were children.

It was after mid-day when they heard whistling in the wood, and saw Boris come out of it and cross the lawn. The men sprang to meet him, but Scylla stood still against the door of the house.

"Quickly," he said—"Kralin is caught on the little island by the tide. See, I have his keys. He dropped them. I have told him what I know about him and that it would send him to prison; and I have made your peace, such peace, with him. He will do nothing now. And he is expecting you to lunch. He cannot leave the island till the tide goes out. He is standing on it, shouting. But I do not know that he is there. You must go over as though you were expecting him. And Scylla, you must get rid of Adrian. While you, Felix, will get the papers. Here are his keys."

Warm cordial of revenge, of action, poured into Felix. He took the keys, took his sister's arm and swung her up; and no one but Boris saw, as the two sprang off, that the look in her eyes had changed. Star-dark and charged with awe as they had been all day. While Felix's were suddenly star-bright.

"Remember. He is expecting us to lunch. Our differences are settled. Picus and I have gone to meet him." He saw them skim away like lapwings. Once they were out of sight, he led Picus into the wood, out of earshot of anything but the trees.

"Scylla knows already," he said. "Do you know, Picus? Kralin will not come back. He was stunned and fell into the pool at the back of the cave. But we must pretend that he is coming back. Go back and tell Nanna. Tell her that we are going to his house for lunch, that we are now going to meet him, who went for a walk along the coast. And you must say that it is true to yourself. Till you believe it. Tell the story to yourself. In half-an-hour, when we do not find him, you must begin to be unquiet. A very little unquiet.

This is what you have to play, Picus. Picus, do you understand? He sent me back to invite you. We are not really anxious, not for some time yet. Not until the big tide and the strong wind with the voice like a bull blow his body up the *siffleuse*—"

"Be quiet, Boris." Then, looking at him, Picus saw that it was not hysteria, but rapture.

—"How does Scylla know?" (How had he known she had known? How did he know now that he had known himself all the time, that his time-sequences had gone into reverse so perfectly that he had not troubled to consider it?)

—"How did you do it, Boris?"

"Do you want to know *now*?"

"Only if I'd better. And I had better not. But now what we have to do is to tell the same story. I burned your note."

"*Bien.* Then I will tell you what we have to tell. We walked upon the cliffs along the coast and discussed an agreement between us and some employment he could give me. We sat down on the grass. Below us we saw the little island, still to be reached on foot. He said to me that his wife had greatly loved this island, and that he would go there and remember her alone. He climbed down the cliff. (It can just be done there. I have tried it.) I did not wait for him. I said I would take his message back to you, and we would return and meet him. To give him time, I went for a walk—yes—to the rabbit-warren, a little inland. It is all right, I *have* been there. There I stayed, watching the rabbit-play, from where the island cannot be seen. Then I came up to the house to tell you. It is without fault. When he fell into the water in the inner cave, he was not yet dead.

"Attention, Picus. We are going to meet him now, meet the man who has been mourning for his wife, your cousin, on an island which she loved. We walk, we expect, we stare, we pause, we call—"

At the end of the wood they met a shepherd and asked him if he had seen a gentleman anywhere on the cliffs or below them on the rocks. The shepherd had seen no one about that morning. They walked along the edge of the rising cliffs till the island came in sight, and between the island and the shore ran a hundred yards of shallow bright water. "In there," said Boris, pointing to the island. Picus repeated to himself, "In there." In the island tomb. But neither of them knew that. They were walking to meet a kinsman, who had gone out there dry-shod to meditate in a place dear to his dead wife. He heard Boris say to himself: "I spoke of Felicity." Wondered what sort of pre-funeral discourse had been forced upon Kralin. How had the man faced his death? Had he stared or whimpered, fought or entreated? Boris was intact. He could hardly have protested much.

A few minutes later, for the benefit of possible spectators and for their own, they were calling "Kralin! Kralin!" A gull-noise it made, repeated. "Kralin! Kralin." They followed it with a perfect mime of bewilderment, not yet growing to anxiety, but to annoyance. "Damn the man," said Picus to the earth. Until they set off back to the house by two different ways, with gestures of separation to show that they did not intend to miss him. Entering the wood by a side track, Picus noticed that he was almost forgetting that the man was dead.

At the house he went at once into the kitchen, to tell Nanna that they would not be back to lunch. How they must have missed Kralin, and would go over to his house to wait for him. How Mr. Boris had found a way out, how Kralin had agreed and their troubles were over. That if he came back their way, she was to send him across the valley quickly to join them at his house. The old nurse, topping and tailing gooseberries, did not look up from her work. Boris followed him into the kitchen.

"I cannot see him anywhere. Where is it that he has got to?" The old nurse looked up at him.

"Is that you, Mr. Boris dear? Be off with you to Mr. Adrian's house. If the man who married Miss Felicity doesn't come, you had best tell the coast-guards. The tide will be in by then." They left the kitchen softly. Crossing the first field, Boris said:

"When will his body come up?"

"I don't know. The tide may pull it out to sea, and it will never be found."

"Then it will not blow out from the top?" Picus explained how that could only happen if there was a great storm, and the blow-hole worked in a jet with the strength of the Atlantic behind it.

The sea was entering the cave, swilling round it and falling back; swilling round it faster and faster; mounting to the brim of the dividing rock. Spilling over it, a few drops, then a lip of water, splashed and then stirred the laden pool within. Until a sudden water-crest broke in on it, setting its weeds awave, stirring the body of the man who lay on its white floor. Stirred the body, shifted it; and now with its full rush was lifting it as the sea piled up the long gallery of the cave.

That is what they did not know. They were going to have their lunch and wait for him; for a man just out of sight, meditating in some cleft in a rock, or walking the downs in remorse for his wife, or hiding because he intended them some discourtesy.

In the warm dust of the lane, it seemed a long way from the sea. As though there was no sea. Telling themselves that they were hungry (Boris *was* hungry), and that Kralin must be somewhere. —He might have returned, by some trick, before them, and had no business to keep them waiting—they opened the garden gate. On the threshold, Felix met them.

"Scylla's taken Adrian for a walk. I wish it had been for a ride. S.A. comes in useful. I've got the lot. Out of the safe. Went down the lane—no good trusting Adrian anywhere near them, and they're under the hay in the barn." Scylla and Adrian came in.

"We are very obedient to you, Boris. Have you time now to tell us what it is all about?"

"Plenty," said Picus, "unless Kralin is cut off somewhere by the tide, he seems to have disappeared."

"Let us eat our lunch," said Boris.

"I must know what has happened," said Adrian. They followed one another into the dining-room.

"Wait," said Boris to Adrian, "he will tell you himself when he returns."

PARIS-SENNAN
1930–32

AFTERWORD

Brightness Falls from the Air

In 1927 Mary Butts wrote in her journal, "Eliot and I are working on a parallel.... But what is interesting is that he is working on the Sans Grail, on its negative side, the Waste land."[1] Appearing six years after T.S. Eliot's poem *The Waste Land,* Mary Butts's visionary grail romance, *Armed with Madness,* like Eliot's poem, captures the spiritual climate of the 'twenties and shows the influence of Jesse Weston's *From Ritual to Romance.* In addition to the need for and possibility of personal renewal and transformation, Butts's novel presents their actual occurence. It explores the correspondence of divine and human in six people's lives. Although some of the description of place and landscape recalls Butts's family home, Salterns, near Poole Harbor in Dorset where she was born in 1890, and also the environs of Corfe Castle, a favorite haunt, it is not the autobiographical details or physical facts which signify in her stories, but rather what one of her poems terms the "high-strung moment,"[2] when, as Virgil Thomson puts it, "the persons observed are caught up by something, inner or outer, so irresistible that their highest powers and all their lowest conditionings are exposed."[3] Without this occurence, there is no clarification, only the form of ritual or of romance. The purpose of ritual, to paraphrase Jane Harrison (whose works Mary Butts had read), is to make the individual one with the god, to make possible the attainment of divine life. Cleansed and consecrated by its performance, the neophyte is reborn: "Thou art become God from Man"; "Thou shalt be God instead of mortal" state two Orphic tablets.[4] Harrison traces ancient ritual in Greece from savage rites to Orphism, and indicates the relation of these rites to Christian ritual and also to drama. She speculates how the worshippers of Dionysos, in believing they were possessed by the god, were but a step from the conviction

> "that they were actually identified with him, actually *became* him ... a conviction shared by all orgiastic religions, and one doubtless that had its rise in the physical sensations of intoxication ... [which] would go far to promote such a faith, but there is little

> doubt that it was fostered, if not originated, by the pantomimic character of ancient ritual. . . . It is a natural primitive instinct of worship to try by all manner of disguise to identify yourself more and more with the god who thrilled you."[5]

Harrison feels that this "savage doctrine of divine possession, induced by intoxication and in part by mimetic ritual," found "a higher, more spiritual meaning" in Orphism. Priest of Dionysos, Orpheus "altered the conception of what a god was"; he sought to obtain the godhead not by physical intoxication but by spiritual ecstasy, not by drunkenness but abstinence and purification.[6] And Orpheus was a man, not a god.

Robert McAlmon remembered the ecstatic atmosphere Butts breathed,[7] and ecstasy and abstinence are certainly practised by her characters. Even when they do become merely physically intoxicated, something else appears to be their object. Butts describes the Greek gods, in her essay *Traps for Unbelievers,* as "projections of ideal human mana . . . not gods come down to man, but gods who were man and God,"[8] pointing out that "in common with the christian, the classic mind at its best insisted that, though it was possible for the divine and the human to mix, 'man is not God.'" The failure to distinguish between them leads to the horror of the kings of Persia, the Ptolemies, the Roman emperors, and, in the modern age, the Hollywood stars: "Human nature was not meant for that strain."

Butts's characters neither fall into what she describes as the "old weakness" of Christian monotheism's "insufficient insistence on the wild, enchanting, incalculable force in nature, the mana of things, the non-moral, beautiful, subtle energy in man and in everything else, on which the virtue of everything depends," nor into the danger of polytheism's "mana-worship," an absorption into things. Picus's and Scylla's associations with Zeus and Leda, their identification with birds and wood, typical of the mythic world, never wipe out their individuality. Scylla's brooding and hatching of situations, of "Truth [which] isn't every one's breakfast egg," Picus's whistling, his ability to communicate with animals and his quiet aloofness, are not labored. Gault Cliff is "Bari . . . the warm wood" and Baldur's wood, but it also remains Gault Cliff.

Butts's awareness of the supernatural, which she says played an "extreme part . . . from the beginning, in my life," along with her belief in God, Apollo, and Artemis,[9] her investigations into the occult, and her knowledge and practise of transcendental magic reflect the period's interest in these subjects. Though like many writers and artists of the 'twenties she confronts the problems of disbelief and excessive subjectivity, the end of humanism and the fear that there is "*nothing* but physical adventure"[10]—and feels that a "revaluation of values," a "discovery of a new value, a different way of apprehending everything," is coming or needed[11]—there is the conviction in her work, as one of her characters puts it, that "we are taking part in events, only part of which are happening on the earth we see."[12] This conviction and the sensation of it are partly explained by and give rise to the ritualistic aspect of her writings, without which plot, characters, and even language can seem "indecent," as Virginia Woolf called *Armed with Madness.* Indeed, beside the slight talent Butts seems to have had for forming and cultivating associations which might have furthered her literary career and reputation, it is this nature of her subject matter and its treatment which have most hindered her being more widely appreciated and known. Handling myth and religion with equal seriousness while being also highly critical of their conventional interpretation or practice, Butts's work challenges a merely literary or religious reading, and her inconclusive use of myth and religious symbols makes scant sense from any orthodox viewpoint, secular or nonsecular.

In his memoir of the 'twenties, Douglas Goldring writes of Mary Butts's "almost overwhelming 'personal atmosphere,'"[13] and describes her as "a natural surrealist, with a flair for everything queer in art and life, a trememdous zest for parties and a child-like delight in all the more exotic forms of naughtiness."[14] This flair, zest, and delight achieve their essence in her writing in *Armed with Madness* with its snatches of songs and poetry, the characters' dancing, feasting, and little jokes, and the language: vivid, visual, direct, sometimes cryptic and jazzy, condensed, unexpected.

The telling of the story, as well as the story itself, is a bit chaotic, unplanned and out of hand, creating a sensation of madness, of something greater disordering and confusing the characters and the book, and allowing for a transformation typical of the myth and poetry and Celtic art Mary Butts loved. Little is inanimate. Picus lets out a breath and waits for the wood's answer; now the characters and now the scenery—gods, nature, objects—are center stage, and sight is seldom lost of either. This coexistence of art and life, heavenly and earthly, is possible because they form for Butts a realm similar to that of the grail kingdom whose delights, the poet Wolfram says, are like those of the kingdom of heaven whose dominions include "whatsoever the air touches."[15] The madness of the 'twenties, the bewilderment and anger and desperation as well as the high spirit, is also the madness of trying to live the truth of myths and legends, which madness arms Scylla and Picus. Rather than just despair and confusion and romantic notions gone sour, these two receive illumination and union through their identification with what they love: the presences of their own place. Fortified by these, they are better able to confront the greater madness centering around their cousin Felicity's life and death in the sequel to *Armed with Madness.*

II

Not long after Mary Butts's marriage in 1930 to her second husband, the cartoonist Gabriel Aitken, at one time a close asociate of Siegfried Sassoon and a friend of the Sitwells, the couple moved to Sennen on the Cornwall coast, not far from Land's End. Even today Sennen Cove seems an isolated spot, especially off-season and in dark weather. Though it has been built up since the 'thirties, it has not become tourist-ridden like other nearby seashore resorts. There is a long, sandy beach, several hotels and bed-and-breakfast establishments, a few stores, the small St. Sennen's church, a housing development at the approach to the town, post office and gas station, tea shop and pub, and, on the cliffs above the North Atlantic, a mixture of old and new houses. There are very few trees. Except for the whirr of vehicles along the highway, the predominant sound is the wind, always cool if not cold, carrying the smells of the ocean and the grasses, and, except for a few buildings out of character with the surroundings, the predominant feature is the thrust and heave of the land before the sea. It can be warm out of the wind, and in parts of Cornwall tropical plants and lush gardens grow; but Mary Butts chose an inhospitable dwelling, as removed from the amenities she had sometimes enjoyed as her books were in style and subject matter from most of her more popular contemporaries.

The society of stream, birds, rabbits, foxes, the diffused light, the scent of the turf and salt air, and the ancient sites on the moors close by were another world from the London and Paris of Butts's youth where she had met and known, among others, Jean Cocteau, Ford Madox Ford, Kay Boyle, Hemingway, Bryher, and Ezra Pound. But as her writings make plain, the natural world had always been sacred to her. Perhaps as the bonds and companionship of human society gave way in her own life and in the world at large before that "Black Death of the spirit sweeping over Europe,"[16] she found comfort in the creatures and land of a place not unlike her native Dorset. Certainly her books suggest so, especially *Death of Felicity Taverner.* The character Felicity, dead before the story begins, embodies, as her name implies, that conjunction of the seen and unseen sought and fought for by her cousins, and hated by all whose desire for power is thwarted by such concurrence.

Arguably her greatest novel—and more subdued and traditional than *Armed with Madness*—it brings together Boris Polteratsky (of another book, *Imaginary Letters*), Felix, Scylla, and Picus, against Felicity's family and husband, who are probably responsible for her death, in a struggle to preserve Felicity's reputation and the land she loved. A crucifixion lies at the heart of this novel as it does of *Armed with Madness,* as if to underline the ritual of transformation, the difficulty with which it is effected. Yet unlike the clarity, peace and communion achieved through Scylla's crucifixion in *Armed with Madness,* the sacrifice of Felicity and the response of her community to the malice projected against her leave unresolved the question of how to offset evil.

A line of Thomas Nashe, "Brightness falls from the air," recurs in Butts's stories, expressing not just the loss of beauty, innocence, and everything associated with the good, but also the power of these elemental forces to resurrect their ruin. Felicity is lost in Mary Butts's life and world, as her journals, poems, stories, essays and novels record; and what is at stake, at last, is the disappearance of the sacred itself, that relationship to what is not personal at all and yet without which there is no "magic of person or place."[17] In her last novels, *The Macedonian* (1933), *Scenes from the Life of Cleopatra* (1935), and the beginning of a book about Julian the Apostate on which she was at work at the time of her death in 1937, Butts departs from her own time and familiar things and plunges deeply into the world of myth as though urgently to reach the source or form behind the forms, to glimpse, as her poem "Pythian Ode" quotes, *Quod inferius sicut superius est,* the coincidence of what is above with what is below.

In her memoir, *The Crystal Cabinet,* titled after one of Blake's poems, Mary Butts names a desire, intuitive since childhood and present in her books (even though on this subject "the best you could say—or write—was no more than an indirection"[18]), to live inside and outside the mind at once.

> "I was seeing my mind as though it were a cabinet . . . on the whole an empty cabinet, a crystal cabinet like the one Blake wanted to live inside and outside of at once. Perhaps that was what learning to live meant, really learning. Not the half-learning, which seemed as much as most people learned. Anyone can live outside it, and a very few, like the duller saints, altogether inside. But to do what Blake said—and be inside and outside the cabinet at once? Wasn't that what some one called the 'same thing and simultaneous possession of eternal life'? Wasn't that what Delphi had tried to show to the ancient world?"[19]

Here, she sensed, was the answer to the question left hanging at the end of these two novels, as well as in her own experience and the world, even though the path to this insight was unclear; and her writing, like H.D.'s, was "[her] own way to the Garden of the Hesperides,"[20] her great life adventure.

—BARBARA WAGSTAFF

[1] Mary Butts, "Selections from the Journal," ed. Robert H. Byington and Glen E. Morgan, *Art and Literature,* 7 (1966), p. 172.

[2] Mary Butts, "Rites de Passage," *Pagany* II.3 (July-Sept. 1931): p. 62–63.

[3] Virgil Thomson, *Virgil Thomson* (New York: Alfred A. Knopf, 1966), p. 87.

[4] Jane Harrison, Prolegomena to the Study of Greek Religion (New York: The World Publishing Company, 1966), pp. 583, 585.

[5] Harrison, p. 474.

[6] Harrison, pp. 475–76.

[7] Robert McAlmon and Kay Boyle, *Being Geniuses Together* (New York: Doubleday & Co., Inc., 1968), p. 124.

[8] Mary Butts, *Traps for Unbelievers* (London: Desmond Harmsworth, 1932), p. 42.
[9] Mary Butts, *The Crystal Cabinet* (Boston: Beacon Press, 1988), p. 132.
[10] *Armed with Madness,* p. 90
[11] *Armed with Madness,* p. 9
[12] *Armed with Madness,* p. 140
[13] Douglas Goldring, *The Nineteen-Twenties* (London: Nicholson and Watson, 1945), p. 210.
[14] Douglas Goldring, *Odd Man Out* (London: Chapman and Hall, Ltd., 1935), p. 281.
[15] Wolfram von Eschenbach, *Parzival,* trans. H.M. Mustard and C.E. Passage (New York: Random House, 1961), p. 137.
[16] *The Crystal Cabinet,* p. 133.
[17] Mary Butts, "Magic of Person and Place," *The Bookman* 85 (December 1933), pp. 141–43.
[18] *The Crystal Cabinet,* p. 137.
[19] Ibid., p. 237.
[20] Ibid., p. 231.

A NOTE ON THIS EDITION

Two first editions of *Armed with Madness* exist, both issued in 1928: the Wishart (London), and the variant Boni (New York). *Death of Felicty Taverner* was presented only by Wishart (London), in 1932. Discrepancies in punctuation and spelling within and between those early editions are extensive, and to our knowledge original proofsheets are unavailable. For this edition of both novels, punctuation conforms generally to the Wishart edition of *Armed with Madness.* Occasionally, felicitous typography or usage has been adapted from the Boni edition. Obvious spelling errors have been corrected, and internal consistency has been enforced whenever the author's intention could be adduced. Clear idiosyncrasies in spelling and style are maintained. A very few textual changes have been made where attributions, parenthetical expressions, or misattributed quotations have occurred. The Oxford English Dictionary served as chief arbiter for spellings. The publisher wishes to thank Kathleen Peifer and Alexandra Langley for their efforts as copy editors and proofreaders. In addition, grateful acknowledgment is made to Robert Kelly, for first suggesting the work of Mary Butts for Recovered Classics editions; to Camilla Bagg, for her authorization in behalf of the Mary Butts estate; and to Christopher Wagstaff, for the loan of *Armed with Madness* texts.

The text of this book has been set in a Mergenthaler Linotron version of Baskerville. The design is by Bruce McPherson. William Kalvin at Delmas Type, Ann Arbor, performed the text typography. The book has been printed on pH neutral paper and sewn into signatures. Of this first printing, there are 1700 copies bound in paper covers and jackets, and 300 copies bound in cloth over boards with mylar jackets.